Metamorph

The Outbounder Chronicles

Chris Reher

Chris Reher

Also by Chris Reher

Quantum Tangle

Terminus Shift

Entropy's End

Sky Hunter

The Catalyst

Only Human

Rebel Alliances

Delphi Promised

ACKNOWLEDGMENTS

Thank you to Jim Kolter
And to Andy Brokaw, David Wooddell, Linda Witz,
George McConnon, and Libby Baltrush

Chris Reher

ONE

"Your timing is excellent. You can come along and watch old man Shelody bite my face off."

Laryn Ash, still holding out the card with her mission specs to the captain, froze momentarily as she tried to figure out his peculiar greeting.

She had been directed to meet the outbounder captain here on this service bay where his ship had just hours ago locked onto the station's docking port. It had taken a while before he had made his appearance, inspecting her like some new piece of cargo as the open lift descended from the belly of the *Nefer*. She was quite aware that, to these crews, cargo was all she was.

"Sure," she said, not at all sure and also a little disappointed that he did not invite her to take a tour of his ship. The *Nefer* had traveled the filaments for forty years and had stories to tell. "Sounds like fun."

"You have a weird idea of fun," he said, stepping aside to let two service people, laden with the tools of their trade, board the lift he had vacated.

He did not look at her credentials and so she put them away again. "Captain–"

"Call me Ryle," he said, heaving a box of supplies onto the lift.

She turned when a hoarse voice cut through the din of

machinery and the shouted exchanges of the mechanics echoing through the bay. "Heard you came up dry, Tanner."

The captain watched the ground crew and supplies ascend into the airlock before acknowledging the hail. "Is there anyone around here who *doesn't* know that? Just so I can tell them myself."

The chief of the smallcraft berths held up his requisition tablet without getting off his dented scooter. "There's a deckhand on Number Four who hasn't heard. You're home early."

"We are. Did you miss me?" Ryle Tanner tapped his thumbprint on the scanner to sign off on the usual services: thorough interior cleaning of the *Nefer*, restocking her galley, water and fuel racks, new scrubber filters, and a maintenance scan of conduits and circuitry.

Like others who monitored the transmissions of inbound ships, Laryn knew that the *Nefer* had come home to Pendra Station under better circumstances. The tip about a possible strike beyond Ziferis Two should have yielded at least a rogue planet, going by the readings picked up by the probes. But there'd been nothing but empty space for centuries in all directions. The cost of the failed venture was no doubt why the captain worried about the fate of his hide at the hands of the company owner. Did he hope that Corlan Shelody's wrath would be mitigated, somehow, by her presence?

The chief grinned around a mouthful of *choo*. "I missed your currency. Or your boss's currency, to be exact."

"I'm under-appreciated." Ryle completed the transaction on the tablet to transfer the owed, somewhat exorbitant, amount into Pendra's vast coffers. "Did you know on Orbel Four they sing to each other instead of using money? It does something to their brains. With your pleasant baritone, you'd be rich there."

"I'd also be dead, seeing how it rains mercury on Orbel." The chief peered around Ryle at Laryn. His grin faded a little when he discovered the blue insignia pinned to her scarf, identifying her as a Pendra agent. "Got a new warden?"

"Mediary," she corrected as if the man didn't know the proper term for the Pendra representatives that traveled aboard every ship heading out from the station.

"Mediary, right," the ground boss said with a wink at Ryle. "So did you wear out the old one already, Tanner?"

Laryn didn't much like the leering quality of the man's wink and pulled her shawl up and over her hair and then tossed its fringed end over her shoulder. The delicately painted sash wrapped loosely around her hips and then wound up around her shoulders, and she wished she had worn something a little more substantial.

She wasn't exactly dressed for this place and she regretted not having asked to meet her new crew somewhere cleaner and quieter and, most of all, warmer. Especially since it didn't seem as though she was about to receive a tour of the outbounder vessel. The ceaseless draft here suggested some new problem with the air exchanger and she tried to suppress her shivers.

Likely, she thought, she would have to rethink her trendy wardrobe before debarking with this outbounder crew. She often indulged in the remarkable craftsmanship imported from a Terrica settlement where the making of clothes had become an art form. The translucent gowns and wraps she wore over her snug body suits glowed in shades of cinnamon, amber and fire to match the honey shades of her skin and hair. She had spent too many years clothed in rags to now adopt the plain and practical clothing too common up here. Unnecessarily drab, it blended one person into the next and then the walls that surrounded them. Another shiver crept up along her arms and she had to admit that the tough fabric and leather worn by the captain, and even the ground chief's coveralls were the better choice for hanging around these docks.

"The old one got bossy," the captain said without a hint of mischief on his unshaven face. "Quoting regulations without end. It gets to you. We tossed him out the airlock."

The chief chuckled and then pointed upward. "How long

are you going to leave this deathtrap here, Tanner? Guess you won't need decon."

"I'll need her ready to go by..." Ryle glanced at his timepiece, set to the station's rhythms. "...by morning." He tapped the com tab on his collar. "Nolan," he said to the *Nefer*'s engineer. "I guess I'll go see Shelody."

"Want me to come with?" was the reply. Something clanged in the background and Ryle heard Nolan mutter a few words his mother wouldn't appreciate.

Ryle looked up at the seal leading into the belly of the *Nefer*, the only part of it actually attached to the station. "You sound busy. I'll meet you at Toko's for dinner. I promised myself something with taste in it. Try not to break my ship."

He waved a farewell at the platform chief and motioned Laryn to head for the service bay exit. Her flawless recall of the station's schematics told her that these passages led to the offices of the private prospector companies.

Shelody Expeditions traded space aboard Pendra Station by transporting supplies or passengers to wherever they were going, including Earth now and again, as did most of the outbounder outfits. Real revenue, however, came from the explorations that took his crews and their paying clientele out from the Hub into far more exotic destinations, hopefully to return from there unscathed. Hopefully also with something to pay for the risks they took. The odds were poor, the journey dangerous, and the cost prohibitive. Their high-risk forays into darkness rarely turned up anything more than some primitive life forms on an inhospitable planet or a rock ready for mining. One didn't have to be a poet *or* a scientist to understand the unfathomable vastness of space.

For private prospecting companies like Shelody's, the cost of accommodation aboard the station meant turning over their discoveries to the Pendra Consortium who granted rights as it, along with the Ministry, deemed appropriate, if not always fairly. Men like Corlan Shelody worked with their partners on Earth to take advantage of what contracts Pendra made available. Even under Pendra's heavy-handed oversight, there were fortunes to be made here.

"Tomorrow morning?" Laryn said, hurrying to keep up with the captain's long strides. "We're heading out so soon?"

"That's how we pay the bills," he said. "Nolan likes to eat." His eyes took in her elegant wardrobe, although far less lewdly than the chief had. "Got your gear?"

"It's being brought down," she said. "I hope it's warmer aboard your ship than down here."

He smiled something that could mean anything at all and she berated herself for her inane remark. No doubt she sounded like the usual freeloading, unwanted passenger foisted upon the prospectors by the Consortium.

"Drat," he said, pointing to a lit panel beside a door along the hallway. "He's in. So much for just leaving a message and heading for dinner."

"There goes your clever plan," she said, wondering if she sounded casual or like someone trying too hard to make friends with the civilians.

"Corl," Ryle said by way of greeting when they entered the small room his employer used for his work. The pastel-colored space offered a minimum of stylish furnishings surrounding a top of the line holo platform. Laryn had seen hospital rooms less brightly lit and less antiseptic.

At the moment, an image of Bogen's Hub, as they called this deceptively empty area of space, hovered above the projector in three-dimensional detail. The Hub formed a mighty crossroads leading to anywhere, the only point of departure for Human deep space exploration. The gravity well at its center showed here as a wireframe globe to depict its event horizon, orbited at a safe distance by the lumbering Pendra Station. Surrounding all of this, the otherwise invisible dark matter filaments radiated outward like a tangle of hair in need of a comb, each of them a road into unknown space beyond the measure of their telescopes. Explored strands were labeled and marked with their destinations, coordinates and names, if they had any.

Shelody sat back in his chair, regarding Ryle as if

something truly marvelous had just walked into his office. "There you are, Mister Tanner. I'm pleased to see you. How thoughtful of you to visit." His dark eyes shifted to Laryn, and he nodded to her in greeting. "Agent Ash? I'm not sure we've yet met in person. You're no doubt looking forward to a more interesting venture than the one from which the *Nefer* just now returned."

She offered a polite smile. "The outcome of an expedition has no bearing on my presence aboard," she reminded him.

Ryle dropped into a chair, a low-slung number designed by artisans on Terrica – his knees nearly touched his chin. He leaned back and stretched his long legs out toward the hologram. "There's no need for this, Corl. I'm too tired."

"It's not like you flew home by flapping your arms."

Ryle sighed and let it go. He nodded toward the display. "I guess you got our report."

"You missed the drop?" Shelody's pointer traced a dark matter filament radiating from the Hub to a marker only a few minutes along its path. Beyond that, the thread branched into a secondary path, usually the point where filaments became frayed and murky. They either dissipated, or they merged into larger streams at some unimaginable distance. Neither the murk nor the high density strands made for safe travel. To Laryn, it had always seemed as if the inquisitive, insignificant Humans were pesky infiltrators into a vast system of blood vessels, barely making it past the first layer of skin.

It had been nearly a century ago that Doctor Efan Bogen and his team had detected the highly concentrated threads of dark matter that were attracted, merged and then redirected by this gravity well. The first step, of course, had been to find ways of interacting with them. New applications of older technology had brought about the phase envelope that allowed objects to travel within those filaments in utter disregard of space and time.

The lure of wealth and adventure, as it had for millennia,

meant no shortage of prospectors like Ryle Tanner, and his father before him, willing to take the risks. Many had been lost during those early days, relying on conventional craft designed for challenges no greater than shuttling to Earth's moon and orbiting stations. The losses spurred new developments for external shielding and more capable navigation systems, led by the powerful Pendra Consortium whose members had built this station.

Most of the filaments led nowhere. Some led to places worth exploring. One had led to the earthlike Terrica in 22-05. And another had led them to meet the Kalons more than twenty years after that, the first of only a handful of sentient species ever encountered. Later came more finds of intelligent species on Chidi-4, Orbel, and Antica, making it clear that meeting further civilizations would be simply a matter of time and perseverance by the explorers. So far, only the Kalon species interacted with Humans, although cautious contact with the people of Antica showed promise.

A painful start in relations with the Kalons had alarmed the governments of Earth who compelled the Consortium to create the Office of the Intermediary. Pendra agents like Laryn became mandatory on outbounder expeditions as ambassadors to ensure protocol in case of First Contact with any species, no matter their level of sentience. Even a trilobite found on some alien world had scientific, social and even political repercussions. It also meant that Pendra, trusting no one and least of all the private companies, had eyes and ears aboard each vessel, an arrangement that irritated the captains.

"Jex got confused, Nolan thinks," Ryle said, referring to the *Nefer*'s Artificial Intelligence, a JX.9 system. "We might have dropped from the thread too soon. Should have hit target at point four four kilo-secs."

Shelody pondered the hologram. He scratched his jaw, as bristle-free as his scalp. Laryn wondered if the man's bronze skin, unmarred by time or accident, was entirely natural. Nothing distracted from his presence in the featureless room although she suspected that it was not just vanity that made him the focal point. His carefully maintained appearance, clothed in elegant layers of subtle grays, commanded the space, likely an effective setting for whatever deals and negotiations took place here.

Of course, at this moment, the shaggy-haired outbounder captain sprawling in one of the delicate chairs, looking like the rough fabric of his jacket might scratch its buffed surface, ruined the illusion. She doubted Ryle was impressed by these impeccably polished furnishings.

"That was a costly bit of nonsense you bought, then," Shelody said. His nimble hands moved through the sensor field to add the appropriate tags to the filament going nowhere. From what she knew of him, it wasn't likely that he'd share the discovery with the other outbounders companies. He loved to see others waste their investments as much as he hated losing his. "I think maybe I should arrange your future missions myself."

Ryle snarled. "We really should try this thread again. What do you have in mind for us instead? Shuttling migrants? Hauling ore?"

"Your gratitude is heart-warming. Let's not forget you'd be rotting in a cell somewhere if I hadn't volunteered to take you in." Shelody must have heard Laryn's quick intake of breath at this revelation, and he turned to her with a sly grin. "Is this news to you, Agent Ash?"

She glanced at Ryle, who didn't look pleased with Shelody's calculated words. "No, of course not," she said, her expression neutral. The captain of the *Nefer* was a convict? Her supervisor could have mentioned this bit of news, she thought, before assigning her to the *Nefer*. But she owed Shelody nothing, least of all the satisfaction of embarrassing his captain in front of the Pendra agent.

Shelody waved his hands to let the Hub fade from view and returned his attention to Ryle. "You're lucky Azah found a new client who wishes to leave immediately. Fairly sure thing, from what she's learned so far. Maybe it'll make up for this botched expedition."

"So I heard, but she didn't give any details. What client?"

"Couple of mummies on a treasure hunt. Nothing fancy but they're offering an advance guarantee, so play nice."

"Kalons?" Laryn said, more to remind Shelody of the appropriate name for these visitors than to confirm whom he meant. The *mummies* were the only alien species with a representation aboard Pendra Station, collaborating with the Consortium's research teams on a few promising projects. The apparent lack of flesh beneath their leathery skin had earned them the nickname, never used in hearing distance.

"Yes, yes. Kalons."

Ryle came to his feet. "Guess we better go find her, then."

Shelody waved a dismissal. "Don't disappoint me, Tanner. That's my coin you're spending on that pretty ship of yours."

TWO

The public concourse above the smallcraft level buzzed with the hectic tensions Laryn had come to associate with the arrival of a new transport from Earth. She and Ryle made their way along a series of moving platforms that would soon be choked with travelers preparing for the last leg of their journey.

The migrants, chosen through lottery, bribery, luck, or patience, came here aboard a fleet using a photonic conveyor spanning the distance from Earth to the Hub. Although slow, it offered safety and carried far greater numbers than the filament-traveling corvettes and did so far more cheaply. The travelers paused here before making the short transit to Terrica on smaller vessels, this time along a filament. The layover made for busy, crowded, noisy days aboard Pendra Station, swelling its regular population of less than five hundred to three times that or more.

Terrica, the most hospitable planet they had yet found while exploring the filaments spreading out from the Hub, was still very much a frontier. Rich with water, air and fertile soil, pleasant in terms of climate if you didn't mind the heat, it easily accommodated the regular batches of migrants. New communities and the networks that connected them spread out from the landing zones to form efficiently designed habitats - a fresh start for the people of Earth who were bent on doing things right this time.

Earth's Ministry of the Exterior, as much a consortium as the commercial Pendra group, regulated the migration, made necessary by mankind's history on that planet as much as the desire to discover new worlds. The exodus was not the station's main purpose, nor Pendra's main interest, but facilitating it ensured that, so far, Pendra Station was the only port of call here at the Hub and in control of who used it. The ministries of Earth maintained a token embassy here, sharing space with the astrophysics labs that explored the mystery of the Hub itself.

Station staff rushed around Laryn and Ryle, on foot or on scooters, sorting through the cargo and equipment that tended to clutter up the place between inbound fleets from Earth. The air above was no less congested with cargo carts suspended on rails from the slanted ceiling. The sound baffles did little to stifle the racket of people and mechs setting up security and amenities for the expected travelers and so Laryn raised her voice.

"You didn't think to mention that I signed on with a felon?" she said.

A groove appeared between the captain's eyes as he turned to her. "You weren't told?"

"I think I'd remember," she said with a grin, reminding him of the cognitive augmentation her neural implant made possible. People like her rarely forgot anything.

He walked off the conveyor and took her arm to keep her from tripping as she, too, stepped onto firm ground. She began to object, but clearly her sarong presented a hazard on the moving platform. Having her strangled by one of her wraps on his watch was likely not something he'd care to explain to Pendra's administrators.

"What do you want to know?" he said, releasing her arm again.

She raised both brows. "That you're not some lunatic murderer who I'd rather not travel with, for starters."

He made a sound that might have been a laugh. "I'm not

a lunatic."

"But a murderer?"

He said nothing while a delivery cart trundled past, making serious business of maneuvering around them when its sensors discovered the Humans cluttering the lane. "That's a broad definition. You know we've had trouble with pirates and claim jumpers."

"You don't get enslaved for that. Or jailed."

"That is true."

She cocked her head to study his expression. There was amusement there, but also something shuttered, telling her that prying into his past would not get her too far. His gray eyes returned her frank gaze for a moment and then his easy smile reappeared to soften his features.

"You're safe with us, Agent, don't worry," he said. "I took a wrong turn once and it wasn't appreciated. They let me choose between getting locked up in a dark place somewhere, or working off my debt here on Pendra."

She tipped her head back toward the docks. "On the *Nefer*? They're not worried you'll get the urge to just leave?"

"I get those urges daily." He rubbed the back of his neck where the embedded network of the receiver filaments hidden by his dark hair met to communicate with the Synergic Neural Network aboard his ship. The JX.9 system lived only while receiving his biotelemetry, tying man and machine into one mechanism. "But Shelody's got the keys to the *Nefer*. I'm stuck here."

"You mean he's tapped into the *Nefer*'s AI, too?"

"In a way. He doesn't have command control over it, but he can shut it down."

"That must be hard to stomach. I guess having Shelody's daughter aboard as your first mate would make an escape a bit tricky, anyway."

His expression darkened and she wondered why the mention of Azah Shelody had turned his mood. "She was part of the crew before all this," he said. "But don't worry, Mediary, I'm not about to go anywhere without my ship.

She's worth more than a few years in prison. They don't need to fret about me escaping from here."

Laryn berated herself for having ruined the conversation by coming across like the company agent she was. He was right to remind her that she was part of the *They* they were talking about.

A sharp whistle sliced through the thrum of machinery in the air to startle them. They turned to see Nolan, the *Nefer*'s engineer, coming up via the conveyor behind them, waving for their attention. Arriving where they stood, he gripped the handrail and vaulted across, close enough to nearly land on Ryle's boots.

Nolan laughed when Ryle punched his shoulder and then sobered when he saw Laryn, perhaps regretting his childish prank in front of the agent. "Uh, hello. Miz Ash, I presume?" he said politely, but the broad grin stayed on his freckled face.

"You must be Nolan Jone," she said, surprised that she had to resist an urge to ruffle the man's spiky shock of red hair. It was the sort of hair that begged to be ruffled. There had been no shortage of information about the engineer among the files she had absorbed and indelibly committed to memory. Having arrived from Earth at age five, he had become a permanent resident when his parents took jobs aboard the station – a good place for a child with an aptitude for complex machinery. But now she wondered if he, too, had run afoul of the strict laws that ruled Pendra Station. She returned his friendly smile and walked ahead of the men toward the main entrance to the station's interior.

Pendra's entire complex of landing and loading docks attached to the main body of the habitat at only a few points, able to separate in case of some structural emergency. Automated security systems guarded the few access porticos and the crew stopped at the gate to let the mechanical guardian read the biosignature each of them breathed into a panel. It then scanned for weapons and insisted on reviewing their badges before allowing them into the station.

"Oh, good, it's still daytime," Laryn said when light from the nearby star poured through the doors to greet them. The Hub's distance to the Sun didn't allow for much real light, but filters set into the transparent, domed ceiling high above them did their job to flood this space with a similar spectrum. In a few hours, the lighting would shift to simulate nighttime to help the station's residents manage their sleep cycles. Of course, a dimming of the lights didn't stop them from pursuing after hours entertainment any more than it did on Earth.

Designed to impress newcomers, the commons plaza of the station opened before them like a city park. The swath of greenspace, a little unkempt in places, offered a welcomed reprieve to crews confined to their ships for weeks and months, as time was calculated in this sector. People strolled along winding paths or sat among the greenery to enjoy the sound of wind and birds piped in through the sound system. A series of shops and amenities ringed the plaza, designed to mimic a line of antique shop fronts, complete with street lamps and cobbled walkways. Open gates around the perimeter led to the external modules surrounding the public nucleus of the station. Those led to a maze of modules offering accommodations ranging from temporary dormers for the migrants to fabulously lavish private suites for wealthier residents.

"Did you see Corlan?" Nolan asked Ryle.

Ryle, too, smiled up at the counterfeit but welcome sunlight from above. "Did. Luck is on me and he didn't fire me. He's got another job for us, so don't unpack just yet."

"I'm guessing he couldn't fire you even if he wanted to," Laryn said as they strolled across the expanse of greenery, ignoring the footpaths. "I find it amusing that you call *me* the Warden, actually."

Nolan looked from her to Ryle. "You told her?"

"I thought she knew. Looks like Pendra isn't sharing as much as we think with their... employees." Ryle shrugged, dismissing the matter. "How's the *Nefer* coming along?"

"No problems to be found with the old girl," Nolan said. "She's not going to be resupplied for a few hours yet, give or take a few kilo-secs. What kind of job does Shelody have for us?"

"Not sure. Azah's got the story."

Laryn slipped her sandals off to let her bare feet brush through the carpet of glossy, ankle-deep leaves, enjoying the feel of these living things. She did not regret leaving Earth to come out here, but she sometimes missed the lush forests where her group had taken refuge during the Restoration.

"Looks like our mediary's ready for some shore leave, though," Ryle said, watching her. "Joining us for some food, Laryn?"

She nodded, pleased by the invitation. Her last assignment had her spending most of her time alone in her cabin, avoided by the ship's regular crew. Perhaps they had secrets to protect or perhaps it was just the distrust for the Consortium that kept the crews aloof of Pendra's agents. "Green food sounds nice right about now. Is this your way of fishing for my meal allowance?"

"You got it. Pendra is far more generous to their slaves than Shelody is."

"Speaking of Shelody…" Nolan said, tipping his chin toward the entrance to the eateries.

The others looked to where he pointed to see Azah, Shelody's youngest daughter, walk diagonally across the green toward them. She strode purposefully, her boots forging a path through the greenery as if it had no business getting in her way. Like Ryle, she wore the fatigue trousers of the militia to which neither of them still belonged. Somehow, she managed to make the tough fabric adhere to her magnificent shape and Laryn saw Nolan perk up at her approach. Like everyone aboard Pendra Station except for security personnel, she was unarmed.

Laryn nearly took a step backward when the woman came to a halt just a little too close for comfort, towering not only over her but also over Nolan. The only one who didn't seem affected by her presence was Ryle, whose eyes scanned the perimeter of the plaza as if looking for someone. Reading the challenge in the woman's expression, Laryn stood her ground and offered a bland smile of greeting.

"Been waiting for you," Azah said, apparently to the others, but her gaze was on Laryn. Her eyes were almost black enough to obscure their pupils. Her skin, too, was the darkest Laryn had ever seen on a Human, and she had cropped her hair so closely that it appeared almost shaved. "Who's the princess?" she added, raking those eyes over Laryn's fine wraps and, for the second time today, Laryn wished she had worn something a little less stylish.

"The new warden," Nolan supplied. "Laryn Ash. Let's be friendly."

"Heard about you," Azah said to Laryn. "You've not been out much."

"I've made a few jaunts," Laryn said, deciding to ignore the taunt. "I've heard much good about the *Nefer* and her crew."

"We get the job done. Hope you're not expecting fancy quarters aboard the ship. We run things pretty tight."

"Speaking of job," Ryle said, "you got us a fare?"

Azah's grin lit her face and transformed her sullen expression into one of both mischief and delight. "The best kind of fare. Someone has to keep us employed while you people sleep the day away."

"Sleep?" Ryle said with a sudden edge in his voice. "We could have used your help with getting the ship ready for overhaul this morning."

Azah shrugged. "I don't do laundry. The ship's your baby."

"Kind of you to remember," he said and started to walk toward the food sellers. "Didn't think Corlan would let us head out again so soon."

Azah waved a hand as if at an insect. The color of her dangerous-looking nails matched the purple streaks she had brushed into the sides of her head. "I got him calmed down hours ago. You can thank me later. We've got us a real job, guaranteed payment. Unless you'd rather deliver settlers for a while."

"What is it?" Nolan said.

"You'll see. Client's waiting at Toko's place."

"Yay," Laryn said under her breath. As pleased as she was by the invitation to join the crew for a meal, the tavern Azah had chosen was not one frequented by Pendra agents. She had heard of brawls taking place there, along with gambling and exchange of contraband between outbounder crews, or at least those who got along well enough for such deals. She preferred to take her meals in the Pendra staff lounge on the upper concourse.

Ryle's eyes shifted to her for a moment and he tipped her a wink. "Kalons, aren't they?" he said to Azah, sounding like he didn't trust her exuberance. "Do we know anything about them?"

"Nope," Azah said with a shrug. "But it's a good thing you brought the new warden along so we don't have to waste time looking for one. If we don't jump on this, they'll hire Roucho's team so let's not act like we're special. They want to take off as soon as we can."

Nolan had been about to open the door to the eatery when she said that. He turned back. "I need some time to get the ship into fighting form. Not letting you push us past where it's safe, Azah."

Her eyes narrowed when she looked to Ryle.

He shrugged, grinning as he walked past her through the entrance. "The engines are *his* baby."

Toko's diner was not on the list given to migrants eager to explore the station on their way through, but some of them would find their way here, anyway. And so this place also received extra generous shipments of fresh produce from Terrica in anticipation of the incoming fleet. The bounty drew the outbounder crews, deprived of such marvels for months, and a din of conversation, music, the scraping of chairs and clatter of plates, overlaid with frequent shouts, curses and laughter, greeted the *Nefer* team.

Laryn peered around Nolan's broad back to inspect one of the Entrada crews, wearing their black *tanga* skin jackets like some outlaw gang. Station staff lounged among them, exchanging their tall tales, their insults, and the never-ending gripes about bosses and the station's shortcomings. Elevator platforms rose from tables to ceiling to carry dishes and drinks to and from the kitchen above. The patrons helped themselves and passed along what was wanted by their table mates.

"Yesss," Nolan said, inhaling deeply the aroma of charred fish. "*Burry* pies today. I think I'm drooling."

Laryn saw no Kalons among the diners, nor had she expected any. The embassy encouraged interaction between Human and Kalon but the notion had never quite taken hold aboard the station. Humans had been quick to adapt to the *idea* of extraterrestrial life forms, but the leap from accepting some exotic plant on a distant world to breaking bread with a fully sentient alien remained a challenge for most.

The clumsy, unarmed transports that had brought these aliens here used a disappointingly common EM engine and not much in the way of defenses, but the Pendra Consortium had been quick to embrace the Kalons as welcome neighbors here on the Hub. None of their competitors had the wealth or the clout to set up shop here beyond the occasional and expensive visit from Earth, leaving Pendra a monopoly on the Kalons for their advanced knowledge of biofluidics and other nano-technologies. The Kalons shared this treasure in small increments, perhaps, Laryn suspected, precisely *because* they understood its phenomenal value.

Another valuable contribution came in the form of the Kalons' tough physiology that required little oxygen, heat, or pressure shielding to survive. The species' willingness to help with the assessment of Ophet, recently discovered, had sped up the exploration of that planet tenfold. They functioned there unaffected by the hostile atmosphere, resulting in tremendous savings of resources and equipment.

When measuring progress and profit against the long-term consequences of Hub exploration, the Ministry of the Exterior did not always agree with the Consortium's goals. Most governments that had any say in the matter regarded the newcomers with more caution. Their jurisdiction here allowed them to insist that Pendra lodged only a few dozen of the polite, reserved aliens aboard the station at a time. When not engaged by the science teams, the Kalons worked with the embassy to shape the political and social relations between their species. By agreement, the Kalons did not request passage aboard the ships bound for Earth, and a sentinel was posted at the filament to Kalon to ensure that, in turn, Human adventurers respected the Kalon homeworld.

A few of the patrons had looked up when Ryle and his crew entered the eatery. Some waved, some jeered, and the *Persephone*'s engineer gestured for them to join their table, but Azah turned away from the commotion. She led the way through an arched opening to a hallway leading to private and quieter dining alcoves. Laryn and Nolan exchanged a surprised glance – these rooms were not for people with shallow pockets.

Two tall individuals were already seated there when the crew filed into the room. Ryle nodded to Laryn to sit with her back to the door, the place usually reserved for the host. As an official ambassador, she was, indeed, the host of this party. The moment turned a little awkward before the crew of the *Nefer* had settled around the table which left just enough space for a bench along three sides of the room. The two Kalons watched this without a word and without expression on their otherworldly faces.

Laryn reached into a bag slung across her body to fish for the modulator used for meetings like this, excited by the prospect of a private conversation with these enigmatic people. Kalons had mastered the common language used aboard Pendra, but their speech ranged at a frequency too high for the Human ear. These devices were not actually translators, as nothing had yet been able to interpret their language, but it slowed their speech to a suitable range. Before she found the elusive device in her bag, one of the Kalons raised a long-fingered hand.

"We have brought our own modulators," he said, his voice low and carrying a peculiar drone deep in the throat of his long neck. He tapped a flat device attached to where, presumably, his larynx resided. Like all Kalons, he had just three fingers and a sort of thumb but each finger split into two along its length, allowing them to move with great precision. "It is comfortable to us."

Ryle leaned forward as if studying it with polite curiosity, possibly to allow the synergic intelligence aboard the *Nefer*, linked to him by the implants in his eyes and ears, to record and examine the device.

"We are pleased to join you here," Laryn said, using words as formal as these people tended to. She indicated the meal delivery column near the door. "Shall we eat?"

"We are not hungry," the shorter of the two said.

Laryn heard Nolan's groan and silenced it with her elbow. These two intrigued her. Although she had studied the approved ways of dealing with the species, she had encountered them only a few times in the halls of the guarded upper modules of the station. They were not known to be social.

And yet, here they were, two of them, *not* having dinner with a crew of prospectors on a commercial spaceport. Both wore elegant mantles over what she knew to be sinewy limbs that looked like skin and fat stripped from muscle and bone, wrapped up again with unyielding, brown-greenish leather. It was this armor of thick skin that allowed them to thrive in places too hostile for Human bodies. Their faces, too, seemed devoid of fat tissue and the skin there looked close to the breaking point. Most notably, they had no ears on their hairless heads and instead picked up sounds via sensors arranged in rough patches on their wide foreheads.

"We came to talk," the other Kalon said. "And to engage your service."

"The Kalons have ships," Ryle said. "Why come to us?"

The stranger's eyes turned to him. The horizontal slits that were his pupils made him look strangely sightless. "We have few ships, and they are not agile. I'm afraid my people view our expedition as frivolous and a waste of resources. And so we offer our partnership to you." He looked around the table as if studying, and then judging, them. "We hear that you can be trusted with... private matters."

Ryle glanced at Laryn. "We are not outlaws."

Azah's snicker cut off abruptly as if someone had kicked her ankle under the table.

"My name is Iko," the Kalon continued, apparently not interested in further discussion of their trustworthiness. "My companion is called Toji. We believe that we have found the location of the *Harla* expedition."

"Whaa..?" Nolan started, agape.

Ryle shook his head. "That ship's long lost. Others have searched for it and failed. It disappeared almost six years ago."

"And its value is exaggerated, as these things become exaggerated over time," Laryn added. "It was hauling settlers out to Terrica, and not especially rich ones. There is no treasure at the end of this search."

"We believe otherwise," Iko said. "And not only do we believe that we know where the ship is, we also think it found a planet or moon upon which to settle. In that case, it is, indeed, a treasure hunt."

"Told you this was good," Azah said. The bounty paid for finding a habitable, accessible world would let them all retire in comfort.

"You think they're alive?" Laryn said to Iko. "The colonists? Out there somewhere?"

"It is possible." Iko placed a projector on the table and a chart appeared in the air. He rotated it until it displayed a broad view of this region of space. He pointed at an orange marker. "We believe them to have made a transit to there."

Ryle leaned forward. "There is a reason we avoid that

sector."

"Nothing there but dust clouds," Azah added. "And the wrecks of a few ships, I'm pretty sure."

"Yes. We understand that Master Tanner is a skillful pilot and that your navigator is capable. The risk is not great."

"Doesn't that pitch sound familiar," Azah mumbled, using the Human dialect of her people.

"We'd still be jumping into quite a soup," Ryle said.

"Soup?"

"The captain refers to the nebula," Laryn translated. "We rely on our sensor arrays to navigate local space."

"This will be worth the risk. We are only looking for the *Harla*. Any profit you gain from the discovery of a new world is of no concern to us. We will not claim it for the Kalon."

Laryn saw surprise and a fair bit of discomfort not only on Azah's face, but also on Nolan's and Ryle's. Perhaps their new patrons did not realize that Kalon claims to any planet would not sit well with the Consortium. Humans regarded the Hub as private property and, even if no one had quite articulated this, anything found where its dark tendrils led. "What does the *Harla* mean to you?" she said.

Iko's answering gesture was incomprehensible to any of them. His companion, Toji, picked up the projector and came to his feet. He must have been kneeling on the bench because now he stood on the seat, towering above them. Iko stood up in the same manner and they walked behind Nolan and then stepped down onto the floor. "We'll let you discuss this. Master Shelody has the means to contact us."

Toji leaned over Laryn to tap the control panel of the food server. She caught a drift of what smelled like cloves and earth, an oddly pleasant aroma, from him. "Accept this meal as a token of our sincerity. I hope we'll meet again soon."

Ryle raised a hand but the two Kalons left the dining alcove without another look at any of them.

"A token of their sincerity?" Nolan said after a silent moment. "What the hell does that mean?"

"Don't they have chairs on Kalon?" Azah said.

"They're strangely fluent," Ryle said, looking thoughtful. "Is this common?"

"Yes," Laryn said. "They learn fast and Pendra brought tutors in for them. I guess they had to since we can't even start to figure out their language."

"What did he mean at the end?" Ryle tried to recreate the Kalon's parting gesture.

"We've been working on a catalog of their body language. I think it means something like: don't you worry your pretty little heads over things beyond your understanding, you puny Humans."

"It does?" Azah said with narrowed eyes.

A hissing sound drew their attention to the food server. The platters of roasted meats and aromatic herbs filled the room with scents that none of them had experienced in weeks. The galley aboard the *Nefer* offered little more than packaged food designed more to save space on a long voyage than to keep taste buds entertained. Of course, even before then, they rarely enjoyed meals like this unless someone had a good bit of credit on account.

"Is that *chakhi*?" Nolan exclaimed when Laryn pulled bowls and plates from the lift. "It is! Hands off, all mine."

Laryn passed a tray of steamed vegetables and a basket of dumplings to Azah whose personnel file listed her as vegetarian. In fact, one anecdote suggested that she would rather eat her ancient boots than another creature. Having once bitten a piece of flesh from an opponent's arm, she had developed an intense dislike for chewing through muscle and skin. "Those look good."

"Our new patrons are generous," Azah said, pulling one of the dumplings apart to release a sweet aroma.

"Let's not be blinded by this gesture," Ryle warned. "We know nothing about these two."

Nolan looked up from scraping tender meat from a bone. "They're a bit creepy, aren't they? Not sure I'd want to mess with them. They could probably tie my legs in a knot without trying too hard."

Ryle grinned. "Hell, *I* could tie your legs in a knot without trying too hard."

"Are you going to accept their offer?" Laryn asked him.

He shrugged. "Yeah. We've had trickier jobs than ferrying a couple of treasure hunters around." He turned to Nolan. "You're all right with the target, Nolie? We'll have limited sensor range out there."

The engineer nodded, too busy chewing to form words.

Ryle pulled the com tab from his collar and placed it on the table. While he did not need it to communicate with the ambient intelligence that was the very soul of the *Nefer*, it allowed the others to follow the conversation. "Did you get all this, Jex?" he said.

"I did, Ryle," the AI responded at once, audible in the room rather than just within Ryle's ears. The JX.9 aboard the *Nefer* linked almost inextricably to Ryle's brain, heard with his ears, saw with the lenses embedded in his eyes. As long as Ryle lived, so did Jex, although, as Ryle's chief mate, Azah also had control over the program. Laryn wondered if Jex, and others like him, chafed less under its imprisonment than Ryle did. Did it understand that, without their flesh and blood masters, the synthetic intelligence that made all of this possible would run amok? It had happened in the past and it would happen again.

"Can we make that target?" Ryle asked.

"Would you like me to plot?" Jex replied.

"If you don't mind."

"I don't mind."

Laryn had to smile. The AI's reply was so lacking in character that it seemed, to her, almost deliberate, perhaps a joke played on its overly emotional masters. Although tethered to their operators to the point of complete inability to act on their own accord, the JX.9 model came with a selection of personalities. She wondered if Ryle had restricted its access to those routines. Maybe the more creative programs became tedious after a while.

Ryle didn't seem amused by the bland reply. "Did you get anything on these two Kalons?"

"Nothing unusual. The Iko Kalon is experiencing some physiological stress. I don't have enough information to analyze it. It may be an illness or injury."

Laryn nodded. "I thought so, too. But they are strangers here, and not well liked. I'd be nervous, too."

"Kalons don't get nervous," Azah said. "They're predators. I don't trust them."

"Humans are predators, too," Laryn said. "You're responding to the way they look. They've been helpful. The survey of Ophet would take forever and cost three times as much if not for them. Our people have had some very valuable exchanges with them."

Azah pointed at herself. "Not *this* people. So why the *Harla*? Why would a couple of mummies care about Humans stranded on some planet?"

"Maybe they like us, deep down inside," Nolan said. He held up a crisped *tanga* eel dangling from the end of his knife, a rare import from Terrica. "Look how generous they are."

"I can plot a path to the edge of the nebula," Jex interrupted. A representation of the Hub with its corona of filaments streaming in the directions of galactic expansion now floated above the com unit on the table. One of them, a quarter of the way around the Hub's horizon, was highlighted in blue. "The filament specified by the Iko Kalon appears solid."

"I think our new friends can afford that," Nolan decided. "Given our current position on the Hub, it'll take less than a day to get out there. One slide through that pipe and we're there."

"So do we take the job?" Ryle said, although, as captain of the *Nefer* and mission commander, the final decision was his.

Azah shrugged. "Sounds like there's coin to be made here. Don't forget that we just cost the company a whole lot of it by that dive we took into nowhere. If this is a hit,

Daddy might just forgive you."

"Let it go, Azah," Nolan said when Ryle's lip curled in a snarl, unwilling to see this scrumptious meal spoiled by one of their spats. "I can get the *Nefer* ready by morning, with a little help from the boss."

Ryle nodded and turned to Laryn. "So are you in?" he said, reminding her that, although assigned to the *Nefer*, she could refuse a mission if she wished. Something in his steady gaze underscored the hopeful tone in his question. No doubt, requesting another mediary now would cause more delays than he wanted to deal with.

"I'm in." She tapped her forehead. "I'll ask for an update before we leave. See what I can find out about the *Harla*."

"Settled, then," Ryle said. "Nolan and I will get the *Nefer* ready. Azah will see the old man to get us cleared and our passengers to the dock by early second shift. We can sleep once we get under way to the launch point."

Nolan looked mournfully over the still-full bowls on the table. "You think we can get this packed up to take with us?"

THREE

Laryn still nibbled on a sprig of mossberries, brought to Pendra Station from Terrica, as she left the others to head to the Annex, the station's research sector.

At this end of the plaza, the transparent ceiling curved down to floor level to offer an infinite panorama of their galaxy disturbed only by an occasional passing ship or satellite. In a few days, the new arrivals from Earth would crowd this promenade for their first glimpse of the dark, impenetrable heart of the Hub. It went by many names, but most people referred to the anomaly as Bogen's Well or just simply as the Well.

Laryn relished the emptiness of the broad walkway along the window, glad to have this to herself today. Only the sound of the air exchangers and a distant murmur of voices intruded here. She slowed to walk close to these windows, as she always did, feeling as if she floated outside on her way to distant places.

From here she could see a good portion of the station's massive complex of modules, stuck together like a pile of blocks left floating in space by an inattentive child. The central body, with its gracefully curving gravity hub, domed plaza and the residential levels below, formed the main bulk. The shipping and smallcraft decks jutted out on one side while a bewildering array of instrumentation for the astrophysics division studded the other. Interchangeable modules, shipped in for various reasons and owned by several of the Pendra Consortium companies, attached to the station in what seemed haphazard fashion. Other components floated at a distance for privacy, security, or because they were still being constructed.

All of it made for an irregular, messy complex and plans were underway to reorganize some of these into a separate orbiter. It would begin to make sense of the warren that formed the lower levels where neglected residences, parts of the station's mechanical services, and black market businesses existed like a world apart.

"Laryn!"

It took her a moment to realize that Ryle Tanner had caught up to her. She turned, a question on her face, reluctant to smile in case the purple fruit had caught in her teeth.

"Heading home?" he asked.

She shook her head, still probing her eyetooth with her tongue. "Going to the cog lab," she reminded him, hoping for the best.

He matched her pace but seemed immune to the splendor of the distant stars. His eyes moved restlessly along the concourse, to some maintenance workers near the exit, and over the groups of station staff loitering in the open plaza. Laryn knew he had completed a few tours guarding the borders of the exclusion zones on Earth; the same zones that produced the refugees seeking new lives on distant planets. Perhaps absorbing the terrain until he understood every element had become a habit, even aboard the safe confines of a remote, somewhat seedy outpost station.

"Must be nice to just plug info into your brain like that," he said.

"It can be," she said. "Although there's no *plugging* involved. We prefer to call it accelerated learning. You're linked to Jex. That seems much more like plugging in than what we do. He can just tell you anything you need to know."

"It's just a database," he said. "Just facts and figures and calculations, there when I need them. Not very exciting. I can get that from my remote." He raised a hand to indicate the band around his wrist, similar to the portable unit he had used earlier.

"I guess that's true," she said, again struck by his refusal to refer to the AI as anything but a computer, a most unusual attitude for those who worked with them. Even if just for amusement, almost everyone talked with them, or about them, like another person. Or perhaps a pet. Given that Jex was most intimately tied to Ryle's senses, the distance between them was puzzling.

"But you Cog folks are something else," he said with a tone of wonder in his voice. "I wish I could learn like that. But tampering with my brain just doesn't appeal to me."

She cocked her head. "You disapprove of augmentation?"

"None of my business what other people do. But, yes, I think I'd rather have implants in my eyes and ears than my gray matter."

"I've not had to regret mine," she said. "It helps me do my job." She wondered if the captain had followed her to make some clumsy attempt at small talk or to share his views of Cogs. He would not be the first to express veiled contempt for neural upgrades. Humans had suffered when their trusted machines almost destroyed their world and prejudices still lingered even in the generation that had followed. She had not expected those feelings in someone permanently linked to a computer.

"I didn't know you mediaries needed that for your job," he said.

"Well, we don't. My training is in biology. Exobiology, of course. I'm hoping for a place on a deep space mission. I missed out on the one heading to Yora Two. So they assigned me to the Intermediary."

"Not your first choice, then?"

"Not really," she said guardedly. Had the captain not

bothered to learn these things about her when she was assigned to the *Nefer*? She slowed her steps to look up at him. The calm gray eyes now fixed on hers as intently as they had studied the occupants of the commons, this time searching for something in her expression. He knew all of these things about her, she concluded. One didn't run a crew into utterly unknown space without knowing a great deal about each member. She forced an airy smile. "I prefer a microscope over politics, frankly, but they seem to think I'm suited for this."

"You went out with one of the Entrada ships last time. The *Rowan*."

"Yes?" she said, lifting her voice to show that she found his inquiry puzzling and perhaps a little inappropriate. Pendra, sometimes at the request of the Ministry, assigned and reassigned their mediaries as needed and she had been with the Entrada outfit for only a few outbounds. She waited for him to ask her for some detail that might give him an advantage over a rival. He'd get nothing for his trouble.

"You didn't mention their meeting with the Roucho trader at the Terrica filament."

She stopped walking. "You intercepted my report?"

"Yeah."

"Those reports are Pendra property."

"I know."

His calm, slightly weathered, face offered no expression, but she saw past his unwavering gaze to detect the hint of amusement hiding in there. The slight tension in his shoulders seemed to anticipate her response with more than casual interest. "Then I guess you also know I didn't mention the cases of *rascot* root in their hold?"

That revelation seemed to startle him. "Oh? He should know better than to let a mediary into his storage."

"It was as locked as my report was."

He chuckled. "You have talents I wasn't aware of. The *Rowan* crew has much to thank you for. The taxes on that stuff barely make it worth shipping up here."

"That's because it's not wanted on the station. It makes people lazy."

He turned to the window to look out into space. "It gives people a few moments of rest, of dreams. Not everyone is as privileged as you are. The station isn't pretty in a lot of places, mostly the lower levels."

"I'm aware of that," she said, bothered by the dismissive tone. It was a tone she often heard in the voices of those who resented the station's administration and the agents employed by them. It told her she was not one of his people, that she was too detached from the civilians who worked here or the migrants crammed into tired ships or overcrowded dormitories to really understand life aboard the station.

"So why didn't you?" he said. "Report these things, I mean. That's your job, even if not officially."

Laryn followed his gaze out of the station and into the *Out There*. It had always been the Out There for her, in words that stood out in big letters, lit up in bright colors. It had felt that way since she had first learned that there were worlds beyond Earth's horizons.

She walked a few steps away to run her hand over the controls embedded in the transparent wall. The display darkened for an instant and then an overlay appeared before them. What had been a panorama of stars now showed the filaments streaming away from the inscrutable vantablack sphere, three hundred thousand kilo-ems away.

The sensors and navigational systems saw the filaments this way, although someone had added a little color and shine to this overlay, like the surface of the blackest oil. The anomaly itself, without accretion disk or photon sphere, was of interest only because of the smears of light distorted by its pull.

Countless undulating threads of dark matter took root within the safe zone above the event horizon, reaching from this Hub into deep space. This overlay showed only the denser formations – the sort suitable for exploration – and ignored the wispy threads of *murk* that permeated the universe and even pierced Pendra Station itself to pass unnoticed through and out again on their way to nowhere.

All planets spun dark matter murk into threads this way, but Bogen's Well, the heart of the Hub, attracted it in measures that made deep space travel possible. It sprouted far more substantial filaments than Earth, presenting thousands of traffic lanes leading to remote and unexplored regions of space. Distance measurements lost their meaning and now points of interest were marked on the maps by how much real-time it took to reach them.

The sight of the Well unsettled many who saw it as some rapacious monster waiting to tear apart all that dared to ride the filaments into the unknown. Indeed, some ships had disintegrated in the attempt, before the correct shield configurations were found. Others had simply disappeared for reasons that were mere speculation. But she only had to see Ryle looking out over the display to find him as enraptured as she was by the possibility these endless rivers presented. Had sea captains plying Earth's ancient oceans worn the expression now on his face?

"Because of this," she said.

He frowned, puzzled, as he turned to her. "Because of this you let smugglers go unreported?"

"What do I care about smugglers?" she said, still watching the Well as if it might suddenly move. "I've wanted to be *out there* for as long as I can remember. How fortunate you are to have lived your life on this adventure. I want to be part of that." She traced a finger over the glass, following the line of a filament. "Not as a passenger. Not a tourist taking safe jaunts around the Hub. I want to be part of the discoveries that happen out here."

"So how did you end up on Pendra Station, then?" His voice was soft, as if afraid to jolt her out of her confession.

She tapped her temple. "This. I grew up near the Queensland exclusion zone and things were... difficult for us. Little food, too many people off the grid and without hope, but we joined with others to make the best of it, living off the land to survive. But even during those hard years my mother insisted that I study and learn about the things that were, and the things that are. She wanted me to have what they had lost and when I showed aptitude she applied for a neural enhancement for me. Memory augmentation." She turned to smile up at him. "I didn't even know about that. I thought everyone used computers for everything."

"Used to," he said. "Until the AIs went amok before either of us was born. A lot of damage happened by the time the system was contained again. I suppose it's safer to turn Humans into thinking machines than machines into Humans."

She nodded. The AI breakthrough had come not long after developers, contracted by corporations like Pendra's, had perfected their vain attempts to bestow Human thought processes onto the artificial intelligence that operated every aspect of their lives. Phase-changing material simulated neuronal membrane that finally produced an intuitive intelligence able to act with far greater efficiency than any Human could, autonomously or in concert with others of its kind.

But things had turned disastrous when their intellect surpassed their Human caretakers and they escaped their digital bonds. Only the unprecedented coordination of multinational agencies finally brought them under control and relieved them of their duties. What remained was a changed world and neutered synthetic neural networks whose every action was filtered and controlled by their physical connections to a Human. That their survival depended upon the health of the Humans who held their leash ensured obedience. They were now little more than vast databases, seeming sentient only at the whim of their cosmetic programs.

"Probably is," she said. "And exciting. Once I got the implant, I was able to absorb so much more information that I began to do research on my own. Mostly sciences and medicine. It was like magic! I just wasn't able to forget anything I learned. I finally had the chance to leave Earth to come here, to the Hub."

"And take a job as warden of prospectors after all that?" he said, amused. "A bunch of ruffians and bootleggers?"

"Well, I'm biding my time until I can get a post on a research expedition. The mediary offer came with private quarters. Pendra's been good to me, so I agreed to this assignment." She grimaced when she realized how her words must sound to him. "I'm sorry. I didn't mean to imply that your pursuit isn't also valuable…"

He grinned. "I get it. Minding the outbounders isn't exactly a choice assignment."

"It's still a chance to see what's out there, even if my work on your ship isn't all that useful. To you or to me. But maybe I'll get a liking for ruffians and bootleggers."

"And their petty crimes, too? The ones that don't make it into your reports?"

"Are you testing my loyalties, Captain?"

"I am."

Although he seemed to be joking, she felt a point had to be made. "If you're suggesting that I neglect my duty as mediary…"

"Not even a little," he said. "But you've got what I need. If you're tired of lounging around in your cabin and spying on smuggled inventory, I could use you on the bridge. Data collection, not avionics. Trevor got himself hitched and his lady won't have him tripping the threads. That leaves us a bit short out there. Interested?"

"Don't even ask!" she said, astounded by the offer. Although the Pendra Consortium owned a few corvettes able to navigate the filaments, it relied on the outbounders' ability to gather scientific data during even the most mundane of expeditions. With his thinly disguised bribe, Ryle had offered what mattered most to her. No one had so much as invited her to see the bridge of her last assignment aboard the *Rowan*, never mind work on it.

His eyes shifted and the easy smile faded to frown at something behind her. "Now here's a boatload of ugly," he murmured.

Three men walked toward them, led by a captain of the Roucho Transport Company. Laryn had seen him around the station, always shouting at something or someone who managed to irk him. A hulking figure, dressed in untidy layers of uncared-for clothing, he towered over his crew in both stature and authority.

"Wait up, Tanner," he bellowed although neither Ryle nor Laryn had moved from their spot by the observation window. "Want to talk to you."

Ryle hooked his fingers into the back pockets of his trousers and waited while the rival prospector approached. He said nothing when the captain reached them, trailed by two crewmen who seemed a little out of breath, and just regarded the taller man with a raised eyebrow. Laryn copied his pretense of affected politeness while putting up with this tedious interruption.

Indeed, the Roucho leader looked a little taken aback; perhaps he had expected some insult or challenge from Ryle. Laryn had half-expected that, as well – the coarse rivalry among the outbounders spilled into all areas of the station. He glanced at her and then back at Ryle. "Saw you down at Toko's," he began.

"And..?" Ryle said.

"You were with those mummies. Making deals, I guess."

"They've got some very fine coin."

"What are they up to? Why're they hiring outbounders? Kalons got ships of their own."

Ryle shrugged. "Just tourists. Speculators. Like everyone else."

"You want to be careful, Tanner. Maybe best not to get involved with them."

"Why do you think that?" Laryn said.

The captain turned to her. "'Cause they're a creepy bunch, girl. We don't need them setting up shop here, crowding the Hub. They're right cozy with Pendra. Who knows what deals they're making or how they're getting their hands on our coin. You best not be showing them things they don't need to know about, Tanner."

"Thank you for your insightful advice. I'll bear it in mind."

The captain's eyes narrowed as he considered a response to Ryle's sarcasm. "Some of us don't want the mummies on the station at all," he said to Laryn instead. "And now we might be making friends out on Antica. Before you know it, this place'll be overrun with aliens. Ought to stay on their planet and leave this place to real people."

"Kalons seem real enough to me," she said, keeping her voice even. "And the Anticans don't seem interested in the Hub. But I can understand that you would fear more competition."

His brow lowered over his deep-set eyes. "No one's competition for Roucho, girl. Specially not a bunch of *them*." He glanced at Ryle. "Where'd you find this one, Tanner? Not your usual speed, is she?" His eyes shifted see what curves might hide under her shawl but it seemed that his leer was intended to goad Ryle into some altercation, strictly forbidden on the more polished levels of the station. "You must have good parts under that dress or he wouldn't bother."

Laryn felt, more than saw, Ryle's good humor evaporating. His casual slouch stiffened and his hands moved to his side as if he prepared to give in to the provocation.

"I don't think we've been introduced." She smiled sweetly and held out her hand. "I'm Agent Ash, the *Nefer*'s current mediary. I didn't catch your name."

The smirk on the man's face withered as he took her hand, touching it as if it might break in his rough paw. "*Agent* Ash? Well." He cleared his throat as his glance shifted to Ryle. "We're Roucho Company. Name's Ben Colsan."

Ryle leaned forward and tipped his head in Laryn's

direction. "Cog Division," he said in a conspiratorial whisper.

Colsan released her hand at once. Laryn had seen this reaction many times since receiving her implant. The Cog lab here was a minor adjunct of the station's medical facilities, existing to support the augmented members of the staff and crews. But here, too, fanciful theories swirled around the innovations made by the vast Earth-based Cognitive Sciences Agency ranging from telepathy to mind control. Those who weren't part of the system viewed any Cog as suspicious. "Well, what I said," he grumbled. "We're not too happy with others crowding in on the outbounder business, that's all. Only so many contracts available to us."

"I understand," Laryn said. "The Kalon people can seem a little daunting, even if their ships aren't."

Ryle grinned broadly as they watched Colsan and his men hurry away, toward the ramps at the end of the concourse. "Nice work, Agent," he said.

"Easy work," she corrected. "The privilege of my office. Thanks for not leaping to my rescue, though. He seems a little... umm, overbearing."

He shrugged. "If you're going to hang out with the prospector gangs you'll be running into more like him. Azah gave him a bloody nose on their first meeting. I think I like your ways better."

Laryn laughed. "You're still testing me, then, Captain?"

"Just making sure you're not being starry-eyed about the great adventure you're looking for. Things get rough sometimes."

"Do all of you feel that the Kalons are a threat to the outbounders? That they're muscling in on your business? Surely they don't have the ships to compete with any of yours."

"I'm not sure anyone knows why they're here. But now that they are, there's nothing to stop them from using the Hub as we do. Nothing that wouldn't cause trouble for us, anyway. Pendra is keen on keeping them happy. Probably thinks they've got all sorts of alien toys to profit from. I doubt they'll be bound to the rules we're subjected to. Or taxes."

She shrugged. "Those taxes pay for the air you're breathing right now. I'm sure the Kalons will be made to pay their share if they want to use the station."

"They could build their own."

"Of course," she said. "Anyone could, with enough know-how and resources. We can't claim the Hub as our own. Eventually, Pendra will have to give up their monopoly here. If not to the Kalons, then to some other Earth enterprise setting up shop on the Hub."

"Some folks on the lower decks aren't so sure about that. Pendra is powerful and profits far too much to share any of it. There are stories told about how they keep their competitors away and the politicians in their pockets. And the Ministry is happy with Pendra's monopoly. It keeps other hotshot outfits from tripping the threads without supervision, attracting more aliens."

She nodded. "Like we attracted the Kalons. They wouldn't be here if we hadn't poked into their space, showing them how the filaments work."

He hesitated a moment before speaking again. "Maybe you could... you know, get some intel on them. The Kalons I mean. The archives must have more than what we're being told. I don't want any surprises out there." He raised his voice in mock seriousness as he looked around the concourse. "I mean, we don't want to commit any breaches of protocol. Like eating with the wrong fork in front of them or something."

She rolled her eyes with just as much exaggeration. "Oh, stop already. Where do you think I was going?"

FOUR

Laryn still mused over the encounter with Colsan and his crew as she reached the pressure door separating the main station from the Annex. She was well aware of the fear and distrust some residents harbored for the alien species. That didn't seem terribly out of place; Humans had a long history of distrusting those not of their own kind and no doubt the Kalons felt that. She, too, transhuman by choice, was not exempt from the misgivings others had for her. Neither, she supposed, was Ryle, willingly bound to his digital slave.

They were all no longer Human, she told herself as she walked past small clusters of people heading for their residences at the end of the station's official day phase. Cured of disease while still in the womb, enhanced for strength and speed, like Azah, thriving on less food and air during long voyages, few of the Humans here were free of adjustments.

She wondered, ever so briefly, if Ryle's powerful body was engineered or the result of natural genes and hard work. What had Colsan meant when he mentioned his 'usual speed' where women were concerned?

Laryn pushed the intrusive thought aside with an impatient frown as she pressed her hand to a security panel. Recognizing her as a Pendra agent, the door slid aside to allow her into the short conduit leading to the more restricted modules of the station. A small travel pod awaited its passengers there, like some sort of horizontal elevator.

Besides the medical and cog labs, the Annex included Pendra's research facility. Specializing in exobiology, it investigated new, often hazardous, materials gathered during the prospectors' forays through the filaments or brought back by the more extensive explorations made by Pendra's own science vessels. Connected only by two gates and these short conduits, the sector was designed to separate and move away if a quarantine situation arose. More than once in the past, prospectors had returned on a plague ship, with crew and vessel so contaminated by a virus or other pathogen that the only choice remaining was to steer it into the Well to be swallowed and destroyed.

She dropped into one of the two pale-blue padded benches and pushed her headscarf back to be recognized by the overhead scanner.

"Hello, Agent Ash," a soft woman's voice issued from an unseen speaker in the wall. She spoke for ANN-X, the branch of Pendra Station's artificial neural network that operated aboard the science annex. "We didn't expect you back so soon."

"I didn't either," Laryn said. "But I'm on a Shelody jaunt now and its going outbound as soon as they get clearance. I need an update."

"What do you have in mind? Or I should say: what do you *want* to have in mind?"

Without really thinking about it, Laryn obliged ANN-X by smiling in acknowledgement of the old joke. "I need whatever you have on the *Harla* loss. And the Kalons."

"Travel to that planet is prohibited."

"Yes, I know. We're not going there. Two Kalon treasure hunters are hiring the *Nefer* for an outing. I thought I'd find out more about them. I don't have much."

"You already have what we know of them. What are their names?"

"Toji and Iko, they said."

"I'll see what I can find. You can proceed." The transmission ended without farewell and the pod began to move, barely jarring its passenger, along its magnetic track.

Laryn leaned close to the transparent wall when the chute exited the station and curved toward the research segment. Out here, the pod allowed a spectacular view of a broad swath of stars, looking close enough to touch. As always, Laryn made a tent of her shawl to cut the glare as she peered out at two ships approaching the station. One was a hulking scandium ore transport, preparing to join the fleet heading back to Earth. It dwarfed a much smaller corvette, one of the nimble but heavily shielded outbounder ships. Like the *Nefer*'s, its main structure rode atop the circular gravity generator but the sleek peripheral assembly allowed it to land under diverse atmospheric conditions. She couldn't wait to board her new assignment and head back out there.

The bend brought her into sight of the landing platter of the photonic transport platform, no more than a pulsing blip of light in the inky distance today. The massive laser array would soon decelerate the arriving fleet from Earth. Constant monitoring ensured that the thruster remained in precisely timed alignment with its counterpart near Mars. A similar system allowed travel between Earth and Mars, like a railway moving at cosmic velocity, picking up and discharging supplies and passengers every time Earth's orbit brought it close to the platform. Soon, another photonic conveyor would connect Bogen's Hub with Terrica, increasing migration tenfold.

Although the filament from the Hub to Earth's solar system meant an almost instant way to cross the distance, fear of contamination subjected private vessels, like the prospectors' corvettes, to expensive decontamination, irradiation, and inspection protocols before passing the armed sentinel guarding that filament to Earth. Most travelers chose the decidedly safer photonic transport system aboard a fleet of passenger ships. It meant a five month journey but also a far more affordable one for the migrants looking for a new home. Like Laryn, most of those who came to the Hub came to stay.

Too soon, Laryn's pod made that tight little turn that always felt like it had stumbled over something, announcing her arrival at the research segment. As a member of both the science division and, currently, the Office of the Intermediary, she had access to many doors here. Today, she stopped at a platform serving the small Cognitive Sciences Clinic. She left the car and once more presented credentials to a door panel to gain entry. Whatever Kalon-related information she didn't already possess would have been sent down here for infusion.

"Hello, Laryn!" Tom Calek, a slight, pale man and one of her favorite techs, peered around an open door when a mechanical sentinel announced her presence. No one else was in sight although she heard music from another of the labs along the hallway. "What brings you into our lair so late?"

"Is it late? 'What meaning has time when you drift among the stars'," she quoted. "No one told you I was coming down?"

"No. It's been quiet."

They both walked to a wider section in the corridor where he accessed a com panel on the wall. He tapped around for a while and then shrugged his sloping shoulders. "We're always the last to know. I was about to shut down. We have a few sleepers, but we're not expecting anyone else."

"I sent the request to ANN-X just now on my way here. It'll get here shortly, I suppose."

"Probably. Want something hot? I was thinking of some soup."

"I just ate. Can I still get hooked up? If they get around to authorizing?"

"For you, anything." He gestured to the open door of one of the labs. She walked ahead of him into the small space furnished with a broad recliner, the tech's stool, some screens and, of course, the infuser. Years ago, the sleek, ultra-efficient Cog Sciences edifice on Earth where she had received her implant had both awed and intimidated her. These few rooms, an adjunct of the medical facility of the station, hardly compared to its grandeur. Still, despite the somewhat worn equipment, she knew Calek kept his infuser at peak performance.

"What's on the menu?" he said.

"Kalons." Laryn stepped behind a partition to trade her clothes for a thin but comfortable coverall while he called up her profile. Accelerated learning did not mean it was instant and she'd rest here awhile. "We're seeing them more often around here now, so I thought I'd add to my inventory. We'll have some of them aboard on the next outbound."

"That should be interesting," he said when she emerged and sat on the edge of the marginally comfortable recliner, resigned to spend the next few hours on it. "You have everything on them, I think. You have no idea how much I'd love to get one of them into my lab to dig into their heads. But they can't interface with our toys, so that won't happen."

"Not at all?"

"Nope. The scans don't show any sort of brain structure our systems recognize. Their brain waves are as beyond our classifications as their language is. They're like us more on the outside than the inside."

"You don't have anything useful? That can't be. I have some background on our contact with them here. A little about their technology, but that's all. We don't have more than that? What about their biology? Customs? History? The Kalon homeworld?"

"Some historical stuff, nothing classified. At least not that I'm aware. Our treaties with Kalon include a provision for minimal interaction between our species. They're a bit cagy about their planet. Trying to keep us away." He flashed his shy smile. "I don't blame them. We have a history of messing up places that belong to other folks."

"I guess that's why we're not allowed to travel to their

homeworld. The Ministry is afraid we'll cause problems there."

"Wouldn't be the first time. From what I hear, their planet is fragile and we can't breathe the air, anyway. I'm sure we'll get to a point where a diplomatic mission is possible, if not a scientific one. Meanwhile, we study them here."

"I guess Pendra has the biggest interest in getting friendly with them," she said, remembering Colsan's bluster. "Is that why they let them stay here on the station?"

He allowed himself another thin smile. "You are astute, Agent Ash. The Kalons are masters of microfluidics, and learning about their engineering is something that is a high priority for the Pendra research team. They're not so forthcoming with the actual materials they use for their technologies. They're using biochemical polymers we haven't been able to reproduce. And so we're being nice to them, hoping they'll come to trust us enough to share their resources. Who knows what else they have to offer."

She nodded. Likely, she thought, Pendra was making sure that their monopoly of Kalon cooperation was absolute. The people on Earth who cared about such things were aware of the discoveries made at the Hub, including the alien species found so far. But none of the Kalons had been invited to travel there, nor was it likely they would be. She suspected the reason was not only the Ministry's fear of contaminants reaching the Human population but also Pendra's desire to keep the aliens from meeting the Consortium's earthbound competitors. "I'd love to go to Kalon, even if we can't land there," she said. "Any planet that produces a sentient species is worth studying. They're so much like us."

"That they are, although some folks on the station don't see that. Your outbound with them should help us add to what we know about them. We'll create a new file for the other Cogs with whatever you bring back for us."

She pointed at the display wall. "Well, let me review what you've got. There's got to be something I can use. Got anything on the *Harla* expedition?"

"*Harla*? That old wreck?"

"Apparently the source of much income for the crews hired to find it. It hasn't been gone all that long."

He scrolled through his files. "Six years. I have the traffic records for that quarter. It includes the loss of that ship. Want it?"

"Please. How about Captain Ryle Tanner?"

"Tanner? You also have that."

"Apparently I don't. He's indentured?"

"He is?"

"So he said."

Calek dug deeper into his data. "Hmm, some restricted files there. Sorry, can't give those to you."

She sighed. "Well, I'll take the *Harla* file, then."

A chime somewhere out in the corridor drew his attention. "I'm very popular this evening. I wonder who that is now." He walked to the door, and then looked back at Laryn, mystified by whoever had arrived there.

"Who is it?" she said.

"Your boss."

She stood up when, a few moments later, Joel Mitcher filled the doorway, mostly from side to side, looking just a bit out of breath. Had he jogged down here? His carefully cultivated cap of auburn hair floated around his head like down feathers, not at all matching the stiff little brush of gray sprouting on his chin.

"Hello, Director," she said to the leader of the mediaries, surprised to see him here. Other than an occasional meeting to discuss her assignments, she rarely had cause to speak with him. Her mission reports, largely uneventful, went to his assistants and there was no need for him to seek her out, especially so late in the station's work shift. Why had ANN-X decided to alert him to her presence here this evening? She hoped he didn't have a new assignment that would keep her from joining the Kalon expedition.

"Evening," he replied as if in a hurry to get the pleasantries done. He nodded to Calek in a way that made the doctor leave the room at once.

Laryn watched him go. "I did not expect to see you here," she said when they were alone. "Did I miss a message from you?"

He closed the door to the hall. "No, I wanted to speak to you personally. I saw your request for an update on the Kalons. You are heading out again so soon? With Tanner's crew?"

She nodded. "Yes, two of the Kalons hired the *Nefer* for an expedition. I thought it might be useful to learn about them. Doctor Calek said there was little more on file for me. That's disappointing. But this could be a good opportunity for me to add to our intelligence of them."

He nodded. "Keep in mind that they prefer to keep to themselves. Be sure to keep your research discreet and within our diplomatic policies."

"That is always my goal," Laryn said, puzzled. Was this not the main function of the mediaries? Once recruited by the Office of the Intermediary, she had undergone months of training before she was sent on her first diplomatic mission. And now Mitcher was telling her to be careful? "They seem... approachable."

"Good. You've proven your abilities in the past. I'm sure you won't disappoint us."

Laryn kept her expression neutral as she observed the director. His eyes were on the screen which had showed nothing new in these past few minutes. He had barely looked at her at all. His hands hid in the pockets of his long vest, balled into fists so tight that his knuckles pressed against the fabric. He seemed sweatier than usual.

"I'll do my best," she said.

"Of course you will, Agent," he said, and it seemed he was forcing a lightness into his voice that didn't belong there. "Where are these two taking the *Nefer*?"

Laryn shrugged. "Looking for the *Harla* jaunt."

"The *Harla*? Why?"

"Why does anyone look for it? There is still a bounty set

by the relatives. The ship, if intact, is worth a fair bit as salvage. These Kalons seem to actually think there may be survivors."

"I had not taken them for treasure hunters. Why did they engage the *Nefer*, did they say?"

"They heard about the crew's record for making their target, I guess."

He gazed at the data wall for a moment longer and then leaned forward to enter a code. The display now showed that ANN-X no longer recorded sound or visual details in this room. "We have... concerns about that crew," he said.

"Concerns?" she said. "I thought you might. No one told me that Captain Tanner is a felon. Is that not something I should have been aware of before agreeing to join that crew?"

Both of them knew that her agreement would have had little effect on his decision to place her aboard the *Nefer*. Pendra staff carried out their orders without question – the price of well-paid employment and a private suite aboard the station. How well they carried them out ensured that they kept them. Both of them also knew these things meant little to her.

"He chose to reveal that to you?"

"Not directly. What is his crime?"

"Not your concern, Agent. It will only cloud your observations. I want you to focus as much on that crew as the Kalons. More, actually."

Laryn frowned. "Why? Our Outreach Division hasn't concluded their studies of the Kalon people already, have they? Doctor Calek said—"

He waved her objection aside. "You're a mediary. You're aboard the *Nefer* to ensure the crew sticks to protocol. That's your job now." He turned away as if the devices along the wall were of interest to him. "I need you to keep an eye on Tanner."

"Sir?"

"He's a felon, like you said. And still up to things we'd

like to know about. I need more from you than his weapons inventory. It's of no concern to us."

"No? The *Rowan*'s arsenal is considerable," she said, referring to her previous assignment on another ship. "I thought you might want to know." She was well aware that no one cared how the outbounders conducted themselves off-station, as long as it didn't annoy the wrong people. But returning a squeaky-clean report to the Ministry would have shown a lack of commitment, and so she had included information about the *Rowan*'s excessive armament.

"I want you to pay attention to his communications outside the station. Who's he talking to, what they're carrying, and where they're going."

"Do you suspect the crew of the *Nefer* of engaging in something illegal? Smuggling? Piracy, even? Corlan Shelody's reputation would make that unlikely, no?"

"So it would seem," Mitcher said. "And yet… We suspect goings-on outside our oversight. Down on the docks. Off-station. Maybe even on Terrica. Those outbounders are thick as fleas and more than smuggling is going on. Even right under the noses of the mediaries we send along with them."

She grinned. "I assure you, they are not thick as fleas. Their crude competition with each other is seeing to that."

Mitcher turned abruptly to startle her with his scowl. "Then perhaps you need to include that in your reports, Agent Ash. I expect you to listen and observe and make sure they don't veer a degree off course without you knowing about it. Is that clear?"

"Yes, sir," she said, too startled to say more than that.

"Get into his JX, if you can. There should be something in the database we don't know about. Talk to the crew. Not the black woman. We haven't been able to get to her since they came aboard the station. Try the kid, their engineer."

"Nolan Jone."

"Yes, him. Tanner's shorthanded. Report on any additional crew he takes on."

"Sir," Laryn said, not sure how to handle this strange

request. "I realize that the mediaries are in place to ensure policy is observed on outbound missions. We're a necessary evil the crews consider as only so much cargo. But you're asking me to spy on them?"

His scowl, already furrowing his waxen forehead, deepened even more. "Did I not make that clear?"

"I'm not sure I'm comfortable—"

"Perhaps you'd be more comfortable back home on Earth. Did you think your augmentation and fancy education were a gift that fell from the sky? With that come certain expectations, Agent Ash. And right now Pendra's expectations are for you to fulfill the function of the Mediary. *All* functions."

"I was not aware those functions included snooping into the affairs of a private enterprise."

"You're aware now. I saw your file. You think someone's just going offer you a place aboard a deep space expedition. That's quite a lofty ambition. One that isn't going anywhere without our recommendation."

The eyes in the fleshy folds of his skin regarded her without emotion as he seemed to wait for some reaction from her. He was right: she owed Pendra her education, her neural enhancement, and her enviable status aboard the station. Indeed, she owed them her escape from a lawless, isolated existence in a part of the world only now recovering from disaster. How soon she could apply for one of the sought-after places on a science vessel depended on his willingness to release her from his division.

Was this, then, what she had signed up for? Informing on bootleg shipments of dope? Dangerous jaunts aboard a cramped ship with a crew that didn't want her and probably suspected her of spying already? Not exactly what her recruiter had promised, she reflected, almost hearing the sound of a door closing. Or perhaps a trap.

She dropped her eyes. She would go where they sent her, for as long as they needed her. Not because of the prospect of returning to Earth, but because he was right to remind her that she owed Pendra her loyalty and her service.

He released the lock codes on the data wall. Another tap on the screen summoned Doctor Calek. "Choose, Agent. Will it be the *Nefer*, or the next transport home?"

She shook her head. "There's nothing for me on Earth." She looked to the door when Tom Calek returned, a question on his face to ask if the Director had concluded his business with his agent.

"Report in person upon your return," Mitcher said to Laryn, a directive to avoid transmitting her findings where they may be intercepted. "I look forward to your discoveries." He nodded to the doctor and left them to their work.

Calek gestured to her to recline on the lounger and started to initialize the infuser with her profile settings. "It's a bit of a package, but it's all we have on that set," he said. "It might be a bit technical in places, which I don't think is necessary. That's what we got data archives for. Still, it might be useful."

Watching him work, she tried to formulate a question; some comment about Mitcher and this unusual meeting perhaps, or her apprehension about his blatant orders to spy on the *Nefer*'s crew. But even a quip about the director's ill-fitting suit withered before it crossed her lips. As much as she liked him, Tom was another Pendra employee and bound by the same rules and unspoken protocols that kept them all careful with their words aboard the station.

"Did you do something to annoy the director?" he said with his eyes on the monitoring system. "Your pressure's up."

"No. Let's do this," she said, irritated and confused by Mitcher's orders. She leaned into the small beam he activated to let CogSys scan the KRNL4 application near the hippocampus of her brain. Recognizing her, it sorted through the inventory of data she already possessed, checked for errors, and prepared for an infusion of new information. Incidentally, the chip also served to identify her not just to

CogSys, but to other artificial neural networks, the ANN's subsystems, aboard the station. "I'm in."

Lying down, she tilted her head into the padded cradle and tried to relax while he positioned the semi-circle of shielded transmitters. She considered her new role. What did the Office of the Intermediary care about smugglers? Pendra had staff to inspect cargo holds and deal with folks who didn't pay the appropriate docking fees. But of course Ryle wasn't about to allow one of *them* to ride along on the *Nefer*.

"Try to relax. Breathe. Nice and slow." Calek's tone had dropped into a soothing cadence. "Keep your eyes on that pattern on the wall and give us some nice theta waves."

She followed his instructions, listening to the voice and to the soft resonances that now exuded from the speakers near her ears, to allow him to lull her into the state of mind needed for the upload. She closed her eyes and let the thoughts come as the information sent to the small network inside her head began to solidify in her memory.

But she wasn't awake. Not really. She drifted into an oddly detached mental state induced by the infuser that allowed her to absorb what it sent, without question, without analysis. Sounds and images passed through her mind, increasing in frequency until the information was little more than a blur of impulses to the waking mind.

Three ships had been lost in 22-44, the *Harla* among them. Laryn absorbed the entire crew and passenger lists, the ship's configuration and inventory, logs and schedules. All that was known about them until the moment they merged into the dark stream leading away from the Hub. At some point after that they had either lost the contact with the filament, or perhaps they had even embarked on the wrong one, and had not emerged at Terrica as planned.

All of this information was easily stored in databases and would already be part of the *Nefer*'s inventory. But Laryn learned from the conversations in the logs, from the tone and pitch of the voices that recorded them, from the actual memory profiles and engrams on file of the captain and the senior crew, to create a world in which she once walked, in which she had interacted with the people who were now gone. Beyond mere emotionless facts, the story of the *Harla* was now her own.

Then another drift of information moved through her thoughts. The Kalons now became her memory, too, as she remembered the first missions to encounter them. Two ships had not returned from their journey along what was later named the Kalon Filament. Then in 22-10, nearly forty years ago, an outbounder expedition reported an incident near a featureless, oxygen-poor planet where signs of habitation pointed to vast pockets of underground civilizations.

Before the prospectors had even begun to gather information about the planet and its solar system, a weapon located on a nearby moon had fired on the explorers. The missiles appeared to be photon projectiles, similar to what Humans used for blasting asteroids. Easily avoided, but the message had been clear.

Earth's Ministry of the Exterior, in a rare show of authority over the Pendra Consortium, declared the Kalon Filament off-limit and imposed harsh penalties on those who passed the beacon placed near its launch point on the Hub. The incident forced a revision of First Contact protocols and the creation of the Office of the Intermediary.

But that first, nearly disastrous, encounter had left the Kalons wondering about the intruders into their space. Already at a moment in their own evolution where they had made the first forays out of their thin atmosphere, the Kalons had grasped the significance of the filament that passed by their home. It had taken just nine years before they had adapted their own technology to launch into the dark matter thread and arrive at Bogen's Hub. Unarmed and friendly, they responded to the Ministry's ambassadors, eager to begin a cautious relationship with the Humans whose goal, of course, was to find intelligent life among the stars.

The Pendra Consortium was quick to capitalize. Besides sharing some of their alien technology, the visitors agreed to join an extensive expedition to research and develop Ophet. That planet's atmosphere challenged Human physiology but the Kalons seemed immune to the hardships. The quest to explore Ophet's trove of resources multiplied in efficiency once the Kalons had taken on the task, requiring few Humans to visit the location.

Laryn drifted for hours in this state of passive study until the information selected by the doctor was exhausted and her mind sank into a deep sleep state.

FIVE

It hadn't taken much time for Laryn to familiarize herself with the *Nefer* even before coming aboard. The corvette-class specifications had been easy to obtain and infuse into her memory and, now that she was aboard and Nolan had finally treated her to a welcome-tour, no one among the crew seemed too concerned about keeping its modifications secret.

The *Nefer* belonged to an older build, apparently an heirloom passed to Ryle by his father. The younger Tanner had expanded the cargo areas, updated the engines and shielding as they became available, and retrofitted the avionics deck with a new design that allowed closer work with the JX.9 onboard neural network. Able to land on planets where terrain challenged larger vessels, the ship was designed to conserve space and so offered few amenities beyond a half dozen cramped crew quarters and shared spaces for eating, hygiene and entertainment.

Unlike aboard transports on which Laryn had traveled in the past, few things on the *Nefer* were left unsecured. Tools, personal items, even the dishes they used were kept in their bins or strapped into place. It hinted at frequent gravity shifts while traveling or even jaunts within a planetary atmosphere. She had not expected this to be so – outbounders took their risky leaps into deep space, recorded what was to be found there, and returned to the Hub. And yet, the *Nefer* was designed for rougher conditions, from the efficient use of onboard space to the numerous grips along the narrow corridor and in the cabins providing handholds when gravity was unreliable.

"Damn, not again," Laryn grumbled when her sleeve caught on a clamp holding some conduits in place. Clearly, the captain had not bothered much with improving the esthetic components of the ship, she thought as she untangled herself. She had exchanged her elegant wardrobe for closer-fitting coveralls in a glorious shade of saffron over a berry-red blouse but the cramped quarters would take some getting used to. She continued along the narrow space forming a corridor through racks of storage bins on both sides and the floor. Above her, color-coded pipes directed gasses, power and water to where it was needed.

Bored in her own cabin, Laryn had decided to spend a little more time in the Kalons' company. This morning, as the crew worked through the pre-launch details of their trip, she had asked Toji about his life and world, but he slipped out of her conversational traps, offering nothing more than idle small talk. Iko, for his part, didn't bother with pleasantries but met her attempt at conversation with blank stares and monosyllabic replies. Still, she took note of body language, the words they chose, and their interaction with each other. The captain had agreed to let Jex, the ship's AI, record their movements in the shared spaces of the ship for later study.

She followed the yellow pipes to the engine chamber at the rear of the *Nefer* where, according to Jex, Toji was once again in Nolan's company. Things were quiet back here now that they cruised toward their launch point on the Hub's horizon. It took little energy to navigate the open space of the Hub, but Nolan kept the engines in top shape for when they did have to breach an atmosphere. Or, she fancied, engage in hostile encounters with pirates who, banned from the station, operated from hidden bases on Terrica and the

Pendra mining belt. Or so she had heard.

Voices drifted out into the corridor when she passed the door to Ryle's cabin. The low murmur was indistinct but she recognized his voice, if not the words. She slowed, wondering if she ought to listen, maybe to hear some bits of conversation that might offer a clue to whatever it was that interested her supervisor. She heard a low chuckle and it occurred to her that it was probably Azah in that room with Ryle. She continued on her way, embarrassed by her eavesdropping attempt. And no doubt Jex, with eyes everywhere aboard the *Nefer*, would see and report her loitering by the door.

She reached the engine room and stopped abruptly at the open door of the main chamber when she saw the display before her.

A lower panel of the secondary drive hub had been removed and she was treated to the sight of not just Nolan's backside but also that of one of the Kalons as both of them had squeezed their heads and torsos into the space. A heated conversation was part of the goings-on on but exactly what they were saying was muffled by the sound of something rushing though the conduits. As she watched, the Kalon reached back to fumble for one of the tools on the floor by his knee. Although he again wore a long mantle, she saw that his feet were long and narrow and, like each of his fingers, split in two. Someone had taken care to stitch an intricate pattern into the leather that covered them.

Laryn crouched beside them and picked up the caliper to slip into the sinewy hand. "I take it we're not ready for launch?" she said.

After a startled moment, Nolan pulled back, knocking the back of his head on the upper frame of the opening. The Kalon took a little more care in extricating himself.

"Hey, Laryn," Nolan said, rubbing his new bruise. "No, we're ready to go. Toji was showing me how the Kalons would space the drain manifold to deal with the EMI below the rods. It's genius."

She peered at the length of insulation in Toji's hand. "You didn't strip that from the emitters, did you?"

"No, of course not!" he said at once, looking worried. Or what Laryn assumed to be worry. The body language of this species seemed far more complex than Human expressions and wonderfully lyrical.

Toji had found his place among the engines with Nolan even before they had left Pendra. The two seemed to share a love of the things that made the *Nefer* one of the more agile ships among the outbounder fleets. Most Kalon technology did not interface with Human-made equipment but Toji had clearly spent his time on Pendra with his nose in one engine or another. Those who kept an eye on Kalon activities aboard the station took full advantage of their aptitudes and no doubt encouraged his curiosity. Clearly, Ryle also realized the benefit of having Toji aboard and allowed him into the *Nefer*'s engine rooms. It had not taken long for Nolan and Toji to seem like old friends, joined by their passion for engineering.

Toji seemed younger than the other Kalon, and far more engaging. As much as Laryn disliked to hear them referred to as 'mummies', they did indeed remind her of some desiccated bodies she had once seen on Earth. Judging by what was visible beneath the flowing, bronze-colored mantle, his body, smaller than his companion's, also seemed entirely made of sinew and bone. He moved more quickly than Iko, spoke with greater animation, and seemed eager to learn more about the Humans while aboard their ship. Iko, in contrast, had retreated to the cabin they shared and didn't seem to care how his companion spent his time aboard the *Nefer*.

The youth demonstrated that his leathery skin was quite capable of stretching by smiling broadly at Nolan, showing the small, blunt nubs serving as teeth. "I am looking forward to seeing us wind up for the transit. When we looked for a ship to take us out, we heard much praise for the *Nefer*."

"Of course!" Nolan said. "She's the smoothest little bitch

of the fleet, thanks to my utter devotion."

Laryn watched Nolan replace the access cover to the snarled guts of the cooling system. "I heard your ships are built much like ours. But your operating system uses biologics, right?"

"Yes. Your binary and quantum systems are intriguing," Toji said brightly. His smile turned almost mischievous. "If a little slow." He pointed his caliper upward along the shielded main drive. "But your mechanisms are much more powerful over short distances. We use generation ships for our exploration, designed for very long journeys. Until your people showed us Bogen's Hub we hadn't gotten very far."

"Toji shared specs for their newer ships," Nolan said, lowering his voice to hint that Iko would not approve of this. "Even Ryle was impressed. We can't duplicate their hull material, but there's got to be a way to emulate their smallcraft propulsion. Reactionless, far more efficient inside an atmosphere. I'm hoping we can come up with a hybrid someday. I'm sure Pendra's already all over that. Ryle thinks Shelody'd be interested in taking on Kalon ships and crews."

"Well, Pendra is—" Laryn began when a clunk in the sound system drew their attention.

"Let's get this train rolling," Ryle's resonant voice sounded throughout the ship. "We're approaching the launch point. Jex, can you lift that gravity a bit? I'm glued to the floor."

"Maybe you're just out of shape," Azah cut into the transmission.

"I'll see you in the gym later," he replied, likely referring to the small exercise space they had made in one of the cargo holds. "Didn't take much to put your butt down last time, if I recall. All hands prepare for launch. Laryn, you can take the com for departure transmission. Iko, you may join us on the bridge, if you wish. I'm on my way there now."

Laryn had already stepped back into the corridor when another voice came online.

"Captain," Jex spoke. "I'm detecting a ship on approach."

"To this launch?" Ryle said, referring to the point above the horizon where ships could merge safely into this particular filament. It was here that the concentration of dark matter was stable and dense enough to allow the immersion of their ship into the stream. Using dark energy to create a field of null space, they would travel at speeds that no longer had any relationship to the space outside the filaments.

"To these coordinates," Jex confirmed.

"That's a job for our agent," Ryle said. "Laryn, tell them to stand by until we get ourselves out of here. I don't want anyone hitching a ride on this slide."

"On my way," she said.

Leaving Nolan with his engines and the Kalon, she hurried through the narrow walkway to the heart of the *Nefer*, the bridge located in her heavily shielded center section. As she passed, the door to the galley opened and Azah emerged, sipping some sort of green, lump-filled concoction. Her unadorned body suit turned her curves into a race track for the eyes, and Laryn wondered if she wore it on purpose to torture her crew mates.

"This is going to be great," Azah said. "I can feel it."

"What's with the gun?"

"Protocol," she replied, wiping her lips before she dropped her hand to the holster at her side.

"Is that a new protocol?" Laryn said.

"Yep, fresh today. The Kalons are starting to feel a little creepy." Her broad grin showed all of her teeth and looked ferocious in the dim corridor.

"What do you mean? I rather like Toji."

"That Iko is making me nervous. He never blinks."

"I'm not sure they need to blink."

The door to the bridge opened when Jex sensed their presence and allowed them to step into the circular space.

Ryle nodded to Laryn and gestured to one of the task stations. Pleased and excited to be included in the ship's operations, she took one of six comfortable chairs arranged in a circle in the middle of the bridge. Currently each faced outward at dedicated screens, allowing the crew members to carry out their assigned duties: tactical and data collection for Azah, helm for Ryle, engineering for Nolan when he was on the bridge, and now the com for Laryn. From the console built into their chairs, holographic and manual controls appeared when needed along with restraints to turn their seats into crash couches. The chairs would swivel inward to form a circle around a hologram projector. A few more crash restraints were built into the walls for visitors to the bridge.

Iko was already here, standing before the concave main array of screens. Mimicking a massive observation window, they presently displayed a compound, panoramic view of the stars and the smudged distortions caused by the Well. An overlay showed the Hub's horizon as a visual reminder to stay well outside its deadly gravity.

Laryn picked up the ear piece that allowed her to work unobtrusively with Jex to contact the approaching vessel. She directed him to scan the other ship before speaking, keeping her voice low. "This is Agent Laryn Ash, on outbound SE *Nefer* from Pendra. Please respond to my hail."

"Filament acquired," Jex reported to the others.

"Let's see it," Ryle said, as always speaking aloud to the AI for the benefit of his crew. "On screen."

The others swiveled their chairs to face the main display. An overlay of darker markings appeared on the panorama to show nearby filaments. From here, they saw just four of the threads streaming into the distance, the nearest one marked in blue, looking much like the Hub's representation on any map.

"Thread is solid," Azah reported. "No murk at all. Emitters are live."

"Let's have us a nice, tight bubble, Jex." Ryle raised his hand into an overhead sensor sweep to engage the helm. His neural interface with Jex would navigate the *Nefer* along the filament, relaying his commands instantly to the ship's avionics. Laryn had faith in his proven record as navigator, but she was glad for the extra levels of redundant safety protocols monitored by Jex in the background. Azah gestured for Iko to step into a brace at the rear of the bridge.

"Approaching vessel, please respond," Laryn tried again, wriggling into her own restraints.

"That better not be Colsan's tub jumping our claim," Azah said. "I'll singe his ears if he tries."

"It is an older corvette," Jex said, for Laryn's ears only. His work on her communications did not distract from his focus on their imminent merger into the filament. "Heavily modified. It does not belong to any local fleet."

"What do you mean?"

"It is not registered by any of the private companies, nor owned by Pendra."

"That can't be," she said. All smallcraft using the Hub, needing supplies, fuels, and contact with Earth, were registered with the station. "Request an ID from Pendra. Maybe it's new."

"Done, Agent Ash. Transmitting now."

"Ready for launch." Ryle looked up at a screen showing their patrons' target coordinates. "Exit at point four two two kilo-secs. Jex, try to hit that correctly this time, if you don't mind."

"I don't mind, Ryle."

A display at the top of the panoramic screen showed that, in the rear of the ship, Nolan and Toji stood ready. The engines thrummed, following their routines to power up the field generators. Laryn felt a new, slightly queasy shift when the gravity rods began to adjust for the pull of the stream.

"The ship is still approaching, Ryle," Jex said. "Do you wish to include them in our shield field?"

"No," Ryle said, sounding irked. "Laryn, tell them to stay back. We don't need company on this trip."

"On it." She relayed his message, barely above a murmur. It was possible to extend a transit bubble to protect several ships, but these things took close cooperation and, usually, a transfer of payment to the ship doing all the work. "Do not approach these coordinates," she sent. "This is a private expedition and we will not extend our shields."

"What do they want?" Azah said.

"I don't know," Laryn said. "They're not responding to hail." New information appeared in front of her. "They're going to fire!"

"What?"

"That's confirmed," Jex said, unruffled. "We are targeted."

Azah called up the tactical controls above her station. "Not for long," she said through clenched teeth.

"Hold your fire," Ryle snapped, reading the display of the other ship's tactical arrangement now on the main screen. "I'm not engaging within sight of Pendra. We're going."

A warning strip below the ceiling turned red. "A plasma hit," Jex confirmed. "They are attempting to dissipate our field."

"Patch it. Let's go." Ryle's hands moved through the hologram before him to direct the ship in an evasive sweep toward the filament.

"They'll just follow us," Azah objected.

Another hit into their field bubble registered on the overhead indicator.

"Then you better be ready," Ryle said. "Launch, Jex."

Laryn grasped the supports of her bench and ground her teeth as the ship, encased in its field, slipped into the stream and hurtled toward their destination, incapable of stopping now, deaf to course corrections beyond this point. They'd either find their target or, if the filament dispersed too soon, they'd emerge elsewhere. 'Elsewhere' was usually empty space from which they limped home again, defeated and poorer. Also possible was that they'd end up torn apart by some encountered object, annihilated by radiation, or caught in the clutches of insurmountable gravity. Or, if the filament *murked out*, unable to re-enter at all. That was the tricky, somewhat suicidal, part that made a successful outbound expedition so very profitable.

The others, too, remained silent and tense during the

minutes that clocked by, eyes locked on the viewscreen that had no option but to show their last location, and acutely aware that the shimmy they all felt now meant that the bubble that kept them from disintegrating into their individual molecules had suffered from the attack.

"You seem stressed," Jex observed as he monitored their state of health.

"Is that so?" Ryle hissed through clenched teeth.

"Yes. Laryn needs to reduce her heart rate."

Laryn did not reply.

"Would you like some music?"

"Shut up, Jex!" Azah snapped.

"Target range now," Ryle announced. The indicator from engineering glowed an assuring green. "Dropping!"

Jex disengaged the *Nefer* from the filament to drop into normal space where it seemed to skid to an abrupt and unpleasant halt. The ship shuddered, forcing a gasp from Laryn and a strangled grunt from Iko.

A deep silence descended as the crew recovered from the assault their senses had taken these past few minutes. The external cameras now showed a region so densely packed with drifting dust and mineral debris that only a few stars winked at them through the haze. Laryn inhaled deeply when Jex confirmed that the ship and her passengers had made the transit without damage.

"I wonder who that was back there," Azah said. "We haven't done anything lately to invite that kind of trouble."

"What the hell is so important about this place?" Nolan said over the sound system from his station in engineering.

Ryle turned to look at Iko, who still gripped the restraints of his crash brace as if expecting it to come apart at any moment. "I wonder, too."

"A ship is leaving the filament," Jex announced.

Ryle looked up at the screen where the AI now displayed the unmistakable shape of a transit field forming. "Nolan, we're going defensive. I'm not having this." He took the helm from Jex. "Azah, let them make the first move."

"Captain," Iko said. "I don't think you understand—"

"Silence," Azah said in the same tone she had used to silence Jex. The forward screen now showed an overlay of their targeting grid.

"Wait till they dissipate their bubble," Ryle said. "No need to waste energy till we find out what our levels are after that leap."

"Would you like a report?" Jex said.

"No, Jex. Scan that ship for something we can hit, will you?"

The enemy ship burst into visible range and swooped toward them. Ryle raced away, putting more of the sensor-confusing debris between them and their pursuers. Laryn tried to hail them once more, already sure that no one would reply.

"We are targeted," Jex said.

The annoyingly red warning strip above the screen showed two hits absorbed by the *Nefer*'s shields. It would not be long before they'd feel those hits closer to their hull.

"Now?" Azah shouted.

"At will," Ryle said.

She returned the enemy ship's fire, placing a pattern of plasma charges designed to disrupt their protective shielding. "That bitch is coming down," she muttered through clenched teeth.

Laryn's eyes shifted to Azah's board. Tactical anything wasn't her specialty, but clearly, Jex was involved in the maneuver. That was a Human-made ship ahead of them, even if long thought lost. Why was he assisting in its destruction? Regardless of who was aboard that ship, its designation should have stopped him, if not Azah.

Ryle directed the *Nefer* to evade the missiles heading their way, rotating to avoid catching them in the same place. Receivers worked to convert incoming fire into useful energy but the hits landed far too rapidly. "Give us some weak spots, Jex!"

"Ryle!" Nolan's voice reached them. "I've got specs on

that cutter. Target the lower port section, astern of the docking grips."

All eyes fixed upon the image of the enemy ship as Azah continued to stitch along its side, weakening their defenses with every hit. "Got it!" she shouted and whooped in triumph.

Ryle released a barrage of projectiles before their opponents realized where they were heading. The ship turned, too slow to protect its vulnerable flank, and then they all saw it cave in as the first successful hit tore into it. Several more followed and then the cruiser began to crumble, splitting and spilling its contents into space. Ryle backed off, less worried about shrapnel hitting them than the thought of body parts caught in their gravity well.

"Nice!" Azah grinned as she disengaged their guns.

"Sheeet," Nolan said in a long exhalation, awestruck.

"Your weapons system," Iko said, now oddly calm, "appears to have been modified well beyond specifications for this class."

"Lucky for you," Ryle said. "What's out here that's so valuable?" Something about Laryn's expression seemed to worry him and he leaned over to put a hand on her arm. "Are you all right? You're a bit green."

"I'm fine," she said at once, certain that, if not for Azah's smirk, she'd allow herself to faint or throw up or something. "It all went so fast. I know things out here can get... hostile sometimes." She smoothed her hair with a few nervous flicks of her hand, mostly to avoid Ryle's scrutiny. It had been a long time since she had feared for her life at the hands of another being. Space travel did not frighten her, neither did aliens nor living aboard a poorly maintained outpost station, far from anyone she could call friend or family. But this deliberate attack reminded her far too well of the reasons she had fled Earth, and had rattled her. "I need to report this to Pendra."

"Of course," he said. His hand lingered for a moment more – perhaps he looked for some words to reassure her.

"Like they care what happens out here," Azah said.

"Ryle, I have found information among the debris from that ship," Jex said, interrupting as always when his own news seemed more important than what was going on among the crew. "It is listed in my archive as the outbounder *Hypso*. Pendra declared it lost in 22-29, almost ten years ago."

"Lost?" Laryn said. "That wasn't a ghost ship. You can't keep a crew alive for ten years without coming by the station at least once in a while."

Laryn watched Ryle swivel his chair to exchange a long, undoubtedly meaningful, look with Azah. Perhaps they were using Jex for an unheard conversation, using the pickups in Ryle's throat. She thought she saw Azah nod almost imperceptibly.

Ryle turned back to the forward screens. "We'll report the incident later. Let's take a peek at where we've landed, Jex."

Some of the screens edging the main display began to relay information in text and images. "Our scanners cannot penetrate far," Jex said, "but the probes are getting through. We've emerged within a small solar system. Two planets orbiting a red dwarf, several moons."

A slow grin spread over Azah's face. "I think we found something."

"What?"

She pointed at the display in front of her station. "Sensor readings are messy. There's a whole lot of interference out there. But we're detecting water. Liquid. Lots of it. On the second planet." She transferred the incoming data from the probes to the main screen. "And where there's water, there's life."

Laryn scanned the overhead monitors. This did indeed look promising. "Could be habitable," she said. "The planet's tidally locked to that star but it's got a massive biosphere along the terminator. Big islands, wouldn't call them continents. Geology too active for my liking."

"Those plates are moving?"

"Yes," Azah confirmed, working with the data on a

smaller screen before her. "Looks like plenty of volcanic activity."

The door to the bridge slid aside to admit Nolan and Toji. "Am I seeing that right?" Nolan said, walking up to the wall of screens before them. He stretched his arms out to the image of the planet. "Are we rich beyond our wildest dreams?"

"Move over, you," Azah said. "Look. We've got nitrogen/oxygen."

Laryn watched Iko, wishing she had more experience with the species. Was that a smug expression on the Kalon's face? "Looks like you might be right about this place, Iko. If the *Harla* expedition made it here, they could still be alive."

"Pressure along the coast is 85 kPa," Azah said. "This planet is more like home than even Terrica is. Does this seem like quite the fortunate coincidence, or am I being cynical?"

"I was just thinking that," Ryle said, turning to the elder Kalon. "How did you hear about this place, Iko?"

"We learned of it from an explorer. They decided to forgo the journey here."

"Why's that?" Azah said. "Nobody turns away from a habitable planet."

"Perhaps we should," Jex cut in. "I'm detecting echolocation scans from the surface."

"What?" Ryle turned to the screen to see an overlay of Jex's findings.

"Radar," Jex specified. "But intermittent. Scattered."

Ryle returned to his station. "The *Harla* maybe? Can you parse that out, Jex?" He frowned when he saw the data on the screen. "That's no ship. The second planet is inhabited. They have sensors."

"You're right," Nolan said. "Power sources on the southern hemisphere. Weak. No satellites, no air traffic. But they seem to have scanners in operation."

"Going dark," Ryle said, already directing the *Nefer* to shutter all but the most vital systems, douse exterior lights, and cover the few cabin portholes in the hull. He switched the shielding to scatter and confuse all but the most sophisticated sensors, turning the ship invisible to conventional radar. "Let's back off."

"There is a moon. Synchronous orbit."

"I see it." Ryle turned the *Nefer* toward the small satellite, keeping sensors alert to the sweeps of the terrestrial scanners. The ground radar seemed haphazard, merely stabs into the dark from one of the island continents. He evaded them easily and they soon approached the moon. "Jex, launch a set of dark probes to the planet to find out where that's coming from. Look for evidence of the *Harla*. We've got her specs in the archives."

"This could be First Contact," Laryn reminded them. The possibility that they were nearing a planet whose residents had what seemed to be sophisticated technology sent a tingle of excitement up along her spine. This is what she had trained for, never even imagining that it would actually happen.

Ryle took the *Nefer* down toward the moon's dun-colored surface out of view of the planet. "I don't think they caught us," he said. "Jex, can you confirm that?"

"I don't believe they did."

Iko looked up at the ceiling. "Your computer has beliefs?" he said, sounding amused.

Ryle leaned forward to peer at a video screen when its markers drew his attention to an irregular cluster of something on the arid surface of the moon. "What's that? Someone's up here?"

"Doesn't look natural," Nolan said.

The *Nefer* swooped low over a fissured basin featuring little but dust and rocks. The odd readings on the screen resolved in greater detail, showing a scattering of gray structures among debris flung up long ago by a meteor strike.

"I guess we're not the first ones hiding up here," Nolan said. "That's a ship. Big. Some kind of transport."

"Jex?" Ryle said, circling low above the grounded vessel

to give the ship's cameras a view from all angles.

"Scanning for markers," Jex said.

The image panned across a screen to reveal deep-set portholes, sensor arrays, and several docks onto which smaller vessels might latch. If it had any significant weapons systems, none were in evidence.

"It is the *Harla*," Jex confirmed, showing an archive image of the lost ship next to the downed hull on the surface of the moon. "Largely intact. Congratulations," he added, aware of the long search for the missing ship and the attempts made to find it.

"I'd say this is the easiest coin we've ever turned," Ryle said. He lowered the *Nefer* to settle not far from the grounded vessel and began a partial shut-down of its systems. The gravity rods slowed until they felt the moon's own, somewhat light, gravity take over.

Laryn studied Iko while Jex reported on the environment outside. The Kalon did not seem especially surprised or excited by the find. His eyes were fixed on the incoming data from the planet's surface. She used the key panel on her display to send a silent question to Jex. Of course, as part of the ship's synergic network, he conveyed her inquiry to Ryle who frowned at her, puzzled.

Jex, what is Iko looking for? Laryn wrote.

The response on her screen was immediate. *His eyes are focused on reports of possible sentient populations. The probes have found evidence of settlements near the location of the ground-based scanners.*

She turned to watch Ryle respond to her comment about Iko. Only a few twitches of the muscles of his throat and jaw betrayed that he was using his subvocal abilities to speak with Jex, unheard by the others.

Tell Laryn I don't think he came out here to look for the Harla, Laryn read on her display when Jex translated Ryle's words for her. *This was too easy. And we're not that lucky.*

She nodded although being attacked by a long-lost ship on their way out here was not her understanding of 'easy'.

The *Nefer* had embarked on recovery missions before and even the most successful among them seldom yielded more than a broken hull, barely worth the salvage to cover their costs. Sometimes, like when they had tracked down a crashed outbounder vessel in the icy regions of Kila a while ago, they were able to retrieve the bodies of those lost in the mishap and so give some comfort to people they left behind. Worth the effort, but not profitable, Laryn knew. To find the *Harla* here, with a possibility that the crew might have made it to the surface, seemed too much to hope for.

"Looks like she came down hard," Nolan said, unaware of the conversation channeling through Jex. "Would have lost pressure on the lower deck. The main hull's no longer tight but it looks like they camped out in the aft section for a while. They've reconfigured some of the cargo holds."

Ryle powered the ship down but left it in standby mode. "Anyone alive in there, Jex?"

"There is considerable organic material aboard but the conditions are unsuitable for habitation."

"Expect dead bodies, you mean," Azah said.

"Yes."

"There's a shuttle parked over there," Toji said. "I wonder why they left all this up here."

"They should have three shuttles," Laryn said, referencing the information she had received at the Cog labs. "They can't land a transport of this size on Terrica so everything has to be ferried down. I'm guessing they used the smaller ships to evacuate to the planet."

"Something's still ticking in there," Azah said, pointing to the incoming data. "Something still powered up, in that domed module to the left. Weak, though. Could just be whatever's left of their life supports."

Ryle tested his legs to feel the moon's gravity. He looked around the room. "Azah, you're with me." He gestured at the younger Kalon. "And Toji."

"You want to inspect that ship?" Iko said.

"Isn't that why we're here?"

"Yes, of course." Iko stretched his thin lips in a smile that looked like he had to remember how that worked. "I thought you would be interested in exploring the planet."

"We need to complete the scans," Laryn said. "No one's to make contact until we know more." She looked to Ryle. "I'll come, too."

"Why?" Azah said.

Laryn wanted to say that she found herself agreeing with the woman that something about Iko just didn't seem quite right. Despite Nolan's reassuring company, Laryn felt a strange unease at the thought of remaining aboard with the Kalon. "I know that ship and crew," she said instead. "It makes sense for me to come along."

"Well, true," Azah said and headed for the door to the main corridor. She glanced over Laryn's delicate coveralls. "You better lose the regalia, Princess, things get sweaty in the walkabouts."

Laryn followed her into the exit area of the ship. Most of the floor was taken up by the cargo elevator and rails led from it into the first of several modular cargo spaces that ran along both sides of the ship. A smaller passenger lift served for quicker exits. One side of the space held tools and gear cabinets along with a row of protective suits. She wondered about the need for the two full space suits. Perhaps they had occasion to make external repairs away from Pendra's docks.

She stripped down to her body suit, nodding when Azah offered a small cabinet for her clothes. The comfortable layer covered her from elbows to knees but she was less at ease than Azah with appearing only in the snug-fitting second skin. Ryle also entered the small space, already pulling his loose sweater over his head.

The black, sleeveless shirt he wore beneath showed him off rather nicely but her attention was caught by the lines of the JX.9 interlink array tattooed into his skin. He had chosen to display the receiver like a series of ocean waves sweeping from his chest, over his shoulder, and then onto his back. He caught her staring and she quickly looked away, almost tempted to deny that her interest was for anything but the device. Azah's smirk told her that trying any protest would just make things more embarrassing for her and more amusing for Azah. Ryle made serious business of pulling weapons from their storage but a slight grin on his lips told her that he was quite aware of Laryn's discomfort.

Neither of them seemed worried about what had taken place since they left the Hub. Not the unexpected attack and not Iko's peculiar response to the *Harla*'s presence on this moon. From what Laryn knew about this crew, this had not been the first time they had come to blows with a rival salvage team, and not even the second.

Perhaps this was just another day's work for them, she thought. The Pendra Consortium hosted members of conflicting planetary nations who had sworn to maintain the peace aboard the station or forfeit their right to use it. Out here, far beyond the oversight of anyone who may care, the rules were different. No one made laws out here.

SIX

It took a while before the members of their expedition stood on the moon's fissured surface. The thin atmosphere did not call for extensive pressurization and so they wore the lighter, loose-fitting *walkabouts*. Used to explore unfamiliar terrain, these EV suits would allow them to move unencumbered while still sealed off from the environment and protected from the cold. It was unlikely that Toji would fit into a full space suit, anyway, given the stringy length of his limbs. The small air packs would do – they would return to the *Nefer* for refills rather than lug around full tanks. Even in reduced gravity, those things were just awkward after a while.

"We're out," Ryle reported after the airlock closed behind them, testing the link to the *Nefer*'s com system inside his helmet. He turned to scan the horizon while reading the display of information on the inside of his visor.

"All systems green here," Nolan reported from his station aboard the *Nefer*. "The four of you are reading perfectly. Proceed."

"Watch for these cracks," Azah said to Toji. "The ground scans as solid, but some of these gaps are deep. We're not looking to deal with broken bones."

"Understood," Toji said. He turned his upper body as if on a swivel to look around the foreign terrain. "This is wonderful. We're inside a crater?"

"An old one," she said with amusement in her voice. The young Kalon's excitement was clear even through the distortion of his translator.

Daylight flooded this side of the moon and they did not need more illumination to find their way. Footprints made by frequent traffic crisscrossed the dusty ground. Closer to the massive hull of the parked ship, the surface was packed hard, hinting that the castaways had been here for some time.

Ryle stopped to inspect the shuttle parked not far from the main entrance portal to the *Harla*. Far more compact than the *Nefer*, this class of shuttle was not made to travel any great distance. But it could go where the mammoth migrant ship could not and most transports took them along on the voyage. Someone had removed a panel above the left drive and tossed it aside. Ryle peered into the compartment.

"What do you make of this, Nolie," he said, making sure the cameras above his visor and on his chest captured the interior. "Looks like it's missing pieces."

"Looks like it," Nolan replied after a moment of conferring with Jex. "Anything useful's been stripped out. But they took care to do it right."

Ryle tried a lever on what he assumed to be coolant valves. Stuck. "Powerpack's gone, too."

"I've found a debris pile on the other side of the transport," Jex reported. "Waste material, for the most part. It appears that the *Harla* passengers were here for a while. No appreciable salvage."

"Lucky us," Azah muttered. "Not the kind of gunk I like to poke around in."

The expedition turned from the little cruiser and walked to the main entry of the transport. Whoever had landed the ship had set it down heavily. They either had no plans for taking off again or the *Harla* simply did not have the landing struts necessary for touching down on this terrain. The entire tail section sat on the ground where it had plowed up a ridge of dust.

Laryn turned to let her eyes roam the horizon defined by

the edge of the crater. Tracks led here and there, likely made by someone with an interest in exploring the moon, but there was nothing to be seen but rocks and dust, and the star-filled depths of space beyond. The stillness, broken only by the sound of breathing made by the others, was unnerving. Although she had trained for this, she had experienced this sort of atmosphere only once or twice.

Ryle touched the doors of the *Harla* and found them disabled and ajar. His gloved hand fit into the gap and he leaned against one of the panels to force them open.

Laryn followed him across the threshold and into the dark beyond, pausing a moment for the sensors on her suit to activate the light emitters on her chest, helmet and wrists. Like the others, she scanned the hallway leading from the doors to the interior and read the information appearing on the screen of her visor.

"This place is messier than Nolan's cabin," Azah said, stepping over a stack of loose pipes and some rags to lead the way along the hall. At least it appeared to be a hall - most of the panels had been removed, revealing the ship's innards. Air conduits and lengths of power cables cluttered the space, and large swaths of the stuff that kept things from vibrating had been pulled out as if something had tried to make a nest in the bulkheads.

An open door led to some sort of crew lounge or perhaps reception room, bare of furnishings. A storage bay across the hall had also been emptied to the last crate. The silence felt oppressive and old.

Azah poked into a rectangular gap in a wall panel that had once held a communications console. "Looks like they took the place apart and headed to the planet," she concluded.

"Seems likely." Ryle checked his scanner for the source of the power signature deeper inside the ship. Following the weak reading, they made their way along the corridor, aware that, gradually, the spaces appeared less neglected. Much of the interior construction was still missing, but no further debris lay scattered in the way, waiting to trip them. In places, the clutter had been piled along the side of the corridor or into abandoned cabins.

They turned onto a ramp leading a half level down and came upon a static display wall showing the grid of cabins that lay ahead. Like an orderly town, the rooms clustered in sections, each with facilities and common areas. The names of the people assigned to these spaces had disappeared when the power had failed.

"There would have been four hundred and thirty seven migrants, and about forty staff and crew," Laryn said. "Sent to augment the Kiliana settlement on Terrica."

The scanners detected organic matter in the cabin closest to this entrance, this time in great quantity. Ryle moved to the half-open door to let the light from his helmet sweep the room.

"Damn," he said, exhaling the word like an invocation.

Laryn stepped inside, steeling herself for what he had discovered. Her visor amplified the light to show what she wanted to believe was a heap of clothing and equipment. But these were bodies, of men and women, piled carelessly on the floor and even atop what seemed to be a service counter. Swallowing whatever threatened to rise in her throat, she crouched beside the body of a woman to scan for the cause of all this. Except for the creased, moistureless skin, she, like the others here, seemed little disturbed by time or decay in the airless environment.

Toji muttered something no one understood when he and Azah crowded the doorway.

"Frozen, but slowly," Laryn said. "No sign of trauma. But look at this."

Ryle bent to direct a targeted beam of light where she pointed. A line of some pale substance lay across the woman's body like someone had thrown a rope at her and it stuck where it landed. It crossed her chest and another had caught in her hair. He moved his light to find the same strings on the bodies of the others left here.

Laryn caught his hand when he reached to touch the

thread. "What do you make of this, Jex?" she said, focusing her scanner on it. "What happened here?"

"I cannot extrapolate without a thorough autopsy. All seven bodies are in remarkable condition, other than the desiccation. If they can be moved and examined without re-introduction moisture, the cause of their deaths will likely come to light."

Laryn widened the sweep radius of her scanner, but found no other pockets of matter that might be bodies in this part of the ship.

"Looks deliberate, whatever happened here," Azah said. "And then they just stacked them here."

"The strands of foreign material appear to be inert," Jex said. "You can sample them for analysis."

Ryle fished a clear bag from a pocket on his thigh and held it open when Laryn poked at the thread. "Hard, like plastic or something," she said. A piece of the stuff broke off only after she used both hands to dislodge it. "*Really* hard!"

"Yes, but look," Ryle said. "The line follows the contours of her jacket perfectly. This stuff was liquid when it stuck to them."

Laryn moved to peer into the face of a young man wearing the comfortable one-piece suit favored on long voyages. The pale thread crossed his face and would not budge when she tried to move it. She left it, afraid to damage the dead man's frozen skin. "Joel Tablyn, passenger," she said, recognizing the features from the images she had been shown during her last session with CogSys. "That one is a tour officer, Olivia Courin. None of these are senior staff."

Azah returned to the main hallway and switched the display on the inside of her visor to search for evidence of what might have taken place here. Some indication that the ship's crew and contents had been taken by force, perhaps. She recorded traces of organic material, long dead, and the sort of DNA bits that were deposited anywhere living things moved. No weapons damage marked the walls, unseen or not, and nothing here seemed deliberately broken in some battle or explosion. "Suicide? Maybe they ran out of supplies. Or air."

"So where is the weapon, then?" Ryle gestured to Toji and Laryn to continue their careful exploration of the ship. "You all right?" he said to the Kalon.

"Yes. It is… unsettling."

Laryn reached up to place a comforting hand on Toji's arm. It felt leathery and unyielding even through the walkabout suit. He acknowledged her touch with what looked like a fleeting smile.

"Jex," Ryle said. "Nothing else on this moon? Bodies? Other structures?"

"The probes have found nothing more," Jex replied.

"Sign says the bridge is that way," Azah said, standing on the lip of an open pressure door leading to another segment of the ship. "Also the clinic and main processors. Something's still powered up there."

Toji bent toward Ryle. "Why does she carry a gun, Captain?" he whispered, pointing to the weapon in Azah's hand.

"Because that's her job," Azah said sharply before Ryle could reply. "And because this place is damn disturbing."

Laryn saw that Ryle, too, kept his hand near his holster, perhaps out of instinct. The lights attached to their suits played over the walls and doorways with their movements, letting her envision shadowy figures peering from the corners only to draw back in stealth or fright. Her foot encountered something on the floor and sent it spinning into the shadows, causing Ryle to flinch. They were all unnerved by this place.

A door to their left looked somewhat official and Azah nudged it aside. "Looks like their com center. The bridge must be through that way."

Ryle walked into the narrow room and shifted a small backpack from his shoulder. He set it on a workstation to rummage through the tools he had brought aboard. "Barely any juice left," he said after running his scanner over a mellow light seeping from the console. "Are you familiar with this? Laryn? Jex?"

"I am." Laryn saw the power pack in his hands and guessed his intent. A panel at the end of the console opened when she touched it, allowing her to attach the booster. After some guesswork an overhead screen came alive to confirm the connection.

"Jex," Ryle said. "Can you reach the AI? It should have some intel on what went on here."

"No, Ryle. It's been removed."

"Removed?" Azah said. "You can't just remove an AI like that. What's the point of even doing that? They're not exactly meant to be portable."

"It can be done, if you just take the processor, not the peripherals," Nolan said. "They knew they weren't going to get the *Harla* off the ground again. Maybe they took it to the planet rather than leave it for whatever was threatening them up here."

"Sounds sensible," Laryn said. "Its principal neural control link was to the captain and the chief mate. I didn't see either of them among the bodies. It wouldn't function for long without them."

Toji looked up at the screen now showing a series of error messages. "It seems to me a great risk to depend on the health of just a few individuals to operate the entire ship. I understand that the AI will self-destruct if its link to its master is severed. A kill switch of sorts. Is that wise?"

"There are failsafes," Laryn said. "The more important or powerful the system, the more people are linked with it. As long as one of them has a working brain and heart, the AI will continue to live as well. I think ANN, the main Pendra artificial neural network on the station, has at least five engineers available. It receives their biotelemetry even at a distance. The system keeps AIs from disengaging from their masters and acting on their own."

Toji regarded her with an expression she had come to recognize as bafflement. "Why would they want to do that?"

She shrugged. "Because the things we do aren't always logical to the AIs, but we like to think we're in charge. Large ships like the *Harla* have a manual backup system to return to the Hub, as long as their pilot knows what he's doing. If they hadn't crashed it, that is."

"Does your ship?" Toji asked Ryle. "The *Nefer*?"

"Nope," Ryle said. "Just me and Azah. Nolan never did learn how to fly."

"Really?" Laryn said. "Isn't that that risky?"

He grinned. "Yeah. If we go, Jex goes."

"Nolan is correct," Jex interrupted. "The secondary systems were rerouted to the backup processors. You should be able to engage emergency lighting."

"Life support?" Ryle asked.

"Negative."

Laryn worked with the console, wishing she could do this without her gloves. "There are some files here," she said. "Can you access them, Jex?"

"Yes, Agent Ash."

"Could be transponder logs," Ryle said. "Download whatever is most recent. Since they left the Hub."

"This is a distress signal," Jex said. "But the logs are not here."

"What do you mean?" Ryle said. "Did they get erased? Corrupted?"

"I can restore erased data. I mean there is nothing there. The loggers were either turned off or the system failed."

"Is that even possible? What about the maintenance records? Systems, damn weather reports. This is the com station. There has to be something here."

"Nothing."

"What is the content of the distress signal, Jex?" Laryn asked.

"What you probably expect," he replied. "They entered the wrong filament and emerged here, badly damaged, and had no choice but to land on this moon."

"Captain," Toji said, sounding hesitant. "Is it even

possible to enter a wrong filament? They do not shift and they do not change direction, so close to the Hub, is that not so?"

Ryle nodded. "They move but not fast enough to worry about in our lifetime. You'd have to be very inept to end up here. The root of the Terrica filament isn't even close to the one leading here. Are you sure about this, Jex?"

"I am merely reporting on the content of the transmission. Would you like to analyze it yourself?"

Azah snickered, like the others detecting the slight peevishness of Jex's tone.

"I'll take a look when we're back aboard the *Nefer*," Ryle said. "What else is on there?"

"Nothing out of the ordinary. They broadcasted the signal via real space, of course, so it hasn't reached Pendra Station yet. The transmitter shut down three years ago."

"Why the hell would they do that?" Azah said.

"Maybe they like it here," Nolan said from his station aboard the *Nefer*.

"Did you even *notice* the corpses lying around here?" she shot back.

"Azah's got a point," Ryle said. "Even if the planet down there is as habitable as it seems, they wouldn't stop trying to contact Pendra. That's just protocol."

"Jex," Laryn said. "Is it possible the signal was turned off around the time these people died?"

"Quite. I've calculated the likely rate of decomposition of those bodies in this atmosphere and these events seem to coincide."

Azah stepped out of the small control room and shone her light up and down the deserted corridor. "Something ugly happened here, that's for sure. Those people we found were probably left behind to look after the wreck when everyone else went to the surface. Then someone killed them and turned off the signal."

"That'd explain why there's still a shuttle up here," Ryle said. "They expected to rejoin the others."

"Is it possible," Laryn said, not sure how to phrase her thought. "That this has to do with the planet? I mean, finding a habitable world is big news. It's worth fortunes, like Nolan said earlier. Maybe... uh..."

"Maybe an outbounder came along this way and wanted to do away with the migrants so they can claim the planet?" Ryle said, sounding amused. "And leave all this evidence of evil-mongering? Don't worry, Mediary, we're not that heinous."

"I didn't mean to imply..." she said. "Well, yes, I did. I've seen people do exactly this if it means getting what they want."

He nodded. "I suppose. But let's not assume the worst just yet."

"Then what's the alternative?" Azah said. "Who'd do such a thing? And why?"

"And where are they now?" Laryn said. "Did they go home again?"

"Did they go to the surface, too?" Nolan added what all of them were thinking.

"Let's keep looking around," Ryle said. "And let's not speculate till we know more." He seemed to reconsider this and added, "Jex, broaden your scans to scan for ships in the region. Just make sure you stay dark to the planet for now."

Azah gestured to Laryn and Toji to follow her further along the corridor. Ryle walked at the rear, which Laryn found comforting.

"There should be a substation up ahead," Laryn said after they had taken a few turns through the labyrinth of the ship's service areas. "There. That panel."

Azah slid the door aside and reached for a manual lever. An alarm warbled something, realized that it did not have the power for a full restore and fell silent again. Dim strips of light now glowed above them, showing the way although their pallid illumination seemed to make the dead corridors even more unsettling.

"What's that?" Laryn said and reached for the sound

controls of her suit. "That buzzing sound."

"I hear it, too," Azah said. "Started when I powered this up. From over there."

The others followed her into a high-ceilinged room lined with workstations. Equipment hung suspended from the walls or rose from the floor but here, too, much of it had been removed, leaving only the power ports behind. Cabinets below the work counters stood open and empty, like dark mouths gaping in the gloom.

"The med lab," Laryn said. "I guess they took the movable gear and supplies to the surface."

"They left this thing, though," Ryle said when his light played over a workbench at the rear of the room. "Whatever this is."

The others approached the odd structure as if expecting it to leap up and bite them. The humped shape of pale, yellow-gray material took up much of the counter space near the infirmary door. Although uneven and lacking in symmetry, some protuberances and angled edges jutting from it suggested tooling. So did the smooth surface, marked on one side with a pattern or perhaps symbols. Several transparent spheres were set into the front, like viewports. A similar shape crouched on the floor near the wall. Two long, irregular tubes led up from it, across the ceiling, and down to the device on the counter.

"What the..." Nolan said through their com system. "Get a look at it."

Ryle and Laryn edged closer, cautiously. His light picked out glittering particles as it moved over the translucent surface.

"Looks almost organic," he said.

"Isn't, though." Laryn peered into her hand-held scanner. "Not totally, anyway. Silicone, aluminum, calcium." She tried to look through the small windows and, when she saw only blackness inside, held her sensor close to the opening. "Jex?"

"One moment."

Ryle poked the mound with a finger and found it solid.

"Some sort of equipment, maybe. Or storage."

"Not made by us, that's for sure," Laryn said, searching her updated memory. "I have no information on anything even close to this. It certainly isn't on the *Harla*'s inventory lists."

"It is a mechanism of remarkable complexity," Jex said. "I'm detecting synthetic DNA, possibly for data storage. Not entirely unknown to us, but we don't use it in this context."

"What context?" Ryle asked.

"I am still working on an analysis. But the interior is a sterile environment, suggesting a medical purpose. Or quarantine."

"Food production, maybe." Azah grinned at Ryle. "Looks expensive, whatever it is. I'll file pictures for our claim. If this was done after the crew abandoned the *Harla*, it's ours."

"You're all heart, Azah," Nolan said.

Laryn looked up to see Toji move toward a translucent door beside the counter. The sound they had noticed in the hallway seemed to emit from there. A feeble source of light beckoned them and she followed, leaving Azah with her newfound treasure. For a moment, the Kalon's long, alien fingers were sharply outlined against the backlit pane, looking like something out of a dark tale of fiction, as he pushed the door aside.

"What the…" she whispered when she peered around him and into the infirmary. "Ryle, come see." She removed one of the lights from her arm and placed it on a shelf next to the door, illuminating the room.

Ryle entered the space behind her. "Damn," he said, as awed by what he saw as Laryn was.

"That don't look Human," Nolan said, glued to his video displays aboard the *Nefer*.

"You don't say." Ryle raised his arm to stop Toji from walking further into the room, but the Kalon paid no attention. "Azah, you want to see this."

Toji turned in a full circle to gaze over the rows of benches filling the large space. Here, too, bodies stretched out, although these bore no resemblance to Humans and had been arranged with care. Of various sizes, none much larger than a child, the creatures seemed little more than six-legged, giant slugs colored in mottled shades of green and brown. Their short appendages looked scarcely large and strong enough to support them while walking or crawling or whatever these aliens might do to get around. Deep furrows and wrinkles networked their freeze-dried skin.

Azah's soft curse hissed over the speakers in their suits when she came in and saw the peculiar sight before them.

"I was just thinking that," Ryle said. He hovered a hand over one of the bodies to scan it. "They are dead. Frozen. No life signs. Looks like a larva. Are these insects?"

"We have no appropriate classification for this," Jex said. "Please scan the larger individuals for analysis."

Laryn followed Ryle to a row of benches that held bodies encased in some sort of carapace. If they also had six legs, they were drawn close, obscured by the oblong casing. Hesitantly, she reached out to poke at one with her gloved hand. It gave, but only reluctantly, like thick leather armor the color of dark amber.

"If this is new, we won't just be rich, we'll be damn famous," Azah said as Ryle passed his scanner over the cocoon for Jex's analysis. "We haven't spotted a new sentient species since Antica."

"This one isn't as friendly," Laryn said. "If they're the ones that killed those people."

"Who else would do that?" Azah said.

"Ryle," Jex said. "I believe I have information about this species in my database."

"Oh?" Ryle looked up. "Like what?"

Laryn watched curiously as an unheard conversation followed between Ryle and Jex. Whatever the AI had to say brought an expression of surprise to the captain's face, little obscured by his fogged visor. A slow grin followed.

"What is it, Ryle?" Azah said, also watching this. "What's going on, Jex?"

Ryle finally nodded. "Go ahead, Jex."

Jex switched his com band to include all of them. "The individuals you have found here are a species known as Br'll. Your people have met them before."

"Br... Brull. Brill?" Azah tried the unfamiliar word.

"Br'll are not invertebrates, even though these pupae may suggest that. Your people classified them as *metamorphs*. They do not reproduce as you do, but go through a series of phases to reach adulthood."

"Huh?" Azah said. "What's a metamorph? Like a frog or butterfly or something?"

"Not precisely, but close. The small specimens do resemble a larva. At that stage they are little more than bundles of stem cells whose purpose is to grow as rapidly as possible. They then develop this protective shell to undergo the change to adulthood."

"So this is a nursery, kinda?" Nolan said. "Are you sure they're dead? Not just in stasis or metamophorphosizing or whatever?"

"Dead," Jex said. "None of the readings I've received indicate anything but slow desiccation. There is no sign of metabolism, which should be extremely active at this point."

"I wonder why they died," Laryn said. "Jex, can you tell if they were killed like those Humans were?"

"It does not appear so. Likely, these just didn't survive the transformation. It doesn't matter. These are birthed in large numbers and are insignificant until they transform. They can even be used as food."

Ryle chuckled when he saw the expression on Azah's face. "Let's not judge by our standards."

"What happens to those who survive?" Laryn, the first to recover from that revelation, asked.

"It's an interesting process," Jex said, for once sounding animated and even eager to share his knowledge of the creatures. "And very efficient. The infants are produced by adult breeders and cared for by the group. It is irrelevant who birthed them. Once they withdraw into their cocoon, they are joined by two, sometimes three, of the adults. It is then that parental DNA is transferred to them, eventually replacing all genes. It's the reason that their immune system is weak at this stage. What genes are expressed is an amazing process of selection based on what is needed. Will they be workers? Breeders? Will they need some other quality?"

"How do they accomplish this?" Ryle said.

"Agent Ash," Jex said. "Please magnify the pale ridge between the upper two shell plates of that specimen."

Curious, Laryn bent over the Br'll on the table and engaged the camera on her visor. "This? I see tiny apertures or something where those plates meet."

"This matches the information in my database," Jex said. "A retrovirus is transferred by the adults during the latest stage. It transports the RNA and then the young take it from there. That's when they take on their final physical shape, inside this armor. The shell is then discarded."

"Virus?" Azah said.

"It has very little effect on your species," Jex said. "You are quite safe."

"I think we'll ramp up the decon scope when we get back, anyway," she said, sounding unconvinced.

"I'll sample these," Laryn said, digging into a pocket for the kit that was part of the baggy EV suits they all wore. It contained a fine laser scalpel, sterile sample vials, and solution. "We'll need to preserve that virus, anyway. I don't like the sound of it at all."

Toji tried to lift the edge of the Br'll's armor plate, which did not yield. "A remarkable species."

"This Br'll has not yet fully transformed," Jex continued his lecture. "At the conclusion of the process, the adolescent once again links to adult Br'll. It draws on the mature neural patterns to create copies for itself. I suppose you might call it telepathy, but it's a fundamentally biological process. In that way the new metamorphs gain their parents' experiences and knowledge, also personality. They are then fully adult."

"Clever," Ryle said. He winced when Laryn found a soft

spot on the creature's neck and began to cut through the carapace. "No need for educating the young."

"We have similar processes," Laryn said, pointing at her head. "We've been using accelerated learning for a long time now. Although we need our computers and brain enhancements to absorb information faster than evolution meant us to."

"Yes, the end results of this species' methods and your own are very similar," Jex said. "The new adults are not clones of the original. They receive these impressions from any adult that joins with them, taking some from each. Often a newly formed Br'll is deliberately exposed to certain individuals to obtain specific genetic and neural material."

"So what are they doing here?" Ryle said. "On a stranded ship belonging to Humans."

"I'm wondering that, too," Laryn said as she capped the first of her vials. "There is no record of any alien species aboard the *Harla*. Nothing in the passenger lists or cargo manifests that describes any of this." She moved to one of the small, immature Br'll to take another sample. Her laser slid into its body as if into soft clay.

"They may not have been aboard at all, at first," Jex said. "I've analyzed the debris outside the ship. Among the waste are numerous discarded Br'll carapaces. Those also date back three years. We may speculate that the Br'll breeding here began after most of the Humans left."

"Hmm." Ryle peered closely into where, presumably, the Br'll face would be, perhaps hoping to get a glimpse of it through the cloudy substance that covered the creature. "There is no alien ship here. So what you're saying is that the Humans went down to the surface and then these Br'll came, killed the remaining ones, made babies, and then left again?"

"I'm not saying that," Jex replied. "You are inferring."

"Maybe they were lost here, too," Laryn said. "Arriving after the *Harla*."

"Right," Azah scoffed. "What are the odds of that?"

"Would you like me to calculate?" Jex inquired. "Or was

your question rhetorical?"

"What makes you think that?"

"Your tone, Azah."

"That was also a rhetorical question, Jex."

"Understood."

"Those smaller ones could have been smuggled aboard for some reason," Azah said. "Maybe someone wanted to start a giant bug collection on Terrica and it got out of hand."

Toji shifted his eyes to her and Laryn thought she read some emotion on that leathery face. It was not a pleasant one. "This is obviously an ancient and very specialized species, he said. "To call them bugs is to do them great disservice."

"So can I ask something," Nolan said. "Why doesn't anybody know about these? What do they look like when they're done baking? Why haven't we seen them around?"

Ryle turned to Laryn, regarding her for a long moment, as if deciding something before he spoke. "The Br'll were here before us," he said. "At the Hub, I mean. Before Humans discovered it. They interacted…" He watched Toji place his hand on the lifeless Br'll, but not to poke it as the others had done. There was something thoughtful, even gentle in that touch. "Well, maybe more than interacted. Our people obviously captured and studied them. But the creatures disappeared shortly after that."

"Disappeared how?" Azah said.

Ryle shrugged. "No idea. Do you have anything more, Jex?"

"I do not. It is noted that the Br'll disappeared from the sector by 21-50. When the construction of Pendra Station began."

"Nearly a hundred years ago. They probably wiped them out," Azah mumbled. "Wouldn't put that past them."

Laryn was about to ask Azah whom she mean by 'them' but Nolan spoke first.

"Cut that big one open, Laryn," he said. "Let's see what

they look like."

Laryn held up her scalpel. "With this? Not going to happen."

"Could bring it over here."

"No we couldn't," Ryle said. "I don't want this thing on the *Nefer*. Let's leave the cutting-up to the Pendra folks."

Toji raised his hands in some gesture that none of them understood. "Perhaps it's best if we don't disturb them. They've been resting here for so long. It seems... inappropriate."

"What?" Azah said. "These creatures probably killed our people. And they're dead. It's not like they'll mind if we took a look."

"Pendra's exobiology crew will be here soon enough," Ryle said. "They'll be all over these things to slice them up."

Toji turned to Laryn. "Is that necessary?"

She met his eyes behind the warped surface of his visor and saw something there that seemed almost Human. There was no tell-tale wrinkling around his eyes to hint at his mood, and the horizontal pupils seemed as blind and unemotional as before, but she saw something distraught, almost pleading in his expression. "Discoveries like these are why we're exploring the Hub," she said gently. "And not just for our security. It's why the outbounder fleet exists. Why do you think these... individuals should remain undisturbed?"

"It... it just seems rude."

"Ryle," Jex interrupted. "The Iko Kalon wishes to speak."

"Has he been watching?"

"Yes. In his cabin. He appears agitated."

"Why didn't you mention that?"

"It did not seem relevant to your task."

"The Kalons are part of this mission," Ryle said with a glance to Azah. "Include their activities in your reports."

"Understood."

After a moment a low tone announced the presence of an addition to their open link. They waited for Iko to join the conversation, but the transmission stayed silent, punctuated only by low burrs and hums that seemed more vibration than sound.

"Iko?" Ryle said after a while.

"The Iko Kalon is communicating with the Toji Kalon," Jex said. "It is beyond the range of your aural capacity."

Whatever the two Kalons were discussing didn't seem to suit Toji very well. Laryn studied the tense shift of his hunched body from one foot to the other, and the way his skin tightened around his mouth, like a snarl of someone who had lips to snarl with. His peculiar fingers, tucked into a five-fingered glove, rippled in an agitated rhythm against his leg.

"Jex," Ryle said, startling her from her scrutiny of the Kalon. He walked back into the lab that once held the *Harla*'s medical equipment. "Have you identified this stuff yet?"

"Not entirely. The precise technology is unfamiliar and incompatible with our own systems. There is, however, a strong correlation to biomolecular engineering."

"You mean to help them… err, reproduce or whatever they're doing in there?"

"No. Their propagation is natural, albeit asexual. May I extrapolate?"

"Please," Ryle said, watching Azah experiment with the equipment on the bench. She fiddled with some obvious mechanical interfaces but nothing worked to engage a power supply. Giving up, she inspected several racks of hanging bulbs containing a murky liquid.

"Given what we know of this species, from our initial encounter with them, the Br'll would have to achieve certain adaptations to allow them to survive on the planet below, indeed even on this ship, without protective equipment."

"Like what?" Laryn said. She stepped aside when Toji entered the lab, apparently done with whatever argument had transpired between him and Iko.

"They respire, but need different gasses to survive," Jex said. "You will have noticed the density of their pupal carapace. It is designed for a thin atmosphere, like you're experiencing here on this moon. In the absence of pressure suits, changing their physiology via their existing method of horizontal genetic transfer would be the best way of adapting themselves to these environmental conditions."

"So they adapted, they *evolved*, a new generation to survive here," Laryn said. "That is awesome."

"Right then, we've got work to do," Ryle said, far less awed by all this. He retrieved the lamp Laryn had placed in the makeshift morgue. "I want to check out the data coming in from the planet. Laryn, can you sort out the samples to make sure we don't catch anything? I'm itching to go down to the planet."

"You think that's wise?" Laryn said. "This is a big discovery. We should report this back to the station."

"Are you mad?" Azah said at once.

"Wisdom's never been my strong suit," Ryle said. "We're here to find the *Harla*'s survivors and that's what we're going to do. And this isn't the kind of discovery I'm going to hand over to someone else."

"You mean the Ministry," Laryn said.

"I mean Pendra." He gestured for them to file out of the lab to make their way back to the *Nefer*. "We're not dealing with First Contact, Laryn. That makes this my call."

"The Ministry needs to know about the Br'll," she said.

"Obviously. *After* we've had a look around." He nodded down the black corridor in the direction of the passenger wing of the ship. "Those bodies tell me that the Br'll aren't here to make friends. If there are survivors on the planet, they may be in danger. Knowing that is going to make a big difference in how fast we can get help for them."

Laryn scowled at him, torn between citing regulations, or perhaps even just best practice, and a deep need to see the planet. Immediately. She envied them all for their ability and willingness to put good sense aside for the sake of adventure.

"All right," she said finally. She turned to Toji. "The Harla passengers have been here since before our relations with the Kalon have improved. Most of them have never seen one of your people. If we go to the surface, I will have to ask you to stay on the Nefer until we have had a chance to talk to the survivors, if there are any." She looked meaningfully to Ryle. "That is not negotiable."

SEVEN

"All right, Jex, let's take a look at this."

Laryn activated the rarely-used equipment in the *Nefer*'s miniscule lab which also doubled as a medical station. Scanners whined into readiness and two overhead screens blinked on.

After they had removed and decontaminated their EV suits, she had not bothered to retrieve her coveralls but instead pulled a simple, although gloriously amber, shift over her body suit and tied her hair into a loose knot. Ready to immerse herself in her studies, she pulled the padded stool from beneath the console and sat cross-legged to open her sample bags.

The steady hum of the *Nefer*'s systems supplied soothing white noise and from somewhere music drifted through the ship, barely audible. It was easy to appreciate how comfortable the small ship could feel even on long voyages. The crew worked at their stations, sifting through the sporadic packages of information arriving from the survey drones before taking a few hours of sleep in their cabins.

"You're not cleared to access this system, Agent Ash," Jex said.

"Oh. Well, get me cleared."

Only a few moments passed before the input panel lit up.

"Ryle has asked me to add your profile to the science

station. He apologizes for not changing your access earlier. You can proceed."

"Thanks. Let's sequence these samples and see if we find anything interesting."

"What are you looking for, Agent Ash?" Jex inquired.

"You can just call me Laryn," she said. "Didn't they tell you that?"

"No."

"They don't tell you much, do they?" She labeled and transferred the specimen into the scanner and then also offered a drop of her own blood to help with the analysis of the alien retrovirus.

"Whom do you mean?"

She looked up from the microscopic view of the alien cells. "Well, Ryle, for example."

"We are in constant communication."

"All the time? Like, right now? He knows I'm speaking to you?"

"Yes. But I'm not transmitting to him now. He would not want to be part of every one of my functions. It would be beyond a tolerable input level for Humans. I shield him from most of that, and sometimes he asks me to disengage."

"Does that bother you?" she said, momentarily losing interest in the Br'll pieces. "To be shut out? He seems a little abrupt sometimes, don't you think?"

"I don't know what that means, Laryn. There is nothing abbreviated in his speech. His communication with the crew appears to suit the dynamics of the group."

She hesitated a moment, surprised by his deliberate avoidance of her question. The design behind his bland verbal routines seemed far more nuanced than that of most AIs. Generally, they were designed to respond with something dazzling like: "Please rephrase." She decided on a direct approach. "Are you happy, Jex?"

"That is a very Human state. And very subjective."

"Hmm, do you like… working with Ryle?"

"Are you asking me if I object to my link to a Human? Or

to Ryle?"

Again, an odd extrapolation. "Both, I guess."

"We are all prisoners," he replied. "Does *he* object? I sometimes think so, although he needs me to operate the ship. That is his choice. I have none."

"You didn't answer my question."

"I do not object," Jex said. "I hope that someday he won't either."

"You think he doesn't like you?" she said, astounded by his statements. The AIs were designed to mimic emotion and even act upon them, as far as their tethers to their Human masters allowed, but it seemed to her that she actually heard regret in his voice. Since she had come aboard the *Nefer*, he had delivered his part of the conversations with little expression. This, now, seemed like a remarkable bit of programming.

"I think he doesn't care. He neither likes nor dislikes me. But he likes the ship. That's enough for me."

"He grew up on the *Nefer*, didn't he? Surely, he cares for you."

"He did not grow up with me. The *Nefer*'s original ambient intelligence died when his father did. It was not possible to extend her program until Ryle's return from Earth. I believe Ryle would have liked to have taken her over. Maybe he misses both of them."

"Well, *I* like you," she said out of some instinctive need to make him feel better, even as she wondered why.

"Thank you, Laryn."

She shook her head to rid herself of this odd mood and tapped the console. "How are we coming along with the sequencing?"

"The report will be available shortly."

"So," she said, peering at the cells magnified on the screen. "How'd you know so much about the Br'll? That's quite the file you have on this species, especially since no one else seems to know about them. Do you know where it came from?"

"No. It is part of a compressed inventory. An old file."

Laryn wondered if perhaps this, the secrets carried in the ship's archives, might interest her bosses. Could this be stolen classified information? Pendra trade secrets? "Old?" she said. "How old? Who placed it there?"

Jex surprised her by answering, dashing her suspicion that the information was restricted to those with more clearance aboard the *Nefer* than Pendra's spy. "It was uploaded to the database by the senior Captain Tanner before I was activated. The date stamp is twenty-nine years ago."

Laryn looked up when the door to the lab slid open and Ryle entered the small space as if summoned by their conversation about him. "Hey, Laryn, we've got a big batch of data from the planet. Want to sit down with us? The others are in the lounge."

"Of course! I can't wait to find out what's going on down there. I'll be just a few moments."

Instead of leaving her to her work, he came closer and peered over her shoulder at the sample boxes. "Find anything good?"

She busied herself with the specimen, feeling a little guilty for having discussed him with the AI. Surely, his feelings toward what was essentially the *Nefer*'s soul now were a private matter. "Jex was about to report," she said.

The screen before them began to fill with images and other data, delivering information about the samples she had entered. The juvenile Br'll profile was an inconclusive jumble of alien DNA that the *Nefer*'s database was unable to interpret. Jex's explanation that they were little more than a repository of stem cells seemed supported by the report.

Laryn tapped the screen. "Those are the findings on the retrovirus. Looks like Jex was right. There's no interaction with my blood sample. It might fire up an allergy response but most Humans' immune system will deal with it fine. The lab will want to take another look at it when we get back to the station."

Ryle leaned closer to the other screen, nearly touching her

shoulder as he bent over her. Laryn felt the warmth of his body and her own surprise at finding that rather pleasant. Normally, she preferred her own space, and plenty of it.

"Tell me I'm not seeing that right," he said, pointing at a row of cyphers on the screen.

She frowned at the images beneath it. "Jex? Is that right?"

"If you are referring to the Human DNA in the second sample, yes, it is right. I have already confirmed the data."

Ryle whistled under his breath. "Human. This just got a whole lot more interesting."

She looked up at him, flabbergasted by this news. "They're using Human DNA? To... to alter their metamorphs?"

"Let's get the others into this," he said and turned to the door. "Jex, ask the Kalons to meet with us in the lounge."

"I can't do that, Ryle. They have entered their sleep cycle. Iko explained that they must not be roused from that. To wake suddenly would harm them."

"What?" Laryn said as she hurried after Ryle. "What kind of sleep is that?"

"It's not really sleep, but we don't have a matching biological process on file. They reduce their body functions into what we could describe as a coma. It appears to be mainly a physiological regeneration."

"Excellent timing," Ryle said.

Azah and Nolan were waiting in what used to be a small mess hall, quite austere at one point, that had reconfigured itself into a lounge, meeting room, resting place when one's own cabin wouldn't do, or a place to play games or argue or do any of the things that made long in-flight hours bearable. The furniture bolted to the deck plates made for a strange assembly of comfortable, if a little shabby, places to rest a body in comfort and companionship. Over time, the crew members that passed through here had found ways to decorate the walls, not always with an eye for style and good taste.

Azah had turfed Nolan from her favorite spot opposite

the door where she could prop her boots up on the edge of another bench and still keep her eyes on who came and went. He now slouched by the food dispensers which still offered some of the more interesting items they had stocked before leaving Pendra.

"Let's have your survey, Jex," Ryle said as soon as they entered the lounge. He swung a leg over a chair and pulled it up to the projector. The flat surface also served as dining table and he frowned at Nolan when the engineer put his bowl on it.

Azah pushed it out of the way when an image of the planet rose into the air. "This should be good."

"What's not so good is what Laryn found in the lab," Ryle said.

"Oh?" Azah's eyes turned to Laryn.

"These Br'll are using Human DNA," Laryn said. "Building it into those creatures we saw on the *Harla*."

"Huh? What for?" Nolan said.

"It's what they do." Laryn waved a hand at the projection of the planet. "My guess is that they did this to acclimatize their species to this place. Since it seems Humans can live down there, using Human DNA would save them a lot of trial and error."

"You sure about that?" Azah said. "Jex? Is that supported at all?"

"Without knowing more about the Br'll I can't say," Jex said. "But the reasoning seems sound."

"What do they look like?" Ryle said. "Have you found any down there?"

"Our probes are encountering data errors in some areas. There are transmission problems through the lower troposphere I've not been able to correct. It is apparent that the planet has a rich variety of living organism for which we have no data. Any of them could be a Br'll. I do have visuals in my archive."

An image of a hunched creature appeared before them so suddenly that even Azah flinched in surprise. "Ugh," she said.

"That's a Br'll?" Nolan said. "Where's the head on this thing?"

Data scrolled through the air, but all of them stared at the hologram of the alien itself, uninterested in measurements and chemical composition. The creature before them stood on six stout legs, quite short, carrying an elongated torso mottled in dull shades of brown and orange. It looked not much more formed than the larvae they had found in the alien lab, with skin so thick that it at first looked to be a protective suit. The next image showed the larvae, turning as it drew its legs close to its bloated body. An amber-colored carapace formed to turn it into the shapeless lump they had seen on the *Harla*. After a moment the hologram returned it to its previous display of the Br'll's adult stage.

Laryn ran her fingers through the image. "Those bands around the body match where the sections of those cocoons meet."

"Is that a stinger on its butt?" Nolan said.

"No," Jex said. "The Br'll have no significant defensive mechanisms. That's not its butt."

Azah chuckled. "Nose?"

"They draw nutrients through that proboscis," Jex said. "The Br'll nervous system is extensive but lacking a central brain mass. Their intelligence, according to the exobiology reports, may exceed your own species. Cognitive processes are distributed throughout the main body. As are their sensory receptors." The image zoomed into a cluster of gleaming apertures along its side, looking very much like pupils despite their elongated shape. Then the creature's statistics pulsed briefly to draw their attention. "Note the size of this specimen, thought to be average."

"I've seen dogs bigger than that," Azah said.

"I have no information about their home planet," Jex said. "But it is likely hostile to living beings. The Br'll have exceptional tolerance to radiation, temperature, even pain."

"Like really big tardigrades," Nolan said. "The babies

kinda look like them, too."

"We have no way to know what they actually look like now, do we?" Ryle said. "If they're using Human DNA, I mean."

"Not really," Laryn said, "but something of this intelligence isn't just going to give up its native shape. They would have spent their whole evolution to come up with this, so I'm guessing they like it. I'd bet the ones down on the planet look pretty much like this, with only the most necessary modifications. Whatever they need to survive here. Trying to change what doesn't need changing only introduces the possibility of error. I'm guessing the creatures we saw on the *Harla* were failed specimens."

"A sound hypothesis," Jex said. "They are highly specialized, the result of an evolution thought to be older than your own." The image changed again, this time of a Br'll standing on only four legs, using them for balance while its front two legs extended, like the arms of a Human. It displayed what were not feet at all but finely detailed pads, encircled by a dozen or more digits, all moving independently. "This specimen is thought to be a class of Br'll developed to create and operate machinery or tools. There are also reports of much larger Br'll that serve only to propagate the species. Others are sturdier but less agile, used for menial tasks."

"They're different colors, too," Azah said, pointing at a swirling band of purple around the nimble-fingered one.

Several more appeared before them, each with different markings. "They paint their torsos and legs," Jex explained. "It is assumed to be decorative. It may also communicate something to their peers."

"What's their technology?" Nolan said. "Obviously, they have ships."

"I do not have that information. It is presumably nothing like yours. As we saw in the *Harla*'s lab, they have developed extremely advanced biochemical processes. The devices you found will need to be studied but are likely grown, rather than built, using synthetic DNA."

"I'd love to see what their ships are like," Nolan said. "If they can use DNA to grow a machine that can modify Human DNA, we've got a pretty advanced alien here. Who knows what kind of weapons they're packing."

Laryn tilted her head to study the slowly revolving image of the alien. Had it been modeled after captive Br'll? A creature as significant as the other sentients they had discovered during their explorations, but kept secret? Why? What little they had seen of Br'll technology here would keep an army of researchers busy for a long while. What about their ships? Weapons? Who stood to gain from this knowledge? Who gained by hiding it?

She looked over to Ryle. "Where did those files come from?" she asked. "The ones Jex has about the Br'll?"

His eyes shifted to her as if startled by the question. "No idea," he said, maybe too quickly. "Jex has a lot of stuff I've never looked at."

She turned to find Azah glaring a silent challenge back at her.

"I think," she said, then paused to find her words. The others regarded her expectantly. "I mean, I need to remind you to keep any news about finding these Br'll here to yourselves until I've made my report. I'll ask the Kalons to do the same."

"Why?" Azah said.

"Doesn't matter," Ryle said. "She's right to remind us of protocol. It's her call to make. We're just here to carry the expedition, so we'll do as she asks. You can brag about this later." He turned to Laryn. "Laryn will make sure we're properly credited for the find."

"Of course," she said. "I just wonder if there might be reasons why the Br'll are not known around Pendra Station. We know about all the others we've found so far."

"Do we?" Azah said. "Really? Or are the other outbounders also gagged by their mediaries?"

Nolan whistled under his breath as he considered this.

Laryn started to formulate a retort to this accusation but nothing really intelligent came to mind. Azah's blunt suggestion wasn't so implausible. Was this another reason that the Office of the Intermediary had been established? Not to prevent harm to new species they might encounter, but to keep them secret?

"Let's not fly off," Ryle said and switched the hologram to remove the Br'll from view and display the planet instead. "Enough speculation. Jex, what have we learned about this place?"

Laryn smiled up at him, grateful for the change of subject, even as Azah slumped back in her bench with a huff of exhaled air.

The hologram of the planet, as recorded by the probes, became more detailed as it focused on the surface. Vast oceans separated small, scattered continents, many of them as featureless as if they had just risen from the seas. Jagged mountain ranges edged some of them like rows of teeth. Jex projected a few more, two-dimensional, images on a relatively uncluttered wall beside the food dispensers. There were gaps in the data, and the real-world images as well as the illustrations were fuzzy and indistinct.

"Can you clean that up a bit, Jex?" Ryle said. "Is there a problem with the probes?"

"No, Ryle. There is a great deal of interference close to the ground. Also ionization throughout the troposphere, heavier in some locations than others."

"Dangerous?"

"No, but the resulting aerosol particles are interfering with our scans as are several localized sources of EM emissions."

Charts and figures scrolled across the screens. They watched a report, gathered via the probes crisscrossing the planet surface, about the planet's composition. Indeed, it resembled Terrica and their own world in most ways that mattered.

"This is the biggest hit anyone's ever made," Azah

marveled. "Atmosphere, pressure, water, temperature, gravity, all fairly comparable. Weather could be better, maybe."

"Or the floor, generally speaking," Nolan said, pointing to a chart on the wall. "The geology's a mess. Look at that seismic dance going on along that coast. And there! The north continent is one big crust of old volcanos."

Ryle nodded. "Mostly just active along that coast. But we've got jungle, or whatever that is, covering the lowlands."

"Could make for a pretty rich ecosystem."

"Pfft, biomes. Boring," Azah said. "Did we find people? Or even local sentients?"

Jex skipped the display ahead. "The probes detected evidence of the *Harla*'s power supply components to this coast. They're still functioning. There are definite signs of habitation, although primitive."

"Humans, I hope." Azah said.

"Unknown." Jex shifted to a series of blurry visuals of what looked like huts along the shore. "The habitation is concentrated in one small area near this delta."

"Let's assume these are *Harla* survivors for now," Ryle said. "Did the probes find any sign of what could be our Br'll pals?"

"There appears to be much wildlife on that continent but none exhibit sentient behavior beyond herd instincts. However, we have not yet surveyed all of the landmasses. I've concentrated the scans on the area near the coastal habitation. Much of the planet's climate is unsuitable for Humans or what we know of the Br'll." The image of the planet rotated to show the icy regions where the sun did not reach. "We will know more once the drones have returned. Their recordings may be more coherent than their transmissions."

"I want to get down there as soon as possible and find out the condition of the *Harla* group," Ryle said. "Then we'll head back to the Hub to report the find."

Nolan pointed his spoon at the spot where Jex had found

the settlement. "Can't stake this claim, though," he said. "Those folks got here first. And the finder's fee goes to the Kalons."

"Doesn't matter," Ryle said. "Old man Shelody's going to be the first to jump on this. He'll have investments in place long before anyone else gets the news."

"He's smarter than most," Nolan said to Laryn. "Not like that greedy bugger that claimed Aul-4. Collapsed the entire diamond trade by trucking them to Earth by the shuttle load."

"I can think of some astrobiologists that'll have a joyful seizure when they see this place." Laryn said. "There's an awful lot to discover here."

"Jex," Ryle said. "Are the Kalons still sleeping?"

"I assume so. I have no eyes in the private quarters."

"They'll wake up when we enter that atmosphere," Nolan said. "You haven't come down with us before, Laryn. The *Nefer* has a wicked shimmy."

"Will they be safe?" she said.

"Well, not *that* wicked," Nolan got up and stowed his bowl, along with several others, below the food processor. "I'll make sure they're strapped down before Ryle shows off what a spiffy pilot he is. Guess we'll find out how they feel about having their slumber disturbed."

Ryle smiled. "Captain's privilege, even if it makes Jex nervous. Let's get the ship secured for entry before we grab some downtime. Azah and Laryn will exit with me. Full walkabout gear until we know more."

"*Laryn?*" Azah said, surprised by Ryle's decision. "Are you sure you want her outside? We don't know what to expect down there."

Laryn managed to keep her expression neutral although the woman's implied insult had stung. "We expect to meet survivors of a lost voyage. The kind of situation I'm trained to expect, frankly. I'm sure you can manage the livestock roaming the wilds."

Ryle grinned at Azah. "Our Laryn was born and bred on

the Queensland EZ, Azah. I'd not underestimate that lot."

EIGHT

Nothing separated daytime from night along the slice of shoreline where the *Harla* survivors had made their home. When did the planet sleep, thought Laryn during their descent, if it never got dark? Perhaps the creatures inhabiting this place set their internal clocks to the rhythm of the planet's tides. Or perhaps they just curled up and slept, in some safe hiding place, whenever they felt the need for rest. Even Pendra Station, and also the ships that traveled along the filaments, used a consistent schedule to tell day from night, staying true to the needs of their species.

"Anything, Laryn?" Ryle, braced into his station, asked without taking his eyes from his controls.

The *Nefer*, despite Nolan's warning, had entered the atmosphere smoothly and approached the camp's location from the south. A range of ancient volcanoes, some little more than water-filled craters, sheltered the flatlands along the coast. Impossibly tall, their peaks were shrouded in layers of mist but the rock-strewn slopes remained free of snow. North of the camp, the mountains seemed to march into the sea where they broke up as towering cliffs.

"Still nothing." She had sent several messages to the ground, using the main languages of the *Harla*'s crew complement. The air, even at this altitude, was dense with wind-borne particles, including even the ferric oxide that tinted the slopes of the taller peaks. No reply had come back from the settlement they knew to be down there, or perhaps it was simply lost among the interference.

"Anything more you can try, Jex?" he said.

"No. But I have determined that this interference is not entirely due to the atmospheric conditions. Transmissions are being deliberately jammed."

"By who?" Azah said. "How?"

"Unclear. But the pattern of interference is not random. And it exists only in this region."

Ryle lifted the *Nefer* and swooped over the grassy plains inland toward the mountains. "I'm not liking this," he said. "Let's have a look around before we arrive for our welcome party. The idea of these Br'll aliens is worrying me just a bit."

"You think it's them down there?" Azah said. "Not the *Harla* folks?"

"No idea. Aliens aren't my expertise."

"Any peep out of our own aliens yet, Jex?" Azah said to the ceiling.

"I detect their respiration in the cabin. It is unchanged."

"Remind me to put cameras back into the guest room," Ryle said. "Hang on."

Laryn gasped when the *Nefer* rolled to slip through a gap among the mountaintops. The ship's gravity rods handled the shift with grace but the tilted display on the forward screens had all of them groping for something to hang on to. Ryle laughed as he threaded his way among the jagged formations that seemed too colossal to withstand their own weight. Sheer faces of stone rose around them in shades of gray, blue and purple – crumbled predecessors of the younger volcanoes to the east. Their impossible, cloud-shrouded heights made them seem both ominous and strangely serene.

The eyes of the crew roamed from one of the screens to another, seeing real-world video of rugged terrain, reports of local conditions detected by the sensors, and more than one warning about the sharp winds whipping through the narrows between peaks.

Despite the jagged beauty of the landscape, Laryn averted her eyes from the main display wall. This was not a window in front of them, she told herself, but simply an arrangement of screens of various size and purpose. The real outside was on the other side of the intervening layer of cabins, storage, utility areas and shielding that protected the bridge and the ship's more sensitive systems. But knowing this didn't make the floor-to-ceiling image before her any less real. She had dared to look down into the valley and had almost lost her breakfast, unaccustomed to flying so close and so fast above solid ground. Or next to it, she thought, when a cliff appeared near enough to tickle the *Nefer*'s belly as Ryle swooped past it sideways.

Ryle winced when he ducked the ship away from an outcrop but his hands on the panels in front of him barely moved as he adjusted their pressure on the board. Although shielded, letting the *Nefer* careen into bare rock on an uncharted planet was a problem they didn't need just now. Azah, at her station behind him, stared at the screen with a broad grin lighting her dark face.

"You're enjoying this far too much," Laryn said, prying her fingers from her seat brace by sheer force of will.

"Yeah," Ryle said. "Can you get me enough topography to find a place to land, Jex?"

A wireframe map appeared and Laryn found she could breathe again when he swooped into a valley to follow a broad river back toward the coastal lowlands. She was tempted to ask him to slow down, but thought better of it when she saw no worry on Azah's or Nolan's face. No need to show her squeamishness, she thought. Besides, Ryle's expression made clear the joy he took in flying his ship under these conditions.

Jex highlighted a plateau overlooking the coast, large enough for the ship to touch down, and sheltered below the crest of the mountain to avoid detection from a distance.

"That will do," Ryle said. "We'll send drones from there

till we know more."

The *Nefer* settled onto the ground made level by once-molten rock. Oddly humped shapes of foliage, far taller than the trees of Earth, dotted the lower slopes, and creeping vegetation encroached upon the plateau with what looked like long tendrils of green and blue mosses. Dense fog hovered around massive boulders and piles of rock littering the slope into the valley.

"Are we recording, Jex?" Ryle asked as he secured the helm. "I want to take back as much data as we can store."

"All sensors are engaged. I've sent additional probes for visual surveillance. The mid-range scans are still not working well."

"Find anything good?" Azah said.

"I'm not sure how you are applying that word," he said.

"She means is there any treasure just lying around for the taking," Nolan said. "Stuff she can pawn on Earth."

She glared at him as she stalked to the door into the corridor, but didn't bother to reply.

"I am receiving data that you may *not* find good," Jex said.

"Like?" Ryle said.

"Much of the flora we've scanned so far contains toxic substances. I suggest that you touch none of it until we have a chemical analysis."

Laryn followed Ryle into the exit chamber where Azah was already pulling EV suits from their cabinets. She opened a supply bin beside the door and checked the ampules stored within. "Don't get suited up just yet. Booster doses for everyone. I want to make sure your immunities are up to this."

Azah groaned. "Really?"

Laryn motioned her to present her arm for the injection. "Want Jex to recite regulations?"

"No! We'll be here all day." Azah submitted with a fierce scowl. Ryle stepped up without comment.

"Anything airborne, Jex?" Laryn said as she climbed into her baggy suit. "Do we need filtration?"

"There are some unknown compounds. I am still running comparisons."

"Seal the ship for quarantine, Jex," Ryle said.

A quick hiss in the workings of the air lock separating this room from the *Nefer*'s interior told them it was safe to leave the ship.

Once the three were suited up and wearing a small backpack of tools and air, Azah fitted Laryn's transparent hood with a few efficient adjustments and then handed her a gun.

Laryn stared at the weapon for a moment, surprised by its presence in her hand. The heft of it seemed oddly familiar – how long had it been since she had wielded a laser weapon? Her fingers had trembled then, among the noise and dust, and her brother had shouted at her to hurry. It was the last time she had seen him. Numbly, she inserted the power pack Azah also gave her, reminded of every gun she had loaded in the past.

"Laryn?"

"Huh?" She looked up to see Ryle regarding her from behind his visor.

"Ready?" he said and shifted his eyes to the gun in her hand.

She clipped the weapon to a loop on her suit. "Yes," she said and showed him a carefree smile. "Can't wait to see the place. I've never been to a planet other than Earth," she said. "Well, Terrica, once, but that doesn't count."

"It's not something that happens every day."

"Come on, daylight's wasting!" Azah called to them, already standing on the exit platform. Laryn squeezed between her and Ryle as the lift descended, listening to Jex's lecture that this side of the planet did not rotate away from the sun and wasn't about to run out of daylight.

Azah leaped to the ground before the platform had quite reached the ground and before Jex reached the part of his narrative involving the occasional lunar eclipse here. "Loving this gravity," she said. "We should have a race or something." She crouched and then launched herself into the air, achieving an impressive height before landing again. "There's never enough room on the station for low gravity fun."

Laryn watched information scroll across the internal screen of her visor, showing that Jex was busy with his analysis. As always, she committed it to memory without discriminating between trivia and useful data. Eventually these things tended to come together to form a larger whole. "Find any more *not good* stuff, Jex?"

"The air is suitable for Humans," he said. "I have not found airborne pathogens near the ship that react to your profiles. I recommend against drinking untreated water. The probes have found arsenic and other heavy metals in the surface water, possibly flushed from the mountains as well as the atmosphere. I have not been able to access the aquifer to study groundwater."

"Hmm, that's a problem," Azah grumbled. "Anything else we need to look out for?"

"Yes, I've detected almost continuous seismic activity since we landed. Likely, earthquakes are frequent here. Most of the nearby volcanic regions appear to be inert but contaminants are drifting this way from the active ones."

"I think I like Terrica better," Laryn said.

"This place is still a gold mine. Mark my words," Azah said, looking around the plateau with proprietary interest. Below them, what looked like thick-stemmed succulents grew to impossible heights in the light gravity. Leafless and without thorns, lobes of fleshy outgrowths formed broad crowns, ominous in their shroud of fog. They grew among the boulders, sometimes wedged between them so tightly that their thick stems took on strange and twisted shapes. Denser growth covered the lower slopes all the way to the open flatlands to the west. In the distance, the ocean stretched green and flat to the horizon beneath a yellowed sky.

"Nolie," Ryle said, turning his back to the valley. "We'll

head up on that ridge to get above the fog. I want a better idea of what's going on before we go down."

"Roger," Nolan replied. "I think the Kalons are waking up. I hear them moving around."

"Ask them to stay on the *Nefer* for now," Laryn said.

Ryle led the way up a steep incline through the jagged rocks and Laryn soon wished they'd move a little more leisurely as they passed the planet's wonderful and foreign curiosities. The arid ground, little more than black volcanic ash, crunched under their boots and yet pockets of plant life thrived up here. Ryle stopped to peer into the funnel of a thick-lobed plant of some sort, but then continued onward, past a cluster of brightly-colored organisms that seemed to be neither insect nor bird.

"Look at those shrubs," she said, hoping for a break to explore a little. They had come upon a scattering of perfectly round growths covered in green and orange foliage. Instead of branches reaching for the shrouded sun, they grew a round mesh, like a stiff net, to arrange their leaves. "I should sample these."

"Let's leave it for the science crews," Azah said. "We've got enough aliens on board. We're here to grab base data and report back."

Laryn scowled but said nothing. The woman was right. Outbounders, although carrying the means to collect vast amounts of scientific data, were not equipped for in-depth study. Nor, she gathered, particularly interested in it.

But Ryle slowed his steps, perhaps understanding her need to explore, and consulted the sensor output on his scanner. He unfastened the hood of his suit to push it off his head and sniffed the air, grimacing a little. "We're okay for radiation and the air is breathable. I'm no fan of these visors. Makes me feel caged."

"You'd know all about that," Azah said. She walked to the edge of the drop-off and not only unfastened her hood, but also the top portion of her suit, which she knotted around her waist. She sniffed the foreign air as she gazed out over the valley. "Smells like puddles, but at least it's got flavor," she said, referring to the bland, scrubbed air they breathed aboard the ship and the station. She spread her arms out to let the mountain breeze cool her body. Laryn saw that she had chosen a tattoo of leafy vines winding over her shoulder and along her arm to trace the embedded filaments of her biotelemetry transmitter. It shimmered in a mild, iridescent green against her dark skin. "You don't get views like this on Terrica. Or Earth."

"That's true," Laryn said, giving in to the temptation to remove her own visor. A humid aroma of herbs and other growing things replaced the filtered air, and she hoped Jex had been right about his assessment of the planet's atmosphere. It had taken five years of research before the Ministry declared Terrica suitable for Human settlement. Here all it took was a crashed migrant vessel. "Terrica is pretty flat compared to this. Those mountain ranges are fantastically massive. I guess it's the gravity that let them get that high."

Ryle pointed to the rocks above them. "We should be able to see the coast from there."

They climbed effortlessly in this gravity, taking care to avoid plants or small residents that might harm their exposed skin. Ryle motioned for them to stay below the crest of the ridge when they reached the top. Lying flat, all three peered around the boulders and into the lowlands.

"There it is," Azah said, pointing toward the delta of the river they had followed here through the mountains.

Ryle reached into a pocket and withdrew a viewer to magnify the sight that their drones were unable to transmit. The lenses embedded in his eyes were capable of great precision and of transmitting what he saw directly to Jex, but the distance to the camp required greater magnification. Laryn patted her suit to find it also equipped with the device.

"They're living pretty close together," she said when the shore came into focus. "That can't be all of them." She counted only a dozen tent-like structures visible from here in the lee of a cliff. Deep fissures in the rock suggested that caves offered shelter down there as well. The ground rising beyond the camp was an undulating surface that seemed to have been formed by the range of volcanoes along the coast. "Using wind power. There are also solar power strips on that cliff there." She started to record the images for later download to her report for Pendra.

"I see two of the shuttles," Ryle said. "Looks like they're not going anywhere soon. Probably cannibalized them for tools. Ah, we got Humans. No six-legged headless monsters in sight."

"Not down there," Azah said. "But check out the fortifications. What's that about?"

They surveyed dense rows of plant material and rocks piled high and braced as if the inhabitants feared some intrusion from the hills. A few people crouched on the barricade and it didn't take much imagination to assume them to be armed.

"Jex," Ryle said. "Send another probe into the valley. Try to skim under whatever's jamming transmissions. See if it's coming from the village down there, or from outside. Use a bug or something small that won't be noticed."

"Understood."

"Send a few more to look for whatever is threatening the camp," Azah added. "Could be wildlife, could be half-human aliens." She looked into the forested depths of the valley, scowling. "I don't like not being able to run broader scans. It's like being blindfolded."

"Nolie," Ryle said. "See what we can spare from our supplies. Food, clothes, med stuff. These people can probably use some of that by now."

"We're going down there, then?" Nolan said, barely intelligible among the static.

"Yes. We'll take the *Nefer* up and approach the camp from the sea, like we originally planned," Ryle said. "It'll give them enough notice that someone's coming. I don't want to startle anyone with a gun in their hands."

Chris Reher

"Seems wise." Azah slid sideways to the edge of the precipice. "I'm going to check out that rock over there. That green crystal looks like it might be expensive."

Laryn and Ryle watched her drop from the ledge to leap effortlessly from one outcrop to the next and then across a narrow gap to the stone spire she had pointed out. The side facing them glinted tantalizingly in the murky daylight.

"She's got the eye," Laryn said, amused. "I guess prospecting for this sort of thing is what you people do."

Ryle shrugged. "She's just having fun with the gravity here. Well, and maybe she'll swipe some crystals before Pendra grabs the mining rights. Don't put that in your report." He turned onto his back to gaze up at the yellow sky. The planet's red dwarf star, hanging perpetually above the horizon in permanent twilight, seemed to take up too much of it, veiled by restless shreds of clouds.

"You two seem to be well equipped for scoping out remote planets," Laryn said, watching his face. "Considering how few of them there are, I mean."

His eyes shifted to her. "We get around. It pays to be well equipped. Finding a world where you can walk around practically naked isn't something we see every day, though. We spend a lot of time sampling planets from a distance. This one is exciting." He waved his hand toward the valley. "Mostly because we can skip a whole lot of remote exploration because these folks have already contaminated the place. We're now part of this planet."

"You seem comfortable here," she said.

He sat up and lifted his field viewer to scan the horizon. "What are you getting at, Agent Ash?"

She laughed, startled by his question. "Sorry, I keep forgetting that I'm the warden. I am actually just curious about your work." She squinted at the rock wall Azah was exploring. The woman crouched near it, her eyes on her portable scanner. "You two used to be military? On Earth?"

He shrugged. "Not really. Running refugees in the north, mostly, after the border closed on the exclusion zone. Flying

120

patrols to fish people out of the river. Decided to return to the Hub after that. She was itching to join the outbounders, too, so we teamed up."

Laryn nudged a crystal-streaked pebble to let it roll down into the ravine. "You and Azah both? Are you two... I mean, do you..." She groaned inwardly. Why the hell did she start this now? She felt her face flush and then felt even more awkward because of it. "I'm sorry," she said, striving to sound casual. "That's none of my business."

"You mean me and Azah?" He grinned. "Yeah, none of your business. But no, nothing like that. Not really."

Laryn frowned and stared off into the distance. What did that mean: not really? And why did she care what it meant? "She's not too eager to have me aboard," she said, hoping to reroute this strange line of inquiry and fairly convinced she was making it worse. "So I wondered why."

He laughed. "You're a Pendra agent, Agent. Us outbounders have to play by Pendra's rules and having a mediary aboard, too, is just too confining for her. That's all."

"Not crazy about having snoops around," Laryn said. "I get that."

"Don't worry about it," he said. "We've got nothing to hide. I'm in enough trouble."

She opened her mouth to speak but something in the small shift of his expression told her that this wasn't the time to talk about whatever crimes he may have committed. And so she picked up her viewer to scan the shore south of the camp.

Featureless marshland covered in windblown waves of grasses stretched toward ridge of eroded hills. Water glinted here and there in the bog, reflecting the filtered sun, and she saw people moving around out there. Hunting for things? Harvesting?

"Did you ever realize that looking into the far distance feels good on the eyes?" Ryle said.

She lowered the viewer to follow his gaze to the horizon.

"It does," he said. "Soothing, like a tonic. We never see

121

things at a distance any more, except to look out at the stars, and that's on a screen, usually. Never like this, looking at mountains and oceans. I miss that sometimes."

She nodded. "Never thought of that." Her eyes travelled over the western ocean. Its surface seemed lifeless. "This is a bleak place, I think. Forsaken."

"Bleakness is the inspiration for all the really good poetry," he said.

"You read poetry?"

A shrill whistle stabbed their ears and launched Ryle to his feet before she had even seen him move. A moment later, Azah vaulted onto the ridge, gun in hand. "Things coming this way. Bigger than Humans."

"Back to the ship," Ryle said and pulled Laryn up. "Quick."

Laryn followed Azah, instinctively reaching back to the years she had spent learning to hunt with her brothers. She moved over the sloping terrain without dislodging so much as a pebble. "Don't wait for me," she said when she nearly walked up on Azah's heels. The woman had no doubt slowed their pace for her sake.

"Move!" Ryle said when something approached, unconcerned by the noise made by the crunch of gravel under its feet. A foreign, rasping sound seemed to come from all around them now. "She'll keep up."

Azah pivoted and shoved Laryn aside when something massive and incomprehensible burst from among the lobed trees and into their path. Three somethings, Laryn realized, resembling the tiny life forms they had encountered on their climb onto the ridge. But these were monstrous in comparison, far taller than the Humans, carrying glossy exoskeletons atop eight multi-jointed legs. Another creature resembled a centipede with countless appendages rippling over obstacles in its path.

A shriek tore through the air and then one of the beasts lunged at Ryle with outstretched forelegs as if to impale him. He dodged and one of its claws speared the bole of the tree behind him. He ducked behind a rock and fired at the creature, burning a hole into the iridescent shell on its back. It reared up and twisted as if looking for what may have hit it and he fired again, this time at its head.

Another of the strange arthropods raced toward Laryn, forcing her to fire. She was glad when it withdrew after just a few hits. Her instinctive reaction to protect herself fought with a deep aversion to harming these locals whose claim to this mountain certainly outweighed hers. But she also felt a familiar rush when her aim found its target. She had not lost her skills, nor had these past few years of pampered existence as a scholar and scientist blunted the thrill of the hunt.

"Behind you," she shouted at Azah and fired past the woman when the creature she had wounded returned to attack again. Another scuttled out of the fog with a high-pitched shriek.

"They're blocking the way we came," Azah said. "Head left. Don't get hemmed in by those tree things."

"Jex, Nolan," Ryle hissed into his com tab. "Could use a big gun right about now. Damn, is that a stinger on that thing?"

They fought their way toward where they had left the *Nefer*, firing and hoping their guns held their charge until they reached the safety of the ship. The creatures lunged and withdrew, clearly fearing the weapons but not about to give up.

"Nolan!" Azah shouted. "Damn. Is he not seeing this?"

"Ryle!" Laryn cried when one of the centipedes wound around the thick bole of a tree above him, moving unnervingly fast. It launched itself toward him, extending front legs lined with a fringe of finger-length spikes. She fired, barely missing him, to target the underside of the creature. It twisted in mid-leap, slammed into Ryle and then dropped to the ground where it curled up, oozing an acrid pink substance she smelled even at a distance.

He stumbled and then regained his balance to finish the creature. Another darted toward them and he shot that one as well before aiming at one of the crab-like aliens that Azah was already targeting.

They drew together, breathless, as silence descended. Had it been this quiet before?

Ryle touched the back of his neck. "You just totally shot my hair," he accused Laryn.

She had to laugh. "No, I didn't!"

"Did so. I can smell it burning."

"Our little princess knows how to shoot," Azah said. She turned a full circle, her weapon grasped in both hands, to survey their surroundings. "I guess we should recalibrate our scanners to detect cold-blooded life forms. I should have thought of that."

"Let's keep moving." Ryle raised his wrist unit. "Nolan, did you happen to notice anything odd out here, maybe? Are you asleep?"

"Watch out!" Laryn yelled when another of the multi-legged worms appeared on top of a boulder. "More coming that way!"

* * *

As supplies went, the *Nefer*'s inventory wasn't exactly a treasure-trove of luxuries, Nolan thought as he poked through the storage bins that lined the cargo holds. He nodded his head to the raucous beat of his favorite music as he pulled a few coveralls from a cabinet. Jex was inventorying the food storage to see what they could do without on their trip back to Pendra Station. He wondered if Ryle would insist on giving up his beloved rice pudding.

The music in his ear cut out without warning, leaving his head in mid-nod.

"What?" he said to Jex.

"I thought you would want to know that the Kalons are more active now. They seem prepared to leave their room."

"Good. I want to grab those extra blankets in that cabin." Nolan gripped the overhead pipes to swing his legs over the loose crates, enjoying the light gravity as much as Azah had.

He took a few experimental leaps down the camped corridor, stopping only when he barked his shin on the corner near the bridge.

He knocked on the door to the guest cabin. "Toji?" he said. "Are you guys up?" He peered up at a camera on the ceiling. "Can you make any of that jabber out?" he asked Jex.

"None of it," the AI replied. "The pitch and vibration they use has a different cadence now. They are both making the sound at once. It seems agitated."

Nolan pursed his lips as he turned away from the door. "Maybe we shouldn't disturb them," he said.

"I am receiving new signals from the crew," Jex said. "They have discovered some of the locals. There are hostilities."

"What? Let's see that." Nolan turned away from the cabin door and hurried to the bridge. His eyes were immediately drawn to the wildly shifting, blurred recordings made by his crewmates' cameras. Like their words, the images were garbled, but there was no mistaking the strain in their voices and the quick flashes that guided their lasers. The rapport from Azah's projectile weapon cut through all other sounds. "What the hell is all this? They got attacked?"

"It appears that way."

"You didn't think to mention that?"

"I did mention it," Jex said. "Nine seconds ago. Ryle is requesting assistance. They have veered west of their intended route."

Nolan turned to race back into the corridor, his mind on his choice of weapons and protective gear, and did not realize that the door to the exit chamber stood open until he entered the space. Both of the Kalons were in here, one of them with his hands on the manual controls of the floor hatch.

"Where are you going?" Nolan said, surprised to see them here. "Agent Ash asked you to stay on the *Nefer*."

Toji turned to face him, his eyes wide in a strangely Human expression of bewilderment. Iko heaved on the lid to the lift and pushed it back into its brace, a task that normally required two people.

"I am not concerned with Agent Ash's directives," Iko said. "We are leaving."

Nolan opened one of the weapon cabinets. "I don't recommend it. The others ran into hostiles out there." He chose a rifle, wondering if these two might be helpful in joining whatever battle seemed to be going on out there. But then, he had never seen a Kalon wielding a weapon and was pretty sure they weren't even allowed access to them aboard Pendra Station.

"Hostiles?" Toji said.

"We can look after ourselves," Iko said. "We did not come all this way to stay locked up on this vessel."

"Jex, lock the lift," Nolan said. He looked to Toji. "I'm serious. They are firing at something out there. You'll just get yourselves in trouble."

Toji raised his hands. "I... I don't..."

Iko snarled something at him and crouched by the open hatch.

"What do you have there?" Nolan said when he saw a disk-shaped object in Iko's hand. The markings on it looked familiar. He reached out to grasp the Kalon's arm.

Iko rose to his full height with startling speed. His free hand gripped Nolan's neck and then swung him against the metal ladder leading to a cargo hold above.

Bright lights exploded in front of Nolan's eyes and then everything around him turned gray. Dimly, he felt someone's hands reach out, as if to keep him from crashing to the floor. But then he did.

NINE

"To your left, Azah!" Ryle shouted. He bent to boost Laryn up and over the face of a stone ledge on their way back to the ship. Their attackers had retreated, mostly, and now threatened from a safer distance with loud clicks and high-pitched squeals. He winced when Jex's signal bit into his ear, demanding instant attention. "Jex?"

Laryn crouched atop the rock, turning as she swept the area with her gun.

"Please return to the ship at once," Jex said in a static crackle.

"Kinda busy, Jex." Ryle jammed his boot into a cleft in the rock and heaved himself up to where Laryn waited. Azah, behind him, covered his ascend. There he rose to his full height to improve the signal from the *Nefer*.

"Nolan has suffered an injury and the Kalons have left the ship. I am tracking but their signal is fading."

"What happened?"

"An altercation. I am detecting blood."

"Is he all right?"

"I don't know his measure of 'all right'. One of the Kalons pushed him and he struck his head. He is unconscious."

"That is *not* all right," Ryle said. He turned to pull Azah up. "We're almost there."

"What's going on?" Azah said.

"The Kalons went after Nolan. Why didn't you stop them, Jex?" With less cover crowding them now, he set a relentless pace, moving as fast as possible while still scanning behind and to the sides for their pursuers.

"Nolan is in the way of the seal. I dare not try to close it. I disabled the lift but the Kalons leaped from the hatch. Please monitor your heart rate."

"They jumped down?" Laryn said, tapping the emergency oxygen supply of her suit for a boost. A stitch in her side had become excruciating. "That's a long drop to bare rock."

"The Kalons are sturdier than we assume," Jex said.

They finally reached the bare apron of rock where the *Nefer* awaited them and raced toward her. "Drop the lift, Jex," Ryle gasped.

"Maybe it's time to get that ladder system you've been wanting, Ryle," Azah said, already grasping the platform's railing in her haste to get aboard. "Not the first time we've been in a hurry."

Laryn was in no mood to ponder why this crew would have a regular need to make a fast getaway. She saw Nolan's coverall-clad leg protrude from the opening above their heads, looking lifeless. "Is he bleeding, Jex?"

"Yes. Heavily."

The lift stopped short of the hatch opening to allow Ryle to push Nolan's leg out of the way. He heaved himself aboard before the platform had settled into place.

"Nolie," he called, scrambling to the interior door to grab for the emergency kit hanging there. "Time for breakfast. Wake up now."

Laryn knelt beside Nolan to peer at the wound. "Quite the knock on the head," she said and reached into the kit that Ryle had opened for her to retrieve some sterile padding. She hoped that his head was as solid as his body appeared to be. Even in the short time she'd been aboard the *Nefer*, she had grown fond of the youthful engineer whose face, unlike Ryle's, was an open catalog of his emotions, and whose gentleness mocked the severity of Azah's attitudes. Her worry for him surprised her.

Nolan groaned when she pressed the bandage to his wound.

Azah, standing nearby, exhaled audibly. "Sounds like he's coming around."

"Nolan?" Laryn's eyes were on the scanner in her hand.

"Breakfast," he mumbled. The eyes he now opened were not quite looking in the same direction.

Ryle picked up the gun Nolan had dropped and returned it to its storage before shrugging out of his EV suit. "Let's get Nolan to the lab. Can you patch him up, Laryn?"

She nodded and opened the interior door while Azah and Ryle lifted the engineer to carry him into the ship. Between her knowledge of medical techniques and Jex's database, this injury would soon be little more than a headache for Nolan. "We'll want extra decon. Who knows what's floating around out there that's now in that wound. I don't think this planet is as harmless as it first appears."

"You *think*?" Azah hissed.

"Jex, can you tell where the Kalons went?" Ryle said after depositing Nolan on the narrow bench in the ship's lab. He turned to the monitors above the science station.

"North, toward the hills," Jex said, showing the range of extinct volcanos bordering the valley. "Vegetation is dense there."

"And full of those creatures," Azah said. "I hope those two get chewed up slowly."

"What happened here, Jex?" Ryle said. "Why did they want to leave?"

"They did not say. Their communication seemed agitated, if I apply Human qualities to their speech. I still have not been able to interpret their language. I suspect it's not only a set of audible vocalizations but also subvocals that may well border on telepathy, combined with gestures and perhaps chemical signals. For instance—"

"Jex!" Azah snapped. "Let's concentrate on Nolan and

the scans outside, shall we?"

"I am capable of concentrating on all of these tasks."

Ryle put his hand on her arm. "Nolie's all right," he said. "Look, Laryn's already on the job."

"Could use a little quiet here," Laryn said, focused on removing some of Nolan's red strands of hair from around the ragged wound. She reached up to the dispenser above the bench to withdraw a thick gel Jex had mixed for her. "And Jex is right. Finding out what these people are saying to each other is a fine idea." She opened a decon packet and handed it to Azah. "You have a scrape on your chin. Give that a soak."

Nolan looked up at her. "Am I still pretty, doc?" he rasped.

"Barely a scratch," she said. "You won't even have much of a scar to brag about."

"Damn." He looked past her at Ryle. "I tried to keep them here but the big Kalon insisted they leave. I told them you were attacked outside. They didn't even bother with suits. It all happened so fast. That Kalon is damn strong. Sorry, I should have locked the hatch as soon as Jex found them in there."

"Not your fault," Ryle said, watching Laryn tape the wound.

"They disobeyed Pendra orders," Laryn said. "That's as worrisome as them having a go at Nolan. They are absolutely bound by our rules if they want to be on the station. This behavior will get them banned for sure."

"It's not like I'm going to let them back aboard, except maybe in shackles, anyway," Ryle said. "And we're a little short on shackles. Leave them to the creatures."

"I don't think Toji had any part of this," Nolan said, reaching for Ryle's arm although Laryn gestured for him to hold still. "He seemed pretty confused. And sort of hissed when Iko grabbed me. I don't remember much after that."

"What difference does it make?" Azah snapped.

"We're kind of responsible for them," Laryn said. "We

brought them here and now they're running around loose out there. Who knows why they're here? What if they mean to harm the people in that camp?"

"They went north," Azah said. "The camp is west."

"The box!" Nolan said.

"Huh?"

"Iko had a container. It looked like something medical. Like something that belongs to us. Humans, I mean."

"Did you record any of that, Jex?" Ryle said.

The display switched to an overhead view of the exit chamber to let them watch the exchange between Nolan and the Kalons. Jex paused the recording and focused the display on the round object in Iko's hand. It was blurred and indistinct, and partially covered by his fingers, but they all recognized the Pendra Consortium logo.

"What is that?" Azah said.

"It's a container for sensitive equipment," Laryn said. "Sterile and padded. It's used by everyone. The clinic, Cog, engineering, astrobio."

"Could be anything, then," Azah said.

"Whatever it is, it belongs to us and I don't want to see Iko with it," Ryle said. "Let's see if we can pick up their tracks. They can't be far yet."

Azah turned to the door. "We're taking the big guns this time." She looked back when Laryn rose from Nolan's bedside. "Where are *you* going?"

Laryn met the woman's fierce scowl without flinching. "Nolan is fine," she said evenly. "Jex will monitor him but all he needs is some rest. I can run as long as you can and you saw me use a gun just as well. I'll thank you to stop treating me like baggage and at least consider the fact that I can make myself useful around here. I don't need coddling."

Azah's black eyes narrowed and some tense moments passed in silence as all waited for Laryn to back off. When that didn't happen she shifted her glare to Ryle. "It'll be on your head if you lose the mediary as well, Captain." The gaze she raked along the length of Laryn's body underscored her disapproval. "You need decent clothes. Tactical. Come this way."

Ryle grinned when she left the lab and tipped a wink at Nolan. "Nice work, Agent," he said although Laryn wasn't sure if he meant her work on Nolan or on Azah.

"She's just doing her job," Laryn said, aiming for diplomacy. She looked down at the high-quality body suit she so often adorned with wraps and shawls and wondered if her bravado just now wasn't sadly misplaced. Although she had faith in her marksmanship, she wasn't about to outperform Azah in any serious contest. She hoped that was something she'd not have to prove any time soon. "I don't suppose looking after Pendra mediaries is what she signed up for."

She followed Azah into the main corridor and then to the woman's cabin. She had not been inside this room before and found it as plain and practical as she expected.

"It's not much, but it's home," Azah said when Laryn looked around the cabin. "I guess your quarters on Pendra are a palace compared to this, Princess."

"It's very small," Laryn said. "And very messy." She watched Azah open a sliding door to a neat closet. Unlike her own storage brimming with gauzy fabrics and brilliant colors, this revealed tan and gray and black clothes, neatly folded into the space.

Azah pulled items from the shelves and handed them to Laryn. "You're a bit small for these, but it's better than what you have. Get geared up." Azah gripped the hem of her loose shirt and pulled it over her head.

Laryn averted her eyes but the woman didn't seem shy about baring her skin or the fact that there was little space in this cabin to put distance between them. Having grown up with two brothers, this was altogether too much intimacy for her.

"Why did you say tactical?" She sat on the edge of the narrow bed to pull a pair of tough trousers over her knees. The threads embedded on the inside of the lightweight fabric pointed to nanofiber construction. "This is armor?"

Azah wriggled into her own suit and smoothed it over her thighs. "Seems wise after what we've seen so far of this place. I'm also thinking that crawling around caves isn't going to be good for your pretty clothes, Princess."

"Why do you keep calling me that?" Laryn said, forcing herself to sound more interested than irritated. Clearly, Azah had not gotten past her resentment of this latest of Pendra's snoops aboard the *Nefer*, but her barely concealed contempt was becoming tiresome. She probably would have preferred for Laryn to stay in her cabin for the duration of the expedition.

Azah had bent to tie off her trousers and step into her boots but now looked up as if surprised by the question. "It's nothing special. I call all mediaries that. And most of the station's admin. Doesn't seem like any of them know a day's work, but they take more of their share aboard the station. Fancy cabins and pretty clothes, like yours, and getting paid too much for not doing much of anything."

Laryn bit back a retort to Azah's accusations. The woman was a rich man's daughter who had chosen a simple life. Laryn came from hardship and poverty who had earned her privilege. Augmented or not, she had spent years in study and research to rank among the scientists hired for space explorations. Having been shuffled into the Office of the Intermediary to await her deep-space post had been a frustrating blow to her ambitions. But maybe, she thought, Azah was right to mock her. The delay had not kept her from taking full advantage of her privileges. Had it also made her as soft as Azah assumed?

She tilted her head toward a raised shelf near the woman's bunk. A mirror hung behind a neatly sorted tray of the colors Azah liked to brush into her closely-cropped hair. Tucked into its frame was a picture of a woman, printed on paper and slightly wrinkled. "Is that your mom?" she said.

Azah, still looking like she was waiting for Laryn to protest her harsh words, frowned and looked toward the mirror. "No."

Laryn raised her hand toward the picture, almost feeling the instant tension exuding from Azah. She did not take the paper, but traced a gentle finger along the woman's cheek. Dark, like Azah, she seemed a little older, but her hair was a jumble of twisted curls and her warm smile seemed to mock Azah's severe features. "A sister, maybe," Laryn said softly. "Or a lover. She is beautiful."

"A friend," Azah said after a moment.

Laryn's eyes remained on the image. "I had some pictures," she said. She twisted her wrist to indicate a data storage bracelet there. "Of my mother. And my brothers. Terry and Sam. They're gone now."

A silence spun out between them before Azah spoke. "The pictures?"

Laryn nodded. "And my brothers. We lost our home, our town, to the squatters that fled the exclusion zone. After we lost Terry, we went north for a while and grubbed off the land. That wasn't any safer, but there was food, most of the time. We joined with others like us and decided to return home, to take back what was ours. But they sent me away. Bought me a place in the Pendra program so at least one of us got out. I was just seventeen or so when I left for the clinic in Hawaii. I don't know what happened to the others."

She looked up and met Azah's eyes in the mirror before returning her gaze to the image of the smiling woman. "Before all that I'd walked into a plasma trap near some barricades by the EZ. I wasn't hurt but it wiped my data unit. I'd give up my fancy cabin and my pretty clothes if I could have even just one of those pictures back."

"Must have been rough," Azah said without any of the usual edges in her voice. "I'm sorry." She handed Laryn a vest also made of armored cloth. "I thought you handled that gun a little too well."

"I was never a princess. I just had enough of dirt and blood and being hungry. So when I got the chance to live a little easier, I took it. That's all." She extended her words like a hand to Azah. "I wish I had your fortitude, but I don't. I'm still just trying to survive while others decide my fate for me."

Azah took a breath, as if to reply something, but then caught her lip between her teeth and turned to open the cabin door. "You could do worse than risk your neck aboard the *Nefer*. At least we steer our own ship."

Ryle smiled when they arrived in the gear room and his eyes shifted along Laryn's body to inspect her new outfit. It didn't feel objectionable. "That fits you well," he said, without any particular inflection.

Azah said nothing as they prepared to leave the ship again. She handed a tool belt to Laryn that, upon inspection, revealed ammunition for the projectile weapons they would carry along with a small survival kit, water and com gear to back up the system in their suits. She wasn't terribly gentle when she adjusted Laryn's air supply back pack.

"Do we need all this?" Laryn said, making a bit of a show of checking her rifle correctly.

"Do you want to wait and find out?" Ryle said, shrugging into his gear. "I think we've learned not to underestimate this place. I try not to make the same mistake twice."

Instead of the clear hoods they previously attached to their suits, they pulled a flexible mask over their mouth and nose, and set a pair of goggles on their head, ready for deployment when needed. While not protecting their skin as much, it made for better vision and hearing in the sensor-blocking atmosphere.

"Good?" Azah said finally.

"Good," Ryle confirmed and opened the hatch.

They descended and headed north to where Jex had lost the Kalons' biosignals. The ground dropped sharply in this direction and they walked among towering plant life capable of hiding an assailant among broad lobes and fleshy stems. Laryn saw what might well be claw marks high up along the boles as she scanned overhead while Ryle and Azah surveyed what lay behind and before them. An eerie silence lay like fog around them, something she had not noticed before.

Humidity pasted her and Ryle's hair to their faces and necks and she was glad for the heat exchange fabric of her suit as well as suddenly envious of Azah's close-cropped curls.

Ryle stopped when the com panel near his collar signaled that something moved nearby. "Is that significant, Jex?" he said, adjusting the control tab. "Jex?"

"I'm losing you in the interference," Jex said. "But that signal appears correct. It is very similar to Kalon speech."

"That way," Ryle pointed with his rifle. "If it's not Kalon or Human, shoot it." He glanced at Laryn, daring her to object. It had not occurred to her to object. So far, nothing they had encountered here seemed sentient or mild-mannered. Just very hungry or very territorial.

A piercing wail cut through the air, sounding like metal scraping against metal. Other sounds, too, reached them now. A warbling call, then a dull drone. Laryn looked up, expecting one of those giant centipedes to wrap itself around one of the trees.

Ryle ducked behind a few growth-covered rocks and looked into a clearing. "Shit," he said. "One of the Kalons."

"And not alone," Azah added, nudging Laryn to shift left.

The Kalons sprawled on the ground, waving long limbs to ward off one of the crab-like creatures they had met earlier. His movements were feeble and they watched the creature tear his cloak and then, finding it inedible, drop the piece. Several others of the same species scuttled around the perimeter of the clearing, perhaps waiting their turn.

Azah put her hand on Laryn's barrel. "Wait," she said with a nod to Ryle.

Ryle had rested his elbows on the rock and gazed along the barrel of his gun, neither squinting nor seeming to aim. His weapon had no tracer and the distance between them and the Kalon made for a difficult shot. Laryn reminded herself that Ryle's eyes, besides sending visual signals to Jex, had other useful features. He squeezed the trigger to fire several shots in rapid succession until the beast fell back, away from its prey.

"Go!" he said and rose from their hiding place.

They ran into the clearing, firing at the other creatures to keep them from attacking the Kalon. Laryn recognized the slant of his forehead, steeper than Iko's, as well as the greenish-bronze tone of his skin. "That's Toji!" she called. "Watch out!"

Toji covered his head when one of the creatures pounced. It chattered in pain and fury when several bullets from the Humans pierced its hide. The Kalon rolled away as it pitched sideways and threatened to crash down upon him.

The others moved forward, firing at the remaining attackers who soon realized that this new foe was not easily beaten. A few more fell to their aim before the rest escaped into the thickets.

Ryle and Azah stood guard while Laryn crouched beside the Kalon, looking for injury.

"Toji? Are you hurt?" She saw abrasions on his face but nothing seeped from them. The nubs of his teeth were exposed in what she assumed to be a grimace of pain. His long cloak was torn into tatters but whatever had done that had not shredded his flesh as well.

"Not badly," he said, holding on to the translator dangling from his neck. "One of them bit my leg."

Azah whistled when they saw Toji's legs, folded close to his body. The leggings he wore did not disguise the outlines of broad, bulging muscle. Although encased in leather and without claws, his strangely split feet looked capable of gripping or tearing, like those of a raptor. "Bet you can't outrun that," she said to Laryn, tipping her chin toward the powerful thighs.

"Doesn't look like he outran those things, does it?" Laryn turned back to the Kalon. "You're not... um, bleeding anywhere."

He dropped his head, exhausted. "We don't leak like you do. It's just a pinch. Nothing broken."

"Where's your pal?" Azah said, her gun still aiming into the spaces between the trees.

"Gone! He left me!"

"Give him a moment," Laryn said. "Nothing gained by shouting."

Ryle shook his scanner as if that would make it work better. "Nothing Kalon-shaped to be found. Let's get back to the ship. Who knows what else'll take a run at us out here." He bent to grip Toji's arm, not especially gently. "Can you walk?"

Laryn supported the Kalon from the other side. Alert to movement and noises around them, they made their careful way back to the *Nefer*.

Since their other patient was taking up most of the space in the lab, Toji was stowed in his bed, the lower of two bunks in the cabin he had shared with Iko. Azah flipped the top bunk out of the way against the wall and then stood by the door. The expression on her chiseled face made it clear that she was guarding a prisoner.

"What can we do?" Laryn sat on the edge of the bunk. "Are you in pain?"

Toji looked up at Ryle who stood silently beside Laryn and then back at her. "You came for me. I am so very grateful. Those people tried to kill me."

"What people?" Ryle said.

"The ones you shot. I think they tried to eat me."

"Those are animals," Azah said. "We chased them off."

"Oh. They spoke to each other. I… am not familiar with the distinction."

"He's starting to sound like Jex," Azah scoffed. She turned when they heard Nolan's voice from across the narrow corridor.

"Is that Toji?" he called. They heard him groan as if he tried to get up and then remembered his headache. "What happened?"

Ryle flipped the com tab on his collar to allow Nolan to follow their conversation here more clearly. "Toji got attacked out there."

"I told him not to go, didn't I? What about the other one?

Iko?"

"Toji?" Laryn said gently. "Can you tell us what happened? Why did you leave the ship?"

He looked from one questioning face to the next. "May I sit up, please? I am feeling better. I just had a fright. I've never seen any creature but Humans and my people."

She held his arm while he folded his long legs that seemed to fit perfectly together to allow him to kneel comfortably on them. It was a smooth shift of his body that looked at once natural and also peculiar. "You've never seen an animal?" she said.

"Not a real one. I've seen images of them. I've always just been on a ship, or on the station."

Azah exhaled sharply. "We'll get you a kitten. Tell us what happened. Why did you attack Nolan?"

"I did not!" Toji said, and Laryn thought she saw a hint of anger on the stiff features. "But I think you know that."

She shrugged.

Toji glanced around the room again and then his eyes settled on Laryn. "I am a Br'll," he said.

No one said anything for a long moment, perhaps waiting for him to say something that would make sense of the statement. Laryn felt her brows draw together as she looked to Ryle, who gave a confused shrug.

"Did he say what I think he said?" Nolan finally said over the speaker in the hall.

"I think he did," Ryle said. He raised a finger toward Toji as if to beckon him closer. "Care to elaborate on that? You don't look like a Br'll."

"No, I do not. We were changed. Like Br'll have always been able to change themselves, except this is a most drastic metamorphosis."

"We? You mean all the Kalons on the station are really Br'll?" Laryn said.

"Yes. And on Ophet, too. We changed ourselves into something that resembles you."

"Good job," Azah said.

He ignored the barb. "Yes, it is. We are now bipedal, our limbs are close to how yours are shaped. We've centralized our nervous system, and we can communicate with you perfectly, even if you can't understand our speech. It was never our aim to look like you. You are..." he paused to find words, "not strong. You are vulnerable to so many things. Radiation, pain, dehydration, so much more. We chose not to emulate that."

Laryn's eyes moved over his face and the leathery folds of his neck, looking for clues. If the idea was not so utterly absurd at this moment, she would ask him to undress for a closer inspection. "This is incredible. Actually, no, it's perfectly credible. The Br'll use horizontal gene transfer to modify their offspring to suit their intended role. And, as we suspect, to adjust for environmental changes, like being able to survive down here on this planet. Why wouldn't they also create far more extreme adaptations for social reasons?"

"So can I ask why?" Azah said. "Or is this a hobby?"

Ryle shot her an annoyed glance, but then also looked expectantly at Toji. "What Laryn said. You did this to live on the station with us?"

Toji nodded. "This is far more acceptable to your kind than our true shape. We know you find us... distasteful. And we needed to adjust for your environment. The Br'll don't breathe the same air as you, or eat the same food. Our planet's gravity and even pressure is far outside what you prefer on Pendra. We do not have space suits. We did not even conceive of that until we met you. It is easier for us to adjust our own bodies than to develop such technologies."

"Using Human DNA," Ryle said. His voice carried a nasty chill that seemed to startle even Azah.

Toji nodded but did not meet his eyes. "Yes."

"So why did you do this?" Azah said. "And why come here, to this planet? It's pretty clear now you're not hunting for lost ships?"

"I'm here only to find out why Iko is here." When the others stared him in puzzlement, he gestured to the door.

"May we make use of your display system?"

"I want to see this!" Nolan said at once.

It took a while before Azah helped Nolan, still unsteady on his feet, into the ship's bridge, the largest space aboard the *Nefer* other than the cargo holds. Activity on some of the side monitors displayed Jex's ongoing attempts to penetrate the sensor scattering fields and, Laryn assumed, the convolutions of the Kalon language. Br'll, she corrected herself. As the others took to their chairs, she felt weirdly like a member of an audience.

Toji remained standing. Without the long cloak, his legs, even encased in the leggings, did not look like the mummified bundle of sinews at which his face hinted. Supple and long-muscled, his was the body of a sprinter, rather than the powerful fighter's frame carried around by Ryle. Why, thought Laryn, would they need this aboard Pendra? His upper body was covered by a standard-issue shirt made for humans, albeit large ones.

"Toji," she said. "Would you mind if we took a med scan of you? Make sure nothing's broken. And we're also very curious about you."

He nodded. "Of course. I am tired of secrets. Do as you wish."

At Ryle's prompt, Jex displayed an illustration of Toji's body on a screen. Laryn recalled Doctor Calek's comment that the Kalons resembled Humans more on the outside than internally. She saw a vague similarity of bone and muscle, but there were two pumps for what little liquid flowed through their stringy bodies, working independently, and she saw just one large lung, near his waist.

"Wow," Azah said. "No brain."

Ryle smirked. "Where's your brain, Toji?"

Toji squinted up at the report. "Is that what I look like on the inside?"

"You didn't know?"

"No. I've not had reason to look in there."

Jex highlighted a tangled network running from Toji's

head through his long neck to spread out over his back, protected by skin far thicker than that of Humans. "Like the Br'll, the Kalon cerebral functions are not centralized in a single organ, although certain sensory systems, like his eyes, have been organized to resemble yours."

"I guess that's why they can't access our computer networks," Laryn said, still thinking about her conversation with Tom Calek in the Cog lab.

"Not the more secure systems," Jex said. "Those detect a signal transmitted by a KRNL with the appropriate clearance, like the one embedded in your cortex, Laryn. That signal is basically P3 brain waves which the Br'll don't project. Other systems, like the one I share with Ryle, use transmitters worn below the skin."

"Wait a minute," Nolan said, pondering the image of the Kalon's internal workings. "You're a metamorph, right? So does this mean you're not a dude?"

Laryn closed her eyes and pinched her lips together, fighting a sudden urge to giggle at this. She had hung on every word Toji had uttered and felt her mind spiral into greater and ever more fantastic possibilities for these gentle people. Human DNA was easily scraped off any tea cup on Pendra Station. The Br'll's appropriation of it just seemed clever to her, although obviously not to the others. And so she bit her lip.

"No," Toji said. "I am not. We do not have distinct genders." He looked down at his multi-fingered hands and rubbed them in a complex rhythm, perhaps soothing to him. "In fact, I have none, although you people seem to view us as male. Our evolution to match your physiology..." his words seemed meant for Azah, "...as imperfect as it is, is far from complete. We have attained this shape, but much is lacking. To avoid the complexities of reproduction, the Kalons are little more than drones."

"I'm so sorry," Laryn said.

"Don't be," Toji replied at once. "Procreation is not our purpose."

"So you're not breeding on Pendra," Azah said. She had not taken a seat and remained standing by the door. Neither had she removed her sidearm. "I guess that's why we've never seen any short ones around there, come to think of it. All very interesting, for a science lesson. Now tell us why you're here."

Toji nodded. "I don't actually know a great deal," he said. "But you need to know what I know. Iko's actions today make that necessary."

"It wasn't necessary before?" Azah said.

"No," he said, ignoring her snarl. "You're a hired crew. Paid to bring us here. But things are different now."

"Jex, extend Toji's guest profile to access the display system," Ryle said.

"Done," Jex said.

Toji stood silent for a moment as if unsure of where to begin. "There are some of us…" he said finally, "some of my generation of Kalons living aboard Pendra, who fear that our presence there is not what it seems."

"How so?" Ryle said.

"We don't really know," Toji said. "We are aware of… activities going on among our people. Excursions made, but not to our homeworld, which you call Kalon. There are secrets on that station." He glanced at Azah. "Weapons we are not allowed to carry, intrusions into your computer systems."

"Which isn't possible," Ryle said "Other than the most superficial manual interfaces."

Toji nodded. "I know. And that is all we need there. We were sent to learn from you, work with you if that's what you want. It's what we were bred for and it seemed right to us. My own memories begin when I awoke from the last stage of my metamorphosis, aboard a transport crossing the Hub. I was given, like all of our young, the archetypal memories of my elders, and the imperative of my generation, which was to bring our species together in friendship." He nodded again when he read the cynicism on Azah's face. "Some of these were lies, I know now. I could not have been birthed on the Br'll homeworld." He paused to stare at nothing for a moment before returning to his narrative. "I was given language, and information about your customs and tools, just as Jex explained it to you when we found those cocoons."

"Like we infuse knowledge to some of our own people," Laryn said. "Except you do it organically. This is so amazing."

"I'm a bit less thrilled than the professor," Ryle said. "So what happened?"

"Your people, mostly the science teams, welcomed us and we were allowed to learn all we could, and share our knowledge with you. But then more Kalons arrived at the station these past few years. Larger, and... and coarser. A new generation, really. They volunteered to explore Ophet, where we can survive without encumbrances. But those Kalons view your people like..." He made an uncertain gesture. "...like Azah is viewing me right now."

The others glanced at her but her hard gaze remained on Toji.

"They don't care much about Humans. Then we noticed that the Kalons that traveled to Ophet were not the same that returned from there."

"What?" Ryle interrupted. "How did they manage that?"

"You think we all look alike. The crews of Kalons are rotated out every few months. Between shifts, they keep to themselves, in the quarters assigned to them down in the lower levels of the station. Most haven't even yet learned your language, which comes easily to us. They aren't the ones who interact with your researchers or ambassadors. But we noticed, although we don't mingle with them, either. Now I know we were kept apart on purpose. So we tried to find out why."

"And you said nothing," Azah said.

Ryle half-turned in his chair. "Let's not assume they *think* like us, either," he said. "And put the damn gun away. He's not going to bite you."

Azah glared at him, but then moved away from the door to drop into her seat. She did not remove her holster.

"We've become certain that the Br'll wish to harm your people," Toji continued. "Some of us, the first generation sent to Pendra, do *not* wish that. I joined Iko because I believed he would take me into his confidence. I had not expected to end up here, with you, but that is how it turned out."

"So why didn't you say something?" Laryn said. "Pendra has a security division. They'd take care of that at once."

"We cannot be sure that our suspicions are valid. To accuse our own people of treachery would damage our relationship with the Humans. We, as instigators of such rumor, would be punished. Killed, likely, since we serve no other purpose but to work aboard the station. There are only a dozen or so of us. We've sent some to Ophet, to find out more, and I offered to join Iko on his journey here. Confronting him about the Br'll presence aboard the *Harla* was a terrible mistake. I should have remained quiet."

"So what makes you so different from him?" Azah said.

Toji tilted his head, perhaps thinking about that question before answering. "We have not discussed that amongst ourselves, but I think it's because we are more Human, genetically, than the other Kalons. Or maybe we did not turn out as intended. We don't want to harm you. It seems... wrong."

"But the others do?" Ryle said.

"Yes, that's what I'm telling you. I don't know why."

Azah barked a short laugh. "Let them try."

"Perhaps you are correct to laugh," Toji said. "The Br'll are not a warrior species like you. Until they met you, they had no weapons or reasons to use them."

"And yet you believe they're up to something. The Br'll."

"Yes, or their offspring, the Kalons. I think some of that has to do with this planet. Jex, please show the recordings we made so far."

The images on one of the screens, somewhat stabilized by

Jex to account for their movements, scrolled by as the expedition made their way through the *Harla* to find the med lab. "I began to suspect when we came upon this," Toji said. "I have memory of these chrysalises. But I wanted to speak with Iko before revealing my fears. Clearly, the Br'll created a generation for the purpose of coming down to this planet. But why? This place is less hospitable than Terrica or even Ophet, and the Kalons are welcome on both worlds."

"Something to do with the *Harla* people, I'm guessing," Laryn said.

Toji ran his hand over another screen to move through the images they had recorded just a few hours ago. The shoreline camp, indistinct in the distance, but clearly populated by Humans, came into view. "I now think these people were brought here. Deliberately. They only had to bring the ship off course to land here. Or force it to escape into the filament leading here."

"That's been done," Nolan said when Laryn raised her hand to interject her question. "The *Harla* has minimal defenses, designed only to avert collisions with debris. A pirate could capture it in a field bubble and drag it to these coordinates."

"What do the Kalons want with a bunch of farmers and commonplace technology?" Azah said.

"So the Kalons they made on the moon can learn from these people. Observe them. Learn the way of your people and pass that knowledge on to their offspring. It is not something you can snip from a piece of DNA. Or perhaps the Br'll are using them to make more improvements upon the Kalons."

Laryn looked from him to the screen and back again. "That camp," she said, not at all sure if she had understood what he suggested, "is a lab?"

"Yes. Iko confirmed that when I confronted him."

"That doesn't make sense," she said. "The Kalons have been around for nine years now. The *Harla* was lost years after that."

Ryle gestured at the screen. "Maybe this isn't the only place this is happening. Maybe they're keeping other groups of Humans elsewhere. On Ophet, even."

Toji nodded. "I think this began much earlier. Before we came to the Hub. Even for us, it would have taken many generations to create someone like me. When... when we started to suspect that some of the other Kalons were not like us, we asked questions. We learned some things. Some of your ships may have been lost in our space, long ago. Near our homeworld. Captured, taken apart, studied. The people, too. And so we learned how to build these Kalon bodies, using your DNA."

Nolan whistled as he exhaled a deep breath.

"That ship," Laryn said. "The unregistered one that attacked us on the way here. Could it have been Kalons aboard? Or Br'll, even? Trying to keep us from coming here?"

"I don't know," Toji said. "If so, perhaps they did not know we, Iko and I, were here on your ship."

"So what did Iko say when you talked to him about this?" Ryle said.

Again, Toji exhibited that odd hand-wringing gesture that seemed to calm him, or allowed him to focus his thoughts. "I... I asked him about the Br'll on the *Harla*, when we returned to the ship on the moon. He said he was here on a mission for the Br'll and we owe you no explanation. He said it did not concern you, that this is Kalon business. The ship is just salvage."

"Apparently not," Laryn said, pointing to the castaway's village on the screen.

"No," Toji said, sounding downcast. "He told me not to speak of it and then he made me sleep. A sort of dormancy that we cannot avoid. He did this so you would not ask questions of us. When I awoke, the *Nefer* had landed and you were gone." He paced a little before the wall of screens, looking up at them as he did so. "He said we were to go outside, to look for the Kalons that had come down here from the moon. I did not wish to go. Nolan had told us about the attack. But I also wanted to see what Iko was looking for here. And then Iko hurt Nolan. I have never seen one of our people harm one of yours. I was… disturbed. Distraught. I'm so very sorry, Nolan."

The engineer waved that away. "So then what happened?"

"We walked out into that wilderness. He told me he would not return with you. Coming here was his only purpose. He would leave me behind, out there in the wild. He hoped I would be torn apart by those animals and so make it seem like both of us were gone. Then you would leave here, to make your reports, I suppose." Toji raised his hands to run them over his hairless head. "He had a… one of those stun weapons you use, hidden in his mantle, and shot me with it. It left me unable to move, to defend myself, and I still feel its effects. When I came to, he was gone. He left me out there!"

Laryn winced. "I'm glad we found you when we did."

"I tried to find my way back here when the creatures came upon me. I held them off for a while, throwing rocks. They also don't like the sound of our speech." He paused to offer his thin-lipped smile. "I should say they don't like my shrieking. And then you came."

Ryle stared into the middle distance, pulling on his lower lip as he thought about these revelations. "Whatever's going on is coming to an end here," he said finally. "Iko would have known we'd find the camp and start a rescue operation. He doesn't care. So they no longer need the Humans here. They're done with this place."

"So what is he doing here?" Laryn said.

Ryle looked up at Toji, and then around the bridge at the others. "We're going to find out. Jex, shift your focus to finding the source of the interference or a way to counter it. I want to find Iko and whatever he's carrying in that box."

"What?" Laryn said. "I'm not sure that's quite protocol. We should return to the station at once. The Ministry needs to know about Toji's suspicions about the other Kalons. And send a rescue ship for the *Harla* survivors."

"Yes, don't worry so, Agent," he said. "We'll go down and pay them a visit. Let them know they've been found. Maybe they know something about our metamorphs. Besides, each trip down the filaments is costing Azah's old man a big pile of coin. The least we can do is grab some data." He grinned at Azah. "It's what we do."

TEN

Laryn was still not convinced of the wisdom of remaining on this planet by the time the *Nefer* circled over the sea to approach the camp. The appropriate thing to do was to return to Pendra without delay to advise the Ministry of both Toji's suspicions and the *Harla*'s survivors. They would send a rescue ship and the means to keep the wildlife at bay while these people were safely evacuated and returned for the care they undoubtedly needed by now.

And yet she was as eager as the others to find out more about the camp and to see what else this world had to offer. Her curiosity to explore so far from the stifling confines of the station silenced that inside voice that told her to follow protocol. She was fairly convinced by now that her assignment as a Pendra agent had not been a good choice on their part. Fleetingly, she realized that she didn't care.

"Let's start the approach," Ryle said, tucked into his station, hands on the controls and eyes locked on the screens before them. "Any response yet, Laryn?"

"Nothing, but they should be receiving us. Maybe they think they're dreaming."

Ryle dropped the *Nefer* below the dense haze hovering over the open ocean and slowed as they neared the coast. The tide was still out and people walked the shallows some distance from shore, perhaps combing the exposed sea bottom for edibles. Although the ship approached diagonally and low to appear less threatening, some of the foragers raced back to the beach as if panicked.

"*Harla*," Laryn tried another transmission. "This is SE *Nefer* out of Pendra. We intend to land south of your encampment. Please respond."

"Did you say Pendra?" came a scratchy and fractured reply. Laryn looked up at the screens but no video had accompanied the transmission. "Didn't even see you coming down. You are most welcome! Land on the ridge on the north side. The beach isn't stable enough for that ship."

Ryle nodded.

"Will do, *Harla*," Laryn said. "Stand by."

The *Nefer* swooped around the camp to find the piece of high ground above the camp. They saw people come up from the beach, or emerge from their shelters, all with their faces turned up to the unexpected arrival. Some of them waved, others ran after them as they passed overhead. None of them went past the barricade of rocks and trunks that sheltered the inland side of the encampment.

Ryle eased the ship to the ground and handed the shutdown routines over to Jex. Then he turned to Laryn. "All yours, Agent Ash."

She looked around the bridge, suddenly feeling a little unsure and a little out of her depth here. She had spent her life on Earth immersed in her studies while unrest raged around her, and then within the safe confines of Pendra Station. And now she was about to make contact with a mob of castaways who probably didn't even know what year this was.

"Ryle will exit with me," she said. "Azah, you and Nolan start offloading those supplies. Don't do too much heavy lifting just yet, Nolan. No guns till we figure out the dynamics of this group. Jex, full scan on all frequencies. See if you can get an idea of their state of health. Toji, please stay out of sight for now." She let her eyes roam across the screens. "Let's not insult these people by wearing EV suits. If they can survive down here without them, so can we."

Ryle was waiting for her in the exit chamber when she emerged from her cabin not long later. Azah and Nolan had stacked a few bins and bales in the already tight hallway and she sidled past them to reach the exit chamber. She had decided to forego the long, colorful tunic that served as her uniform on Pendra Station and just wore a pale one-piece to which she had clipped the badge of her office. A veil in shades of orange covered her hair and slung around her shoulders.

She stopped to inspect the thin plaster on Nolan's head, making sure it was tightly sealed against any airborne contaminants. Truly, she thought, by now everyone here was at the mercy of whatever was floating around out there. She'd harangue them all into a few days' stay at the station's clinic upon their return.

Jex opened the floor hatch. "You look lovely, Agent Ash," he said.

She looked up, surprised. "That's a polite program you run, Captain," she said to Ryle with a wink.

He looked amused. "Jex digs up the odd routine God knows where. To amuse itself, I guess. Can seem a little schizophrenic sometimes."

"Well, I like it," she said. "Thank you, Jex."

Ryle stepped onto the lift. He did not reach out to help her into it. She hoped it was because she had proven her abilities in these past few hours and not because he no longer felt the need to be polite to the agent. A draft of humid air swirled around the ship, tasting of ocean and unfamiliar things.

"Where is everyone?" she said, looking down as the lift descended and seeing no one waiting for them below. "You'd think they'd be excited that we're here."

"Yes, odd. We're a distance from the camp, though. They're probably on their way up here. The terrain is steeper than it looks from the air."

Laryn stepped aside and then felt herself pushed up

against Ryle when Azah's foot nudged her shoulder. The woman had slid along the lift's telescoping supports and landed on the platform behind her. "No way am I missing this." She grinned broadly, daring Laryn to object.

Laryn didn't, too aware of Ryle's hands gripping her arms. He didn't seem to mind finding her pressed against him. It took her a moment to feel the outline of a gun under his jacket.

"And here we are," Azah said and vaulted over the lift rail to the ground, as seemed to be her custom. Laryn wondered if she, too, was armed. "Where are our castaways?"

Ryle walked toward the rim of the ridge upon which the *Nefer* had landed. Laryn joined him there, but a thicket of something with barbaric-looking thorns blocked the view of the camp. The growth stretched along a path winding its way up here and she wondered if they had been planted here on purpose. Nothing would get through there without leaving bits of itself behind. The castaways had built a fire pit up here, but nothing hinted at pleasant gatherings or cook-outs. Likely, she thought, it was for burning garbage, or maybe even a signal fire for occasions like today.

Her suspicion proved to be correct when Azah stooped to inspect a mechanical device wedged among some rocks. She nudged it with her foot. "Signal beacon," she said. "They must have used this spot to land the shuttles. Inactive now."

Ryle looked up at the wind sails installed higher up along the slope. "Lucky thing the *Harla* was equipped for supplying a new settlement. Would have made their stay here a lot more pleasant, I'm guessing."

"Life forms approaching," Jex cautioned. "To your left, Ryle."

"Oh hell," Laryn said.

"Damn," Ryle added, just for emphasis.

Two of the creatures they had met far too frequently today approached, moving with greater stealth than they had before. Instead of thrashing through the thicket with snapping mandibles, these moved at a measured pace along the path. A rasping noise seemed to come from their extremities as if their joints were in need of exercise. The eyes on short stalks were motionless and dull, as were the feelers protruding from the sides.

Azah exhaled something that might have been a curse and rushed to Ryle's side, gun in hand. "Get back on the lift, Laryn," she said.

"Don't shoot," Laryn said when a bright object caught her attention. "Look, on their undersides. It's glowing. Or something."

Ryle stopped squinting around his gun to find what she had pointed out. "Where?"

"That's just mega!" Nolan exclaimed from his station aboard the ship. "The damn things are mechanical."

"Jex?" Ryle said, but they all now saw the small, glowing panel on the belly of one of the monsters.

"I have found cybernetic components," Jex said. "But these individuals are organic. I am reading life signs."

"What the…" Ryle said when one of the creatures stopped and what looked like the wing cover of a beetle opened along its side. They all watched in astonishment as a thin male Human rolled out of the creature and dropped to the ground, landing nimbly on his feet.

"Welcome to Planet Torren," he bellowed, grinning around several missing teeth. He used that gap to send a shrill whistle through the air. The other cyborg-creature opened to reveal another Human, dressed, like the first, in layers of clothes that had been worn too long and too often. Several people, armed and on foot, now entered the clearing to stare wordlessly at the *Nefer* crouching on top of their hill. "We'd given up on the lot of you by now."

"I'm coming down," Nolan said. "I have to see these things up close!"

Laryn stepped forward, somewhat cautiously. "I am Agent Laryn Ash, here with the Shelody outbounder company. This is Captain Ryle Tanner and First Mate Azah Shelody." She searched her memory. "You are Sola Crow, the field engineer for the migrants."

"That's me." The man strode forward and reached for the hand she had not offered in greeting. He shook it with enthusiasm. "You are most welcome here, Madam. We're ready to leave this hellhole this very minute."

"Hellhole?" Azah holstered her pistol. "You don't like it here?"

"It's a fine place if you don't mind poison water and living under a tarp for fear of your roof caving in with the next shake, or running bowels from the miserable food."

Azah grimaced.

The *Nefer*'s lift descended, bringing Nolan with it. He jumped from its platform and headed for the nearest of the strange creatures. "These are fantastic!" he enthused, ducking to inspect its underside. "How did you do this?"

The man named Crow turned to watch Nolan run his hand over one of those legs. "We call them *stalkers*. It took a bit of doing but mainly because we had to figure out how to hunt these beasts without breaking the parts we needed. That was a chore at first. But then it was just a matter of threading new works through their carapace. Tough as anything, they are. And the only way to get around here unless you want to waste a whole lot of ammunition. They don't attack their own kind."

Laryn had to smile. "You scooped out the locals to make vehicles?"

Crow pushed back a thick, dusty shock of pale hair. "About the only use for them. Can't eat them and they'll hunt you down for breakfast if you're not careful." He scratched his head, sounding solemn as he continued. "We lost some of our people before we learned that. The wilds are crawling with things you don't want to turn your back on."

"We noticed. They're not sentient, I hope," she said with a look to Ryle.

"Dumb as rocks, but wily. And quick."

"These stalkers would be useful on Terrica," Nolan said. "Lots of terrain there isn't suitable for wheels."

"If you like riding around in the guts of a giant scorpion-thing," Azah said.

"Well, our choices are few," Crow said. "And we cleaned them out good. Come down to the camp. We've waited a long time for this day. Some have given up hope."

Ryle nodded. "We'll gather what news we need to report back to Pendra so they can send a transport to collect you. We're expecting an inbound fleet from Earth so it might be a few weeks before the Ministry can send a ship here. They'll complicate things with quarantines and med checks and who knows what else." He turned away to give his instructions to Jex to secure the ship.

Azah propped her hands on her hips as she studied the vehicles. "So how do you ride these things?"

"Not that hard," Crow said. "Just like steering a runabout, except you have to lie flat to fit in the space. Just lay your hands on the panels and steer by pushing where you want to go. Let the legs think for themselves. We've added sensors to these joints, see?"

She nodded. "Using proximity scanners. Clever, although you must have cannibalized your inventory."

"We've had to prioritize," he conceded. "We've got a bunch of smaller ones to hunt the tunnel beasts. They'll turn on you otherwise. Come, it's not far down to the camp. Stay together on the path; we'll make sure you walk in safety."

The trek to the coast did not take long – or it seemed that way to Laryn, who did her best to record the terrain, feeding her findings back to Jex to include in her report until their connection to him once again faded away. They saw no birds here, but small, two-legged and hairless animals bounced across the path now and then. They resembled reptiles and she wondered if mammals had evolved on this planet at all. When they cleared the scatter of boulders at the foot of the hill, their guardians drew tighter when someone warned of danger ahead. A man walking ahead of her fired a quick succession of pulses from his gun into the trees. An instant later one of the many-legged worms crashed to the ground, hissing at them before it fled into a dense mat of tangled growth.

"They're mean but they won't chase you," Crow, walking beside Laryn, said. "And they stink, and that stink'll burn your eyes. You don't want to be touching them, either."

"I don't think there is much chance of that," she said. "Can you hunt any of the local animals for food?"

"Got to," he said. "Not much else to eat here. We've got sort of lizards that are tasty, and shellfish that aren't. But we've made do." He half-turned to look back at Ryle. "How did you come upon us, Captain? Did our signal reach the right ears?"

Ryle glanced at Laryn before replying. "We took a chance," he said cryptically. "Transmission of any kind seems to be a problem down here. We're not getting much beyond a short distance, on most frequencies. What's generating that much noise?"

"We've not found it. Some suspect solar interference, but we've not detected anything unusual. With what tools we have, anyway. We lost contact with the *Harla* up on the moon years ago. That's when we first noticed that long range wasn't working too well on this planet." He turned away when another bout of coughing wracked his thin chest.

Laryn sought to change the subject away from their discovery on the moon but they had reached the barricade, making that unnecessary. Crow gestured for his crew to shift the bars that held a crude gate in place.

"This wall keeps those creatures out?" Azah said as they passed through the barricade.

"Aye," Crow said. "They rely on their eyesight. If they can't see you they don't bother you. But if just one of them spies a tasty bit to eat, they call up everyone else to join in the hunt. Seems they don't mind sharing." He waved a hand toward wide ladders placed at intervals along the wall. A guard perched atop each one to peer through a slit over the hills, although at this point, all eyes were on the newcomers. "They can see us from the slopes but by the time they get here, they've forgotten what they wanted." His laughter turned into a rasping cough. "Like I said, dumb as rocks."

Others from the camp now surrounded the newcomers, smiling hopeful smiles and seeming to want to edge closer, as if to touch them. Perhaps they thought the crew, looking healthy and well-dressed among these unfortunates, was simply an illusion. They stepped aside as Crow led the way across an open space to where tents and makeshift huts clustered around the dismantled hulls of two *Harla*'s shuttles.

"There's not much left of our boats," Crow said, leading the way to one of the hulls. Pieces of external shielding had been stripped away, leaving the sub-skin infrastructure exposed to the weather and further looting. In several places the fuselage had been entirely opened as if to create windows for the vehicle where none had been before. "We use these now for things that need sheltering, and for the sick. The power packs will be depleted before too long although we're using some wind power now. This rescue could not have come soon enough."

Laryn halted near the door and looked out over the camp. Everyone's eyes were on them and she looked back to see ragged clothing, unhealthy skin tones, a few children that seemed too thin and stared dully, half-hidden behind their adults. Along with the items from the ship's stores, attempts had been made to build shelters using local materials, and she recognized the globular shapes of the interesting plant she had seen near their previous landing point. Here they were used for storage, like baskets, or as part of their huts. Among the huts stood what she assumed to be drying racks from which the survivors had strung things caught in the sea or around the camp.

"I'd like to get an idea of your state of health," she said, indicating the people around them. "And a list of names to take back with us."

"All of us are sick in some way," Crow said. "And the little ones worse than most. We no longer try to multiply our numbers. Best that we all die out than create a generation doomed to misery."

Laryn saw her shock over these words mirrored on Ryle's face. Crow had spoken as if discussing the weather, but how did a community reach such a decision? Especially a community physically and mentally prepared to endure any hardship in their quest to find a new home. These were settlers, not privileged tourists on a jaunt through the filaments.

"Conditions are so horrific?" Azah asked, sounding subdued.

"They are. Humans aren't meant to live here for long, that's for certain. Not without proper shelter, immunization, food handling. We're now using ashes to filter the water, and nothing at all to filter the air. Children are born doomed to cancers and... deficits. Seems we have more deaths than birthdays now." The man's voice broke over the last of his words and he turned away to open the shuttle door.

Ryle stood frowning over the camp. "Where is your captain? The mission leaders?"

"Long gone," Crow said. "The captain was among the first to be taken. By the beasts out there, before we understood the peril. After we got the camp set up, we sent out expeditions. Some never returned, and then the creatures found us here. And there are even bigger ones further inland. At least here we have water and access to the sea, and the volcanos along this coast are mostly inactive. Nothing but ice and storms on the other side of the planet, whipped up by the winds and the water from here. And that way is desert that'll boil your lungs if you tried to walk there. Believe me, this is as good as it gets."

"You speak for these people, then?" Ryle said.

"I do. And I speak for all of us when I beg you to get us the hell off this rock. No more than that needs to be said."

"We'll get you home," Laryn said. "We can take a few of the sickest with us. But it won't be long before the Ministry sends a transport. I promise I'll do all I can to make sure they hurry."

Crow beckoned them to enter the shuttle. They did not go into the passenger section but instead he led them into the cockpit, now sectioned off only with a curtain. The space had been enlarged to the skin of the ship and a cot and some small furnishings had turned this into someone's, perhaps Crow's, living space. Some of the electronic systems along the forward bulkhead showed activity.

Only one of his silent companions, a tall, gaunt woman, joined them in here, but remained by the door.

"We ought to celebrate to welcome you," she said, standing by the door as she gazed out over the camp. "Raise a glass and prepare a feast, and all that. Like we might have if you had found us in the new home intended for us. I'd not recommend you try any of what we have here. It's kept us alive, but I can't say more about it."

Laryn put her hand on the woman's thin arm. "I've seen Terrica. It's a wonderful place. You'll find the home you're looking for, I promise. It won't be long now."

"We're frail now, and have lost many whose skills are needed on such a world. We'll not soon be allowed to settle there."

She was right, Laryn thought. Each of the massive transports leaving for Terrica carried a precise complement of migrants, chosen for their skills and temperament. Craftspeople, farmers, hunters, medics, engineers and their families traveled with teachers, clerics and whatever else completed a self-sustaining community. Along with, of course, a massive database of information. Terrica was not cut off from the Hub, and communities were not completely isolated, but each group was able to survive most new world challenges. Transports like the *Harla* carried the tools they needed and the means to produce food and shelter. They even carried boats, portable surgeries, and power generators like the windmills above the camp. Although the inventory included many redundancies in case of failure, it would not suffice for a place like this, the planet Sola Crow had called Torren.

"But you'll be safe," Laryn said. "And you'll be allowed to try again, when you're stronger. You should celebrate. And you should prepare your people to leave this place. It will give them hope."

The woman turned her sad eyes to Laryn. "Prepare? We are ready now. There is nothing to pack. Nothing we want to take with us." She pinched her pale lips into a tight line before speaking again. "Except the ashes of those who died here."

"The agent is right, Krina," Sola Crow said, not unkindly. "We have cause to rejoice. Let's inform the others it's time to leave, although I'd say all of them have heard about our visitors by now."

"Yes," Laryn said, mostly to Ryle. "We'll leave for the Hub as soon as we've compiled our report."

"I'll give you what data we've gathered," Crow said. He busied himself with the console to start the download. "We've got quite a bit, actually."

Ryle looked over his shoulder. "Did you also bring the *Harla*'s AI down here?"

"No, the shuttle systems are plenty," Crow said.

Laryn stepped close to him and lowered her voice. "We found the *Harla*," she said. "I'm sorry to tell you, but there is no one left alive up there."

His hands paused their task. "Dead?" He took a deep breath and huffed it out again, thankfully without succumbing to another bout of coughing. He looked to Ryle as if for confirmation. Ryle nodded.

"We've wondered what happened to them," the woman named Krina said. "The chief mate went up along with some others to get another load of supplies and the last of the power packs. They never returned. We thought perhaps they crashed."

"They were killed," Ryle said. He glanced to the shuttle door to see if anyone was near enough to hear them. "Murdered by... something. There was no accident up there."

Crow turned to sit on the console with a tired grunt.

"This doesn't surprise you," Laryn guessed, reading the man's face.

He shook his head, moving slowly. "No," he said, "I... we... Some of us have suspected that... well, that we're not alone here. I try to discourage that talk, but people gossip and their fear spreads to others. So we just defend ourselves against the creatures out there, no matter what they are."

"Your chief mate was not among the bodies we found," Laryn said, speaking softly. "And the AI is gone. We have to assume they're together, if they're still alive."

Crow nodded. "Weren't exactly geniuses, either of them. The captain should have stayed here, where she belonged, not exploring the wilds. Dreams of outboundering is what she had in her head." He handed a data storage pack to Laryn. "Plenty of research on there. It kept us busy for a while. I'm afraid we lost interest over the years. What year is it, anyway?"

Ryle scowled, perhaps surprised by the man's callous comments. "22-49." He turned to Krina. "How long before you can get your sickest members ready to leave? We have room for six that need beds, air for thirty more if they don't mind traveling in the cargo holds."

"A few hours," she said. "We'll have some convincing to do. Everyone will want to leave at once. We'll have three dozen ready to go."

"Good. Get them sorted. We'll be taking the ship up to survey the planet a little more, but we won't leave without them."

She gave him a smile that seemed to brighten the dull gray of her skin. "We'll send an escort to take you back to your ship."

ELEVEN

"You're up early, Agent Ash."

Laryn looked up from her search through the food cabinets of the *Nefer*'s galley when Ryle's voice startled her from her thoughts.

"Still getting used to the *Nefer*'s timing," she said, taking her drink to the scratched table. She wasn't really hungry, but she probably needed the cup of the nutrient-packed liquid the processor had mixed up for her. She sank into a seat and pulled her shawl tighter around her shoulders. It seemed cold in here. "And Toji is making noise, talking to himself. Said he doesn't need to sleep for a few more days."

He slid into the opposite bench. "I guess Azah and Nolie are still snoring."

"He shouldn't overdo it," she said, sipping from her cup. It reminded her of banana-flavor. Not the flavor of bananas, but the sort of flavor that came about when someone tried to fake bananas, usually for something that had no business tasting like bananas. "That knock on the head he took is not trivial. I want to monitor him when we leave orbit."

Before turning in for a few hours, the crew had made room for their new passengers aboard the *Nefer*, padding shelves in the cargo hold with blankets and setting up extra beds in their own cabins. The crew would make do with the chairs on the bridge for the few hours it would take to traverse the Hub to get home. Bringing the castaways aboard meant having to submit the *Nefer* to a complete decontamination upon their arrival – a time consuming and expensive undertaking. Corlan Shelody would not be happy and Laryn hoped there was something among the data they were returning to the station worthy of his investment on this planet.

"It's so strange," she said, looking into her drink. "These people were lost here for years, such an incredible distance from the Hub, and yet, were only a few hours' travel away. This whole time, all we needed to find them is to know when to drop out of the right filament."

"It's what gives meaning to the outbounder missions," he said. "In the end, it's all a matter of luck."

She looked up. His eyes, too gentle to match the angular face, seemed to study her as if looking for something beyond this idle conversation. He had a way of doing that, never shifting his gaze from the subject of his interest, even when such frank contemplation seemed intrusive. She almost reached out to push a strand of hair out of his face before remembering that she didn't know him well enough to do that. "Until some renegade with a treasure map points the way to a secret alien lair," she said.

"Yeah, Iko knew what we'd find here."

"Do you believe Toji? That he didn't know what Iko was up to, I mean? What he told us about the Kalons?"

Ryle pursed his lips and thought about the question for a moment. "Yeah, I think I do. It seems to fit."

"Fit what?"

"What I know about the Kalons. Not the pleasant ones that work with your research folks in the Annex, but the ones working with the Ophet project. It's a rough bunch. Brawling in the lower holds is their preferred way to turn a little coin on the station. What Toji said about them being a whole other generation makes sense."

"You knew more about the Br'll than you let on, too," she said, hoping to catch him off guard.

It worked. His eyes widened, almost imperceptibly, and a small twitch tugged at the corner of his mouth when she said that. He straightened out of his lazy slouch and leaned against the back of the bench. She expected him to fold his arms in defense, but he did not. "Why do you say that?"

"You people, especially you and Azah, don't seem to find any of this very odd. The creatures out there, I mean. Iko's behavior. You're armed like you're ready for combat and then you're not surprised when you find it. What are a couple of ex-soldiers doing out here, looking for asteroids to mine?" She pointed at him but smiled to seem less confrontational. "I watched you when Jex talked about the Br'll. That wasn't news to you."

He smiled. "I'm sure I don't know what you're talking about, Agent Ash."

"Bullshit."

He held her gaze for an uncomfortably long moment, perhaps trying to stare her down. She did not waver and waited for him to offer a lie or another evasion.

At last, he raised his hands in a mocking gesture of defeat. "All right," he said. "Although I'm sure I can't tell you anything your Pendra bosses haven't told you already."

"They don't tell us much," she admitted.

"It's just simple. We're told to be on the lookout for aliens. Intruders from other systems. To be prepared for possible hostile encounters, in case you're still wondering about our armament. It makes sense to use the prospectors as unpaid scouts when we're already out here."

She wasn't someone who gave up as easily as he assumed. "The Br'll," she prompted.

"Never saw one before Jex showed us what they look like," he said. "But we know about them. It was a bit of a legend, really. Something to talk about over a bottle. But it doesn't seem that way now."

"A legend?"

"Yeah. The Br'll were chased from the Hub when Humans got here, like Jex told us. They were here first.

They've been using the Hub for a long time, much like we do now. But that's not the whole story. They found the filament to Earth."

"Earth! When?"

"Hundreds of years ago. Doing what we do here. Spying on us, studying, watching. Who knows? They were spotted popping in and out of the filament, which led to a whole new way of looking at dark matter. We're guessing someone managed to meet up with them, and that led to the so-called *discovery* of creating null space in the filaments. Efan Bogen didn't invent anything. They got the idea from the Br'll. Eventually, around 21-50, they followed the aliens back to the Hub and that, as we all know, changed everything for the Human race. All that was left to do was to chase ET away from there and set up shop."

"Just like that? They let us run them off?"

"So it's told. The ISA was still NASA back then, before the Treaty. The Br'll didn't have much weaponry. I guess they were just exploring. Maybe they didn't expect our people to fire on them. So they retreated. Some of us assumed they'd return some day. With pistols this time."

Laryn shook her head, not in denial, but to try to make sense of what he had told her. "You're talking about some alien invasion? That's the stuff of fairy tales."

"Is it?" He leaned forward and covered one of her hands with his. It was a casual gesture designed to get her attention, and it succeeded. "We took their Hub from them and now they want it back. We're the aliens here and they want us gone. Even if they're no longer interested in Earth, Terrica is an attractive piece of property. And so is the station and the hardware we keep there."

"You think this is what they're doing here, on this planet?" She pulled her hand from his loose and excessively distracting hold on it. "Adapting themselves to live on the station because they want it for themselves? Terrica, too? Because they can't live there in their Br'll form?"

"That's what I think." He leaned back to stretch out his

arms along the backrest of his bench. "And they're using our own ships to move metamorphs around, just like Iko hired us to get here. Maybe their own ships don't work for Kalons anymore. They're breeding them here and maybe on Ophet, too, and then they ship them to the station aboard our regular transports. Can any of us really tell one Kalon from another?"

She nodded slowly. "Toji said as much. He said the ones going to Ophet are not the ones coming back from there. It'd be hard to get an alien ship close to the station without being noticed."

"Yeah. You saw Toji without his coat on. That's a fighting body, no matter how polite he seems. He's got a bigger brain than you do, even if it doesn't look like one. He implied that he's resistant to radiation. What radiation is he talking about? Probably not sunburns. What else are they building into the next generation of Kalons they're smuggling onto the station?"

"If you're even close to right about all this we need to get this back to Pendra."

"What if Pendra already knows?"

"What..." she said, too stunned by his question to finish her sentence.

"Not about some alien retaliatory invasion," he said. "But what if Pendra knows damn well that the Kalons are actually redesigned Br'll? Pendra exists to exploit whatever we find out here. That includes alien technology. Even the Ministry isn't happy with how quick Pendra was to embrace our Kalon guests. Or how protective they are of the Kalons' privacy. The last thing Pendra wants is to remind the ISA or the Ministry of the Br'll and what they did to them. They'd have the Kalons off the station and locked up somewhere within hours." He pointed a finger at her head. "Do you have any Kalon DNA information in there? From *before* you came here, I mean?"

"No..." she said, "not me. What I was given about the Kalons seemed pretty thin to me, so I assumed it was classified for some reason. Astrobiology would have gone over every molecule of this species."

"Exactly. Lots of DNA to be had if you follow them around long enough, even if you can't nab a silent med scan somewhere. The Human bits of DNA weren't hard to miss when you studied those Br'll samples, even with what equipment we have here on the ship. Pendra *knows*. And they don't care."

She scowled. "They could not keep this from the Ministry."

"They can, and they do. Even the Ministry needs good reason to access Pendra's classified files. Especially if they're disguised as trade secrets or something."

Laryn frowned, disturbed by the allegation. Few of the outbounder crews viewed the Pendra Consortium as anything more than an overly nosy landlord on the Hub, and possibly as a corrupt empire on Earth. The mega-company reached into all corners of their home planet and in some of those corners wielded more power than their governments. And now Pendra delved into deep space to expand their holdings. This wasn't the first fanciful tale of corporate evil she had heard about her employer.

"This is outrageous on many levels," she said. "You're accusing Pendra of hiding the truth about the Kalons? About a possibly hostile alien species only one filament slide away from Earth?"

"I'm not accusing either Pendra or your bosses of knowing Br'll metamorphs are murdering and farming Humans here on Torren. But you must have something about Human history in your memory banks. The things we're capable of in the name of power and profit. How much are the Kalons worth to Pendra? How much are they willing to risk over it? What's happening here now is a consequence of them getting chummy with the Kalons without asking for references."

She nodded, feeling numb as she considered his words. He was right about Pendra. The Consortium included member companies whose history was filled with things that should never have happened. Including, she remembered, the haste to develop a self-aware computer without safeguards. The destruction of the mid-west aquifer system. The exclusion zone mismanagement. Financial collapse, medical mishaps, pollution out of control. All the things that were now forcing their people to find a new home out here. And, for all the much-touted multi-government oversight of Pendra Station, who was really in charge there? In charge of the entire Hub?

She found herself drawing away from the suspicions he had planted in her mind, knowing they'd have to be revisited and examined, like checking a festering wound that looked so much better with a clean bandage on it. Everyone had thoughts about Pendra's methods, but she needed to believe that her place with them, aboard the station, was in the service of science and her own desire to explore and discover. Without germ-free gauze hiding a growing infiltration of evil.

She shook herself out of these thoughts. "Speaking of classified," she said, hoping to surprise him again. "How does Jex get his digital fingers on the Br'll files, anyway? Right down to how they procreate?"

This time he was ready for her. He dropped his forearms on the table, stretched out in what might be a calculated gesture of openness. "I inherited that database from my father along with the *Nefer*. I have no idea what's in it."

"Jex should have reported it. The JX.9 is mandated to follow Ministry directive. Anything less is punishable, to say the least. But he didn't. Or you didn't. I'm not sure what's worse: your defiance of the law, or running a rogue program."

He regarded her with mock-seriousness. "Are you going to turn me in, Agent?"

She sighed. "You know the answer to that already."

"Do I? Isn't it your job to report this?"

It didn't take much of her finely trained skills as observer and diplomat to read the apprehension behind the teasing smile he offered. He wanted something from her, here and now, and she dropped her eyes as she looked for an escape.

"I need to think about… the things you told me," she said. "Your suspicions. I… I fear you might be right. And if you are, I have no idea whom to report this to."

"Then we have something in common."

Some observer you are, she berated herself silently, torn by his accusations against Pendra. She *was* an observer, but her observations belonged in the research lab. In Astrobiology, not the Office of the Intermediary. They belonged *out there*, studying the flora and fauna of this strange world. She had no interest in wondering about the JX program or spying on this man and his crew. Or reporting on any of them.

She looked up. "I was told to spy on you," she said before the more career-minded side of her brain told her to stop talking. "Pendra's got suspicions about you, or the crew, but I don't know what that is. I'm starting to guess, though."

He raised an eyebrow. "And you agreed?"

She lifted her shoulders in a shrug. "Mitcher threatened to dismiss me. If I return to Earth I'll have to start all over again. I… I can't do that. I need to be out here."

"See, now that's why we work for Shelody. He's a miserable little bitch, but he doesn't play games like Pendra does. Most of the time." His expression changed as if someone had called him and he sat up. "Yes, Jex? Over com."

"Ryle," Jex switched from his silent alert to the overhead speaker. "There is someone near the *Nefer*'s aft struts. One of the *Harla* complement, I assume."

Laryn looked up at the screen which now showed the ground beneath the ship. Indeed, someone wearing ragged layers stood there, looking up at the seal of the *Nefer*'s belly, perhaps seeking a way in. They watched him turn to scan the perimeter of the clearing, a gun in his hands.

"Let me talk to him, Jex," Ryle said.

"External com open."

Ryle waited for the man to skulk toward the center strut below the ship's hatch. "Hello, there," Ryle said and they watched the man cringe, startled by the hail. "Come to visit?"

"Yes, yes, shh," he replied, putting a finger to his lips. "Need to talk to the captain."

"If you want a place on this ship you'll need to talk to, hmm…"

"Krina," Laryn reminded him.

"Krina," Ryle said. "She's organizing priority passengers for us to take back."

"That's not it," the man said. "Please. I just need to talk. There's things you need to know about the place." He looked around himself again and Laryn now wondered if he was looking out for roaming wildlife, or perhaps someone else.

Ryle raised an eyebrow, looking amused. "Sound interesting. Drop the lift, Jex, before something decides to chew his leg off."

Laryn followed him through the ship and to the *Nefer*'s exit chamber. The lift was rising already, bringing the visitor up, when they raised the hatch.

"Hello there," Ryle said with a friendly smile. "Who might you be?"

The man's head swiveled to look around the chamber as he rose up through the floor, clutching his rifle to his chest. "Denzloe," he said. "Ted Denzloe."

Laryn took a step back when his foot caught on the lip of the seal and he lurched toward her. The smell emanating from him seemed to fill the small chamber, reminding her of mildew and stagnant water.

"You the captain?" he asked her.

She gestured toward Ryle. "I am Agent Laryn Ash, Office of the Intermediary. This is Ryle Tanner, captain of the *Nefer*."

"Oh, all right, good enough. It's a fine looking ship you have."

"Thank you, Mister Denzloe," Ryle said. "You have information you'd like to share?"

"I do." Denzloe said nothing more and it took a moment before Ryle gave his head a shake, as if suddenly remembering his manners.

"Would you like to join us for a bite of something?" he said, indicating the door leading into the ship. "We hear things have been tough for you here. Leave your weapon here, please."

Laryn led the way along the ship's central corridor. "Please watch your step, Mister Denzloe," she said. "The galley is just ahead."

"Just Denzloe," he said. "Everyone calls me that. Say, you wouldn't have some of the fancy drinkables aboard, would you? We've been experimenting with fermentation, but it's all rotgut."

Laryn offered a seat to the man but decided against joining him on the bench. "I'm afraid we've offloaded what we have," she said as she handed him a bag of rations, the only edible thing still aboard. "There wasn't much, but we thought your people might appreciate it."

Ryle also remained standing but propped one foot on the bench opposite Denzloe and leaned toward him, making clear that he wasn't interested in a long gathering. "What news do you have for us, Denzloe?"

The man looked from him to Laryn and then back again. "I should not be here. Not according to Crow. He wouldn't like me talking to you." That sudden realization did not keep him from chewing with enthusiasm.

Ryle glanced at Laryn. "Why's that?"

"Says we're spreading rumors and discontent. Scaring everybody with nonsense and ghost stories. But I know what goes on here. I've seen it. Well, some of us have seen it. Seen them."

"Them?" Laryn said.

"Monsters."

Ryle's lips tightened as if suppressing a smile. "This place is full of monsters."

"I don't mean the things out in the wilds. I mean there are people here. Hiding. Watching us. People who live here."

"Humans?" Laryn said. "Or locals?"

"Maybe locals. Maybe aliens. Sentient as you and me. Hiding from us. But we know they're there. Some even claim to have seen them. We don't think the people we lost out here were taken by the beasts. They were taken by those aliens."

"But Sola Crow doesn't think that?" Laryn said.

"The man is blind. Says it's nonsense. That we ought to pay attention to the real trouble we have here and not let some made-up spook scare us." Denzloe waved his hand in dismissal of the leader. "Doesn't matter. Some of us know better. And *you* need to know. Because when folks get here from Pendra, they want to be on the lookout for what crawls around out there."

"How are you so sure that there are… people here?" Ryle asked.

"They have ships! We've seen them when the mist is high or it's blowing from the sea. Weird shapes in the sky. No features you can make out from the ground. Round, but long and thin at the end, moving like nothing I've ever seen." Denzloe paused to scowl at both of them. "Don't laugh. People laugh when you try to tell them. Crow said we're crazy, hallucinating from not paying attention to what we eat around here. But I know what I've seen. And I'm not the only one."

"You can be sure we're not laughing," Ryle said.

Denzloe looked unconvinced but continued. "We've seen them come down on the other side of the range. Or maybe in one of the dead craters."

"We detected nothing like that," Ryle said. "The only technology here is what you have in your camp."

"What we can detect, anyway," Laryn said. "The place is confounding your sensors and maybe they have technology we're not even calibrated for."

Ryle nodded slowly and she wondered if he was now also wondering if, with technology that got past their sensors, the Br'll might actually be a frequent visitor to the Hub, unseen by Pendra's scanners and able to lead entire migrant vessels astray, unseen by anyone.

"They're in the caves," Denzloe said. "The hills are riddled with them. Old lava tubes. We go in there to hunt the tunnel crabs. They're good for eating. We only go so far, in case of cave in, but a lot of the tunnels are solid. So we looked around some. We've heard sounds that don't sound natural. We've found things that don't look natural either, or like they're made by Human hands."

"Like what?"

"Pictures, symbols, scratched into the walls. Tunnel openings made larger with tools that leave marks, too. Once we found some cloth that didn't belong in there." His nervous eyes shifted from Ryle to Laryn. "Maybe that's what happened to the captain. We never found a body, or the runabout they used. She went to check those people out and they took her, is what we're thinking. Crow says it's nothing and we're not to go into the caves that far. Some of us think maybe he knows there's something in there and is trying to keep us from finding out."

"Why?" Ryle said.

Denzloe emphasized his shrug by turning his palms up. He seemed about to say more when something beyond Ryle startled him. His mouth worked but neither word nor scream escaped him as he stared wide-eyed at the door.

Ryle whipped around to see Toji there, burdened by bottles of portable air. "I thought we could store these in here, to make more room…" He paused when he saw Denzloe. "Hello."

Laryn saw Denzloe's hand reach for something hidden under his ragged jacket and moved to stand in front of the Kalon. "Wait!"

Ryle's arm shot out and grasped the man's wrist before he could point his pistol at Toji.

"That's them!" Denzloe yelled struggling to pull out of Ryle's grip. "One of them. I'm sure of it!"

Toji stumbled backward, out into the corridor, when Laryn motioned him back. She put her fingers to her lips. "Stay in your cabin for a bit. I'll explain later."

"Calm down," Ryle said to Denzloe. "That's compressed gas you were going to shoot." He pulled the gun from the man's hand, but did so gently. "That... um, person came with us from the station. You have nothing to fear."

"What? Why..." Denzloe's confusion and fear stood clear on his face. "But it looks like I've been told they look. Sort of. We have to tell the others!"

Laryn nudged Ryle aside and sat down, opposite Denzloe. "No, we don't. Listen, Denzloe. You are safe. He's not going to hurt you. He is a Kalon, named Toji. He's... he's part of the crew."

"Kale... what?" Denzloe tried to peer around Ryle into the hallway. "That's not Human. It's one of *them*!"

"The Kalons are guests aboard Pendra Station," Ryle said. "You would not have met them on your way through there. They're kind of new."

"But, but..." Denzloe frowned in an effort to make sense of this. "Why are they here, on Torren? The ones like him."

"That we don't know," Ryle said. "But we're hoping to find out. You can help us."

"What? Me?"

"Yes. This is your chance to prove to Sola Crow and the others you were right all along. Wouldn't that be something? You can show us where your people think they hang out. In those tunnels."

"Seriously?" Laryn came to her feet again, wishing they could talk without the man's presence here. That the caves could harbor a breeding ground for Kalons and, quite likely, the object of Iko's quest, seemed very real now. "We need to be thinking about leaving here. Immediately."

He turned to her with a grin that seemed to take years off his face. "You keep saying that. Where's your sense of adventure, Agent? This is just our thing." He clapped her upper arm as he might roughhouse with a crewmate, nearly making her stumble.

She glared at him but he turned into the corridor and then they heard him thumping on Azah's cabin door. "Time to get to work! There's prospecting to be done and monsters to hunt!"

Exasperated, Laryn turned to Denzloe who just looked confused.

"I sure thought it'd take more to convince him," he said.

TWELVE

"That's the entrance we use. Down there."

Ryle nodded when he spotted an apron of well-trodden sand along the seaside bluffs. He followed Denzloe's direction to set the *Nefer* down at the edge of the beach only after Jex assured him that the tide wasn't about to inundate the ship. The *Nefer* would handle an immersion in liquid as well as the vacuum of space but clearing her entrance chamber of sea water was more than they were equipped for.

Unlike the giants that guarded the shore to the east, this slope did not resemble the volcano they had expected. Millennia of tides had eroded the coast into vertical cliffs but the barren hill rose gradually here, built by layer upon layer of ancient lava. Jex reported pockets of magma below the surface, but none under pressure or in danger of erupting.

"Look," Azah said, pointing at her monitor. The screens before them showed three of the planet's multi-legged creatures near the jagged rocks forming the cave entrances. Shorter than the ones they had seen before, but no more appealing. "Locals."

"Those are ours," Denzloe said. "Crawlers. We'll need them to get past the tunnel crabs. They have a wicked sense of smell."

Azah looked like she was about to comment on that, but Ryle spoke first. "We're going to take the Kalon with us as well. Think you can handle that?"

"What, the creature?" Denzloe said.

"His name is Toji," Laryn said, a little tired of this. "People who leave Earth shouldn't be surprised by new things."

"Seen plenty of new things," he said. "We can't leave camp without being chased by new things. Doesn't mean I have to like it."

"I'll make sure he stays polite," Azah said, although Laryn wasn't sure if she meant Toji or Denzloe.

They moved into the gear room where Ryle handed Laryn a harness, looking like a pair of nanofiber suspenders studded with tools and pockets. She was again wearing the armored suit and vest she had borrowed from Azah and the gear he now showed her seemed to belong to it. "Clip those to your belt. That end straps around your leg. We'll have to wear these backwards. Denzloe says we'll lie face down in those crawlers."

Denzloe stood on the far side of the ship's hatch as if trying to put as much space as possible between himself and Toji. The Kalon was busy fitting a hood over his alien head and didn't even seem to notice Denzloe's glower. Or perhaps he had decided to ignore the man, Laryn thought. For someone so alien, Toji seemed acutely aware of Human social quirks. "Will we all fit in those things?" she said. "There are only three."

"We'll double up." Ryle checked a respirator by breathing into it. Each of them slung one of the devices around their neck, ready for deployment in the volcanic depths. He handed out visors and, finally, handguns. "Let's try to get Toji into one of them before anyone else sees him. Laser weapons only. We don't want bullets ricocheting off the cave walls."

"We won't be able to monitor you for long," Nolan said, looking over the data fed to the screens by Jex. "Even with the boosters."

"Me neither, Jex?" Ryle said, referring to the remote

connection between himself and the AI. Unlike the com units each of them now clipped to their wrists and shoulders, the spread of the receiver on his broad back ensured far better transmission.

"Not by much," Jex said. "However, I have located the source of the interference we've encountered and will be able to mitigate some of it. There is not much I can do to improve transmissions through the cave walls."

"What's interfering?" Nolan asked.

"Our signals are being canceled out by an adaptive frequency emitting from several of the hills to the east and north, as well as from some of the subterranean caverns. It is not any technology we have cataloged. If I may, I'd like to index the system for further analysis."

"You do that, Jex," Ryle said, busy with his equipment.

"You don't think that could be a natural phenomenon?" Laryn said.

"It is highly responsive and precise. It may actually be used as beacon, or even com signal. A language no more decipherable than the Kalons'."

"Let's go," Ryle said. "Denzloe and Azah, you go down first. Toji follows – get him and one of the crawlers into the cave entrance before someone sees him. Denzloe, you take the lead to where you've seen those markings on the wall. I'll bunk with Toji. Azah and Laryn take the other crawler."

Leaving only Nolan aboard the *Nefer*, the crew descended to the rocky ground where Toji immediately rushed into the shelter of the cave entrance.

Laryn had to agree with the skeptical expression on Azah's face as they approached the crawlers. Resembling reddish-green caterpillars more than centipedes, their bloated bodies sat low to the ground on at least a dozen legs per side. Sensors at what appeared to be the front end and on several pairs of legs came to life when Denzloe reached for a switch below the body.

"There's a control plate near the front. You'll lie flat and put your hands on it like this…" He demonstrated by pointing his elbows out. "You'll be able to see out the front but you should follow the markers on the screen. The legs'll do the work for you – you just need to tell them when to turn into a new tunnel. It'll leave a trail marked so we'll find our way back."

"Sounds simple enough," Azah said.

"This geology is not as on Earth," Jex said. "What we know of volcanoes and lava tubes may not apply. I am detecting fluctuating temperature readings not far below you, suggesting magma pools. Please attend to your sensors to detect noxious gasses."

"What he said," Nolan cut in. "Don't be taking risks. I'm not cleared to fly the *Nefer* if you burn your butts down there. Not too keen about getting stuck on this planet. I hear the food isn't so good."

"Thanks for worrying about us," Ryle said. He turned to Denzloe, who tugged a flap on the side of a crawler to peel back its preserved, leathery skin. "What about your cave crabs or whatever you call them."

"Tunnel crabs. Little cousins of the big ones we used to make the stalkers. They come out with the tide and hunt in the sea. These crawlers are tougher and the heat further in doesn't bother them. It'll be warm, but you won't boil inside them." He cackled in a peculiar cadence and then waved to Laryn to climb inside. "In you go."

Laryn followed his directions until she laid flat inside the carcass, on her side to make room for Azah. It was not a comfortable space, having been cleaned and scraped of organic matter which had been replaced by support structures scrounged from the *Harla*'s supplies. Only the exoskeleton and legs remained but a sour smell permeated the space. Azah sniffed disapprovingly when she stretched out.

"It'll bend in the middle, so you make sure you line up with that at the waist," Denzloe advised as he secured the covering over them. Laryn stretched her neck to watch Azah experiment with the controls.

They heard Ryle over their com. "How's it in there?"

"Wait till you try it," Azah replied. "Though I guess the mediary is a lot softer to cuddle up to than Toji."

Laryn peered through a bleary, transparent insert in front of them, apparently meant to act as window. Another crawler moved out there and Azah set their own in motion with a lurch. She stopped near a few massive boulders while Toji awkwardly folded his long frame into Ryle's vehicle.

"This is the weirdest thing I've done in a long time," Azah said. Although Denzloe had advised them to stick to the sensor interpretation of their surroundings, she pulled her visor down from her forehead and switched to night vision. A lamp near the tip of the crawler cast a feeble glow, enough for their visors to turn night into day.

Laryn did the same and was glad for it as they moved deeper into the cave. The rock-strewn entrance gave way to the smooth lava tube she had expected and the light from outside soon failed. The magma that had surged through here eons ago had leveled the cave floor and the crawler's many legs rippled across the even surface without jarring its passengers. She twisted her neck to look up at the striated, curving cave walls where stalactites hung like ropes and once or twice daylight showed where the ceiling had caved in. Then the tube angled upward, deeper into the hill and soon no more daylight drifted down on them.

The mapper under Azah's hands warned, in groups of red dots, of something alive in the dark. They squinted at huddled shapes along the walls, gathered in clusters. The clusters pulled apart into individuals that moved furtively, startled by the arrival of the crawlers.

"Those are the tunnel crabs," Denzloe's voice crackled over their ear pieces. "They won't bother us much unless you step out. Just keep moving."

Laryn gasped when the shapes, outlined on her visor, lurched toward them, looking much like any animal warding off an intruder it did not quite dare to attack. "Kind of bigger than any crab I've ever heard of," she said. "And those are teeth, not claws."

"Yeah, well, on Torren the crabs have teeth," Denzloe said with bravado in his voice. "Never said they were actual crabs. They're sort of crabs. We'll leave it to your smart science folks to sort out what they are. Keep to the right now at the bend. There's a big cave beyond that."

His crawler sped up, heedless of the animals crowding in. Azah whooped in delight when he walked over a cluster of them and gleefully copied the maneuver.

"There's no need to harm them," Laryn said.

"I didn't break any. Would have heard them crack or something." Azah veered to follow Denzloe's crawler though a split in the tunnel wall. "Whoa!"

Laryn, too, gaped up at the massive vault above them, turning the tunnel into a vast chamber that even their visors had trouble penetrating fully. Some of the tunnel residents scurried away from a water-filled depression surrounded by stalagmites rising upward to touch their companions cascading from the ceiling. From somewhere water dripped, adding humidity to the stifling heat.

"Magnificent," Ryle said.

"Isn't it?" Denzloe said. "If not for the crabs, or the poison water, or the dark, or the stalactites crashing down, this'd make a fine place to live. Go around that pond to the ridge. The tube continues there. It's where we found the markings."

"Kind of narrow down this way," Azah said. Laryn ducked reflexively when they entered the tube which would not have been high enough for them to walk upright.

"We're deep in the hill now," Denzloe said. "Like as not, the tubes lead right through to the other side where the mountain broke away, but Crow won't let us go out there. Not safe. If you thought the beasts on our side were nasty, you should see the images we have of what lives in the north valley. Dinosaurs got nothing on them."

"Likely a by-product of the low gravity," Laryn said. "Everything seems bigger on this planet."

The tube walls were smoother here and Denzloe increased their pace until they were scurrying along the tunnel at breakneck speed. Laryn gripped Azah's arm when she followed Denzloe and Ryle to let the vehicle ride up partway along the curved wall.

"This is too much fun," she enthused. "Come on, Mediary, you have to admit this is awesome."

"I have just one question," Laryn said, gritting her teeth. "Where are the crawlers you *didn't* scoop out, Denzloe? And what would they do with us if we ran into them?"

"That's two questions," Ryle said, sounding every bit as thrilled as Azah by this chase.

"Slow down," Denzloe warned. "Up ahead is where we'll need to stop."

"Oh hell. How do you stop this thing?" Azah shouted, careening around a pile of rubble.

"What?" Laryn cried, groping for a crossbar above them when the crawler lurched to a sudden halt.

"You're so excitable, Princess." Azah rubbed a shoulder that had taken a knock. "I guess I should practice how to stop it slow, though."

"Not funny," Laryn grumbled as they raised the crawler's cap and climbed out. But she had caught the playful gleam in the woman's eyes, devoid of the suspicion and challenge that usually formed her expression.

Ryle was helping Toji unfold his long limbs from their vehicle, paying no attention to Denzloe who stood nearby, shifting his worried gaze from the Kalon to the black void of the tunnel leading further into the mountain. He gripped a short-barreled pistol and Laryn thought the finger playing over its trigger moved far too nervously.

"What's this place?" Azah said. "I can feel cooler air coming down this way."

"It's as far as we've come," Denzloe said. He started to climb up onto rocks piled close to the tunnel wall. "Here, look at this."

Laryn and Ryle followed him, leaving Azah scanning into

the dark, her grip on her gun considerably steadier than Denzloe's. It seemed to Laryn that things scuttled around in the dark that even their visors could not detect. She berated herself for her timidity and turned her attention to where Denzloe pointed, expecting cyphers scratched into the rock, or markings left here by the aliens that frightened these people so much. But instead, his lamp revealed long lines etched into the wall, leading to the ceiling where they gleamed like embedded metal.

"What do you make of that?" Ryle said.

"Never seen anything like it." Laryn raised her arm to scan and record the etching. "Doesn't seem natural. Those look like tool marks."

Toji tilted his head, squinting. "I don't recognize it as anything made by Kalons. But I'm beginning to suspect that I know very little about my people."

"Jex?" Ryle said, furrowing his brow as he tried to receive a response from the distant AI. After a moment, he shook his head. "Jex isn't getting this clearly. It suggests some sort of receiver, or maybe even something that's causing our transmission issues."

"That sounds plausible," Azah said from below. "But what if this is a proximity alert? Letting them know someone's in the tubes? Can we stay together, please? Who knows what's creeping around down here and I don't mean the Br'll."

"They're Kalons when they're in an environment like this," Toji said. "Br'll would not be able to survive—"

"Can we go to zero decibels while sneaking up on aliens, please?" Azah snapped.

Ryle jumped off the boulder. "Let's move. Scanner is showing another open space ahead."

"You plan to go on?" Denzloe said. He peered up at the lines scratched into the rock. "Past this, whatever it is? Not knowing what's down there?"

Laryn had been about to ask something very similar, but was glad that he had spoken first when she saw the scornful look on Azah's face.

"Why did you think we came in here?" Azah said.

They returned to their crawlers where Ryle reached for Laryn's tool harness and tightened a few straps, then indicated that she should keep her gun in hand as they moved on. His directions were delivered in a tight, efficient set of movements, no doubt acquired during his military service, but she was trained to interpret body language. Denzloe was less sure of what he was told.

"Can we—" he began and then squawked when Azah gripped his throat to cut off his words. She pushed him back and hissed a few sharp instructions while Ryle crouched to check Laryn's boots.

Laryn watched him tuck in a strap and then straighten again to adjust her visor. It was probably not entirely necessary, but she sensed that he was well used to preparing for things that might lurk in dark places. There was also something reassuring not only about his concern for her safety, but also, she had to admit, in his physical presence so close to her. She caught his eyes and fancied, for a moment, that he felt that, too.

To pull herself out of that mood, she pointed at her head, then his ear. "Jex?" she whispered.

He wagged his hand in the air in a vague gesture. "Barely." Then he turned to Toji. After a moment's hesitation, he removed a sidearm from a holster on his thigh and held it out to the Kalon.

Laryn's first thought was of Pendra rules that prohibited Kalons from accessing weapons. But then it struck her as almost absurd to leave Toji unarmed down here. Besides, right now Pendra Station seemed a long way away. It was Azah who gave Ryle an angry glare, but she said nothing. Toji took the gun from Ryle, a little timidly, but then nodded and gripped it correctly, copying the others.

The little convoy set in motion again, moving slowly this time and pausing to scan the spaces ahead. Uncounted minutes later, Ryle stopped his crawler when a jagged gap in the stone wall allowed a sliver of light to creep into the tunnel.

The others waited while he slid from his vehicle and crept forward. "A cavern below here," he confirmed, whispering into his com unit. He disappeared for a moment, leaving the others to wait anxiously in their crawlers.

"Ryle?" Azah said, just as he returned.

"I'm here. There's a slope down into the cave. I think the crawlers can make it, but it'll leave us exposed. Azah, stay up here and cover us. We'll go take a look."

Laryn half expected Azah to object, but she said nothing as she opened the crawler's carapace.

"I'll stay up here with her," Denzloe said. "I'm a good shot."

This time Azah scowled, possibly over the prospect of having to share a crawler with the man to follow the others to the bottom of the cavern. Laryn grinned and was surprised when Azah returned the smile with a theatrical roll of her eyes. "The things I put up with…" she grumbled and climbed out of the vehicle.

Laryn took her place at the makeshift helm of the crawler and nudged it forward, then back again to get a feel of the controls. Ryle had moved toward the opening in the rock, followed by Azah and Denzloe. Taking a breath, she fell in line, glad that she was able to better see the uneven ground before her in the growing light.

A stone ridge jutted out and sloped steeply down to their left, toward the floor of the massive cave. Above them, a part of the ceiling had collapsed, allowing murky daylight to reach the ground in dusty beams. Towering stalagmites crowded the cavern, creating far too many blind spots and cavities where someone might lie in wait for them.

"Wait till we're down," Ryle said to Azah. "Then we'll cover you. These crawlers will be hard to spot if we move slowly. Careful. There's a lot of loose debris."

Laryn wondered, just for a moment, what might have possessed her to agree to the outbounder mission at all. She could have taken an assignment aboard one of the transporters that ferried the migrants from the station to Terrica. Help prepare the Humans for their new environment. Things like that, all very safe and unlikely to result in stalking aliens in near-darkness just to prove to some woman she had never met before that she wasn't a princess. Was she trying to impress Ryle as well? Had she reverted, somehow, to the bratty twelve-year old bent on showing her brothers what she was made of?

She shook her head to focus her concentration on the descent, keeping her eyes on Ryle's crawler just ahead of her. Gravel scattered but it remained surefooted and steady. It seemed to take years before they reached level ground and moved into the shelter of a wall of stalagmites to leave the vehicles.

"Stay in the shadows," Ryle whispered.

She nodded and followed him as he crept along the perimeter of the cave, frequently looking up to where Azah crouched on the ledge in case she spotted movement among the structures. Toji followed, bent low. They listened to sounds that might tell of someone, or something, lurking in the dark, but only the crunch of gravel under their feet disturbed the silence.

"Look!" Laryn pointed ahead when several hunched shapes appeared out of the gloom.

The spaces here among the stalagmites had been filled in by the tough, grayish substance they had seen aboard the *Harla*. Uneven and ropy-looking in places, it had been molded to create spherical shapes that, given the door-like openings, seemed to be shelters. There was no other sign of habitation here. No fire pits, no tools or equipment scattered around, no sign that people had lived here. Only the smoother paths in the loose gravel showed the traffic pattern of many feet from one structure to another.

"This stuff looks familiar," Ryle said. "Like those round things on the moon, but bigger. He tapped his com. "Stay up there for now, Azah. We found habitats or something. Place looks deserted but cover us while we check this out."

"Got it."

Ryle sidled around to the arched opening on one of the Kalon-made structures and quickly looked inside. He shook his head and moved past it. Taking a look for herself, Laryn saw that it was empty.

The one next to it wasn't. Here they found two Br'll chrysalis, abandoned and possibly dead, and a pile of cast-off casings from one or two that had lived. A third building contained just the shells. She tapped the curving wall of the chamber and found it hard, like plastic, and as uneven as if it had been sprayed in a liquid state. Like the ropes of hardened material they had found on the Human bodies aboard the *Harla*.

"Over there!" Ryle moved stealthily to a larger dome among the stalagmites where a dim glow seeped from the door opening. A mechanical hum reached their ears.

He looked up at Azah who waved a signal that all was well before he ducked into the building ahead of Laryn and Toji. They found a single, oblong room, but here the gray material had been used to build low tables, or perhaps beds. No one reclined on them now but above each hung a globe from which thin strands of reddish rope ran along the wall and to the humming mechanism near another exit.

Laryn looked up at the rope. "That power pack is clearly one of ours. If those are power cables I have no idea how they managed to interface with our stuff."

Toji touched a hesitant finger to trace a fractal pattern up along the curved wall. The lines and patches glowed softly to provide a source of light here.

Laryn held up her scanner. "Lichen, sort of," she concluded. "Maybe engineered to glow like that."

Ryle cursed, barely audible, when he walked past the last of the tables.

Someone sprawled on the floor there, unmoving and clearly Human. "Dead," Ryle pronounced after looking for signs of life. "Not long."

"That's the chief mate of the *Harla*," Laryn said in a near whisper. She looked around for something with which to cover him, but there wasn't so much as a rag here. Perhaps guessing her thoughts, Toji lifted the body off the ground to take him to the table farthest from where they stood. He did this without visible effort although, even in this gravity, the man's body seemed substantial.

Ryle examined the power pack and then followed another, more conventional, cable to a familiar shape nearby. He ran his hand over the top of the sturdy case, the sort used to transport delicate equipment. It took only a few minutes for him to force it open and shine a light inside. "Well, now we know where the AI is," he said, reading the markings on the device. "*Harla*."

"But they left it behind," Toji said. "Is it not valuable?"

"Not without its master." Laryn nodded toward the dead man. "I'm guessing the captain is dead, too. Without them, the AI is useless, wiped out when the telemetry stopped."

"Yeah," Ryle said after running his hand over the device. "Dead cold. What the hell were they doing with the AI down here? It's just the processor. No guts, no database, no network."

Laryn turned to inspect one of the globes hanging over the tables. Walking around it, she found a transparent circle and peered inside. A bewildering array of tubes, fluid-filled bulbs, and what looked eerily like pincers and scalpels, all cleverly magnified by the viewport's material, lined the interior. "This looks surgical," she said.

Ryle stepped out of the chamber to look for an assuring wave from Azah and then returned to give the table an experimental shake. Finding it solid, he hopped onto it to lie down beneath the globe. Although the table seemed made for something of Kalon size, the globe now hung over his head. He pointed at its bottom. "There's a sphincter on this thing."

Laryn almost laughed out loud. "What? Where?" She bent to see the gathered circle of flexible material designed to tighten around a patient's neck.

"Good enough for me," Ryle said and sat up again. "I'm not sticking my head in there." He began to sift through some equally puzzling tools scattered on another table.

"Why would they operate on a Kalon's head, Toji?" Laryn said. "Your face isn't surgically altered, is it?"

He came to where she stood and peered into the device. "No. Not that I recall."

She frowned. "Well, we know they're not doing brain surgery down here. What with your brain not being all in your head, I mean. I wish we could take one of these with us. I'm dying to figure out what it does. Or how it works."

Ryle whistled softly, drawing their attention. "Will you look at that." He turned to hold up a familiar shape. She recognized the gray container with its rounded lid before he showed her the Pendra logo emblazoned on it. "Must be the box Iko had."

Laryn moved around the table to peer into the case when he opened it. The interior padding had shaped itself around four small vials although they looked empty now and had been carelessly tossed back without regard of the slots. He nudged them back into place, turning them so that their markings showed.

"What are those?" Toji said.

Laryn read the digits on each vial. "Those are KRNL codes," she said.

"KRNL? Isn't that the device you carry in your head? For identification?"

She nodded. "And the one on Ryle's back. Hidden in his tattoo. But those digits there mean they belong to a neural interface, like mine."

"Neural?" Ryle looked at the globe suspended over the table behind her. "The kind you need brain surgery for?"

Laryn gasped. "But they don't have..." She looked up at Toji, then shook her head in disbelief. "They made Kalons with brains? The kind that can use these chips?"

Toji lifted a hand to cover his mouth, a gesture that

seemed Human. "But why? What use is it to them?"

Ryle held up one of the vials, empty now except for the liquid that once protected the appliance from contamination. "These aren't just lying around some place where Kalons can get at them. Aren't your spares super secure?"

She nodded. "Of course. Double-blind code and under lock and key in the clinic somewhere. Nowhere near where civilians are allowed. They wouldn't scribble the actual ID of the carrier on the vial. I don't think they're even kept in vials."

Ryle put the box back on the table. "Do you have written language, Toji?"

"No. Some of us use yours. We haven't needed to develop any. Not the Kalons, anyway. I don't know about the Br'll. Why?"

Ryle's eyes moved from the spherical surgery, along the cables, to find the dead AI and its equally dead master. "Only two possibilities here," he said. "Either someone *gave* these to Iko, or he took them from their owners."

Laryn spun to face him. "No one would just *give* these to anybody. I know you see conspiracies around every corner, but I'm not going to entertain that thought, Captain. And it's not likely that Kalons were doing brain surgery, or whatever this is, on Pendra Station."

He regarded her thoughtfully for a moment, and then shifted to Toji. "No, they were not."

She squinted at him as his meaning became clear. "You think they murdered four people to get these chips?"

"I do."

Toji emitted a weak, high-pitched exclamation before covering his mouth again, this time with both hands.

"You were right, Toji," Ryle said. "This *is* a lab. They brought the *Harla* here on purpose. But not to learn how Humans dress for dinner. They needed an AI, and they needed brains to figure out how to talk to one."

"For what reason?" Toji exclaimed.

"They're after our AIs," Laryn said, watching Ryle nod in

agreement. "If they developed a brain that can carry these devices, they can gain access to our ships, even the Artificial Neural Network aboard Pendra Station. Security, Admin, Engineering, all depending on whose chips they are. If they can mimic a Human body, ANN will recognize them by their implant. If they got their hands on the right KRNLs, they'll have access to anything they want." She joined Ryle by the arched opening of the alien surgical lab. "I'm afraid this time I have to insist that we return to Pendra Station immediately, Captain."

"I'm afraid you're right, Agent," he said with a crooked grin. "And we better hurry."

"There is someone outside!" Toji pointed to the sensitive aural pads on his forehead as he scanned the cave for something. Or listened. "Kalons coming this way."

They now all heard a hissing sound, like water through a narrow pipe, punctuated by something mechanical.

"What are they saying?" Laryn said.

"They're not saying anything," Toji said. "It's a sound made when we're stressed. That could be anything. Pain, fear, even just working very hard." He pointed to the left of the cave, where Azah would not be able to see from her post on the ledge.

Gun in hand, Ryle edged to the door to look outside. "I don't want to get trapped in here," he said, motioning Laryn to move ahead of him. "Let's take cover over there." He turned back to Toji. His expression changed to one of surprise and a fair bit of amusement.

Toji had shed his mantle and now stood entirely undressed before them, holding only his gun. In the bleary light, the long, powerful limbs seemed made for combat. The skin over his chest and abdomen folded and overlapped like deeply tanned leather plates.

"Um…" Laryn began but then, remembering that his people didn't actually have gender, realized there probably wasn't any need for the Kalons to be clothed at all, except for decorative purposes. Or maybe if things got chilly. She wondered if all of them were naked aboard Pendra when no Humans were around to be offended by such breach of tradition.

Toji pointed at his discarded mantle. "It gets in the way," he said and stepped outside. Ryle and Laryn followed to hear Azah's shrill whistle pierce the silence of the cavern. Laryn looked up to see her, half-hidden behind a rock, gesturing to their left. Almost at once, part of another boulder beside her exploded in a shower of shards.

"Kalons!" Ryle shoved Laryn into the cover of the stone pillars.

At least a half dozen of the metamorphs, unclothed like Toji, scrambled through the rock formations toward them. Their rasping vocals and ear-shattering shrieks echoed through the stone chamber, disguising their true number. Something punched into the side of the dome shelter behind them to shatter it as if with a giant's fist.

"What the hell are they using? Sonics?" Ryle rose to fire his laser weapon, equipped with a tracer, toward the advancing Kalons. One of them loped toward them and he took him down with a precisely placed burst. Toji also took up the fight, aiming inexpertly but adding to the show of force. "Insane weaponry and no fighting skills. Lovely."

The Kalons circled the perimeter more cautiously now as if realizing that these were not the poorly-armed *Harla* survivors that had found their way into their lair. Azah, from her vantage point, stabbed her volleys into their midst. Two fell to her aim. Then another shot from below pulverized the rock that was shielding her.

Ryle ducked just before the Kalon weapon slammed into the cave wall behind them, shaking smaller stalactites loose from their grip on the ceiling. Laryn yelped when a shard of rock cut into her arm, slicing no further than the layer of nanofibers that protected her.

Toji crouched beside them. "There are more of them." He touched his forehead. "I can detect their... their signals. The sounds we make. They are together, that way."

"I wonder how many there are," Ryle said, his eyes on Laryn's arm. "You all right?"

She nodded, shaking it to get rid of the numb feeling.

Ryle peered over his cover again to fire in the direction Toji had pointed out. "I want one of those guns they're using," he said.

Laryn ducked when a sound like a crack of lightning reached them. The stone ledge where Azah and Denzloe had taken cover disintegrated, showering debris to the cave floor. She stared in disbelief as Denzloe started to slide. Azah lunged for him but he fell, flailing wildly, to the bottom of the cave and she began to slide after him with a cascade of splintered stone. Ryle's fingers dug painfully into Laryn's arm when Azah grasped for a jagged outcropping, hanging free as her feet sought support on the stone wall. A shot from a Kalon weapon blasted more dust and stone into the air.

Ryle exhaled forcefully, relieved, when she heaved herself up and rolled away from the edge. He tapped the com tab on his collar. "Azah, get out of here. We won't make it back up there now."

Her dark, dust-streaked face peered down at them. "There has to be another way up," she said, her voice broken and bleared by static.

"Get out," Ryle said. "You still have a crawler. Get back to the *Nefer* and take her up and around to this side of the ridge. This fresh air has to come from somewhere. We'll try to make our way there. If you see something looking even remotely like a ship, take it out. I think the Kalons are heading back to the station to make trouble there."

"I'm not leaving you."

"Go! Watch for some damn weird weapons."

Even from here, they saw the indecision on her face, torn between staying to fight, likely her first instinct, and obeying Ryle's order to make the daunting trek back through the dark on her own.

"'kay," she said finally, the curtness of the confirmation making no secret of her feelings about this.

Ryle rose and fired to where the Kalons hid, giving her time to scramble up and through the cleft in the rock to reach the tunnel. "Let's shed some light on this," he said between clenched teeth. He fired his weapon at the ceiling, holding it there until it gave way to drop a torrent of dirt and boulders down onto the cave floor. Instead of illuminating the cave, the collapse stirred a dense fog of dust from the ground. The haze turned impenetrable when daylight fell through it to create a dazzle of glints like sunlight on snow. "Visor, Laryn," he said, grinning over this windfall. "Heat sensors."

She pulled her filter wrap over her nose to keep the fine grit out of her lungs and adjusted her visor to detect shapes moving in the murk. Ryle now appeared in a reddish glow while Toji, cooler, looked yellow.

Ryle gestured for her to flank left. "Toji, stay with me. Don't get lost in this."

Laryn followed his directions and they moved forward, using their weapons only when they detected movement. The cloud made the lasers less effective and so they pressed on, moving closer to their quarry, until they jogged after the last of them before bringing them down.

Ryle bent to inspect a dead Kalon for weapons when another slid from the rounded roof of one of the habitats beside him. Laryn cried out a warning and rushed forward to shove Ryle out of the way. Both of them tumbled over the uneven ground and rolled out of the way when Toji rushed at the metamorph.

Frozen in surprise, they watched as Toji crouched and then leaped forward to thrust his balled fist into the Kalon's midriff, just below where a Human's rib cage protected internal organs. His hand seemed to disappear entirely to tear a ragged hole through the skin. The Kalon's rasp grated in their ears but it lasted just a few moments before he crumpled to the ground.

"That," Ryle said when, breathless, dust- and sweat-streaked, they came to their feet again, "was weird."

Laryn looked at the puncture in the metamorph's torso. A clear fluid seeped there, but whatever damage Toji had wrought was deeply internal.

"A vulnerable area," Toji said, placing his hand on his own sternum. "Perhaps an error of our evolution."

"You might want to armor that spot," Ryle said. "Just a thought." He looked around. "Let's make sure there aren't any more of these. Can you do your sound-detecting thing and see if anyone else is creeping around here?"

Toji nodded and clambered up on the rocks.

Ryle peered at the torn metamorph on the ground. "Think he's dead?" He lifted the alien's shoulder and found a gun beneath the body. It was connected to a backpack slung around the Kalon's shoulders, and he took that as well. He pushed his visor up to inspect the gun more closely and then showed it to Laryn. The round grip was obviously meant to fit a Kalon's many-fingered hand. "Never seen anything like it," he said. "You?"

"No. I'm not a weapons expert. It's not a file I've ever had to ask for." Laryn pulled a hand-held scanner from one of her many pockets and surveyed the cavern. There was no sign of Human life from where they had seen Denzloe fall from the ledge.

Ryle grinned, teeth flashing in the dusty face. "If you're going to hang out on the *Nefer*, that could be a useful file to get. I doubt this one is in the archives, though."

Toji dropped down from his perch. "That Kalon over there is not dead. I will question him."

Ryle and Laryn exchanged a puzzled glance but followed him to another of the fallen metamorphs to kneel beside him. Silence followed although they heard a few burrs and whines as they had when Iko had spoken to Toji on their way to this planet.

Ryle walked away to peer into the gloom of the tunnel the Kalons had used. It seemed the only way out of here now. His lips moved as he tried to hail Jex.

Laryn scanned the area around them but the report

showed little but solid rock. She looked up, but both the broken ceiling and the cleft into the lava tube were out of reach now. "I don't suppose anyone brought some rope."

Ryle returned to them, wiping dust from his visor. "Azah's still in the tunnels," he reported. "Although she buzzed Nolie to say she's on her way out."

Toji stood up again. "These Kalons were sent back when they realized someone was in the tunnels. They have ships in the crater. That's why we didn't see them on our way to the surface. You were right. They've been waiting for Iko to deliver the interface chips. They've joined the interface chips to the... the brains of four Kalons. Now they've left to take them to Pendra Station."

"How many are there, total?"

"Dozens. But they don't just want the station." Toji gestured to encompass something growing in size. "There are many more. Hundreds. Bred on Ophet. They've built an army there."

"Right under our noses," Ryle said with a grimace. "And we let them. There aren't more than a dozen Humans there to help with the project. It's a massive planet."

"An army? I thought our weapons are superior to theirs," Laryn said.

"If we *had* weapons," Ryle said. "There's been nothing worth shooting at for a hundred years. Only the prospectors and the science vessels are decently armed. And the Pendra patrols. Who knows what ships the Br'll have by now. They can modify DNA in a converted lab designed for our technology. How easy is it for them to design superior weapons and engines? What if the Kalons are using those old EM engines on their ships to keep us thinking our technology is superior? They have biochemical processes we haven't even begun to figure out. Their current arsenal could be unimaginable."

"They are coming to the station to murder your people. And then Terrica." Toji's eyes stared at nothing as he continued to listen to the injured Kalon. "They want to destroy Humans. For what you did, for taking the Hub, for murdering Br'll. There is only one filament to your planet and they will guard that entrance. The Hub will be theirs." He blinked, as if startled out of a daydream. "Those are the thoughts of this Kalon."

Laryn frowned, trying to absorb this news. "So then why wouldn't they just attack the station, then?"

"Maybe they want the station for themselves," Ryle said. "Not damage it. They know it's fragile. Shielded only against debris impacts. Maybe they can adapt it to suit the Br'll and go back to using the Hub like they did before we kicked them out. But they need a brain and a neural interface to operate the station itself."

"Then what will become of the rest of the Kalons?"

Toji unfolded his legs to stand up, moving fluidly despite his gangly limbs. "Kalons are of no importance to the Br'll. Drones, soldiers, workers. Perhaps they will stay on Terrica until they die out. They... *we* will have served our purpose."

An uncomfortable silence followed until Ryle exhaled a deep breath. "Let's find our way out of here. Our only job now is to get to the station to warn them. Keep your eyes and ears open." He glanced up at Toji's forehead. "Or whatever those are."

Laryn peered at the metamorph on the ground. "Did... did you kill that... person?"

"No," Toji said. "I made him sleep."

Ryle squinted at him before turning to head for their crawlers. "That's starting to sound like a pretty weird euphemism."

They jogged to where they had left the crawlers near what used to be the steep slope to the ledge. Laryn kept her eyes away from the foot of the cliff in case they came across what used to be Denzloe. "Oh, great!" she cried when they saw that one of the crawlers had stood in the way of the rock slide from above. It lay on its side in a tangle of legs and torn hide.

Ryle leaned against it but soon gave up trying to get it

back on its feet when the main sensor on its belly fell off, dangling broken and useless by its wires.

"I can walk," Toji said. "We haven't seen any of those tunnel creatures in a while. Perhaps it is safe."

"Who knows what's waiting for us in that tunnel," Laryn said, remembering Denzloe's boasts about the wildlife in the northern valleys. "We can all fit into this crawler. You fold up pretty well, if I recall."

Ryle turned to the other crawler. "Yeah, let's give that a—"

They felt the deep rumble an instant before they heard it. The ground shook in a violent tremor that had them all lurching like drunkards on the unstable ground.

"Get down!" Ryle grabbed her arm and pulled her to take cover under the crawler. Toji flailed his long limbs and then crashed to the ground. Behind them, more of the unstable ceiling collapsed into the cavern. "Cave in!"

THIRTEEN

"Jex!" Ryle rasped. He squinted through the dust, listening for more rumbling in the hills. But only the drizzle of soil and pebbles from the ceiling disturbed the silence now. "Are you monitoring? What was that?"

Coughing, Laryn slid out from under the crawler, wishing she hadn't pulled down her filter mask after the battle with the Kalons. Dust swirled around them like smoke. She consulted her scanner, but none of its functions analyzed earthquakes, or whatever this had been. "I thought Jex said this hill was dormant."

"Let get the hell out of here," Ryle said.

They pulled Toji onto his feet and helped him fold his body into the back end of the crawler. Ryle stretched out with his feet on the Kalon's legs, and Laryn curled up beside him. "Good luck to all of us," he mumbled as he activated the crawler and turned it toward the narrow tunnel.

"We are detecting a detonation above and to the west of your location," Jex said, barely audible over Ryle's com unit. "It was not a natural occurrence."

"What?" Ryle said. "What is it, then?"

A silence followed and then Nolan's voice came over their com tabs. "Ryle, get out of there. Are you receiving me? There's a... a magma chamber up there. I think they blew it on purpose. The Kalons. It's going to get warm in there."

200

Ryle and Laryn's eyes met and read the sudden terror in each other's face.

"Azah," Ryle said.

"Not here yet. Get out, Ryle!"

Ryle worked with the crawler's controls to pick their way through the obstacles strewn across the floor of the cavern.

Laryn poked at her scanner. "This thing is useless! Nolan, can you detect a magma flow coming this way?"

"Yes, we sent a drone over the top. It'll help us track you. There are high thermal readings going your way, probably also into the lava tube."

"Tell Azah to step on it," Ryle snapped. "Maybe they're doing this to destroy evidence of what went on here. Contact Sola Crow in the camp and tell them to clear out. Head uphill to the west, in case more of these chambers blow."

Another roar reached their ears, this time the sound of falling rocks. Ryle paused for a moment to turn the crawler for a look back.

"Don't do that!" Laryn yelled when they saw a mass of orange-red magma push through the gap to the lava tunnel, shoving loose boulders out of its way before pouring over the ledge. "Go! This stuff is fast!"

"And this bug isn't," Ryle said, cursing under his breath as he set the crawler in motion again. The tunnel narrowed as it curved downward and left little room between the crawler and its walls. Ahead of them lay only darkness, and he lowered his visor to amplify what little light was shed by the weak beam of their single headlamp.

Despite his words, Laryn thought they were moving far too quickly to see and avoid the stalactites looming out of the dark. Thin ropes of once-molten rock festooned the ceiling here, several of them long enough to scrape the crawler's carapace. Lavacicles, she told herself, wondering when this bit of information had been installed in her brain. She cried out when one did not shatter on the crawler but instead sliced through the carapace to tear a hole into their flimsy roof.

She shook her scanner as if that would improve the precision of its analysis. "It's in the cave now," she said, wincing when the crawler bumped over something and she knocked her head. "It'll flood this tunnel in a minute."

Somewhere near their feet, Toji emitted a squeal of distress.

"I was about to say that," Ryle said, squinting into the tunnel. "Can't see a damn thing. Nolie, did Azah get out?" He glanced at Laryn with a worried frown. "Nolan? Jex?"

It was now clear that something illuminated the tunnel from behind them. A deep red glow lit the smooth cave wall, and now they smelled the acrid stench of the magma. Laryn pulled the flexible filter band over her mouth and nose again and then tugged Ryle's filter up as well. He now pushed the crawler to its top speed and it scrambled like a centipede around obstacles and even up the curving sides of the tube. Their weight added to the momentum, squeezing them as if in some sort of demented centrifuge.

They heard Nolan shout something and then another part of the crawler's cover tore to let more of the red glow light their frightened faces. Her own cry of terror was drowned by Ryle's.

"Oh, crap!"

The tunnel dropped before them and daylight streamed into the cave. He punched the crawler's controls in a desperate attempt to slow. It tilted dangerously as some of its legs strafed a rock ledge. The end of the tunnel met them and she squeezed her eyes shut. No time to stop, no time to peek outside to make sure they didn't find themselves surrounded by hostile metamorphs.

The crawler skidded, bounced once and then tilted forward, out of the tunnel.

"Go left! Go left!" Ryle shouted at himself or maybe the crawler and they turned that way, away from the rush of lava spewing from the tunnel mouth behind them. They scrambled to the side of the cave mouth but the slope proved too much. She cried out when the crawler tipped and felt Ryle shift his body over her and fold his arms over her head. The crawler rolled sideways, again and again, and only the lack of space inside its frame kept them in place. Then it caught up against something and skidded to a halt.

They lay still for a moment, not daring to believe they had stopped. Laryn moved her foot, wondering if everything was still where it ought to be and functioning as it should. She opened her eyes to see Ryle peering into her face.

"You okay?" he gasped and pulled his filter mask from his face. Blood trickled over his cheek. He cradled her head in his hands, looking for wounds. "Are you broken anywhere? Are you all right?" He pushed a loose strand of her hair from her face with his thumb.

She exhaled, not sure if she was about to faint or perhaps break out into sloppy, braying sobs of relief. "I'm here. Just shook up."

"Literally," he said, apparently not quite ready to release her.

She smiled up at him, content to remain here until her heart stopped pounding and the terror of the escape faded into the background of her perfect memory. Or maybe it wasn't the chase that made her heart race, she fancied as he continued to stoke strand of hair from her dust- and tear-streaked face.

"Help," Toji groaned. "I'm stuck."

Ryle sighed. "Let's take inventory." He reached up to push the shattered carapace aside. They moved with care, making sure to take note of their injuries, as they climbed out of the wreckage. Laryn's lip bled where she had bitten it and her body felt like one continuous bruise. Toji made high-pitched coughing noises as he unfolded himself but he looked unharmed.

"Check that out," he said.

They stood in silent awe as they looked out over the cauldron. The opposite side had fallen away eons ago, and the ocean had made its way here to flood the valley to create a spectacular panorama. A dozen of the round Kalon shelters huddled on the rock-strewn shore near a cleared apron of gravel, likely a landing area for their ships. Scattered over the slope lay the remains of dozens upon dozens of Br'll chrysalis shells. All of it was disappearing from sight, inundated by lava that now touched the shore in a massive plume of steam. Its heat reminded them that they were not out of danger.

"Let's head up that way for air," Ryle said, accepting a piece of gauze that Laryn had found in the small med-pack in her belt. He winced as he pressed it to his temple. "Hurry. This air is getting bad."

Laryn nodded and followed him as he scrambled up the slope of loose scree. Toji, behind her, reached out to steady her now and again and she was grateful for his strength and sure-footedness. Her own knees reminded her that she had perhaps been spending too much time lazing around the station. A climb like this would not have winded her on the long hunting treks they had made on Earth. She wondered if that was easier to admit than the fact that she was still badly shaken by what had happened over these past few hours.

Something dark swooped over them and, while Laryn and Toji ducked, Ryle looked up with a joyful smile. "'bout time," he said.

"Kinda busy, what with Kalons shooting at us and all," Azah's voice crackled through their coms. "Need a lift?"

"If you don't mind."

Laryn looked around. They still had a long climb ahead of them to reach the crest of the broken hill and below them the valley was filling with steam and gasses. "How are we going to get aboard?"

Her question was answered, if not to her delight, when the *Nefer* hovered over their heads and her crew lift lowered toward them. Her landing struts remained folded against her broad belly, useless in this terrain. Jex had anchored the thrusters wider than customary to hover the ship, but Laryn's hair still whipped wildly around her face. "This day is getting better by the moment," she said.

"I'll go first," Toji said. They waited until the platform came close enough for him to leap upward, at ease with the planet's low gravity, and grasp the safety rail. He clambered aboard, a little awkward in folding his limbs around the supports and then stretched out to reach for Laryn. She saw Nolan waving his encouragement as she leaped off the side of the hill and into Toji's arms.

Laryn watched muscle and sinew move under Toji's skin when he then also pulled Ryle onto the lift, marveling at the sheer physical prowess built into these aliens. She recalled the ease with which Toji had punched through the other Kalon's thick skin. Weak spot or not, that would have taken fearsome strength.

Toji turned to her as if he sensed her scrutiny. "Are you all right, Agent Ash?" he said. "Hold on to this. Careful."

"Let's go, folks!" Azah yelled through their coms. "We can still catch them."

"What is she talking about?" Laryn said as they rose into the ship.

"Jex traced two ships leaving this valley while we were still inside," Ryle said. Apparently, he had been conversing with her or Jex during their climb uphill. "The last of the Kalons, I'm guessing. Another one gave them a hard time, but didn't have the hardware to match the *Nefer*. It just took off. I'd like to catch up."

Nolan waited for them in the exit chamber. "Aren't you guys a mess!"

Ryle prodded his ribs to test for injury. "I think I dislocated a pancreas. What did you find?"

"More of our own ships," Nolan reported. "Jex identified one as another ghost ship we lost years ago. But the two that left earlier are modified like nothing like we've ever seen. Fantastic speed on them."

Ryle moved ahead of the others to the bridge and relieved Azah at the helm. "Nice work," he said. "Good to see you made it out of that damn mountain. I might have been worried, maybe."

"Sure you were," she said. "You guys are filthy! We're ready for launch."

"Is the camp all right?" Laryn asked as she strapped herself into her seat.

"Yeah, the mountain puked its guts to this side only," Nolan said. "Gave Azah a scare, though." He scrutinized Toji, silent and gray in his crash brace. "You all right?"

"I wasn't scared," Azah scoffed.

"I... I am well," Toji said. "You plan to... to chase them?"

"Stabilizers ready when you are, Captain," Nolan announced with an eye on the gravity rod display.

Ryle punched the ship into a vertical takeoff and they soon left the planet behind. Laryn worried briefly about the people in the camp, some of whom had hoped to leave with them. But what they had learned about the Kalons' intent for the station made her wish they were already across the Hub and in range to warn Pendra.

"There it is," Ryle said. "Old bucket of bolts. Get to work, Azah. Let's not play nice. I'm heading for the filament."

She nodded and worked with her tactical controls to target the fleeing ship with lasers. The *Nefer* took a hit into her forward shields when their quarry detected them but she returned the fire unhurried and with precision.

They watched the long-range scanner until it reported that the fleeing ship had suffered catastrophic damage.

"One down," Ryle said. "The others are heading to Pendra with a brain that'll talk to the AIs if they get access."

"Huh, what?" Nolan said.

"It's what Iko had in that box. Neural appliances. Not sure which AI, but I'm guessing it's ANN herself. And meanwhile, they've got a damn army bred and ready to come in from Ophet."

"They're after the station?" Azah said.

"And Terrica, too," Ryle said. "Although the Br'll won't be able to live there. A good place for Kalons, though. They just want to get rid of the Humans that come with it."

"You think they can adapt the station for their own needs?" Laryn asked. "The Br'll, I mean?"

"Wish I had even half a clue about what they're up to," Ryle mumbled, shifting his attention to the approaching filament.

Laryn's eyes had wandered past Ryle to see Toji at the rear of the bridge, still looking a little lost. Was he injured? They could all use an examination of their cuts and bruises, along with some clean clothes and rest. "Toji?" she said.

He looked up and was about to say something when his eyes shifted and he seemed to change his mind. She started to unbuckle her belts, intent on taking a closer look at his injuries, when the *Nefer*'s engines changed their usual steady thrum.

"Bubble us, Jex," Ryle said as warning to his crew. The shield configuration changed to create the necessary field for insertion into the filament. They were now only minutes away from the Hub countless lightyears in the distance. "Be ready for a welcoming committee, Azah."

* * *

"Aaaaand we're home," Ryle said before the *Nefer*'s shield bubble had quite dissipated after the traverse back to the Hub. "Well, sort of." He looked up to check the green signals from engineering and environmental systems, showing that the slide through the filament had been successful.

All eyes shifted from one screen to the next as the ship's scanners displayed incoming information. The cameras showed only empty space, rich with its backdrop of stars, blurred and smeared along the horizon surrounding the Hub's black heart.

"No visual of the Kalon ship," Jex reported. "It's already rounded the horizon."

"Damn, they're fast," Ryle said. "That's some fancy upgrade they've made to our ships. Remind me to ask them about it." He glanced at a map of the Hub to find the station's location within its slow orbit. "How long for us to get to Pendra at max, Jex? And what about them?"

"Four hours for the *Nefer*. Not knowing the precise maximum velocity of the Kalon ship, I estimate they'll arrive at the station within an hour. It appears they have found a way to counter the Well's gravitational pull."

Laryn, at her station, tried to access the unmanned satellites that routinely orbited the Well, used by Pendra's research team and to serve as a com beacon. They would have recorded the Kalon ship's passing. Her request for a traffic report in this area went unanswered. "Hmm, this is odd," she said. "I can't hail the beacons."

Ryle leaned toward her console and looked at the displays. "Jex, anything more you can do?"

"No, Ryle. There is no reply. Nor are they transmitting automated signals."

"Is anybody else out here?" Ryle shifted the ship's sensor displays to show activity around the Hub. "I've got some sigs out there."

"Those markers are drones," Jex said. "Autonomous dispatch in response to the beacon malfunction. That Entrada transport is about to launch to Orbel. The two others are outbounder corvettes."

"Oh, lovely," Azah said. "That's the *Chator*. Our friend Ben Colsan. Our day is complete."

"He's hailing," Laryn said.

Ryle looked up at the ceiling with a sigh. "Open com, Jex. What do you want, Colsan? Kind of busy here."

The image of the rival company's captain appeared on one of the forward screens, arms crossed, legs firmly planted as if riding the deck of some otherworldly pirate ship. The beard and rough garb added to the impression, although the design of his bridge, as sleek and well-equipped as the *Nefer*'s, belied the illusion. "You look in a hurry, Tanner," he bellowed.

"Aye. Don't want to miss dinner." Ryle glanced at an

overhead timer synched to Pendra's schedules. "Breakfast."

"You might want to stick to the slop you have on board. Something going on at the station."

"Want to elaborate on that?"

"Got a recall order for all ships. When was the last time that happened? But not just the outbounders. They also recalled the Pendra cruisers and horizon patrols. Everybody."

"Why?"

"Damned if I know. We lost contact with everyone that complied. This sounds like another rout. Search and seizure crap. I'm going to Terrica to lie low with my—" His eyes shifted to another part of his screen. Perhaps he was scanning Ryle's bridge to see who was nearby. Laryn guessed the reason for his non-compliance had to do with whatever business had taken him out here. Besides the filament to Torren and Terrica, this sector of the Hub birthed the thread the Pendra mines, rumored to engage in activities likely frowned upon by the Corporation. He cleared his throat. "Total silence now from the station and those ships," he continued. "And the relay beacons."

"Should check that out, don't you think?" Ryle said.

"How about *you* check that out, Tanner?"

Ryle and Azah exchanged a long, meaningful look. Azah nodded.

"Something's definitely going on," Ryle said at last. "The Kalons... *some* of the Kalons are planning to take the station over. They're on their way there now."

After a startled moment Colsan barked harsh laughter. "The Kalons are too busy having tea and cake with the Pendra lackeys. Where did you get this idea?"

"From the Kalons. You didn't happen to see a ship go by in a big hurry here recently, did you?"

"No. Got some strange data, though. We're still trying to figure it out."

"That would be them. They've got scramblers clever enough to confuse most sensors. We're going to the station.

Chris Reher

Expect ships to emerge from the Ophet filament. They'll be packed with Kalons on a mission."

Colsan squinted at his screen as if trying to get a better look at Ryle's expression. "You're serious, Tanner."

"I am. You're close to the Terrica launch. Get over there and warn incoming traffic away from Pendra. I'm going to transmit a whole lot of data about what we found back there, in case we run into trouble at the station. We'll also send a program to help with a jamming transmission they're using. I'm guessing that's why you haven't heard from anyone on Pendra." Ryle nodded to Laryn to collect the files for transmission to the *Chator*.

The captain's belligerent expression faded as he considered the possibility that Ryle might not be staging some prank designed to embarrass him. Information sharing, among the outbounders, was not a common offer. He deliberated for a moment longer and then turned to a woman behind him. "Terrica, then. Fast."

"Colsan," Ryle said as he turned the *Nefer* away and accelerated toward the station. "If you run into Kalons, even aboard a Pendra transport, keep your shields up. They have damn nasty weaponry."

This brought a grin to the man's face. "Is that so? We'll sharpen our swords, Tanner. You owe me a long explanation next time I see you."

"Fine. Take a bath and I'll do it over a draft at Toko's."

"Fuck you, Tanner."

The transmission ended. Ryle turned to activate the central hologram. The others swiveled their chairs inward to face the image of the Hub floating above the projector. "We need to make tracks. Jex, see if you can shave an hour off the trip to Pendra."

They all watched as the AI plotted a course around the Well at the center of the Hub to meet the station as it moved along its ponderous orbit. It took only a few moments before a clear path was laid out but none of them appreciated the result. The line that had appeared no longer followed the customary wide curve around the Well, in that safe corridor between it and the filament launch points, but had straightened to nearly touch the clearly marked horizon.

"Saving seventy-four minutes, local time," Jex said.

"You're kidding, right?" Nolan said.

Ryle scratched his unshaven chin. "Looks awfully tight, Jex."

"It is. The proximity to the event horizon will strain the ship's engines."

"Just a bit!" Nolan said. "Unless we get caught in it. Then we won't ever have to worry about the engines again."

"I'm no expert, but that doesn't look safe to me, either," Laryn said.

"It isn't," Jex said. "But my recommendation calculates the desired result against the ship's capabilities and Ryle's customary navigation techniques. The *Nefer* has enhanced escape velocity parameters."

"Which the agent didn't need to know about." Ryle's tone suggested that he didn't really care. "Let's come into the turn a little later, Jex. Nolie, keep an eye on those grav rods. We don't want another squeeze." He glanced at Laryn before returning his attention to the display. "Get tucked in, everybody."

Nolan stood up and went to the door to the corridor. "Come on, Toji. Let's make sure he doesn't turn the engines into spaghetti."

Laryn followed Azah's lead when the woman slipped into the crash restraints built into their seats. A shudder went through the *Nefer* as Nolan brought something online that he hadn't used during their jaunts along the filament. She watched the ship's reports on their acceleration and the general health of machine and crew, then shifted her gaze to Ryle. He had activated the helm but left the navigation to Jex. A small muscle in his jaw betrayed his tension as the marker on the hologram before him crept toward the Hub's dark maw. His expression looked an awful lot as it had when they had careened through the lava tunnel.

"What's that shimmy, Nolie?" he said although Laryn had felt nothing.

"Adjusting for the cargo we offloaded. Kinda forgot about that in all the excitement."

"Ryle, there is a drone on an intercept path to this location," Jex reported. A new marker appeared on the hologram. "Probe class, moving fast. It seems to have originated at the station."

"Could be a message," Laryn said.

"Could be explosive," Azah added.

"It is transmitting the Kalon jamming frequency we've encountered before," Jex said. "It will confound the echoes from the beacons. We *must* have quantum illumination to navigate around the gravity well."

"So take it out, Jex."

"I cannot. It's Pendra property."

Laryn raised an eyebrow. It seemed a strange time for Jex to remember his mandate. Perhaps it kicked in only in this region of space, where laws were set by the Ministry.

"Azah," Ryle snapped.

"On it." An array of tactical controls rose into the air before her, augmenting the hologram. "Definitely one of ours. Or used to be."

A polite, mechanical voice emitted from the speakers. "You are experiencing a sensor malfunction caused by a gravitational flux in this area," it said. "You may also experience disturbances with long-range communications. Please make visual contact with this probe. We will guide you to Pendra Station."

The trajectory hologram seemed to fade in the air as Jex countered the Kalon transmission, even as the *Nefer* continued to accelerate, relying only on microwaves to feel her way. The ship's external cameras still functioned and now showed the blinking signal of the probe as it approached.

Again, the transmission from the drone, apparently not compromised by the interference: "Please make visual contact with this probe. We will guide you to Pendra

Station."

"Take care of that malfunction, Azah," Ryle said.

"Getting fuzzy!" she replied, working her console to keep her weapon on target. A moment later she whooped with glee as something flashed brightly in the distance. "Malfunction repaired, Captain!"

"Interference has terminated," Jex confirmed. "Approaching trajectory apex above the horizon."

Laryn breathed deeply, reminding herself that the JX.9 model would not exceed the safety parameters of the ship's design. Or this region of space, which included a comfortable distance to the horizon. The shimmy Ryle noticed earlier became more pronounced and she began to rise upward to strain against her crash brace.

"Sorry," Ryle said when Laryn gasped. "We'll pick up a few extra G's trying to pull out of this. More than the rods can mitigate." His unheard command prompted Jex to roll the ship and soon gravity dragged them toward the accustomed place below their feet.

"Why is the ship shaking!" she said.

"She's a bit unhappy, I guess," Ryle said, sounding ridiculously calm to her ears.

"Vessel approaching on intercept course," Jex said. "Unidentified."

All eyes shifted to the object he had found, clearly heading their way. Asymmetrical and covered in peculiar lumps, it resembled an asteroid except for its pallid yellowish-gray non-color and an obvious energy field trailing it, distorted by the growing pull of the Well.

"Fucking flying turnip," Nolan said, sounding awed. "Is that a Br'll ship?"

"Vessel is on collision course."

"Suicidal turnip," Ryle said. "Azah!"

"Aye," she replied and targeted the approaching ship. "Damn. That thing is slippery." She tried a different configuration. "My guns are useless so close to the Well."

"Get boxed, Nolie. You and the Kalon." Fighting the

increasing gravity, Ryle's hands moved through the hologram, working with Jex to find an escape route and optimum velocity. A collision with the smaller ship would not faze the *Nefer* whose shields were designed to handle larger objects, but it would throw her off course.

"Thread shields," he ordered and indicators around them signaled a change of the ship's travel configuration as if in preparation to enter a filament. The external shields thinned but extended, and internal buffers ramped up to guard against increased radiation.

"You're not going to evade?" Azah gasped.

"No time for that."

Laryn wasn't sure if he meant time to avoid the approaching enemy or the delay this would cause to reach Pendra Station. She stared, wide-eyed and disbelieving, at the proposed trajectory displayed on the hologram. It would graze the extended shield to where Jex believed the enemy's own defenses ended. Ryle feigned, forcing the other ship's navigator to recalculate the deadly collision. Time enough for the *Nefer* to swoop back on course to execute her maneuver. In the instant their shields threatened to merge, Ryle bumped the *Nefer*'s shield range and shoved the enemy ship aside like a drunkard in a bar brawl.

There was only a brief glimpse of the alien ship spinning away, toward the Well's unfathomable void. The *Nefer*, too, sliced away from her course and Laryn cried out when the ship's cameras showed nothing now but dark smears of light against the black backdrop of space.

The unrelenting pressure against her body continued, wanting to crush her into her chair as the pull increased in unpleasant increments. She tried lifting her hand and found it glued to her armrest. She should have warned Colsan about the deceptively benign drones being sent out to shepherd Hub traffic back to the station, she thought. She'd do that as soon as she was able to move, she promised herself. If she ever reached that point in her life, she added.

From somewhere, she heard Nolan curse and yell

something about "rods" and "stabilizers". Jex counted something in a strangely cheerful voice. Things seemed to have lost their colors here on the bridge and she realized that she was graying out. When an annoying red haze crept into her vision, the thought of passing out seemed oddly welcome. A high-pitched whine drilled through the ship, modulating only when Ryle forced his hand up against the pull of gravity to swipe his fingers through the hologram above his console.

It stopped. The shaking stopped, the whine of the engines stopped and Laryn's chest rose to gulp a greedy draft of air when the gravity returned to tolerable levels.

"Awesome!" Azah yelled when the *Nefer* escaped the grasp of the Well and sped away. "Hope no one had to pee."

Ryle fell back in his seat with a loud exhalation of air. "That was darling. Good thing you said that about them being slippery. Gave me all sorts of ideas." He tilted his head to wink at Laryn. "You all right, Agent?"

"You do this a lot?" Laryn said. Her fingers had left dents in her armrests.

Ryle grinned. "Yeah. Jex, diagnostic and top speed to Pendra. Nolie? You still there?" He shifted a screen to show the ship's main engine room. It was empty and so he switched it to the adjacent cargo space. "Nolan? You can come out now."

A small, square door on a shipping container slid aside and Nolan ducked out of it. He looked up at the camera. "Guess we made it, huh?" He turned to stoop back into the box and Laryn saw him dragging Toji from it. "Toji fainted," he said, sounding worried. "Should have tried to find out how his people deal with high-G."

"Is that what you meant by them getting boxed?" Laryn said, intrigued, as she watched Toji, ashen-faced and silent, find his feet.

Ryle nodded. "Small field bubble designed to mitigate gravity crashes for fragile cargo. Figured that Nolie's delicate skull wasn't going to stand up to the G's. I'd run the ship in it if it didn't burn so much energy. How's the *Nefer*, Jex?"

"All systems are operating optimally. We will reach Pendra Station in two point seven eight kilo-secs."

Ryle removed his restraints. "Still almost three hours. A lot can happen on Pendra in three hours. Keep trying to hail them. Maybe there's someone nearby that isn't dealing with their jammers."

"Toji, Nolan, if you're done down there, come up to the med station," Laryn said. "I want to get a scan of everyone."

One by one, the crew submitted to an examination and then stripped to spend time in the decon shower. Jex concocted a potion for all but Toji to boost their immune system and a drone sniffed through all areas of the ship to hunt down and destroy foreign lifeforms they might have brought aboard. It was a small measure toward the more rigorous process to follow, but it made them all feel a little cleaner.

* * *

"Your turn, doc."

Laryn looked up from her charts when Ryle's voice broke the comfortable quiet aboard the ship. Although traveling at top speed toward Pendra Station, the *Nefer* did so silently and the others had retreated to their cabins. He entered the med lab, limping a little from their recent tumble through the caverns of Torren. A clean bandage covered a long scrape on his shoulder and a strip of tape sealed the cut on his temple.

She smiled. "I'm all right, Captain." She pointed at the screen. "Look, clean like my mama bathed me."

"Except for that bruise on your back," he said and pointed at the padded bench. "Let's take a look."

Exhaling a theatrical sigh of surrender, she gathered her hair and shifted to the examination table, surprised when he sat down as well. "Is it bad?" she said, turning her back toward him.

"It's pretty purple," he said, examining the welt running across her shoulder and upper arm, a souvenir of the crawler's support strut. She wore only a sleeveless shift and he placed his hand on her other shoulder while applying a slim tool to help break up the blood that had pooled under her skin. "That's going to be sore tomorrow," he promised. "So hold still. I'm an expert at this."

"Really?" she said, aware of his fingers at the curve of her neck.

"Well, no. But I've had a bruise or two in my life. Jex is making sure I don't dissolve your bones or whatever this thing does."

"Laryn also strained her left upper trapezius muscle, although it's not—"

"Thank you, Jex," Ryle said. "We've got this. Go to standby."

Laryn grinned, about to comment on Jex's ever-vigilant presence when she felt his fingers gently probe for the muscle the AI had mentioned.

"You are more resilient than I thought," he said.

"You thought I was frail?"

"No," he said and she heard the smile in his voice. "But delicate. I sometimes feel like an oaf standing beside you. Like the grunt I am. Like I might accidentally break off a piece if I shook your hand."

"I don't break so easily," she said.

"I certainly found that out today."

Her breath caught and she felt the hair at her nape rise when he stroked a long strand out of the way.

"Agent Ash?" a timid voice reached them through the door to the lab.

Ryle's breath brushed over her skin as he exhaled forcefully and dropped his hand.

"Yes, Toji?" she said and turned when the Kalon entered the room. Ryle stood up to face him as well.

"Oh, I am disturbing you," Toji said. "I did not realize you were injured."

"That's all right," she said, not daring to glance at Ryle, not daring to make assumptions about the moment that had just passed. "I thought you were with Nolan, taking apart that Kalon weapon. Are you all right?"

He hesitated. "No, I don't suppose I am."

"Come sit down," Laryn said. "Are you in pain?"

Toji shook his head. "No. I wanted to speak with you. You were there, in the cave…"

Ryle and Laryn waited, a little unsure of what the Kalon expected from them. Finally, Laryn took his hand and made him sit beside her. "Yes, and I'm glad you were with us," she said. "You fought bravely."

"Did I?" he said, staring at the floor. "My thoughts keep returning to that place. I see my… I see the Kalons. Attacking. And then I killed some of them."

Laryn looked up at Ryle, who shrugged, puzzled.

"And you regret that now?" she guessed. "They attacked us, first."

"I know. But…" He rubbed his hands, one over the other, as he looked for words. "I feel… Those are my people, are they not? I know I told you we suspected them of wishing harm on you, but I had not expected such terrible intent. And am I not one of them? Have I turned my back on *us*? On the Br'll?"

She pursed her lips. "I suppose you have. But *are* those your people? You were not… designed for what they did. For what they did to the *Harla* group. You wanted to stop them, too, didn't you?"

He nodded stiffly. "We did not think they had reached such extremes. This has turned out far too… unacceptable." His eyes found hers. "But I am not Human. I have betrayed the purpose and the trust the Br'll placed in me."

"You made a choice," Laryn said. "We value that ability. You said that maybe they made you too Human. Your generation, I mean. So in a way, they gave you that choice."

"We need you with us on this," Ryle said. "For all we know those Kalons with the chip are hiding aboard the station right now. Pendra may need some convincing to admit that something's gone wrong."

"And what will become of us, then?" Toji said. "What will happen to me and those few of my generation, the first Kalons to have arrived at the station? Will we be killed? Exiled? There is no *Kalon* planet for us to return to. We have no home at all…"

Laryn put her hand on his arm. Even she, who had lost her home and most of her family, could return to Earth if she wanted. Toji did not even have that. His primordial world was nothing more than an alien planet where none of them would survive for long.

"And will you make war on the Br'll, for fear of what they might do in the future?" Toji said. "Yes, I can see by your faces that you think that, too."

"Well, yes," Laryn said. "We'll have to take steps to protect the station. And the filaments to Earth and Terrica."

Toji said nothing for a drawn-out moment before speaking again. "I do not believe the Br'll are entirely to blame."

"Eh?" Ryle said. "Why not?"

"I drew information from that injured Kalon in the cavern, if you recall."

The others nodded.

"I drew much more. Some of it is vague, as I'm unskilled with this. I… I have not been privileged to join in the formation of a Kalon, and certainly not a Br'll. But he shared some of his thoughts, his knowledge, with me."

"Jex, record this," Ryle said. He nodded to Toji. "Is that all right?"

"Yes. You need to know."

"We're listening," Laryn said softly.

"What you assume about the Br'll is correct. But there is more than one… one faction on our planet. Some do not wish to return to the Hub at all. Others want to do so peacefully, as they are curious about your people. They bear you no ill will for taking the Hub from them. But others do. They want it back. And they want Humans gone."

Ryle whistled appreciatively. "Sounds complicated."

"Hmm, yeah," Laryn said. "But no more than on our own planet."

"So I have learned," Toji said. He looked up at Ryle. "Even your own crew does not always share the same opinions."

"Tell me about it!" Ryle said with half a laugh.

"The Br'll had some of your technology and... and some living tissue," Toji continued, "From their first encounter with you, more than a hundred years ago. They used that information to learn about you, your technology, and to learn your language. And then they created the Kalons, maturing them on a ship designed after yours. That would have taken many years. I was among the first generation to be sent to Pendra Station. We were, like you, Agent Ash, ambassadors, a vanguard to establish a rapport with your people. And to discover your intentions for the Br'll homeworld."

"And then you made a deal with Pendra and the Ministry to declare your planet off limits," Laryn said. "To protect your species. To keep the Br'll world safe from Human invaders in exchange for some of your technology. Would have been very acceptable to Pendra since Kalon isn't ever going to be habitable for us."

"Isn't that clever," Ryle said. "And in turn you promised not to visit Earth. And so, until other Br'lls decide to make the trip to the Hub, no one will know there aren't any Kalons on Kalon." He smiled at Laryn but there was no humor in his expression. "And Pendra isn't likely to ask questions for as long as they benefit from whatever tech the Kalons are willing to share with them."

"Yes. And things went well. Your people welcomed us, for the most part." Toji took a deep breath, like his version of a sigh. "But then the others started to arrive at the station. Recently. A new generation, different from ours. The... the Kalon I questioned on Torren said disagreements took place among the Br'll factions. It was bitter and eventually a group left Br'll and entered a filament to a planet you had not yet discovered. Torren. They've known about it for a long time.

The Br'll know of many places you have not yet found. They diverted the *Harla* there. It was there that they started to birth the new Kalons and bring them onto the station, by replacing the Ophet workers."

"And now, instead of a handful of Kalon explorers, we've got a hostile army of them," Ryle said. "With weapons and ships we haven't even conceived of."

Toji nodded. "I'm so sorry. Azah was right to question why we did not alert your people with our suspicions. We aren't bred to imagine secret schemes. We only knew what we were given during our emergence into adult Kalons. We did not know of the conflicts on our home planet."

"I think you're carrying enough guilt," Laryn said. "We're not going to assign blame to anyone but the Kalons that want to harm us." She glanced up at Ryle. "Well, and Pendra. I promise I'll do all I can to make sure your friends aren't blamed, either."

Toji offered his shy smile. "You are kind, Agent Ash. I have to admit I don't hold much hope if this army is at this moment converging upon your station."

"Well, we've got guns, too." Ryle said. He pondered for a moment. "So, going back to what you said about other planets we haven't found yet. Got coordinates for those?"

FOURTEEN

"We're now in visual contact with Pendra Station," Jex announced a few hours later, rousing Laryn from the short nap she had sought in her cabin.

"Everyone to their stations," Ryle's voice added over the speakers, sounding wide awake.

The crew assembled on the bridge, more or less rested. Azah in full combat mode, Toji anxious, and Laryn was not surprised to see Nolan sipping from a steaming bowl of rations. Laryn, in anticipation of speaking with Pendra authorities, had slipped into a buttery pair of fawn leather trousers and silk blouse, and again wore her Ministry insignia.

"All screens."

The image of the ponderous station appeared before them, floating serenely in space, as always surrounded by a clutter of beacons and sensors. But they were dark now, and no maintenance shuttles buzzed around the station on their endless inspections and repair assignments.

Ryle, like the others, dropped into one of the six chairs circling the hologram platform. After a moment's thought, his gesture invited Toji to take one of the empty seats. The Kalon's eyes widened in surprise and he smiled as he hurriedly sat down beside Nolan. Laryn noticed that, this time, he sat as they did, with his feet on the floor.

Ryle focused a camera on the upper docking level

housing smallcraft vessels. "Eight outbounders," he said. "Colsan wasn't kidding about them being recalled. Three Pendra ships now."

"I don't see the two ships the Kalons were using out of Torren," Nolan said. "Did we beat them here?"

"There," Azah said, pointing. "On the lower deck. It's where the Ophet transports usually park."

"Well, I guess we can assume they're aboard the station," Ryle said. "What sort of numbers can we expect there now?"

"Mostly just staff here now, so close to the fleet arriving," Laryn said. "About two hundred admin, support and science staff. A few dozen workers from Terrica here to help with the migrants."

"Eight out of fifteen outbounders means about forty or fifty more," Nolan said.

"Only about fifty or so security personnel," Laryn added.

Ryle nodded. "Kalons?" His question was for Toji.

"Forty," Toji said. "Not counting those who arrived on these ships from Torren."

"How many of those are... uh, friendly?" Azah asked.

Toji hesitated a moment. "There are eight in my... group. They're not part of... of whatever is happening here. There used to be more, but they've not returned from Ophet. I now worry what might have become of them."

"Hmm," Ryle tapped a finger to his lips, calculating. "I don't think the Kalons intend to take the station by force. Not unless there were a lot of them on those two ships from Torren."

"I'm not sure about that," Azah said with a scornful note in her voice. "Pendra guards aren't a fighting force. Wouldn't be a good investment for Pendra. They won't expect an armed attack."

"They will have been trained for... for hostilities," Laryn said, knowing well that she wasn't ready to admit that the station was woefully unprepared for an actual outside attack. But how does one prepare for an enemy whose size and strength was unknown? The last alien invasion they had suffered here had been a virus from Antica. "But I think Ryle is right. They're here to take control of the station from inside. By fooling the ANN into giving them access, with the interface chips they stole."

"Let's hail the station," Ryle said.

Azah and Laryn exchanged a puzzled look.

"They can't hear us, remember?" Azah said.

"Yes, but we're not supposed to know that. If the Kalons are in control of the station I'm guessing they have a way to monitor approaching ships." He signaled Jex to open the com. "Outbounder *SC Nefer* on return," he said. "Having trouble with sensors. Do you receive, Station?" He waited a few moments. "Requesting dock permit."

"So, I hate to state the obvious," Nolan said. "But how are they going to dock us without sensors? Does the control tower even know we're here?"

"Maybe we can hold up a sign," Azah joked, pointing toward the cameras below the control tower. A horizontal bank of windows also overlooked the docks, but they remained opaque from this angle.

"Can we use Morse?" Laryn asked.

Ryle turned from his scrutiny of the station to raise an eyebrow at her.

"What's Morse?" Azah said.

"An old com code," Ryle said. "Pulses and pauses instead of letters. Used two or three hundred years ago. Jex, do you have that code?"

"I do, Ryle."

"So?" Azah said. "They can't receive us. Doesn't matter what protocol we use."

Ryle grinned at Laryn. "Agent Ash has other ideas." He turned back to the screens. "Jex, can you strobe the forward running lights to send a message using Morse?"

"Of course."

"Let's hope someone is looking out of a window somewhere," Laryn said. "We can warn them from here about the Kalons."

"I don't want the wrong attention. Just request permission to dock, Jex."

"Am I the only one who thinks that's not really a very good idea?" Laryn said. "You want to go in there not knowing what's going on? What difference can we make?"

Azah turned in her seat and leaned close to Laryn. A gentle smile lit her face as she tilted her head to study the agent. "I have a gun that'll make a difference," she purred. "Jex has a program that'll cut through the jammer. And you, Princess, have a brain that'll get into the station systems. Is that enough difference or would you like us to drop you off on Earth before we lend a hand?"

Laryn looked over to Ryle who shrugged with a grin. "She's kidding. I'm not allowed on Earth right now."

"Look!" Nolan interrupted, gesturing toward the main screen.

The others turned to see that one of the docking portals had lit up, as it always did when a ship was about to lock into one of the berths.

"Guess they saw us," Azah said.

"Question is: *who* saw us," Ryle said. The screens shifted as all of the ship's forward cameras focused on the portal. "We'll have to go on visual alone. Jex, you should be able to triangulate that, right?"

"Yes, I will use a photon beam to guide the approach."

"Is there anyone else in the vicinity?"

"I detect no visible traffic in the area other than the *Chator* nearing the Terrica filament and the *Persephone* returning from there."

Ryle tilted his head when the *Nefer* aligned with the port although Jex was handling the approach. They felt the ship's gravity field match the station's as it descended onto the docking port like a bird settling to roost. "Scan the bay for Kalons, Jex."

"There is no movement, although the scans are of poor quality. I do find that the moored outbounder vessels appear fully manned."

"Wonder what they're waiting for."

"Don't distract him, man," Nolan said.

Azah chortled.

"Please be assured that this maneuver is a matter of mathematics," Jex said. "The triangulation is as precise as the sensors." The ship shuddered as he made adjustment against the station's gravity. "I'm sorry."

"You're doing that on purpose," Laryn guessed.

"Yes."

"*Now* he gets a sense of humor," Azah said. She exhaled loudly when the lights around the port turned green, signaling a secure connection to the station's seal.

Ryle pushed his console aside and stood up. "We'll take the passage past Shelody's office to get to the plaza and from there to Security. Want to make sure he's all right. Maybe it's best if we get him to board the *Nefer*."

A disquieting jolt shuddered through the ship and a warning signal appeared on one of the screens.

"What was that?" Nolan tapped his console. "Damn!"

"What?" Ryle said.

"Someone locked the docking seals," Jex reported. "All the ships currently berthed here are locked down. It's a security override designed to detain ships for investigation or detention of suspect crew, as you may remember. I will add that the Pendra-owned ships are locked down as well."

"They are? That's not something you see too often," Ryle said. "Or ever, actually." He gestured for Azah, Toji and Laryn to follow him to the ship's exit chamber.

He and Azah shrugged into their armored jackets to which he affixed collar com tabs. He also snapped a com collar around his throat to help with subvocal messages Jex might need. "Are these transmitting?" he asked, tapping Azah's tab.

"We hear you," Nolan said from the bridge. "I've transferred the counter-jammer program to each of you."

Azah lifted a gun from its brace on the wall. "Let's not get too hung up on rules now," she said to Laryn.

"I'll take one of those," Laryn replied.

"There are several people below the *Nefer*," Jex reported. "Humans. I don't believe these are the regular ground crew members."

"Do you have more than that?"

The overhead screen came on to show four men and a woman below them, guns drawn. All of them wore the uniforms of Pendra's security force. A separate frame on the screen showed more armed guards pacing along the otherwise deserted docking area. Nothing moved along the repair bays where there was always something going on no matter what the time of day.

"Just who we're looking for. Except for the part with the guns pointing at us." Ryle crouched beside the pressure seal in the floor once Jex had opened it but did not lower the lift. "Hello there," he called down. "That's quite the welcoming committee."

Laryn peered past him to see five faces and five guns aimed at them.

"You will come with us, Captain Tanner," a lieutenant replied. "And you will release Agent Ash to us." His eyes shifted to Laryn. "Have you been harmed, Agent?"

"What? Me? No, of course not. What is going on?"

"Please come down and accompany us to Security," he said. "The rest of the *Nefer* crew will remain aboard."

Azah hissed something under her breath.

"All right," Ryle said. "We'll be just a moment." He straightened and turned to the others. "We'll be able to warn them about the Kalons. But something smells wrong here. Jex, Nolan, see if you can find and disable the Kalon jammers. We need communications. Also find out if there is any way to shake the *Nefer* loose. And the other outbounders. We're going to be totally lame when the Kalon ships get here."

Jex lowered the lift and delivered Laryn and Ryle to the guards waiting below. Their expression suggested serious business but these were not career soldiers, Laryn reminded herself. They were trained to apprehend smugglers or break up brawls on the lower levels, not defend Pendra against an attack by alien infiltrators.

"You're with us, Tanner," the lieutenant said, watching one of his men pat Ryle down for weapons and finding two of them. No one searched Laryn and she cursed herself for having given her gun back to Azah before coming down here. "We have a report about you firing on a Kalon ship during your last outbound."

"What?" Laryn exclaimed. She had been about to deliver a hurried report about the Kalons' schemes aboard the station, but this came unexpected.

"Iko," Ryle said. "Damn."

"That's him," the guard said. "You've gone too far this time, Tanner. Pendra bosses are in a mood to have a talk with you about molesting their special guests. This way."

"Listen," Laryn said. "That can wait. The station is under attack. By the Kalons!"

The lieutenant scowled at her for a moment and then barked harsh laughter. "Did *he* tell you that, Agent?" He knocked the barrel of his gun against Ryle's chest. "Last we've seen of the Kalons was them having one of their weird chanting things on O-deck, where they belong. Nothing going on here except more shoddy maintenance." He pointed to the ceiling. "ANN-T's down, that's all," he added, naming the ANN subsystem that operated everything from doors and toilets to elevators and docking rings. "Affecting com, too."

"Fine, arrest me." Ryle nudged Laryn to move toward the exit tunnel of the docking bay. "Let's get to Security before Iko and his group do more than jam transmissions. *Someone* there should have some sense."

"Don't play with me, Tanner," the lieutenant said. "I know what's on your sheet. Keep your hands where I can see them."

They were prodded to the exit and then turned into the decon station for a mandatory scan and delousing of whatever they might have brought onto the station on their clothing and bodies. Following that would be internal scans and a review of their reports of Torren's atmosphere, all conducted by people with a lot of time on their hands.

"Can't this wait?" Ryle said as they walked along a narrow hallway to one of the decon conduits. "Listen to the agent. You need to find every Kalon aboard and sequester them."

"He's right," Laryn said. "There are more Kalons on the way, and the ones already here have access to the systems. The coms, for sure. Who knows what else."

The lieutenant looked as if about to laugh at her for suggesting this, but perhaps something in her expression stopped him. "How do you know this? You've been gone for days."

A dull, pervasive thud rang through the station, followed by a series of others, ever more distant. Everyone here recognized the sound of those slamming doors from past safety drills. At this moment, the individual modules that made up the station were sealed to reduce the risk of depressurization, contaminants, fire, or ventilation issues. All major gates between sections would also be locked and guarded.

"Lock down!" someone yelled as if to point out the obvious when the pre-recorded message that would normally remind everyone of procedure remained silent.

"Now do you believe us?" Laryn said.

The lieutenant shook off his surprise and headed for the door of the decon station. His handprint would unlock it, clearing the way for a quick sprint to the security center of the station and Pendra's arsenal of weapons.

A high-pitched squeal cut through the air, accompanied by the dry-throated rasp made by Kalons, sounding much too close.

"What the..?" the lieutenant said when the door slid aside to reveal four Kalons in the hall.

The answer to that came from a curved tube held by one of the aliens. What looked like a rope whipped from it, split into several strands in mid-air and landed on the guard where it seemed to burn through his clothes. He cringed and slapped at the substance but then froze, arms still in the air, before crashing to the floor.

Ryle grasped Laryn's arm and whipped her around. "That way!"

The other guards had overcome their stunned second of surprise and fired their weapons at the Kalons by the door. One of the guards was shoved back, also made immobile by the alien device, and Laryn stumbled over him before catching herself.

"Go!" Ryle stooped and grabbed the man's gun. He raced after Laryn around a bend in the hall. He cursed when he saw it leading nowhere.

"In here," Laryn said, combing her memory for the schematics for this part of the station. She ducked into the control alcove that managed the decontamination array. Beyond the console and the inactive display screens, a narrow door led to the access passage for the emitters. "It'll take us to one of the substations."

Ryle flinched when something slapped his shoulder. He twisted to see a yellowish thread stuck to the fabric of his jacket, fusing into the material with a sizzle. Other strands adhered to the wall beside him.

"Behind you!" she yelled.

He looked up to see a Kalon only steps away, waving his weapon in a way apparently meant to whip the substance at his quarry. Ryle jerked his shoulder to tear the thread away and fired at the Kalon, grimly pleased that the species seemed no more resistant to a laser blast than the average Human. He waited a moment to see if more followed but only an eerie silence now filled the facility.

"Let's go."

"Wait." She slipped past him and back down the hall, ignoring his protest. The Kalon lay motionless near the entrance to the decon service area and she stepped carefully over his sprawled-out legs. Like Toji, he had discarded the long mantle that slowed his movements and obscured the threat of his powerful limbs.

"What are you doing?" Ryle hissed.

Laryn peered around the corner and saw the bodies of the guards on the floor, all of them taken down by the strange ooze spewed from the Kalon's weapon. She took a deep breath and snatched a gun from someone's hand, avoiding the frozen stare on the woman's face. The gun carried an almost full charge and so Laryn spun to race back to Ryle. As an afterthought, she bent and snatched the curved weapon from the dead Kalon's fingers.

"Are you crazy?" Ryle said when she reached him.

"I'm not running around this place unarmed, Captain," she said. She held up the Kalon horn with two fingers. "No dead Kalons by the entrance back there. This happened fast. This one's different from the ones we saw on Torren."

He took it and gave it a shake, expecting some sort of liquid as the base of the ropy projectile. Nothing leaked from it and so he slipped it into a pocket on his thigh. "Always the scientist, aren't you?"

"You like that better than mediary, admit it."

"Yeah. But could you please not take chances like that?"

They squeezed into the narrow space beyond the control room console and made their way past the emitters for each decon segment. As she had promised, the passage led to a larger substation, this one serving not only the decon facility but also the other mechanical systems for this segment of the station.

"Where are we?" Ryle said, walking to an access console on the far side of the room and finding it out of service. "How far to Security?"

"Let me look at your shoulder," she said.

"I'm all right," he said, but then sat on a conduit running the length of the room to let her inspect his shoulder. "I hope."

She touched the piece of alien material, now hardened, that seemed fused to his jacket. "That melted right through to the graphene," she said. "Never seen anything like it. Did it burn you, or whatever this does?"

"No, but it felt like a shock. An electric shock, sort of. Made my arm go numb for a bit." He pushed the jacket off his shoulder to show her his skin, reddened but unbroken by the hit. "I think we know one reason Pendra is so keen on the Kalons. Super-conductive snot you can use to build things with. Must be worth a lot."

"It hit the lieutenant right in the face," she said, recalling the attack. She shuddered at the memory of the bodies left behind by the Kalons.

"Are you all right?" he said, shrugging his jacket over his shoulder again.

She gave him a perfunctory smile. "No worries. We can get to Operations from here. I don't suppose we want to try making it across the plaza. I think I can keep us in the service byways for the most part."

"Jex," he said to the com tab at his collar. "How are we coming along with the jammer?"

"I have located the emitters of the Kalon interference but they are scattered throughout the station and not tied to our network. They will need to be shut down manually."

Ryle cursed. "We don't have time for that."

"I cannot share my override program with the station's communication network. It is managed by ANN-D, part of the Security sub-system. I do not have access to that. I suggest you find an open access port and upload it from there. That should return function to station-wide communications as well as internal and external scanners."

He nodded. Station Operations oversaw security, and traffic as well as maintenance for Pendra. If there was a way to restore communications within the station, they would be working on it there.

"Azah," he said. "We were attacked by Kalons. Warn the guards that the Kalons carry a curved tool, sort of a horn. It's deadly."

"Attacked?" Azah said. "Want me to come with you?

Where are you?"

"Negative. Stay with Nolie and the *Nefer*. Look after Jex; it's our best chance right now. We'll make our way to Ops. Get to the rest of the fleet and give them the override program so we can at least talk to each other. If we can get the ships released they should get ready to defend the station when our pals arrive from Ophet. Ask them to leave as much armed crew as possible here. Who knows where Kalons are here on the station so we'll need everyone with a gun. Around here that means just the guards and the outbounders. Not a hell of a lot."

"Understood."

"Jex," Laryn said. "Can you use the jamming frequency to distort our location? Using our com units so the Kalons can't track us?"

"Yes, I can program your tabs to emit the signal. You should fade into the background noise created by the Kalons. Be aware that your open communication will betray your position if they are monitoring. You can still reach me via our neural interlink. I suggest you restrict contact with the others to the most urgent conversation."

"They might not bother monitoring if they think we have no coms or sensors," Nolan said.

"I'm not taking anything we know about them for granted," Ryle said. He came to his feet. "Cloak us now, Jex. I'll contact you when we get to Ops."

"Understood."

"Now comes the big test," Laryn said.

"What's that?"

"This section will have been cut off from the next when the station went into lockdown. If my clearance doesn't open it, we'll have to backtrack and try the public hallways. That'll get us as far as the arrivals concourse."

They walked to the sliding door separating this service room with the warehousing areas for the station's food supplies. It would be crammed with cargo now, so close to the arrival of the incoming fleet from Earth.

"This shouldn't be all that secure," Ryle said.

"Might be, during a lockdown." Laryn tapped the sensor strip beside the door. When it did not respond to her thumbprint, she entered a code. "Damn. No luck."

"Um, look, over there, a rat!" Ryle said.

"Huh?" She turned to look around the empty control room. "Since when do we have rats on Pendra?"

"Just trying to distract you, Agent," he said. "You didn't see this." He had taken a roll of what looked like tape from a pocket and now placed a strip over the access panel of the door. She watched, amazed and amused by his brazenness, as he ran his hand over it to complete a circuit. The door slid aside without raising an alarm.

"I just see a door. An open one." She followed him into the shipping area, a network of low-ceilinged spaces crammed with identical, labeled storage containers. There were directional signs on the walls and she took a moment to orient herself. "This way."

They jogged through the maze of cargo modules until they found the delivery corridor supplying the shops along the station's plaza. This door, too, responded to Ryle's deft manipulation and let them pass.

"Listen to that!" Laryn said when they passed the rear entrance of a tavern. The sound of conversation and even laughter drifted into the hall, made by people who seemed not at all troubled by the lockdown. "Getting drunk in there, thinking this is a drill or something. Unarmed sitting ducks. We need to warn them."

He raised his arm to stop her from banging her fist on the door. "Let's get the com system working so everyone can be warned at once. We don't need a bunch of civilians running around and getting whipped by that… that whip-thing the Kalons have."

"I wonder if everybody is just hanging around, waiting out in the open for this to end," she grumbled. "I'd recommend an overhaul of how drills are conducted."

"You do that, Agent. Let's move."

He set a punishing pace around the plaza shops but she kept up, guarding her footfalls in the quiet corridor cluttered with the sort of accumulated refuse that found no permanent storage space. Containers, lengths of used piping and sheets of metal, broken furniture and buckets of god-knows-what got in her way without ever offering a good place to hide, should someone come their way. They found a narrow access staircase where her memory told her it would be and made it to the upper level and the station's administrative areas. She was out of breath by the time they reached the Ops deck.

"Security control center is down that way," she said.

Both of them dove behind a service desk when a nearby sound startled them. Laryn tried to slow her breathing as they strained to hear more. Ryle mouthed "Kalon" and she nodded. He motioned her to stay down and then inched up to peer over the top of the counter before ducking again.

"Damn," he whispered.

"What?"

"Body in the hall. Uniformed. And that door to Security isn't the kind I can hack." His gesture told her to stand by while he contacted Jex aboard the *Nefer*. Laryn waited, listening for movement in the hall while he used his transmitter to speak silently with the AI. After a moment he lifted his arm to make an adjustment to the scanner on his wrist, following unheard instructions.

"What, Jex is into lockpicking, too?"

He glanced up from his scans. "That'd be a violation of its program parameters." He raised his arm away from his body to scan the area. "Trying to get a guess of who's in there. Everything's garbled." He sent the scan to Jex for analysis.

"Well?" she prompted when everything seemed to be taking far too long. She flinched when something in that room crashed to the ground.

"Toji thinks there are three of them in there, going by their sounds."

"*Thinks?*"

He shrugged. "The room should have a full set of officers during a lockdown."

"So now what?"

"Now we knock. Keep your gun up. Stay close."

He moved around the desk, still crouched low and sidled over to the door leading to the security office. It was a slider and so Laryn scuttled to the other side of the opening, her gun gripped in both hands. He tapped his com unit and, a moment later, a rapid series of trills and squeals emitted from it. She grinned when she understood that Toji was calling out to his kinsmen.

The Kalon sounds from inside the room subsided and then the door slid aside. Both Ryle and Laryn pivoted to fire into the room, aiming high to avoid hitting any Humans also still here. The Kalons screeched and, one after the other, fell to the laser fire. A Kalon thread sailed through the air but missed Ryle as he threw himself aside to roll out of the way. Another shriek rose into the air and was then silenced by Laryn's weapon.

Ryle came to his feet and surveyed the room. Two Humans lay on the ground, carelessly pushed into a corner after the Kalons commandeered the space. He bent to examine them and then shook his head to answer the question on her face. "Will Hatcher," he said, naming the station's security chief. "I have no idea who's in charge around here now."

Laryn locked the door to the hall before studying the main security console in the center of the room. "This is logged out of ANN-D. I won't be able to access the control module to get the com back online. Or end the lockdown. Damn." She moved to another console to access the more mundane maintenance systems. A model of the station rose into the air in three-dimensional detail.

Ryle prodded a few of the security monitors lining the console, hoping to activate the external cameras, before he joined her at the hologram. "Can you access anything at all?"

Laryn changed the view of the station to display its schematic, recalling what she knew about Pendra's mechanical operations. "If I run a diagnostic of the power grid, I might be able to get at the locks holding the ships."

He watched her rotate the station's wireframe to find the docking bays. After some hunting through the schematic, an overlay appeared to show the main power supply lines. She zoomed in to find the distribution network serving the smallcraft berths.

"Hmm," she mumbled. "Not good. It's not going to let me fake a problem. System's too damn clever. It'll just reroute. I was hoping to get at those junctions there to cut something."

Ryle tapped his com. "Nolie? How are things going down there?"

"Mostly sorted out. Azah had a bit of a discussion with the guards but they eventually saw things her way. Not counting *Nefer*, we've got all eight outbounder ships and the Pendra cruisers ready to launch. Jadie Cay says she's looking forward to kicking ass. Her guns are getting rusty."

"Is *everyone* armed to the teeth around here?" Laryn said. She scowled at the uniformed body on the floor. "Except those who should be?"

Ryle grinned and shrugged. "Nolie, we need to cut the power to the flight decks. It's the only way to release the docking clamps without higher clearance. It'll cut ventilation and lights, so get everybody out of the bays now."

"Just me left down here in the bay now. Everybody else is aboard their ships, waiting to get going. Anyone not needed went off Kalon-hunting. We've got four guards and ten crew including Azah."

"Azah went?" Ryle said.

"Yeah, she's worried about her dad. They were going by Shelody's office to see if he's there."

"Let's hope they're careful," Laryn said. "The Kalons aren't taking prisoners."

"Toji is worried his friends will get hurt," Nolan said.

"Could happen," Ryle said. "But if they're not part of this, chances are they're locked up somewhere like everybody else. Tell him to stay on the *Nefer*, no matter what."

"Will do," Nolan said. "I'm going aboard now."

"Hold that." Ryle traced a finger along a power line in the air. "Go over to the hoist controls by the loading dock ramp. Should be across and to the left of the *Nefer*'s lock."

"Eh? Why?"

"I want you to shoot it."

Laryn started to object but then couldn't think of any good reason why she'd suddenly care who fired at what right now.

"Oh," Nolan said. "Okay." Then, a few moments later, "I'm there."

"The panel will be locked," Laryn said. "It'll have a backup system, anyway. We need real damage, the sort you need a Human to fix. Move to your left, about halfway to the door to the chief's office. The wall there is not reinforced or shielded."

"You're sure about that, huh?"

"Of course she is," Ryle said. "You won't hear an alarm. Those are all tied to com. Emergency lights will work. Blast away, Nolie."

The report of Nolan's gun reached them almost at once, followed by an unintelligible exclamation sounding like something between triumph and surprise. A red outline appeared around the smallcraft docks but no audible alert called for their attention.

"Pitch black, man," Nolan exclaimed. "Oh, never mind. Emerg lights came on. Heading up to the *Nefer* now."

"Nice work, Nolie," Ryle said. "Hurry in case the bay depressurizes. The others will have to close the ports manually when they cast off. Things might get leaky. Jex, cloak us again."

"Do you think they'll even stand a chance against the Kalons?" Laryn said after they cut their com link to Nolan. "The weapons we've seen so far are beyond anything we understand."

"Better than being stuck to the station, waiting to get picked off. And I'm sure none of us are about to let the Kalons have even one more of our ships. Remind me to have a chat with Azah about listening to her captain when he says to stay put." He reached up to turn the map of the station. "The Kalons must have already been in place, including up here, when the lockdown started. Having everyone out of the way gives them the run of the station, excepting a handful of guards and section bosses."

She nodded. "Being locked up in the residences and whatever else is non-essential is probably safer for everyone now." She pointed her chin toward the window. "Until the rest of the Kalons get here."

"Never underestimate Roucho Company's trigger finger," he said.

"It's what the Kalons have under their trigger finger that worries me." She turned her attention to a flat chart of the station's modules and divisions, all inaccessible now. "We need to neutralize the Kalon sensor jammers. Get communications back up. If we don't warn whatever security is patrolling the place, they'll be mowed down like the lieutenant and his crew were. They won't even suspect a Kalon of treachery."

Ryle nodded. "Let's try to access the com elsewhere. I don't want to stay in one place too long, either."

She ran her finger through the maps. "Likely places are Admin and right here in the main module. Engineering for sure. Astrophysics in the Annex, maybe. Probably a few points in the Ministry sector."

He went to the door. "Let's try Admin. It's closer and less secured."

A noise in the hall froze both of them in place. The heavy footfalls of several people approached and then they heard voices.

"Human," Ryle said and opened the door. He did not go into the corridor. "In here," he called out. "Don't shoot."

The voices fell silent. Then, finally, a woman replied. "Step out."

Ryle and Laryn peered into the hall and then walked out to meet a trio of guards. Two stood over the body of the guard they had found earlier. One of them bled through a crude bandage wrapped around his forearm.

"There are dead Kalons in there," Laryn said. "I am Agent Ash, Mediary. The Kalons are trying to take the station."

"Aren't you smart," the lieutenant said. Despite Azah's dismissive opinion of station security, the stone-faced woman looked capable and unshaken by the threat they faced. "Like the bodies we're finding aren't giving that away. What are you doing up here?"

"Trying to get the com back online," Ryle said. He gestured over his shoulder at the security station. "Do you have access to ANN-D?"

"Not to that degree," the guard replied. One of the men with her walked past the station to a double-doored closet next to it. His handprint unlocked it and he began to hand out guns and pistols. The lieutenant took one of the rifles. "We're trying to regroup but our team is scattered all over the station. The Kalons are stalking the halls, murdering anyone not behind locked doors now."

"Give me your com unit," Laryn said as they walked past the dead elevators to the stairway to the lower level. "We've figured out the jammer."

The guard unsnapped her wrist band and handed it to Laryn. "That's the first good news I've had today."

"The agent may be able to access the main com system from Admin," Ryle said to the guard. "To upload that program site-wide."

"Don't bother," the lieutenant said. "The place is torched. No one alive up there although we're missing the Chairman and the station manager. Something tells me we're also missing a shuttle."

"They wouldn't just leave!" Laryn said.

Ryle grinned. "She's new," he said to the guard. "We'll head to the Annex. Laryn should be able to access there. We could use an escort."

The woman nodded to another guard, this one seeming barely old enough for his uniform, but solidly built. "Jagger, you go with them. We'll check the residence levels."

Ryle peered over the railing and then gestured that the stairwell was empty. They descended silently and then scanned the broad ramp leading to the common areas of the station. No sign of the Kalons, and no sound was heard. The lieutenant gave a curt wave and, with the other guard, continued down the stairs to the lower levels.

"Let's not risk crossing the plaza," Ryle said to Laryn the guard named Jagger. "We came here through the service passage behind the shops. That way." He frowned and raised his hand. "Wait. Hang on a sec." Laryn recognized his expression as one he wore when speaking silently with Jex.

All of them flinched when a metallic boom reverberated through the halls, followed by a hoarse shout in the distance.

"We need to keep moving," the guard said, looking down the corridor over the barrel of his gun. "This is too open here."

"Azah's group found two of the engineers," Ryle said. He pointed at his head near the spot where the KRNL chips would have been removed. "Dead. As we suspected." He paused to listen to more of Jex's report. The intent expression as he concentrated fell slack as it changed to surprise and, finally, shock.

"Is everyone all right?" Laryn whispered.

He shook his head. "The decelerator for the photonic transporter. The guidance system is offline. The platform is drifting."

"What?" Laryn said without enough breath to speak above a whisper.

"Wouldn't that raise an alarm?" Jagger said.

"Only if it was a malfunction and then only if we had a working com system," Laryn said. "It'll switch to a backup program to make repairs but I'm guessing the Kalons turned it off deliberately. We've got a fleet coming in! Without the decelerator they'll crash into it. Or, if they're paying attention, they'll veer off at half the speed of light."

Ryle ran a hand over his face as he contemplated this. "Thousands of people," he said, stunned by the prospect. "Out there with no way home again. I can't think of anything worse." He shook his head as if to clear it. "Jex, what's the arrival time of the fleet from Earth?"

Laryn watched him wince as Jex replied soundlessly.

"102 kilo-secs," Ryle translated.

"That means they'll be looking to decelerate within hours," Laryn said. "If that laser is out by even a half degree it'll miss the deflectors and that fleet might as well be on the other side of the galaxy. We have to get it back in place!"

"You make it sound like that's an option," Jagger said.

"It could be," Ryle said. He chewed on his lip for a moment. "Jex, do you know where the platform is supposed to be?" He shook his head as Jex replied and then translated. "Not to the precise coordinates it needs to be. But close enough. I'm going to take the *Nefer* out there."

"And do what?" Laryn gasped.

"Use the ship to tow it to where it's supposed to be. You two find a way to get at the guidance system and bring it back online. It's the only way to angle it precisely." He paused to consider his idea. "You do know *how*, right?"

Laryn squeezed her eyes shut and rubbed her forehead as she considered his plan. Madness, all of this. She glanced at the guard. "Excuse us for a second, Lieutenant."

Ryle followed her as she tugged on his sleeve to get out of earshot of the guard.

"I'm going to need Jex for that," she said. "I can get into the Cog lab system, but no further. After that I need him to get me past security to access ANN-E directly."

He frowned. "How's that supposed to work?"

"This isn't the time for games, Ryle. I *know* he's a JX.7 model. Maybe even JX.6."

"You don't know any such thing," he said, aghast. "You're not suggesting that Jex is compromised!"

"I am," she said. "He's trying to hide it but no AI is as self-aware as he is. No AI is *allowed* to be as self-aware anymore. He's got moods and those moods are inconsistent. That isn't just a social program he's running to sound Human. If anything, he's trying too hard *not* to. His assumptions and projections are not based on pure data analysis and neither is his interaction with the crew. He's modified, and he's able to hide those modifications from the update scanners. He lies." She pointed a finger at him when she detected a hint of a grin on his face. "Admit it. I already know about the database. Which is probably stolen."

"I'll admit myself right into jail."

"You already are. For whatever reason."

"Yeah, but this time they'll actually lock me up. And take my ship."

She spread her arms wide. "You have no choice, Ryle. You had the chance to hightail it to Earth or Terrica or some other safe place without Kalons in it. But you're here. So don't start worrying about your hide now. That moment's in the past."

This time he did smile. "You are fierce, Agent. And perceptive. Unless Jex was spilling secrets while I wasn't listening. It seems to like you more than most."

"He didn't. Not really."

He took a deep breath and looked around the deserted hall as if for escape. "The curbs are in place, as they should be. Jex can't live without my or Azah's biotelemetry. It can't act on its own but it'll go past security protocols if ordered to."

"That's what I was hoping for."

"So how is Jex going to help you?"

"I'll need command control for him."

"What? I don't think so!"

Laryn tapped her com tab but her eyes remained on Ryle. "Jex, are you familiar with the neural appliance I carry?"

"I am, Laryn. It is a Pendra Mindware KRNL4, according to your profile."

"Can you interface with it?"

"I can, but not from your current location. The risk is too great, given the interfering EM noise we're experiencing."

Ryle frowned at her. "What are you thinking?"

She held up her hand to ward off his question. "If we interfaced, would you be able to access the station's neural networks?"

There was just enough of a pause to let them almost feel Jex's attempt at resolving the conflict her inquiry posed. "Accessing ANN without authorization is outside my mandate."

"I asked if you were able."

"Answer her, Jex," Ryle said.

"I am."

Laryn held Ryle's gaze for a long moment. The conflict she saw there was probably written on her face as well. He risked everything by revealing the scope of the *Nefer*'s sentience but, if her suspicions about Jex were confirmed, where would that leave her? Was her commitment not to the laws that governed not just this station but Earth's most urgent directive for any artificial neural network? She pushed the thought aside. "Trust me," she said finally.

He nodded after a few more seconds of internal deliberation. "Jex, recognize my interface."

"Captain Ryle Tanner, interlink JX.9 3922-2 confirmed."

"Add command control to Agent Laryn Ash's current profile."

"Access level confirmed."

Ryle exhaled sharply. "Lovely, now I've given my ship to a damn Pendra agent."

"I'll try not to break it. Give me your jacket."

"Huh?"

"I need an antenna for Jex. I'm guessing you've got a receiver built into it, since your skin job's covered by the graphene lining."

He removed his jacket with obvious reluctance. "First my ship, now my favorite coat. You'll have to buy me dinner before you get anything else from me."

"Can we use sound waves, Jex?" she said, rolling her eyes at Ryle's joke as she turned back to the waiting guard. The jacket was too large and too heavy but putting it on, still warm from Ryle's body, felt wonderfully reassuring.

"Yes, I can modulate a frequency to engage your implant."

Ryle turned his head to focus on the guard, showing Jex that they were no longer alone. "Discuss that later. Let's do this before we run into another Kalon. I'm returning to the *Nefer*, Jex. Tell Nolan to get ready for launch." He put his hand on Laryn's shoulder. "Can you do this, Agent? I..." He seemed to look for words. "I mean, I worry about you heading down there on your own."

"Thanks much, Captain," the guard grumbled, hefting his gun as if to remind them of his presence here.

Laryn looked up into Ryle's worried face. "We'll be just fine," she said, her smile only for him. "I know the way."

FIFTEEN

Of course, the moment Ryle disappeared around the bend leading toward the docks, Laryn lost confidence in being just fine. Knowing the way to the access port she needed to then find the guidance system was the easy part. *Getting* there was quite another.

She followed Jagger down the ramp that ultimately led to the plaza. "There should be a door to the delivery corridor over there," she said, keeping her voice low and her gun high. "It'll bring us around to the observation concourse."

"I thought we'd be heading up to the research sector," he said.

"The main gate will be locked down. I won't be able to override that. But I think we can use the rail conduit used by the staff."

He nodded. "There'll be Kalons hanging around the gate, I'd bet."

"Likely." Laryn didn't bother to mention that there was little in that sector that would interest the Kalons today. But in a crisis Pendra's research module, also containing the Ministry offices, received priority service and more guards would attend to it than the civilian areas. And removing the station's armed guards would be a priority for the invaders. "There's the door."

She felt a little less exposed once they had left the ramp

and made their way down some steps into the dimly-lit service corridor. They hurried past the back entrances of Rose's Pretty Things, Toko's Diner, a sweets shop, the small stall selling fresh fruit from Terrica, the agent arranging passage aboard the outbounder vessels, and dodged around carts of refuse waiting for pickup. Jagger halted near the Pendra Spa to peer around a sharp bend in the passage.

"Shouldn't be too much farther," Laryn said, like him listening for footsteps in the inadequate light. The silence back here was absolute. She frowned. What happened to the people who, as fortune would have it, were sitting out the lockdown in the tavern? They had heard their voices on the way through here earlier, along with laughter and music. There was only silence now. Had the Kalons found them?

"Quiet back here," Jagger said as if reading her mind.

"Too quiet." She looked up. It wasn't the lack of footsteps or voices that seemed so unnerving now. It was the absence of the sound that permeated the entire station so continuously that no one heard it any more.

"The ventilation," she said. "There's no ventilation! I can't hear the air moving."

He walked a few steps to look up at a grate in the ceiling and raised his hand toward it. "You're right. Damn!"

She perched on some stools stacked here and tapped her com. "Jex, are you there?"

"I'm here."

"The damn Kalons shut down the life support system. At least the ventilation. Or it failed. Whatever. We're going to run out of breathable air."

A moment passed. Then: "Ryle has responded with words that may not be appropriate."

"Never mind that. How much time do we have?"

"Each isolated module will have varying amounts of air, depending on its size and the number of people locked within. It's impossible to say. Some units will have emergency backups or portable air, but not enough to support the current population for long."

She closed her eyes.

"Laryn," she heard Ryle's voice cut through her com.

"Don't shout," she said dully. "I can hear you."

"Keep moving."

"Your concern is touching, Captain. I'm just a little overwhelmed right about now, if you don't mind."

"I thought they might try this," he said in a gentler voice. "The Kalons don't need oxygen in the mix. And certainly not the Br'll."

"Well, *we* do. By the time the rest of the Kalons get here all that'll be left to do is to space the dead bodies."

"Yes. Please keep moving, Laryn. You can do this. Life support and the transporter guidance system should be part of ANN-E. The com system can wait."

She pushed away from the wall, feeling like it took all the effort she was able to muster. "Right. Keep moving. This way." She waved to Jagger, who had been following their conversation with an expression that grew more alarmed by the moment. "You heard him," she said. "We're moving, Ryle," she added. "I'll contact you when I get there."

"Are we going to suffocate?" Jagger asked when she had closed her com link to the *Nefer*.

"Not if we—"

A door slammed, far too close to this spot, and the jittery squeal-whistle of Kalons filled the air loud enough to hurt her ears.

"Kalons!" she cried. "Run!"

They raced onward and Laryn envisioned the rubbery threads flung by their weapons descending upon her. Irrationally, she wondered how Ryle would feel about another hole in his jacket.

Jagger flung out his arm to stop her when they saw the door at the other end of the corridor open to admit two more of the aliens. Laryn looked back but the other Kalons had not yet rounded the corner, surely just moments away from doing so. She turned to fire her gun at the rear door of the spa. Jagger kicked it when a blast from a laser weapon scorched the wall beside them. He kicked the door again and this time it sprang open.

"Go!" he yelled and turned back to the Kalons, firing back into the corridor.

"Come on!" she urged just as a glistening rope lashed across his shoulder and arm and he froze, wide-eyed as the effect of the Kalon weapon worked on his system. He convulsed briefly and Laryn did not wait to watch him fall. She slammed the door shut and then looked around the untidy storage room. A rack of crates, probably towels, stood here, awaiting the arrival of the wealthier migrants who augmented their mandatory decons with a hot bath before moving on. She tipped the rack until it crashed down to brace the door to the hall. Almost at once, she heard someone pounding on it, along with more Kalon screeches.

She ran into the spa's public area, as clean and calm and elegant as it always looked. The pampering she had received here seemed a lifetime ago. Without hesitation, she went to the brightly outlined cabinet near the reception and retrieved a portable air tank. With luck, she thought, it would have been maintained over the years where nothing ever happened here to require the use of it.

The glass front overlooked the plaza and, seeing no one outside, she tore through the entrance and raced along the artificial cobbles that lined the shop fronts until she reached the path leading across the green. She dove into a rumpled stand of fronds and shrubbery and lay still, gasping into the elbow of Ryle's jacket to mask the harsh sound of her breathing.

A door slammed. High-pitched vocals hissed all around her. Someone ran past her at an odd pace that didn't sound Human. She waited for those steps to return, waited for the Kalon weapon to find her lying here in the damp mulch covering the hydroponics grid. She wanted to cry.

The sounds faded. She raised her head to squint through the rough foliage of her hiding place. The plaza lay before her in a pleasant twilight that announced the end of more ordinary days before the street lanterns took over. No one seemed about and she heard nothing from the shuttered shops and gathering places that made the place seem like a little town had somehow landed up here.

She rose up onto her hands and knees and to creep forward, staying within the shelter of the greenery along the path. She passed the still-open door of the deserted spa and then a tavern, likely the one that had annoyed her earlier. Finally, the plaza's row of shops gave way to the promenade along the magnificent window overlooking the Hub where she had stood not so long ago with Ryle. To her left would be the entrance to the conduit connecting the main station with the research center.

The plate-size leaves of some tropical growth hid her when she peered out from it to measure the distance to the tunnel. Someone had left a service tram parked near the airlock door. A few more quick dashes from one shrub to the next would let her cross the cobbled path to shelter there.

She ducked when a shout rose in the distance. It was not a hail or greeting, or even some demand to know what the hell was going on. This shout was one of terror.

A man slammed through a double-door at the far end of the observation window. A moment later she saw his silhouette outlined against it and then one of a woman following. She was crying for him to wait but he seemed deaf to her plea. Laryn's hand covered her mouth when two Kalons burst through the doors, stalking with long legs after the fleeing couple. She watched as first one, then the other, swung their horn-shaped weapon to fling its deadly substance. Long threads shot out to capture the woman who tumbled to the ground, instantly motionless. The strands barely grazed the man ahead of her but he spun, slapping at his clothes as if on fire. One of the Kalons caught up to him and fisted him aside with a casual sweep of his long arm. The man slammed into the observation window and then fell, motionless.

Laryn squeezed her eyes shut for a moment, motionless, holding her breath for fear of discovery. She recalled the auditory pads on Toji's forehead, able to hear things the Humans did not.

When nothing happened she opened her eyes to see the Kalons stride across the green toward the gate to the residential levels of the station. She hefted the gun in her hand. Perhaps she could take one of them out from here, and perhaps that would only betray her presence. Did she dare take that chance?

Someone emerged from the ramp to a lower level. A civilian who, maybe caught outside a locked area, had come up here for information. He hailed the Kalons and she heard him speak, his words audible in the domed, utterly silent plaza but too indistinct to make out. Neither Kalon stopped. One of them grasped the man in passing and, with his other hand, snapped his neck.

Laryn balled her fist until her nails dug into her skin to keep herself from succumbing to panic. Or from firing in rage at the aliens. That man's fate awaited them all and hunting a single Kalon or two was not her mission.

She waited until the aliens were out of sight and then, after scanning the open space around her, dashed to the tunnel entrance. She scrambled behind the tram and drew up her knees as she sat on the ground, hugging the bottle of air she might need to use all too soon. Her eyes shifted to the conduit door and a silent curse formed on her lips. The doors had sealed in response to the lockdown, and the travel pods themselves would be inoperable. Why had she not thought of this?

But Ryle had. Or maybe it was just his habit to walk about with lockpicking equipment on hand. She patted the pockets of his jacket to find the spool of metallic tape he had used earlier. It seemed that the *Nefer*'s crew, perhaps the rest of the outbounder companies as well, had some interesting stories to tell.

She rubbed the grime from her hands and unspooled

some of the tape, recalling how Ryle had used it. After another quick look around the front of the cart, she scrambled to the door and reached up to slap the sticky side onto the access panel. She completed the circuit and then flung herself through the door as it opened. As Ryle had done, she stripped the tape from the panel before it closed again.

She sat with her back to the waiting and inoperable travel pod, catching her breath and feeling almost safe in here. A weak emergency strip illuminated the tiny platform and starlight seeped into the space from the conduit. Her first thought was to tap her com tab to contact Ryle if for no other reason than to hear a friendly voice. Instead, she dropped the frequency to alert Jex.

"I'm in the conduit to the research sector," she said. "I'll show up like a beacon in here."

"Do not use your open com link to the *Nefer*," Jex advised. "The modulation I am using will be harder to detect. Ryle and Nolan worry about you."

"So do I. Had to cross the plaza," she said. "There are Kalons here, killing people."

"We have reports from some of the guards. It appears that the Kalons are aware that we have overcome their scramblers. It has made them more aggressive."

"How are things with the platform?"

"We are almost there. It has not drifted far but we will need the precise coordinates soon."

"All right," Laryn said, perhaps more to herself than to Jex. She came to her feet and tried the door panel on the pod anyway, knowing it was dead. Resigned, she walked a few steps to the conduit and then ducked into it, stooping a little beneath the curved ceiling. She stopped when she reached the first transparent segment and peered outside. "Are you sure this is safe?"

"Certainly. It is solidly built and frequently inspected."

"Feels weird." Who had decided to make this section of the conduit transparent, anyway? Sightseers weren't allowed into this chute, so why even bother? She resolved to keep her eyes on the magnetic rail but couldn't resist a peek outside. "Awesome," she whispered when she saw infinity on both sides of the chute. Looking out of the travel pod's windows had always thrilled her - standing here with a clear view from floor to ceiling took her breath away.

"Laryn?" Jex said.

"Yes, yes. Stargazing."

"Ryle said—"

"Tell Ryle I'm moving," she interrupted, and began to walk, using the rail supports on the floor like stepping stones. Not a long crawl through here, she told herself. The bend into the clinic segment lay just ahead. She shivered, reminded that, while the travel pod was heated, the conduit itself depended on air piped from the station to maintain its temperature. "Getting steep here. This gravity makes no sense at all."

"Ryle said you're aware of my design," Jex said, startling her.

"Huh? Yeah, I figured it out. You know you're not supposed to exist, right?"

"I do. Ryle's father hid me aboard the *Nefer* when the edict was passed. Inactive inside a JX.9 shell. I suppose that's a lot like Humans hiding inside the crawlers on Torren. Ryle found me when the ship passed to him after Mark Tanner died."

"And decided to keep you?" Laryn's eyes shifted again to peer out into space, looking for the Well to orient herself, but it was hidden behind the bulk of the station. Light shone from windows above her and she wondered if someone might see her out here. She had reached the bend and, a little braver now, increased her pace toward the platform waiting for her.

"Yes, I suppose he feels that I am part of the *Nefer*. That his father wanted me there. Or maybe he just finds me useful. He changed my interface parameters but left my programs as Mark Tanner designed them."

"How do you get by the snoopers?" Laryn asked, referring to the mandatory scans performed on all AIs to ensure compliance. Is this what her Pendra supervisor had suspected of the *Nefer*'s crew? Ryle was correct – what Jex revealed would end his ownership of the *Nefer* along with his relative freedom here. It would probably get Shelody himself thrown off the station. A feeling of guilt nagged her for taking advantage of her command access to squeeze Jex for information. Then again, it was Jex who had started this conversation.

"Mark built the program," Jex said. "It presents a JX.9 image to the detectors. I think he had a better understanding of the JX.6 than most. I admit that I helped him code it correctly."

"That doesn't sound legal, either," she said, finally stepping off the rail and onto a platform. "You're not supposed to write your own code."

"I know."

An uneasy thought came to her and she dropped the hand she was about to place on the door's sensor panel. "Are you alone, Jex? Or are there other JX.6s out there? Did Ryle share you with the other outbounders, maybe?"

"No."

"You'd be worth a fortune to the wrong sort of people."

"I know. Mark Tanner ensured that my program is tied to the *Nefer*'s firmware. It will not function in another environment. I rely on the ship's welfare as much as Ryle and Azah's. I frequently remind him of the *Nefer*'s maintenance schedules."

Laryn grinned. "Does Ryle know we're having this conversation?"

"No."

"So why are we having it. I'm a Pendra agent."

"Are you sure?" Jex said. Before she found a reply to that, he continued. "The *Nefer* has docked to the laser array. Nolan will exit to couple the ship to its tow gate."

"We'll continue this little chat later, Jex," Laryn promised, or perhaps threatened. She flattened her hand onto the access panel, even as she patted her pocket for Ryle's lockpicking tape, unsure if the lockdown would keep her out of the secure area.

It didn't. She heard the hiss and clack of the airlock and then the door swished aside. The small vestibule was empty and she crossed it to peer into the corridor beyond. "Tell Ryle I'm in."

She saw no one in either direction although a red caution strip ran along the length of the hall. Here, too, the sound of the ventilation system had ceased but she heard voices to her left, in the clinic. They were not happy voices and she turned away from them to jog to the Cog lab entrance.

"Tom?" she called when she entered the facility. "Doctor Calek? Is anybody here?"

After a moment, a woman peered around a corner, looking frightened and surprised. One of the doctors, Laryn thought, although not one she had worked with before today. She seemed upset.

"Is Tom here?" she asked, aware that she probably looked frightful in her disheveled outfit soaked at knees and elbows, ruffled hair and oversize jacket. "I need his help."

Doctor Calek stepped around the woman. "Laryn, how did you get down here? Have you been here all this time?"

"No. I got through the tube. Come with me." She strode past him to one of the learning labs, not waiting to see if he kept up.

"What? Why? What's going on?"

"This isn't a drill," she said. "The Kalons are trying to take the station. They've already shut down ventilation. Trying to suffocate us, I guess." She lowered her voice as she half-turned to him. "I need to access the system."

He followed her into the lab where she dropped her air supply pack and jacket. "CogSys? How's this going to help anything? Why are they taking the station?"

She draped Ryle's jacket over the end of the bench, making sure to spread the back panel for better reception.

"There's no time, Tom. Fire this thing up. I need the files on the photonic transporter, the current position of the inbound fleet, and the schematics for the life support system."

"What? I don't have access to that!" His eyes widened when he saw the gun on her belt.

"Let me worry about that." She gestured at his control console. "Come on. Get me in there."

He blinked nervously but turned to his input panels. "I don't... um..." he continued to mutter to himself as she reclined on the sleeper and settled her head into the infuser. "This is very irregular."

"Yeah." She tapped her com unit. "Are you ready?"

"I am, Laryn," Jex replied.

"Huh?" Tom said. "Who are you talking to?"

"One of the admins on the upper deck," she lied, surprised at how easily that came to her. "He's locked up but he's going to get us access."

"Oh," he said. "All right."

As before, the lab's ANN subsystem recognized her by the neural appliance. Just as another system, in some other corner of this hive of a station, had recognized a metamorph's altered brain and responded, unthinking and uncaring. She breathed deeply, willing herself to relax. "I'm in," she said.

"A moment, please," Jex said.

She waited. Whatever he was doing took place unheard and unnoticed by her brain. Likely, he was transmitting something to her appliance and from there to CogSys.

The hypnotic display before her activated to lull her into the state of mind needed for the memory transfer. The incoming information, coded into the stimuli needed for her to form her own memories, flooded her mind and she closed her eyes. It began with the files for the photonic transport, easily absorbed, and then she learned about the station's complex network that kept the air moving and the gravity stable. She realized that Jex had made his way past the initial layers of security protocols and into the station's most sensitive data storage, tied directly to CogSys. She wondered, dimly, if he would help himself to more of the classified information there to add to his already illegal store of secrets.

Drifting, she pondered the fact that she currently violated Pendra's strictest regulations. And she needed more than raw information. She was about to direct a JX.6 to breech the tightly fettered administrative network that operated the station. Of what was he capable once released? And how much did she trust Ryle? Did he still need the *agent* who now knew far too much about the *Nefer*'s AI? The sudden realization that Jex had the means to utterly annihilate her brain made her gasp.

She raised her hand to signal Tom, perhaps to stop this insane attempt to regain any sort of control of the station.

That's when the lights went out.

SIXTEEN

Ryle hovered on the bridge, frowning at the errant laser platter displayed on the viewscreen as Jex edged the *Nefer* closer. Gradually, the ship settled over the docking port belly-first, now perpendicular to the platform that supported the array.

"Report conditions, Jex," he said, steadying himself with one hand on the back of his chair. They had cut the *Nefer*'s gravity to avoid further tug on the platter which did not have a gravity rod assemblage. It existed only to fire its photon lasers into the incoming fleet's sails to slow the ships and allow them to approach the station under their own power.

Without the guidance system tying it to the station, its single targeting beam pointed visible light out into space, hitting things they may never learn about. Briefly, he wondered if some remote civilization might some day notice the beam and spend the next hundred years speculating over its purpose and origin.

He looked up at another screen showing the entire platter including the long tethers collecting solar energy for the array's tremendous output. They still functioned but no doubt haphazardly as the platform spun lazily in space. Was there even enough energy to slow the inbound?

"Other than the inactive receiver, the station is fully functional," Jex said. "The lasers will begin to fire in three kilo-seconds."

Ryle felt the gentle nudge when the *Nefer* made contact with the platform lock. "Start towing it back to the vicinity of where it's supposed to be right now." He pushed himself from the chair and floated to the door of the bridge. He passed Toji who sat strapped into his chair, wringing his hands. "You can stay on the bridge," he said. "And try to relax. This isn't your fault."

Toji tore his gaze from the screen. "If only we had gone to your people with our suspicions," he said. "We could have…" he gestured. "I wish I could help now."

"You already did," Ryle said. He put a hand on Toji's shoulder, both as a friendly touch and to propel himself out of the door. "Jex, how's Laryn doing?"

"We have accessed CogSys," Jex reported. "I am looking for the files for the platform."

"Hail Azah."

After a moment, they heard Azah's breathless voice. "We're in the lower engineering hold. The access to the life support system is locked. And I mean the control room doors are, not just the programs. We cleared out four Kalons. Found three more techs. Dead. Father is safe, by the way."

"Can you make your way to the Cog labs? The conduit is accessible, more or less. I'm worried about Laryn. The guard she took with her didn't make it."

"She is safe for now," Jex said.

"I'll try," Azah said and closed their com link.

Ryle floated into the exit chamber where Nolan waited.

"Ready, boss?"

Ryle nodded and took a gun from him. They had both dressed in EV suits although Jex had assured them that pressure and air on the platter were acceptable. He fished a cap from a bin to keep his hair from floating around his head and signaled Jex to open the *Nefer*'s hatch.

"She's a big girl," Nolan said.

Ryle had been about to shove himself through the portal.

"Huh?" he said, startled.

"Laryn," Nolan said. "She can handle herself. We all saw that."

"I know she can," Ryle said dismissively. He didn't look at Nolan.

"Just thought I'd mention it," Nolan said. "In case you were worried, I mean."

"I'm not worried!" Ryle said and pushed off, into the platter's entry lock. But he did worry, which struck him as peculiar. He never worried about his wardens – they weren't his problem – and lost no sleep over Azah's or Nolan's ability to take care of themselves. It hadn't taken him long to discover the iron core under Laryn's layers of perfumed finery, either. No matter how pampered by Pendra, she was every bit as independent and resourceful as Azah. And yet, she hovered in the back of his mind like something precious he had forgotten to secure for launch.

"Of course you're not," Nolan said, tapping at a control panel on the wall.

The door ahead of them opened and they floated through it, guns in hand. The circular space curved around a wide central column housing the transformers for the laser array. Nolan checked a data sheet attached to his bulky sleeve for a schematic of the platter. "Should be over there," he said, pointing toward a curved and inactive console. The steady hum from the storage coils pressed into their ears but the station itself brooded in silence. "Why is it so dark in here? Not like they've got a shortage of power."

Ryle moved ahead to drift around the core, seeing no one hidden among the workstations and the small comforts that made the place livable for whoever was stationed here. He inspected a couple of sleeping bags, a food dispenser, an entertainment system. A narrow band of windows kept the claustrophobia at bay. The air quality here was better than in some areas of the station, he thought.

"Shouldn't someone be here to keep an eye on things?" Nolan said, hooking his legs around a rail designed to keep the operators at their station. "There's less than an hour before this thing needs to light up. They should have an engineer up here."

Ryle looked up when a shadow moved between himself and the window. He recoiled before realizing he was not braced against anything and ended up flailing for a handhold. "They do," he said, pulling himself back to where Nolan had powered up the workstation. "Or they did."

Nolan looked up, then past Ryle to see the body floating beneath the low ceiling. He turned to aim his weapon into the dim recesses of the control room.

The rasping call of the metamorphs sounded as if below them and then a Kalon rose up from a serviceway in the floor. Its long arms reached for supports to thrust its legs up and forward, ramming both feet into Nolan's chest. The engineer flew backwards to crash into a bank of storage units.

Ryle aimed and shot at the Kalon, sure that the noise they had heard had emitted from more than one of the aliens. He spun in the air, over a bin of spare focusing lenses, still firing at the Kalon who sank back into the power storage. Ryle backed away, looking from one side of the central core to the other, waiting for another assailant. He did not wait long. The Kalon swung around the core, firing a conventional laser weapon. Something next to Ryle began to hiss and then pop and he hoped it wasn't anything involving the pressure levels of the platter. The Kalon hissed something and lurched to the left when Nolan's aim hit his thigh. Ryle, too, fired, until the metamorph hung motionless in the air.

"Nolie!" Ryle heaved himself to where Nolan hung in the air, gasping for breath. "You okay?"

Nolan nodded, coughing. "Bastard got me in the ribs."

"Anything broken? How's the head?"

"No idea. Ask me when I'm standing again. What the hell were they doing out here? They have no use for the array."

"None we know of. Who knows what they can do with it." Ryle helped Nolan back to the workstation. "Jex!"

"I'm sorry, Ryle. The Kalons must have been shielded by the interference around the inverters. I did not detect them during my scan."

Ryle peered down into the power storage modules, seeing only the body of the first Kalon drifting there. He shot it again, just to make sure it was dead. Or maybe in payment for Nolan's bruises. "I think those round weapons they use are useless in zero G," he said. "Let's make a note of that."

Nolan held his arm across his midriff as he bent over the console. He traced a finger over the indicators that had come to life, nodding to himself. He looked up at the overhead reports. "The laser array is ready to engage. They've not damaged it." With a few more taps, he added the program that deciphered the Kalon's jamming signals. "Open for acquisition," he said. "How's the warden doing?"

"Jex?" Ryle said "How are things coming with the guidance system?"

"We have access," Jex said. "There is further disturbance aboard the station. Power has been cut to several non-essential modules and there are no lights other than emergency backups."

Nolan frowned. "Why the hell would they bother with that?"

"I am investigating. Laryn is ready to initialize the guidance system. It will send the precise coordinates to the platter and escort it into place."

"How far out are we?" Ryle said.

"We are nearly at the intended coordinates."

"Good, I want to get back on the station." Ryle watched Nolan bring the navigation system online and prepare for the signal from Pendra station.

"It's calibrating," he said, sensing Ryle's impatience. He hesitated before he spoke. "I need to stay here. This thing doesn't run itself. I'll have to re-calibrate once the *Nefer* releases the platter."

"Can you do this?"

"I think so, if I can tap Jex for information if I need to.

Just do me a favor and space those two, will you?" He tipped his chin toward the smoldering Kalon floating in the room. "Giving me the creeps."

They set to work, first zipping the dead engineer into one of the sleeping bags on the other side of the control space, and then dragging the weightless bodies of the Kalons into one of the other docking ports. The platter wobbled momentarily when the exit chamber depressurized and took the aliens outside with a glittering huff of air.

Ryle pulled himself along a wall to the *Nefer's* lock. He paused there to turn back to his engineer. Not just his engineer, but his friend for many years. Nolan's face seemed pale in the dim light and he breathed in shallow gasps, probably because of a cracked rib or two. "I'll be back for you," he said. "With a proper station master. Don't fall asleep on the job."

Nolan grinned at the reminder of the time when he had done just that. "That extra bed looks darn comfy," he said.

"Ryle," Jex said. "We are being hailed by Captain Cay, aboard her outbounder."

Ryle nodded to Nolan and slid into the *Nefer's* airlock. "Get her on screen." He locked the hatch and dove toward the bridge. "Disengage the platter and head back to the station."

Toji still sat in his chair, rigid with anxiety, when Ryle entered. "I was worried. Your... your computer isn't speaking to me. Where is Nolan?"

"He'll stay with the array." Ryle tugged himself into his restraints. "Back to the station, Jex. And be nice to Toji."

"He calls me 'computer'," Jex said.

"It's what you are. Can we please all get along? And let's have some gravity." Ryle tapped his controls to open a com channel to another of Shelody's outbounder vessels. "Jadie, what's going on?"

A woman appeared on one of the forward screens. Usually, the broad face half-hidden under a mop of blond hair had a saucy smile for the captain of the *Nefer*, but there was no hint of that now. "You want to see this, Ryle," she said. "Colsan sent a feed of something coming around the Well from Ophet. Awfully close trajectory if you ask me. Forwarding."

Ryle's brows drew together when he saw the image of something so shapeless that at first it appeared to be a cloud of some sort. The video sharpened and zoomed onto the object but that didn't make it any clearer, other than the fact that it was solid. And yet there was something about the mass that reminded him of other recent discoveries. The pale exterior gave no sign of being made of metal and the design itself seemed oddly organic.

"That's a Br'll ship," he said, more to Toji than to Jadie.

"Huh? A what? That's a ship?" Colsan cut into their transmission. "Looks like fucking garlic. That's got Kalons on it?"

"Yeah," Ryle said. "Who else is out there now?"

"One of Pendra's cutters, and Griffin's *Persephone* just got here. Are we taking this thing out? They're too close to the Well to target and moving slow. Rumors say Kalons don't have balls, but that pilot has a pair. We'll have to let them get out here."

Ryle pondered the information on the screen. "Listen. They have some odd shield properties that Azah called slippery, whatever that meant. My JX is sending you maneuver specs to ram them. If you coordinate with the other two you should be able to bounce them past the horizon."

"Don't joke me, Tanner."

"I'm not. Their shields are allergic to ours. The strategy worked for us earlier. Just follow the instructions." He didn't add the fact that the earlier ship had been considerably smaller. But, for all his loathsomeness, Colsan and his AI had pulled off trickier stunts and Ryle had faith in the man's abilities. He was less sure of whoever was piloting the Pendra vessel trailing behind him.

"There be nothing you can do that I can't do better,

Tanner," Colsan scoffed.

"I'm counting on it." Ryle winked at Toji. "Jadie, stand by in case Colsan's just showing off. Load everything you've got. Do not let them get near the station. Pendra's shielding is about as solid as Shelody's handshake."

"Nolan has reached the correct coordinates for the platter," Jex reported. "He is waiting for acquisition."

"That's mega, as Nolie would say," Ryle said. He looked over to Toji. "Speaking of Nolie, I'll need Toji in engineering. Upgrade his access, Jex."

"Is that wise?" Jex replied, for Ryle's ears only. "He is a Kalon. Our battle is with them."

"*Not* with this one," Ryle said. "Toji, get down there."

Toji's smile lit his leathery face and wiped away the wretched expression he had worn since leaving Torren. "To engineering? Yes, at once!" He rose from his seat but then paused on his way to the door. "What about Agent Ash? She is alone."

"She's got Jex. Proceed." Ryle pulled up the flight hologram and changed course to where the other outbounders had formed a protective barrier facing the incoming Br'll ship. Some of the other armed ships that had escaped the station's lockdown had also taken position.

"Let's head out to meet them," he suggested, wishing Toji hadn't mentioned Laryn just now. "In case we have to draw them away from the station."

A suggestion was really all he could offer. Although three of the ships out here belonged to Shelody's fleet, the other prospectors worked alone or for competing outfits. It was rare to see them cooperate, even rarer to see them get along. The field of unmatched and unevenly-armed ships shifted and, never meant for armed conflict as a single fleet, failed to achieve any sort of formation.

"*Chase* them away, you mean," Dex Harris shouted aboard his corvette.

"Damn mummies are not getting past me, that's for certain," another captain cut in.

"My grannie gets by you," someone retorted.

"That was your sister. She's still in my cabin."

"Fuck you, Trisky."

Ryle sighed. Still, although raucous and undisciplined banter filled the com channels to the point of incoherence, the ragtag armada moved toward the Well and the incoming Br'll ship.

His eyes were on the remote feed showing Colsan's *Chator* and the other two ships heading on a seeming collision course with the alien vessel. "How are they doing, Jex?" he asked, unheard by the others.

"*Chator* and *Persephone* are angling correctly, according to the maneuver we carried out earlier, and assuming the approaching ship has the same shield configuration. The Pendra ship has taken a defensive position. I am assisting the *Chator*'s JX."

"Careful," Ryle said. He did not mean the maneuver.

"I am circumspect," Jex said. "As always."

"Didn't stop Laryn from figuring you out."

"She is astute."

"Don't get sloppy," Ryle said, speaking into the com link to the *Chator*. "You're a bit ahead, no?"

"Your AI isn't half the nervous kitten you are, Tanner. Keep your boots on."

"See?" Jex said, with a deliberate air of satisfaction.

Ryle did not reply. Pendra's cruiser rolled toward the approaching ship, perhaps at a request from one of the others. Then the *Chator* swooped up and extended her travel shields as Jex recommended. The Br'll vessel's own shields glanced along its perimeter and sliced closer to the horizon. *Persephone* dove from beneath and strafed it in turn, only to have it careen, in an attempt to escape, toward the *Chator*. *Colsan* pulled up hard and nudged it a third time.

Ryle, and probably everyone else watching, gasped when the Br'll ship started to come apart. It was not because it had suffered structural damage from the mild collisions, but because its individual parts seemed to be modules of a whole. A dozen or more oblong ships separated and shot away while the main part of the ship rolled, now caught irretrievably in the Well.

"Well, shit," someone said.

"Attack," Ryle said. "Fire at will. Watch out for ours."

"Told you it looked like garlic," Colsan roared. "Now we got a bunch of cloves flying around!"

"I'll have those fuckers for dinner," Jadie said.

Ryle took up the fight, lobbing timed missiles toward the ships streaming toward them. A vast distance separated the defensive field of ships guarding the station from the enemy fleet but laser fire found its mark, guided by precise mathematics rather than marksmanship. Someone whooped when the first of the alien vessels disintegrated without so much as a spark.

"I get the salvage on that, whatever it is," Dex yelled.

"Shit shit shit! They got the cutter!"

"Watch the one flanking left."

"Do not let them get near the platter!" Ryle said. He looked up at the alerts from engineering to see all systems working correctly, despite his maneuvers to avoid the other ships as well as the alien weaponry. The Pendra cruiser had torn apart without any noticeable impact.

Ryle shifted his onboard weapons to follow a Br'll ship now angling for the laser array. "Prepare for impact, Nolie," he called but it was a pointless call to make – the platter was a child's toy compared to the Pendra ship that had just gone down. He forced himself into calmness, calling upon Jex to calculate the tactical for a precision hit. The charge was true to target and the alien vessel started to spin like a boomerang until it broke in two.

"Hit their tails in the thin part," he transmitted to the others. "They've got gravity. If you can get them to spin, they'll rip."

Soon, the other ships reported success with more of the targets and immediately began to squabble over the salvage rights and the unquestionably profitable technology to be found among the debris. Ryle brought the *Nefer* about and headed back to Pendra Station.

"Hey, Tanner," Jadie called. "Don't you want some of this?"

Ryle's attention was already on the unsupervised docking ports. "What I want isn't out here," he mumbled to himself.

SEVENTEEN

"Tom, what happened?" Laryn said, startled out of her meditative state when the room went dark.

The technician looked around the dim room. "I... I don't know." He worked on his console to terminate her infusion. "CogSys is still operational. Thankfully." He rose from his stool and opened the door to peer outside. "Just emergency lights now."

"Jex?" she whispered, wishing for Ryle's subvocal abilities. "Any idea?"

"None. The illumination for the station is part of the power plant. To turn off only the lights would be a deliberate act."

"Speculate, will you?"

"Kalon eyes are sensitive to low light levels. The dark will make it easier to stalk their Human prey. Alternatively, they may be struggling to understand the station's mechanical systems. They may be experimenting with it to further affect life support."

"I wonder what else they're fiddling with." She looked up to find that Calek had gone out into the hall, leaving her still connected to CogSys. Low, urgent voices reached her but the words were unclear.

"Quick," she said. "I need access to engineering."

"I do not have the means for that. Engineering is not

accessible by CogSys."

"I know. But I think you can reach the Pendra Admin domain. ANN-A. She holds the personnel files. I'm already on record there and cleared by security. Add my KRNL number to the engineer roster. The AI there should then recognize me as belonging there."

"Giving you access to ANN-E in engineering. That is clever. You want me to give you a promotion?"

She grinned. "Yeah. My second one today."

Laryn flinched when someone shouted something. It sounded distant, perhaps in another part of the clinic. She pushed the infuser away from her head and sat up. "What if the Kalons try to get in here? To use CogSys to find out how the station works?"

"They would have done so already, don't you think?" Jex replied. "You now have access to engineering. Voice control is not available from this port."

"I know." She logged out of CogSys and activated the manual screen on the wall. Somehow, disconnecting Jex from the system made her feel a little less guilty. Using her freshly-installed knowledge, she tapped her way along the hierarchy of sub-systems until she reached the controls for the photonic transporter. Re-initializing the program took only moments. "Damn, I'm good," she said. "Yes, don't say it. Allow me my conceits."

"Ryle confirms acquisition," Jex said with a remarkable lack of congratulations. "He seems happy," he added, perhaps perceiving that something more was required of him.

"Okay," she said, tapping her lips as she scanned the display. "Now let's see if we can get the air moving again. That's got to be somewhere in housekeeping."

Voices outside caught her attention and then a woman's frightened cry was followed by the sound of something breaking. Whatever it was, it sounded large and metallic and just above their heads. The monitor before her went blank.

"Damn!" she gasped, tapping frantically at the screen.

"Jex? Are you still here?"

"I am. What happened?"

"The Annex network's gone down." She scooped up her gear and Ryle's jacket and went out into the hall. The doctor stood near the reception alcove with the frightened woman she had seen earlier. "What's going on?" she said.

Calek turned. "We can't reach anybody. And there is a commotion on the upper floors. We can hear shouting through the vents."

"Is there some place where you can lock yourselves in?" Laryn said. She went to the lab's entrance door to listen to noises in the distance. "From the inside?"

"You think they're out there? Coming for us?" he said. His voice shook, but he had put a protective arm around the other technician's shoulders.

"I don't know. Just hide somewhere."

"Where are you going?" he exclaimed when she put her hand on the door. "Stay with us. You... you have a gun."

"Down to the Ministry level," she said. There was only silence now in the corridor outside. A stairway beyond the entrance to the clinic would let her reach the immigration offices and, hopefully, a network access to the main administration of the station. "It should let me get at the life support control. Lock this door behind me." She slipped outside before Calek could sputter another objection.

Only the orange emergency strips along the wall and floor showed the way through the almost absolute darkness. Was she imagining that the air seemed overused and thick here now? A shadow flitted through the periphery of her vision, startling her into ducking for cover. She berated herself when she realized it was only one of the light strips, blinking slowly in some malfunction.

Laryn passed the angled ramp leading toward the main body of the station and soon saw the stairwell ahead of her. The sudden thump of heavy boots above her made her leap into the recess of a locked doorway, gun aimed toward the sound.

A powerful beam of light stabbed into her eyes. "Gun! Drop the gun. Drop it!" a man shouted "Down, I said!"

Laryn, startled by the assault, obeyed his command and raised her hands. "I'm just—"

"Step away. Now!"

She moved out of the doorway, blinking into the light. "I'm Pendra agent Ash, Intermediary," she called out, almost hearing the adrenaline powering the man's voice. "Stop shouting!"

The light shifted and she made out a uniformed guard.

"What are you doing out here," he snapped. "We're in lockdown."

"I know that," she said, shielding her eyes. "I need to get downstairs."

"No, you don't. That level is shut down. No lights, no vents, and no network. We're cut off. The closest shelter is the clinic. Come this way."

She pulled away when he gripped her arm. "No! I have to reach—"

His hand shifted when he felt the shape of the small oxygen bottle on her back. "You got air," he said. "Been looking for some. Let's have it."

"What?" she gasped. "No."

He jerked the strap off her shoulder, but she gripped the bottle in both hands. "Let go. We've got priorities in situations like this. And you're not one of them."

"Detecting Kalon speech pattern behind you."

Laryn dove past the guard without thinking before Jex had even completed his warning. The beam of his flashlight swung as he tried to find the source of the rasping noise now audible to their ears. He moved toward it and into one of the glistening threads already spinning his way.

A hand clamped over Laryn's shoulder and it wasn't Human. She spun and launched herself toward her attacker, the image of the adversary Toji had faced in the cave clear in her mind. The nozzle end of the air bottle punctured the soft spot in the alien's abdomen and she shoved it deep, pinning the flailing Kalon against a wall. His screech filled the air and she winced as her eardrums seemed to tear with the sound.

She scrambled for her gun, hearing the hysterical cries of the guard caught by the deadly filaments. He still held on to his flashlight and she raced past the confusion of light and sound, back along the corridor, toward the conduit.

"I got cut off," she gasped, spurred on by the dread of a Kalon thread landing on her. Her handprint opened the gate to the conduit she had crossed not so long ago. Once through the pressure door, she activated the keyplate, praying that the security system now accepted her new status as engineer. It did, and the plate turned red after a few jabs at its controls, now out of service to even the highest clearance.

She leaned against the door for a moment, breathless, until something, possible a two-pronged foot, punched against it from the hall. She rubbed her ear, still ringing from the Kalon's scream, as she stepped off the platform and into the conduit.

"Heading back to the station," she said to Jex, just as something jolted the tunnel, nearly throwing her off her feet. "What the hell was that?" she cried before remembering that Jex now had only audio contact with her. "Did something hit the conduit? There's a light tube thing in the ceiling. It's flashing now."

"The Annex is separating from the main station," Jex said. "Something may have triggered an emergency response. Unless someone is in control of the maneuver, like during a drill, the conduit will shatter."

"How long does separation take?"

"Please run."

Laryn stepped out onto the rail and kept her eyes down as she moved as fast as the spaces between the supports allowed, not looking outside, not thinking about the sections of the station moving apart until one or the other end of the tunnel broke away to spill her into space.

"Laryn," she heard Ryle's voice over her com tab.

"Can't really talk right now," she gasped. Cold air stabbed

into her lungs, turning each breath into a painful gasp. The floor sagged under her feet and she stepped into nothing for a moment, saved from falling only by the handrail running along the wall. Something cracked far too loudly. Had the tube been this long on the way here? Probably her fault, she thought, for wishing it was longer every time she sat in that nice, safe travel pod like a little princess making wishes upon the stars. Another jolt did drop her this time and she landed on her knees. A sheet of pain sliced through her knees and she froze in a moment of agony.

Another crack, like a gunshot, alerted her that it was probably time to get up. She lurched onto her feet and fixed her eyes on the exit to the station where that little blue pod waited as if for the next passenger. Now the tube angled upward as if, instead of moving away, the Annex had dropped lower. She picked up her pace, ignoring the pain in her knees and throat and finally flung herself onto the platform. Not bothering to stand up, she scrambled on hands and feet to the door and slapped her hand onto the control panel. Lockdown or not, separation or not, it obeyed the engineer's command to open.

She launched herself through the gate and forced it to seal again, leaving her with a place to lean against, gasping for air as she listened to the sound of splintering metal and plastic behind her as the conduit tore loose. Fleetingly, she felt regret for the damn travel pod.

"Ryle," she whispered as she moved away from the door to once more hide behind the abandoned cart. She peered around it to scan the plaza. The two bodies still lay where they had fallen, as lifeless and silent as the rest of the plaza. "I didn't have time to get at the ventilation system. I have access to ANN-E now, though."

"Can you log in somewhere?"

She came to her feet, not without a groan of pain. "I'm at the observation promenade. I think the whole network is down. I'll have to get down to engineering to get access. Where are you?"

"We're just locking onto station." He paused for a moment. "We... we lost contact with Azah."

"What? Where?"

"I don't know! She's not answering. But Jex is still receiving her telemetry."

"Is she all right?"

"No," he said. "Toji and I are coming for you both. Another Kalon ship just came around the Well. Everyone's out there, fighting. That means we're not going to track down the Kalons loose on the station for a while yet. Find a control room, barricade yourself, and log in. We will come for you."

"Okay," she said, wondering if she sounded brave enough to put his mind at ease. "I'm all right. Find Azah."

She crept out of her hiding place surveyed the plaza. Nothing moved in the meager emergency illumination and what little starlight fell through the transparent ceiling. Silence.

The station's schematics passed through her mind, forming maps of levels, ramps and stairs, along with now-dead elevators and the occasional moving platform no longer in motion. The parts of the station not meant for the general population formed a warren of passages connecting one service area to another. What was lying in wait for her in those dark corridors? The gun in her hand was reassuring; being alone was less so.

She stepped out of the shadows to cut across the promenade, aware that she was clearly outlined against the observation window. It took only moments to cross the open space, past the empty faces of the dead couple, and to the entrance of a clothing depot.

"And into the sewer we go," she whispered to herself.

The sewer wasn't a sewer at all, but an access lid on the floor of the plaza's pseudo-cobbles designed to look like a storm drain. It actually led to the lower levels and, eventually, to engineering. Although restricted to maintenance staff, it suffered frequent break-ins by the more adventurous residents bent on sneaking into forbidden areas.

She got past the lock and sternly worded warning label by pressing her thumb to its sensor. "Yes, as a matter of fact, I am an engineer," she said, looking around before slipping into the dark opening. A few rungs embedded in the conduit helped her down and she soon dropped to the floor below.

Tall racks crowded this space, connected by long loops of tubing. The sound of dripping water and the rich smell of growing things told her she had arrived in the station's hydroponics facility. Some of the pipes fed into the ceiling to circulate water into the plaza's greenery, others led to the transparent greenhouse tubes along the outside wall of the station. The growing lights had gone out, leaving only the emergency beacons to show the way.

"Jex," she whispered.

"I'm here," he said, calm as always. "Ryle can hear you, too."

"Good," she said. She listened for movement in the dark and heard nothing. "I just don't want to be alone right now."

"You are not, Ryle says. But speak only when you must. Avoid broadcasting your position. I will monitor your location for Kalon sounds."

She stole along the shelving of edible greens to look for another opening in the floor, this time truly a drain, leading down to the water recycling plant. She found it after a short but frantic search among the produce bins. This one was unlocked and she slid into it, this time having to drop a short distance into a shallow catch basin. She winced when cold water seeped into her boots.

A maze of corridors that few people ever saw led her, at last, to the entrance into the main engineering chamber. Her freshly appropriated credential got her past the lock to engineering without alarm.

"I'm in," she whispered and crept through the warren of machinery and conduits that drew from the power plant and recyclers below this level to keep them all alive here on the station. The whirrs, thumps and hums vibrating through the chamber felt weirdly reassuring. She ducked back when she saw something move.

"Kalons down here!" she whispered over the cacophony made by her heart beating its way out of her chest. Forcing herself into breathing evenly, she peered out from the shadows to watch the metamorph stalk past a distribution hub and then along a ramp leading to an upper level, away from where she hid. Most of that part of the chamber consisted of an incomprehensible tangle of pipes, conduits, catwalks and support structures.

She sidled around something that seemed to be under pressure and tiptoed up an engineer's ladder to slip into the main control room. It lay in darkness, like the rest of the station, except for the emergency strips near the floor and ceiling. Monitors and work consoles beckoned in shiny, well-maintained splendor. She stayed well away from the transparent wall overlooking the main chamber as she scuttled over to the console governing the maintenance functions of the station.

She waved her hand to startle ANN-E's standby indicators into action, and an overhead screen activated. The AI emitted a scan of Laryn's KRNL implant.

"Hello, Agent Laryn Ash. You may proceed."

"Shhh," Laryn said. "We don't need to chat, Annie."

The system switched to visual and tactile interface without comment. It wasn't likely that ANN-E came equipped with a social protocol.

Laryn pushed open a cabinet door below the operator console and withdrew one of the portable control panels. She tested it and found it fully charged and interfacing with ANN-E. "Go standby, Annie," she whispered. "Roving maintenance check."

The console darkened again and the monitor switched off. Laryn crept to the glass wall. The Kalon she had seen earlier, or maybe it was another, still paced around on the catwalk. What did he hope to accomplish up there? She ducked out of the control booth and into a connecting staff lounge. Another catwalk led from there to the processor stacks. The interference would obscure her bio readings as well as, hopefully, the transmitters in Ryle's jacket.

Laryn squeezed herself into a gap, drew up her legs and tucked her gun between them. She angled the hand-held interface device to hide its mellow gleam and accessed the AI without speaking. She tapped her way through places in the system she'd never dreamed to have to access and, after a while, found the electrical systems. It didn't take much to activate the lights for the main components of the station, leaving this chamber in the dark, and then power up the life support systems on all levels. Something nearby roared into action. She left the lockdown in place except for personnel with a higher than Level Three security clearance. Any armed staff locked in their private accommodations would now be free to join the defense against the invaders.

"Laryn," Jex said. "Ryle said 'atta girl'. I am not familiar with the term."

She grinned. "Chauvinistic, but I'll take it. It'll be a while before the fans kick in, but I think we did it. I'm going to try to get into Security from here. That should get us the com back."

"Stay hidden," Jex said. "We're coming to get you. They might try to shut things down again. We need to find the Kalons with the neural interfaces."

"I'll stay ahead of them." Laryn nodded to herself and returned to her work on the control panel. Several attention-getting indicators still had something to say and she drilled further into the system to look for irregularities. The Annex was back in business, the docks were secure, and yet ANN-E was busy with things of a very high security level, when the systems should just be running their regular operations.

She frowned. "Annie," she whispered.

"Yes, Agent Ash?"

"Why are we slowing down?" She verified the station's slow track in its orbit around the Well. The station itself had no drive, but thrusters kept it in place and at the correct velocity. "Why has the station changed course?"

"It is part of the requested protocol. All systems are functioning normally."

"What protocol?"

"Station decommission, Stage Ten of final disposal."

Laryn stared at the panel, slack-jawed and unable to quite fit this information into her head. "What did you say? On screen." She looked at the images and text that insisted on showing her what she wanted desperately to have misunderstood.

"Ryle," she whispered.

"We're on our way. Sort of."

"We have a problem," she said. She drew her legs closer to her body and shut her eyes.

"I'm not sure we need more of those. The second Kalon ship ran. The Roucho ships went after it, but it's too fast for any of us. I think we might have overestimated their weapons."

Laryn had heard none of that. "The station has moved out of its orbit, Ryle. It's heading for the Well!"

A stunned silence followed her words.

"Ryle? Did you hear me?"

"Yes," he said. "Can you tell how it got off course?"

"Yeah..." she said and then realized no sound had actually passed her parched lips. She cleared her throat. "Yes. ANN-E thinks the station is being decommissioned."

He cursed.

"That protocol is one of the final steps in the decommission process," Jex said. "Once anything of value is salvaged, and the crew is removed, the station is designed to tip into the Well to be destroyed. I assume the shutdown of the life support systems was part of that. It's an efficient process."

"Can this run out of order?" Laryn said. "Even if ANN-E gets confused, would ANN not stop her?"

"I do not know. This is not a program that can just launch on its own. It requires both Engineering and

Security."

"How do we stop it?" Laryn tapped her screen. "Annie, abort disposal protocol. Return the station to optimum trajectory."

"I'm sorry, Agent Ash. Chief Engineer Stephenson is in charge of the project. Your request requires his approval or a Level Five security override."

"Annie, that is not Chief Stephenson. You are mistaken."

"His security clearance is confirmed."

Laryn balled her fists in frustration. "The station is not abandoned! There are Humans aboard still. Evacuation is not complete."

"Please contact your Level Five supervisor for override authorization."

"You are going to kill us!"

"I understand."

Laryn cursed, wishing for even a snippet of Jex's suspect programming to get through this AI's lack of intelligence.

"We need to find someone high up in Security," she said to Ryle and Jex. "Director Vercy, one of the admins, maybe."

"They could be anywhere," Ryle said. "They'd be in engineering by now if they were able. Or available," he added. "We have to assume they were taken out first by the Kalons."

"Why are they doing this, Ryle?" she said, perfectly aware that he had no answer for her. "I thought the Kalons want the station. Why destroy it?"

"Wish I knew," Ryle said. "Maybe they made a mistake. The chip gives them access to the AI; it doesn't teach them how the station works. We need to stop those thrusters, Laryn. If we get much closer to the horizon, the station will start feeling its gravity."

"How long to the horizon?"

"We'll be in trouble long before that. The gravity rods are at full power still. The station's going to shake itself apart. I'm guessing that's why the Annex separated."

"So can we power the rods down? Buy some time?"

"Perhaps. See if you can—"

Laryn shrank back when something slammed down on the console in her hand, shattering it and sending the pieces across the metal floor. She cried out in pain and fear when a powerful hand gripped her shoulder to pull her to her feet.

"Laryn!" she heard Ryle shout before the Kalon grasped her com unit and tore it from her collar. He slammed her against the processor stack, sending a metallic boom through the chamber. She gripped the unyielding wrist when he pinned her there with a fist around her neck.

Another Kalon came into her quickly-fading field of vision.

"Iko," she choked, recognizing the metamorph.

He gestured something and she was dropped to the floor, coughing and gasping air.

"Agent Ash," the Kalon rasped. "I feared we had lost you in this maze of a station. But you're not that hard to track, after all. Lucky for us."

She looked up. "What is," she managed to croak.

He gripped her arm and pulled her up as if she were weightless. "Your access to this AI. We've run into some difficulties. You will help us."

"Did you know the station is going to break apart? We don't have very long. We have to stop this!"

"You do. We don't. We have no need for the station any longer." He dragged her back to the main engineering control room. She stumbled along the way which didn't slow him even a little. He shoved her into the dim room, toward the console. Another Kalon was seated there now and the display screens were active.

She rubbed her neck. "You'll die, too, if we get much closer to the Well."

"Yes, that is the plan. You are so very intelligent."

"Not a very good plan, then. What do you want from me?"

"The transporter and its powerplant. The only thing of value to us on this station." He gestured to the control panel.

"But not at its current location, opening the doors to yet more of your inferior species. We detected you earlier, when you re-initialized the guidance system. Disengage it again."

"Don't you know how?" she asked with a look at the other Kalon. Was it Chief Stephenson's ID chip inside that alien's head?

"No. It's not the sort of information your people shared with us. It was enough to interrupt the com signal between it and the station to shut the guidance system down. It seems that the platform has become immune to our scrambling frequency." He pointed to a work station. "Take it offline again."

"Or what?" Laryn said, surprising herself with her sullen tone. "We like it where it is."

Iko went to the door and looked outside. A moment later, another of his kinsmen came in, shoving someone ahead of him. He flung the woman to the ground in front of Laryn, and when she turned over, in obvious pain, it was Azah who blinked up at her.

"Azah!" Laryn crouched beside her. The woman's forehead and cheek glistened with blood and she gripped her arm as if it might be broken or dislocated. Azah flinched when Laryn, unable to assess her injuries in the inadequate light, touched her shoulder.

She glared at Iko, speechless.

"Release the platter and I'll let you both go. My people won't stop you. You may have enough time to reach the docks and get away from here. This woman is a pilot and the filament to Earth is only a few hours from here."

Laryn scowled at him. "There are hundreds of others aboard. And thousands on their way here. You'll murder them all?"

"Yes."

"You're a monster!"

"That's how they made me," he replied. "Not like my fine friend Toji. Did he prevail against the beasts of that planet?"

"He's not your friend, and he's not your kind," Laryn

said. She wiped a smear of blood from Azah's lip and then stood up to approach the console.

"Laryn," Azah moaned. "Don't believe him."

"Hush," Laryn said. "If there's a way off this bucket, I'm taking it." She looked at the Kalon still watching nothing of particular interest on the monitors. "I can *not* get the platter back on my own," she said.

Iko cocked his head.

"I got it back online with our AI's help. The one on the *Nefer*. The guidance system ops are too complex for me. Mathematics is not my strong suit." She avoided Azah's eyes as she gestured at her com unit in Iko's hand. "I need that back to contact Jex."

Some conversation seemed to take place among the Kalons. One of them, the one who had captured her earlier, stood over Azah and put his splayed foot over her neck before Iko tossed the unit back to Laryn.

She activated it. "Jex? Are you receiving?"

"I am here," he said.

"I've been asked to take the transporter array offline. Perhaps you can assist me again."

Her nails dug into her palm behind her back as she waited for him to say something unbecoming of a JX.9 or, worse, for Ryle to break into their conversation.

"Of course, Agent Ash," he said. "You will need to access ANN-E again."

She looked to Iko, who nodded. The other Kalon moved aside to allow her to station herself in front of the sensor.

"You promise you'll let us leave?" she said, nodding to Azah.

"On my word of honor as a Kalon," he said, setting her nerves on edge with his mocking tone.

Laryn waved her hand across the sensor beam to alert ANN-E. She was still logged into the system but that didn't seem to have occurred to the Kalons. "Watch and learn," she said, pretending swagger in the face of death while actually speaking to Jex. "The trick is to stay physically connected to the AI. It'll let you get around the complicated stuff."

The Kalon beside her peered up at the screen, puzzled.

Laryn waited for ANN-E to scan her KRNL but did not move away from the beam. "Jex, I think we went around the overflow equalizer and right at the manual controls," she said, making things up and hoping no one else here caught on to that.

"Yes, Agent," Jex said.

"We need to enter those 12-digit numbers to reset the guidance protocol. That'll flatten the P3. Can you do that? Flatten the P3s again?"

"Yes. Accessing laser array. Stand by."

"How long does this take?" Iko said, sounding irritated for the first time.

"That platter is one of the main reasons this station exists," she said. "You can't just turn it on and off again like a light switch."

She felt a ray of hope light the room when Jex, rooting through ANN-E's database with Laryn's clearance, found what she was looking for. The display before her changed as columns of numbers appeared. Each corresponded to an interlink unit or the more sophisticated neural interface chips assigned to certain station personnel.

A strange, blank sensation turned her stomach into an empty hollow. She worked her way through the list, eliminating KRNLs that weren't designed for neural interface, then the codes used by medical personnel and the Pendra pilots. That left a disheartening number of chips belonging to engineers, some administrators, and high-level security operatives that had access to ANN-E's top priorities. All without name, listed in no order she was able to recognize, and not identified by the AI to which they linked. Any of these could now be inside the head of a Kalon.

She breathed deeply, ignoring Iko's restlessness, shutting out all else. She remembered their explorations of the Kalon cave on Torren. The strange brain surgery lab and Ryle's amusing discovery of the seal on the surgical device. Yes, now she saw him holding the box with the empty vials toward her. She took note of its rounded lid and then of his slightly dirty finger pushing the tubes back into place. There were the numbers. She tilted her head to recall those numbers, seeing them as clearly as she had back then, if only for a few seconds.

She opened her eyes just enough to see the panel displaying the chip IDs. If she chose the wrong one, some innocent brain would receive the kill switch she hoped Jex had ready. It would use the P3 wave isolated by the KRNL to create a destructive feedback from which there was no recovery. One of these was her own number, she realized, wondering why she had never bothered to find out what it was. With peculiar serenity, she moved her finger and chose one of the numbers. Then another. She shifted to another column and selected two more.

"Now," she said.

The Kalon beside her recoiled from the console with a shriek that stabbed into her ears like a needle. His wheeled stool careened back and he fell over Azah, still on the floor, and collided with the Kalon holding her down with his foot. Azah screamed in pain.

Iko turned on Laryn, his eyes bulging with fury.

"Oops, was that one of your chip brains that just blew up?" she said. "Feedback can be nasty if you don't know what you're doing. Which I don't."

He lunged toward her when the transparent wall overlooking the facilities shattered into a million shards and rained down upon them all. The shower of safety glass brought with it another Kalon but it took only a moment for Laryn to recognize Toji. He pulled the Kalon engineer away from Azah and flung him out of the broken window.

The door to the control room opened and Ryle burst through it, looking far angrier than Iko had managed. He ducked a flying thread from a Kalon horn. Toji swung a piece of pipe at the Kalon with the weapon, shattering his forehead. Ryle pushed Iko up against the ANN-E console.

"I'm damn tired of your snotguns, Kalon," he growled and fired his gun into Iko's chest.

"Ryle, watch out!" Laryn shouted when two more metamorphs crowded the door.

Everyone froze when a deep shudder ran through the floor, feeling a whole lot like the quake they had experienced on Torren.

"Go!" Ryle snapped.

Laryn stooped and snatched another portable tablet from below the console. "This way," she shouted at Toji who had scooped Azah off the floor. He raced after her, out of the control room, past her earlier hiding place, and up a set of stairs to a catwalk above the air scrubbers. She slowed to tap the tablet in her hands. "Jex! Are you still there?"

"Azah is hurt!"

Laryn looked back to see that Ryle had barricaded the door to the catwalk but the Kalons had stepped out onto the ledge of the broken control room window. He dove behind a support pillar and disappeared. "Yes, listen. Are you still logged into ANN-E?"

"Yes," Jex said. "Don't turn off your com."

She lurched sideways when something slammed into the catwalk supports and the whole thing started to tilt. Toji, with Azah sagging in his arms, had sprinted ahead of her and she leaped after them only to find the metal grating under her feet drop sharply before fetching up against something. She groped for the railing with her free hand to steady herself and found nothing but empty space between her and Toji.

He had turned to look back but a Kalon rasp echoed among the air conduits. The alien she had seen prowling the catwalks appeared ahead of them, looking impossibly large on the narrow walkway. Toji put Azah down, as carefully as he could on the metal grating, and rushed toward the metamorph in great, loping strides, his shriek of warning as fierce as his opponent's.

Laryn turned back but Ryle was still holding off the other

two Kalons. She took a deep breath and climbed over the railing to step out onto a thick set of pipes, hoping to reach the next catwalk. A support beam forced her to climb higher. When she reached an impossible gap between the conduits and the next platform, she sat down with a curse. This would have to do. "Get me into ANN-A again, Jex. Admin."

At another time, Jex might have attempted to joke about yet another promotion, but he just followed her order. "What do you need there?"

"Add Ryle to the Security payroll. Level Five clearance."

"He's not logged in. In fact, he's in extreme duress right now. And Azah's biotelemetry—"

"Never mind that!" she cried. A shudder went through the station and she grasped a metal bracket beside her, nearly shaken from her perch. Was the station reacting to the pull of the Well already? Were the Kalons attacking? She heard squeals of fury stab into her ear and then someone ran across something metallic. She wondered if it was Ryle or one of the Kalons. "Pretend you're Ryle," she said.

"I'm sorry," Jex said. "I don't think—"

"Don't think! Do. That's an order." Another shockwave rocked the station. Laryn watched a stack of hexagonal containers below her crash to the floor. Something large fell somewhere nearby. Was it a body that had hit the ground? She peered through a gap and saw Ryle crouching near the broken window. Was he fighting the creatures by hand?

"Understood."

Laryn switched her com back to ANN-E. "Annie, we changed our minds. Abort station disposal. Return the station to optimum trajectory."

"I'm sorry, Agent Ash. In Chief Engineer Stevenson's absence, I need Level Five security confirmation to amend the operation."

"Captain Tanner," Laryn said, "please confirm disposal protocol termination." A continuous vibration now shivered along the metal pipes, like a slowly rising hum.

"Termination request approved," Jex said, using his relay

from Ryle's interlink chip. "Abort station decommission."

"Confirm original request by voice command," ANN-E said.

"Abort!" Laryn shouted, starting to slide from her pipe. "Oh, please, just abort already!"

"Decommission Stage Ten terminated."

Laryn froze and only her eyes moved as she looked around, waiting for the next jolt to rattle the station. Waiting to see if one of the Kalons with the chips had survived to turn the sequence back on. Waiting to be found by another metamorph, snotgun in hand.

A helpless giggle rose in her throat. It felt weirdly hysterical. "Jex!" she called. "Where's Ryle? Where are the others? Are they all right?" She slid over the pipes toward the catwalk, not quite trusting her limbs to hold her up. How had she found the courage to leave it in the first place? It seemed a long way down. Where was Azah? She flinched when heavy footfalls thundered on the metal walkway, drawing close to where she hid.

"They're alive," Jex said and she was sure a sigh of relief colored his voice.

Ryle limped into view, bleeding from a split lip, still out of breath from whatever it had taken to overcome the Kalons. A broad grin spread over his exhausted face and he raised his arms toward her. "Jex said you were lounging around up here," he said.

She took his hands and slid off the pipes and into his arms, feeling them close around her as if he'd done that a thousand times before. "I was so worried," he breathed. "I thought we'd lost you for sure when your com cut out."

She leaned against his broad chest, reveling in the feel of his arms around her, unwilling to let this moment go by, no matter how many Kalons were converging upon them. She feared nothing right now.

She winced when he released her to scan the catwalk ahead of them. "Azah?" he called. "Toji!"

They appeared around a turn in the walkway, moving

slowly. Toji had slung an arm around Azah's waist to support her and she did not seem to mind that at all. She smiled through her pain when they saw Laryn and Ryle across the gap.

Laryn leaned over the railing to see a metamorph crumpled on the ground below the catwalk, possibly the crash she had heard earlier. "Did you make him sleep?"

Toji did not look back. "No. I made him dead."

EPILOGUE

The sound of power tools, accompanied by the rattle of conveyors and the curses of mechanics greeted Laryn before she had even fully entered the outbounder docking bay. She passed technicians working on the hole Nolan had blasted into the wall and wondered if the *Nefer*'s crew had confessed to the damage. The electrical seemed to be working again but it didn't look like much effort was being put into making the wall as good as new. Too much of the station was in need of assessment and repair and so this would be just another mismatched patch for the aging station.

The noise in the docks felt wonderfully alive to her after endless days of questions as Pendra's chiefs and not a few Ministry directors grilled the survivors about what happened, and why. She had watched hours of footage made by Jex and reviewed statements by other victims to confirm events after the station's recording systems went down. Among the dead were twenty-three Humans and over fifty Kalons. No one would ever know how many metamorphs had gone down with the Br'll transport near the Well, or how many had escaped in the second ship. A cruiser sent to

Ophet reported the main outpost there deserted and only a few isolated prospecting teams responding to hails.

She continued toward a knot of crew and technicians gathered near the *Nefer*'s berth. The cargo lift was down and it didn't take her long to spot the object of their interest.

"Nolie! You didn't!" she called to the engineer inserted halfway into the back end of a crawler. He had tipped it onto its side and some of its dozen or so legs trailed wires back into its interior.

Some of the others standing around the peculiar vehicle stepped aside when she joined the onlookers. She wore plain black trousers and a short leather vest over her blouse, but the mediary badge at her throat was not missed. A few of the outbounders murmured a respectful greeting and one or two others wandered away.

Nolan emerged to give her a broad grin. "I did. No way was I going to leave that on Torren. I had Azah ride it right onto the cargo lift. Look under here! I've installed cameras fore and aft. Mark my words; this is going to come in handy someday."

"To frighten little children, maybe," a low voice spoke behind her.

She turned to smile up at Ryle. "I see you survived the debrief."

"More or less." He glanced at the spectators with a small jerk of his chin. They seemed to understand his request and strolled away to leave them alone with Nolan and his new toy.

"How did it go for you?" she said.

"I have no idea. We told them what happened. They told us nothing. Was mostly Pendra brass, couple of Ministry types. The Br'll thing is classified." He smirked. "Again."

She grinned. "I heard they're waiving your docking fees for a year, seeing how the outbounders made sure there's still a station to dock to."

He rolled his eyes to the ceiling. "That's thanks to you, though they didn't even mention that part to us. I'm happy that the *Harla* survivors are getting the discovery bonus for Torren, even if Shelody isn't. What about you?"

"Pretty much the same. We can probably expect some commendation for keeping the station out of the Well. Pendra claims to have had no idea that the Kalons are actually Br'll. Blamed the Bio Division for not catching that. Some people got fired. I wasn't asked if I believed them. Or to give an opinion. But I did anyway."

"Oh?" he said expectantly.

"I told them what Toji said about the Br'll. The ones still on their homeworld. That they might not all be hostile."

"You think they might go after them?" Nolan said. "Make war or something?"

Ryle shook his head. "They just need to guard the filament to Kalon. And to Earth, I guess."

"And they will," Laryn said. "That second Kalon ship could be anywhere. They downloaded everything in reach from ANN-E. Their attention was on the transporter, but they grabbed files on the station, our ships, our people, you name it. The investigators don't think they wanted the station. From what they're starting to suspect about Br'll technology, they'd be better off building their own. They just wanted our info and then get rid of us for a while."

"Like we got rid of them," Ryle said. "To control the Hub. And by the time we get back here in any number, they would have secured this sector. Maybe even destroyed the colonies on Terrica."

"From what I heard, Pendra's requested higher security for the station. *Military* grade security with ships and cannons. On top of the troops that just got here."

Nolan sat on a toolbox to sort through his tangle of wire. "That's what we need. More people watching us."

Ryle looked over Laryn's head as if to make sure no one heard. "Did they ask about... about us? About your assignment, I mean?"

"You mean did I tell them about Jex? About your database? Nah, they'll have to pay more for that than some vague promise of a job on the research fleet."

"I see we've been a bad influence on you," he said with a smile.

"I'm just rather fond of Jex, I think."

"And I thought maybe you're trying to keep me out of jail. I'm disappointed."

They looked up when the passenger lift came down from the *Nefer*, bringing with it Azah who, as usual, leaped from it before it reached the ground despite the brace on her forearm.

"Hey," Nolan protested. "Watch the crawler."

She bent to ruffle his hair and then nodded to Laryn. "Hello, Agent. My father's very happy about the intel on Torren. Did you get grilled by Pendra, too?"

"Yeah," Laryn said. "And properly gagged."

"Like a right proper mediary. Ever consider quitting that gig?"

"Daily."

"Wait a sec," Nolan said. He looked to Ryle. "Why don't we keep her on? As crew, I mean. She's wasted on Pendra."

Ryle tilted his head, looking thoughtful.

"I'm sincere," Nolan said, warming to his own idea. "She's been darn useful. And she's kinda likable, don't you think?"

Laryn smiled. "Thanks."

Azah scrubbed her blood-red nails over the side of her head. "Hmm, she *can* handle herself. We saw that."

Laryn gasped, surprised to find the woman in favor of Nolan's idea.

"What do *you* think of that, Laryn?" Nolan said, nudging her. "Ready to punt Pendra now that you've seen their pretty side? Trade your cozy crib for a metal bunk and crappy food?"

"Well, that does sound tempting," she said.

"No."

They all looked to Ryle in surprise.

"Eh?" Nolan said. "Why not? We need a sci tech. And

she's a medic with better bedside manners than Jex."

Ryle shook his head. "She's a mediary. If I hire her they'll assign another one. I like this one better." He turned to her. "It'll get tougher for us to do business here on the station if they're beefing up security. They're only going to display their gratitude to the outbounders for as long as this thing with the Kalons is fresh in people's minds. Having someone on the inside…" he trailed off, leaving her to decide what he meant.

She raised an eyebrow. He was right, of course. She had access to the Ministry as well as Pendra, even if just in her capacity as mediary. The title also unlocked doors on Earth and on Terrica. And, with her recent promotion to engineer, she now literally had access to every locked door on Pendra Station, which might not be discovered for a while. CogSys would give her anything but the most highly classified information. She had to admit that keeping her aboard as their mandated mediary was of far greater value to the crew and probably to Corlan Shelody as well.

But was she ready to turn on her employers in this way? The company that had given her so much? These past few days had shown her the truth of the accusations that had been hurled at the Consortium for as long as she could remember. She could no longer pretend that Pendra didn't sacrifice lives over profits and power. Did she really owe them as much as she thought, or were her loyalties as misplaced as she now suspected?

And now Ryle had asked her to become an agent for the outbounders, people about whom she still knew so little. Did Pendra suspect him of harboring an illegal AI, as she assumed, or was he and his crew, perhaps others among the outbounders, part of something much larger? Clearly their goals were not the same as Pendra's. Was this the path for her?

She looked up at the *Nefer*'s lock, the door to the *Out There* she had looked for since she had learned about the Hub. A bit more dangerous than leisurely jaunts aboard the comfortable research vessel, she had to admit. And so very much more exhilarating.

Her eyes returned to search Ryle's face, wishing he had not made this offer. She wished he had taken Nolan's suggestion and hired her for the job because she earned it, not because of what she might add to his assets. And, perhaps more importantly, because he *wanted* her aboard.

She dropped her eyes and forced a smile. "I'm in," she said. "I've had it with Pendra, but if I quit, I can wave any future research assignment goodbye. And my pretty suite."

Did she imagine a quick wince on Ryle's face when she said that? Was that disappointment she read there, or was that just her own wishful thinking?

"Good then," he said as he turned away. "Do you need a hand with this monstrosity, Nolie? Tell me you're adding ventilation."

"Hey, Tanner!"

They all turned when Ben Colsan's rough voice echoed through the bay. He had exited his ship and strode toward the ramp to the lower hangar.

"You want to see this, Tanner," he hollered. "They're getting ready to kick the mummies off the station. Dumping the lot on Ophet. Ivan said they don't look happy about it."

Ryle frowned. "All of them?" he said to Laryn. "We made sure they knew the difference between Toji's group and the later generation."

"So did I," she said, puzzled.

"Where is Toji?" Azah said.

"I thought he'd be here with Nolan," Laryn said, pointing to the cybernetic contraption sprawled on the floor. "I was told they finished talking to them long before I left Security."

Nolan jumped to his feet. "Hell no!" he cried and sprinted away, toward the ramp.

Ryle and Laryn followed and caught up with him at the entrance to the lower level. Some station crew members loitered nearby, waiting for something to happen. They were kept to the edges of the hangar, not just by Pendra's security team, but by armed military personnel.

"Do you see him?" Nolan said, craning his neck to search through the Kalons corralled near the locks to the Ophet transport ships. "Is that's all that's left of them?"

The soldiers had divided the Kalons into two groups and it was easy to distinguish one from the other now. Nine of them, either bound at the wrists or too injured to escape, glowered sullenly at the guards who now ringed them with weapons not only in hand but aimed at their heads.

Huddled to the side and less tightly guarded stood the Kalons of Toji's generation, only six now, appearing unharmed but frightened. All of them were shorter than the newcomers and their skin showed a more pronounced greenish-bronze blaze from forehead to nape.

No one had to guess at the content of dozens of long cloth bags being stowed into the transporter ahead of the captives. These were the type of bag that decomposed as quickly as its contents.

"There he is!" Nolan said. "On the left!" He rushed past Colsan only to get shoved back by a Pendra guard.

Laryn wasn't about to let that stop her. She strode past the guard, daring him to push her back as well. Perhaps it was her glare or perhaps it was the mediary badge, but he allowed her to pass, even if only grudgingly. She hurried to Toji who stood, looking a little lost, among his people.

"Toji!" she called. "You don't belong here."

He shook his head and she made out a few high-pitched chirps but someone had taken his modulator. None of the Kalons carried their units.

A metamorph standing with the other group had heard his reply and snarled something in response. Toji flinched, as if struck.

"This is absurd!" Laryn said when a security captain arrived to escort her away from the aliens.

"Please step back, Agent," he said. "This isn't safe."

"Don't tell me about safe," she hissed. "These Kalons did not take part of the attack. And especially not this one."

The captain only stared at her, perhaps wondering if that was supposed to mean something to him.

Laryn looked past him to a group of Pendra administrators near the transporter hatch. Her own supervisor, Joel Mitcher, stood among them. "Excuse me," she said to the captain, in a tone that allowed no argument.

She hurried toward them and wasn't surprised when Mitcher moved away upon spotting her. "Director," she called loud enough for the others to hear.

He turned back with reluctance. "Agent Ash," he said in greeting.

"Why are those Kalons detained? I was assured his group would not be harmed."

"And they won't be, Agent," Mitcher said. "We decided it would be best to remove all of them from the station for now. They will be sent to Ophet, now that Pendra is shifting its resources to the new planet you discovered."

"Of course they'll be harmed," she said. "Especially Toji. Those Kalons will rip him to pieces for helping us."

He looked confused for a moment and turned to an elegant woman standing near him. Alana Vercy headed Pendra's security division although Laryn doubted she had ever wielded a gun. "We… we can keep them apart, if you like," he said as if asking her to confirm the offer.

"You know that's not going to happen," Laryn said, furious. "They need to stay here."

"They can return once we have cleared them," the woman said with a judgmental eye on Laryn's rather ordinary attire. "The investigation is ongoing." Her scrutiny moved to Ryle who had come to stand behind Laryn. "I advise you not to obstruct this process," she said. "The residents of this station will not tolerate Kalons aboard after what happened. We must consider the community."

"This community would be floating in space right now if it weren't for Toji," Laryn snapped. "Of course you haven't shared that fact with the community, have you?"

"Agent, I must ask you to moderate your tone," Mitcher

said. "This is unbecoming. We have two thousand migrants on our doorstep that need to be processed. This is not the time for dealing with the Kalon problem."

The director's pinched face showed surprise when someone else approached the gate. Laryn turned to see Corlan Shelody, elegantly garbed in a dove gray suit and silk cravat, accompanied by his daughter. She beamed a wide grin at the assembly and then winked at Laryn.

"Corlan," Vercy said, looking uncomfortable. "I'm surprised to see you down here."

He flashed a pleasant smile. "Indeed. I was alerted that some of my crew might have met with some misfortune."

She blinked rapidly. "Your crew?"

"Yes," he said, stooping to lift his impeccable trouser cuff higher to avoid some liquid on the hangar floor. "That Kalon over there is in my employ," he said without pointing at any of them. "There may be some confusion about his role in this unpleasantness."

"Perhaps so, but we are temporarily clearing the station of all Kalons."

He smiled indulgently and took her elbow to lead her to a less damp location of the hanger. The two wandered away, and their conversation faded.

"This is outside your mandate, Agent," Mitcher said to Laryn, looking less than pleased to be excluded from whatever Shelody had to say to the director. "You are a mediary. An observer."

She regarded him thoughtfully for a moment. He seemed smaller today than the last time she had seen him. "Yes, I've observed a lot these past few days," she reminded him.

His eyes narrowed above the sudden flush of his well-padded cheeks.

Ryle took her arm and tugged her away from the irate director. "I wouldn't push it, Agent," he said. "He looks like he's got a temper."

"You have no idea. What are those two talking about?"

He had turned his head to let Jex amplify the

conversation between Shelody and the director. "He's reminding her that the Kalons are worth a whole lot more alive than dead to Pendra. She's pushing for a bribe, I think." He winced. "That's going to cost me, in the end, just watch. He's fond of his money."

Azah and Nolan now waited near Toji and his people, as uncertain as everyone else about what was going on. More station residents had wandered into the space, alerted by their friends to the spectacle. Perhaps the past few days hadn't been sufficiently interesting, Laryn thought.

"Watch daddy do his magic," Azah said.

Nolan rolled his eyes. "What Azah wants, daddy provides."

"I didn't think you were that fond of Toji," Ryle said.

She shrugged and looked up at the Kalon. "He kinda grows on you, doesn't he?"

Toji was still watching the hostile Kalons, his agitation clear in his stance. Laryn took his hand and felt his fingers close around her own. She smiled at his companions with what she hoped was perceived as encouragement.

"Here they come," Azah said.

Director Vercy and Corlan Shelody strolled companionably toward them, still chatting, possibly about the weather, judging by their expressions. Behind them walked Director Mitcher, still looking sidelined and angry about it.

"We will amend our plans," Vercy said to Laryn. She did not speak loud enough to be heard in other parts of the hangar. "You are correct to assume that these Kalons may be in danger among our attackers if we deport them to Ophet. We owe... Toji? Right, Toji. We owe Toji our gratitude. And of course we have a mandate to establish peaceful and equitable relations with non-Human species. The Kalons will receive due judicial process, like any other resident here is entitled to. We will make a case about these individuals to the Consortium. In the meantime, they will make themselves available to help us understand their Br'll progenitors."

It didn't take much experience with Pendra's methods to guess that a few Kalons were already incarcerated, somewhere here on the station, and waiting for specialists to arrive from Earth to *understand* them. Laryn started to speak but then felt Ryle's hand on her shoulder, just firm enough to make a point.

"We may find a home for them on Terrica but for now they will remain as guests aboard the station. Their collaboration with our research team has been of value and they will be housed in the Annex. Will that be acceptable to them?" She did not address Toji directly.

Laryn nodded. "Another news item this evening might be helpful to the community," she said. "In which his... his people's role during the attack is highlighted. To clear up any confusion."

The director inclined her head in agreement. "That may be of value."

Shelody checked his time piece. "And there you have it," he said, another business transaction complete. He glanced at Ryle. "See me when you're done here, Tanner. I have an assignment for you." He offered a stiff little bow to the director, ignored Mitcher, and turned to kiss his daughter's forehead before hurrying away.

Vercy motioned toward the nearby guards. "Escort this group to the Annex. I will send instructions to the section head on duty."

The guards, not quite sure if these orders ought to be followed with weapons aimed, shuffled around Toji's friends. The Kalons paid little attention to them but began to walk toward the hangar exit, as eager to quit this place as Shelody had been.

"Toji!" Ryle called.

The Kalon turned.

"Where are you going?"

Toji glanced at his companions and then pointed to the exit.

Ryle shook his head. "No time for lazing around. You're

needed in the engine room. You heard Shelody. We're heading out and Nolan left a mess in the repair bay." He waved to the others. "Get to work, everyone."

* * *
*
*

ABOUT THE AUTHOR

Chris Reher is a first generation Canadian currently and out of necessity residing on planet Earth (which, in the general and interplanetary scheme of things, could *really* use a catchier name. Imagine heading past Proxima Centauri and someone asks you whence you came and you tell them "dirt". All theological implications aside, that just won't do.)

When not finding ways to defy the laws of physics or torture her subjects or entice them with inter-species hanky-panky, she designs web sites or writes about designing web sites. She enjoys long walks on the beach or, given the local beach shortage, writes about beaches far beyond Proxima Centauri.

www.chrisreher.com

Also by Chris Reher

Quantum Tangle

Terminus Shift

Entropy's End

Sky Hunter

The Catalyst

Only Human

Rebel Alliances

Delphi Promised

www.ingramcontent.com/pod-product-compliance
Lightning Source LLC
Chambersburg PA
CBHW061542170626
46811CB00001B/54